# THE
# MISBIRTH

D.B. Moffatt

## BeachHouse Books

Saint Charles   Missouri   USA

# COPYRIGHT

ISBN 9781596301030

Library of Congress Control Number: 2016930934

www.beachhousebooks.com

an Imprint of

**Science &**

**Humanities Press**

Saint Charles, MO 63301

# PROLOGUE

Chester White was a bitter young man.

Eleven years earlier, under pressure from his parents, he decided to do the "right" thing and drop out of high school to marry the young girl who claimed to be carrying his child.

The ceremony was simple and brief.

The only people in attendance were the bride and groom's parents and, of course, a Justice of the Peace.

After the marriage, Chester's father loaned him enough money to put a down payment on a struggling vending business.

The father of the bride had seen fit to stake the newlyweds to a year's rent in a small one-bedroom apartment located in another section of their home town.

The year had been 1952.

In the Americana of those days, sometimes the less said about certain social realities the better it was for all involved.

And, thus, began the marriage of Chester and Shirley White.

# CHAPTER ONE

Chester White smiled, as he pulled into the parking lot. It was his final job of the day.

Carver's Bar and Grill was one of his favorite stops. It was located in his hometown of Rutland, New York and mere minutes from his house.

Chester climbed out of the driver's seat and walked to the back of his van. He opened the rear doors, pulled out the dolly transport, and began loading it with the supplies he sold for a living.

Eleven years earlier, when Chester assumed ownership of the business, it had been strictly a nuts and candy vending operation.

In the beginning, he would simply buy those two products from the wholesalers and then traverse his newly purchased route restocking the machines and dutifully collecting his nickels and dimes.

Over the past decade, that scenario had changed.

In addition to nut and candy dispensers, Chester had expanded into cigarette, jukebox, and pinball machines.

More recently, in 1961, after the premier of the movie *The Hustler*, Chester had purchased the distribution rights that made him the sole vendor of pool tables in Rutland and the surrounding areas.

"Everyone under the age of sixty is going to want to be the next Fast Eddie", he had accurately predicted.

What had made the pool table franchise acquisition so unique was the fact that the machines accepted nothing less than quarters to play one game; an unheard of sum of money in the vending business of those days. More importantly, not one customer had complained about the price to play.

He wheeled the now laden dolly towards the rear entrance of Carver's Bar and Grill. Chester surveyed the packed parking lot.

*"It looks like 'Happy Hour' is happier than usual,"* he mused, to himself.

As he approached the back of the building, a screened door swung open.

A kitchen employee held it ajar, not so much out of courtesy or respect, but more out of an instinctive fear of the young man entering.

Chester White was twenty-seven years old. He stood just a glance under the height of six feet. His frame was imposingly muscular. His face was a countenance etched with the lines of an inner rage few men dared to challenge.

Emerging from the kitchen, Chester parked his dolly at the service end of an impressively appointed mahogany and brass bar.

Without prompting, one of the barmaids working the 'Happy Hour' shift immediately approached him.

"What will it be this afternoon, Mr. White?" she asked, cheerfully.

"The usual," was his disengaged response.

"I'll be right back," she promised.

True to her word, the young woman returned with a stainless-steel tumbler filled with ice in one hand and an unopened bottle of Jack Daniels in the other.

She placed both vessels in front of the patron.

"Can I get you anything else?" she asked.

"You'll be the first to know if you can," he answered, dismissively.

With that, the keeper of the spirits made her presence scarce.

Chester White broke the bottle's seal and poured a generous amount into the tumbler. He swirled the concoction to allow for the proper chill and then relished a long, satisfying swig.

He pulled a pack of cigarettes from his shirt pocket, lit a Lucky, and tossed the pack onto the bar.

Exhaling a plume of blue, the route distributor surveyed the Carver's bar scene.

As usual, the late afternoon crowd was divided into two distinct factions.

Seated at the bar were the townies; men and women born and raised in Rutland, New York.

On the other side of the room, congregating in booths and at floor tables, were the "kids".

These young people were mostly college students who traveled from various Connecticut schools to Carver's and other bars in town in order to drink, legally.

Connecticut's drinking age was twenty-one; New York's was eighteen. Rutland was the first New York town over Connecticut's southern border. Hence, its immense popularity among the crew of higher learning from the Constitution State.

Chester White took another long pull from the tumbler and an equally long drag on his cigarette.

A door located behind the mahogany bar opened. A young man emerged and quickly closed it behind him.

After surveying the entire room, he leisurely poured himself a drink and made his way down the bar towards Chester White.

"You're running late today, Chet."

"It takes time to recalibrate the machines," explained the vendor.

"Does that mean a rate change?" asked the young man standing behind the bar.

"Yes," confirmed the vendor.

"Are the prices going up?"

Chester White fixed a stare at his inquisitor.

"J.J., have you ever known the price for pleasure to go down?"

Both men broke into knowing laughter and raised their drinks to toast.

Johnny "Junior" Westfield was only one of two people Chester White considered a friend.

The two had been long-time classmates up until Chester's sudden *decision* to drop out of school.

4

Westfield had successfully graduated high school and then gone on to a four-year private college in upstate New York where he graduated with a degree in business.

Currently, Johnny's job title was "Manager" of Carver's Bar and Grill.

J.J. was of average height, weight, and looks. Truth be known, everything about him was pretty much average except for one thing. He was the first and only son of Jonathan "Big John" Westfield.

In the politer social circles of Rutland, New York, "Big John" was described as a locally prominent businessman. However, behind the closed doors of political decision, the elder Westfield was known as "the man behind the mayors".

The 'mayors' were the men who ran the New York towns that bordered the state of Connecticut. They wielded a great deal of influence when it came to deciding who, and more importantly, who would **not** be granted liquor licenses to conduct business in their respective hamlets.

"Big John" Westfield controlled the sole distribution rights to all forms of alcohol sold in that part of New York state.

With the disparity in legal drinking ages between New York and Connecticut, the purchase price for a liquor license in any of those towns was rumored to be outrageous.

Chester White desperately coveted a piece of the enormously profitable alcohol business.

Although he never admitted it, to himself, this was the only reason Chester continued his friendship with the younger Westfield.

# CHAPTER TWO

"So, how much are you jacking the prices?" asked the now excited manager of Carver's Bar and Grill.

In the vending trade, a general rule of thumb was 10% gross to the "house" for providing equipment space. Assuming no decrease in volume, that meant more money for the establishment with no increase in overhead.

Chester White took another pull from the tumbler. He finished his cigarette and snuffed it in an ashtray. White stared into the eyes of Westfield.

"It's going to be a nickel more for candy, nuts, and pinball. For smokes and tunes, it's going to be a dime. And to play pool, it's another twenty-five cents."

Junior Westfield drained his drink and in the same motion began mixing another.

"You think I'm going to be getting any complaints?" he asked, cautiously.

Chester White continued to stare into the eyes of his former school mate, with an expression that made Westfield very uncomfortable.

"If they don't pay, they don't play. It's really that simple, J.J."

Junior Westfield redirected his attention to the other side of the barroom.

The jukebox was playing the Chiffon's current hit, "He's So Fine".

A couple was standing in front of the machine, happily trying to decide which song to play next.

Johnny shifted his gaze to the pool table.

As always, it was in use. There was a crowd standing two deep, with quarters on the carom watching and anxiously waiting to play the winners.

Westfield looked at Chester White.

"You know, we really should get another pool table in here".

Chester glanced at that section of the room and then motioned for the barmaid.

"Yes, Mr. White?"

"Ice," he ordered and waggled the metallic tumbler in front of the young woman's face.

"Coming right up."

She adroitly pulled a fresh tumbler from an overhead rack, filled it with ice and politely placed it in front of him.

"Will there be anything else, sir?"

"No."

With that, the barmaid was off to fill another drink order at the crowded bar. J.J. Westfield looked quizzically at his old high school buddy.

"I could just have easily gotten that for you."

"But you didn't," admonished the vendor.

Chester reopened the bottle of Jack Daniels and poured generously into the tumbler. Again, he swirled its contents and then relished another swallow.

White refocused his attention on Junior Westfield.

"J.J., the only way you're going to fit another pool table in here is to ditch that shuffleboard game. Is anybody still playing that thing?" asked the vendor, with genuine interest.

Junior Westfield looked resentfully at the idle dinosaur.

"Some of the old-timers do, *when* they come in. And even then, at a nickel a pop who gives a rat's ass!"

"Well, the shuffleboard isn't my piece of equipment, so I can't touch it. But, run the idea of getting rid of it by your old man and I'll have a spanking new pool table in here making you money the very same day."

Johnny "Junior" Westfield's face flushed, with emotion.

His hand trembled as he lifted his glass to drink. Finally, he slammed it on the bar and stared in the direction of Chester White without making direct eye contact.

"I'm the ma, ma, ma manager of Ca, Ca, Ca, Carver's!" he stuttered. "And don't you or anybody else ever fa, fa, fa forget it!"

Chester White remained serenely indifferent towards Junior Westfield's awkward outburst.

"You know something, J.J. At times, I have difficulty remembering that," he smiled. "Anyway, I've got to get to work."

With that, the vendor turned his attention to the well-stocked dolly he had wheeled in, earlier.

Chester picked up two cases of cigarettes and headed towards the front door of Carver's where the cigarette machine was located.

That afternoon's 'Happy Hour' was shifting into second gear. Both the number of patrons and volume of music were on the rise.

The vendor stopped in front of the cigarette machine.

Using the master keys, he removed the front panel and rested it on a near-by window ledge.

Chester White made a mental note of the remaining inventory, as he replenished the machine's supply.

An interesting and recurring pattern had developed in recent months at all his stops.

More filter-tipped and menthol flavored packs were being sold than the traditional non-filtered brands such as Chesterfields, Camels, and his personal favorite, Lucky Strikes.

"*The times they are a changing,*" he hummed, to himself.

The vendor fully understood that future cigarette orders would have to reflect the new trend.

Chester emptied the contents of the change bucket into a bank money bag. He then recalibrated the machine to reflect the ten cent price hike.

As he was about to re-attach the front panel, a bar patron approached.

8

"Hey, man, you want to give me a good deal on some smokes?"

Chester White eyed the college student, with detached disdain.

"Sure. The old price was twenty-five cents a pack. The new price is thirty-five cents a pack. But, if you buy four packs, it'll only cost you a buck and a half. It's called a volume discount."

"That sounds good to me!"

Money and cigarettes exchanged hands.

The collegiate returned to his friends to brag. Chester White returned to the bar to drink.

*"What the hell would the real world do without college students?"* he thought, to himself.

The vendor hoisted a cardboard box from his dolly and placed it on the bar.

He poured more Jack Daniels into the iced tumbler, lit another cigarette, and then started sifting through the newest 45 rpm record releases.

At last, satisfied with his record selections, Chester got up from the bar and made his way through the noisy crowd to the jukebox.

The kids in front of the music machine were happily dancing to Lesley Gore's current smash hit, "It's My Party".

Without hesitation, Chester White literally pulled the plug on Lesley's party.

The abrupt musical silence brought jeers from the startled, and then annoyed barroom throng.

Undaunted, the vendor turned to the crowd and held up both hands.

"Listen, to me. Let me get my work done here as quickly as possible and then I'll let you guys fight over who picks the next ten free plays!"

There were no cheers, but no objections.

Chester White went to work.

Deftly, he opened the glass faced front of the juke box. The vendor chose to collect and secure the money before proceeding with the record exchanges.

Having pre-labeled the new recordings, the transition was fairly seamless. Before closing the front glass he punched the free play button eleven times.

Chester White selected his current favorite song and then locked up the machine.

As he walked away from the jukebox, the music resumed.

"Hey, what the hell is this crap?!" yelled a disgruntled young man.

"Yeah, what is this shit?!" echoed his female dance partner.

Chester White stopped and turned to confront the disappointed couple.

"This *crap* is what the two of you will probably be listening to for the rest of your lives." He resumed his walk back to the bar.

The song was "I Saw Her Standing There."

The band was The Beatles.

The year was 1963.

# CHAPTER THREE

Shirley White sat at the vanity table in her bedroom meticulously applying make-up.

She, reluctantly, turned away from her image in the glass to check the time.

"It's already six-thirty!" she panicked. "If he's late tonight, I swear to God he'll never hear the end of it!"

She returned to the reassuring comfort of her own reflection, in the mirror.

The "he" Shirley referred to was her husband, Chester White. The two had married eleven years earlier, as a result of her unexpected pregnancy.

Shirley was not in love with Chester. Truth be told, she never had been. They had met as a result of circumstances neither one had intentionally planned. It had been a blind date arranged by one of Shirley's closest high school friends, Mary Peterson.

Mary had needed a "chaperone" in order to gain her parents' permission to see the then guy of her dreams. Shirley agreed to spend the night at Mary's house and go on a double date.

The two boys arrived at the Peterson home that evening in order to escort Mary and Shirley to the high school dance. As it turned out, the young man accompanying Mary Peterson's date was none other than, Chester White.

Shirley knew who Chester was, but had never personally met him. He had been described to her as "pretty much a loner and different."

The foursome started the evening as planned, by showing up at the dance. However, at the band's first break, they decided to cut out.

The two couples ended up on Rutland's answer to Lover's Lane. Accompanied by a cooler filled with ice, mixers, and a full bottle of Gordon's Gin, the evening's festivities began, in earnest.

In Shirley's mind, she was forever trapped in an unhappy marriage as a result of one stupid mistake. That night, she had too much to drink and ended up in the back seat with a guy she would not have given a second look at, in the sober light of day.

But her father had been insistent!

"If you're hell bent on doing adult things, you are damn well going to act like one!" had been Mr. Dunn's unwavering decree.

Her mother had no say in the matter.

The thought of terminating her unexpected pregnancy never crossed Shirley's mind. However, even if it had, such a daunting undertaking by a sixteen year old girl in 1952 would have been, at best, risky and at worst, fatal.

After the marriage, Shirley's father found them a one bedroom apartment in a more "suitable" section of Rutland.

He paid the first year's rent in advance and then, for the most part, washed his hands of his eldest child and the entire sordid incident.

Shirley's mother had been somewhat more understanding, especially after the baby's birth.

Mrs. Dunn did her utmost to spend as much time as she could with Shirley and the new-born.

However, those efforts were constantly frowned upon by her husband.

"Martha, the last thing we need is your tacit approval of Shirley's unseemly circumstance negatively influencing our younger daughters!" he had insisted.

The already messy situation was worsened by the fact that Mrs. Dunn did not like Chester White.

"There's something about that young man that just doesn't sit right with me," she confided to close friends.

As a result, the time Mrs. Dunn spent with her daughter and grandchild diminished with the ensuing years.

At first, this abandonment on the part of her parents had shaken Shirley to her emotional core. She had felt alone and neglected.

However, with time, her fears of uncertainty and vulnerability had been replaced with a newfound sense of independence.

Although she refused to admit it, to herself, Shirley's increasing sense of independence was the result of her husband's non-stop work schedule and growing income.

At the time of their marriage, Chester's father had fronted him the money for a down payment on a dying vending route. With long hours and some ingenuity, he had transformed the business into an ever-increasing money maker.

It was for this reason they were able to repay Chester's father and also put a down payment on the three-bedroom house they now lived in. The neighborhood was not exactly up to Shirley's pampered tastes. However, it was a definite step up from the hovel her father had banished them to after the marriage.

Again, Shirley peered at the night table clock.

"Six forty-five!" she fumed. "As usual, the bastard's going to be late!"

She rose from the vanity table and walked towards the bedroom closet.

At the age of twenty-seven, Shirley White was best described as not unattractive.

She was of average height, weight and, with the proper lighting, possessed reasonable facial features. Her most striking attribute was the long auburn hair which she attended to with constant self-appreciation.

Shirley emerged from the bedroom closet and stood in front of a ful-length mirror.

She admired herself in the ornate, champagne-colored dress she had purchased earlier that day expressly for that evening's festivities.

"Mommy, where are you going?"

Standing in the bedroom's doorway was Chester and Shirley White's eleven-year-old daughter.

"Mommy is going out tonight, baby," answered the preoccupied Shirley.

"Why?" questioned the little girl.

"To have fun," said the mother.

"Don't you have fun with me?" asked the child.

"Of course, I do, Patty Cakes. But tonight, mommy is going out to have grown-up fun," explained the mother.

"Oh."

Finally satisfied with her appearance, Shirley turned to face her daughter.

"How does mommy look?"

"Good."

The mother basked in the glow of her daughter's compliment.

After all, Patricia Anne was the second love of Shirley White's life.

# CHAPTER FOUR

After recalibrating the jukebox, Chester White returned to his seat at the bar.

From his dolly, he extracted a mechanical coin counting machine and placed it in front of him.

After some careful adjustments, he began to empty the various coin filled burlap bags into a metallic till located at the top of the device.

Automatically, the nickels, dimes, and quarters sorted themselves into the appropriate plastic canisters and stopped only when filled. Simultaneously, the amount of money in each filled canister was electronically recorded.

Johnny "Junior" Westfield ambled back towards Chester White. He nodded towards the machine.

"Hey, Chet, what the hell is that?" he asked, without curiosity.

"It's a money calculator," said the vendor.

"What does it do?"

"It computes," replied Chester White.

"It does what?"

"It adds by itself," explained the vendor.

"Oh."

Without prompting, the same young barmaid stopped in front of Chester White, picked up the steel tumbler and replenished it with ice.

He looked at her and laughed.

"You're a fast learner."

"Only when I want to be taught," she teased.

With that, she turned and started walking down the back of the bar, purposely, showcasing lines worthy of memorization.

Chester White picked up the bottle of Jack Daniels and melted more ice. He lit a cigarette and then turned his attention to Junior Westfield.

"You want to know something, Johnny?" he asked tapping the coin counting machine.

"Sure, Chet. What's that?"

"Pretty soon machines like this one will be adding up dollar bills."

Junior Westfield had just raised his cocktail glass to finish the remnants of a Seven and Seven when Chester White made his pronouncement.

Convulsively, Junior sprayed what had been in his mouth onto the bar in a spasm of humorous disbelief.

"Chet," he laughed. "If I didn't know any better, I'd swear I was in deep conversation with old Jack Daniels himself!"

Chester White remained contemplatively silent.

Johnny Westfield continued.

"Chet, you're dreaming if you think the day will ever come when people will start stuffing serious cash into vending machines," he said.

Chester White did not get a chance to respond.

A commotion had erupted at the pool table.

Immediately, Johnny Westfield signaled the Carver's Bar and Grill's bouncer to quell the uprising.

Paul "Bounty" Hunter was a man in his middle thirties and a Viet Nam vet. Like so many young men involved in that conflict, Hunter had returned to the country he had so bravely served, a different person.

However, his imposing physical presence and visible bodily scars made him the ideal marshal to keep the peace in Dodge City.

Paul Hunter reported back to Johnny Westfield.

"The pool table isn't taking any more coins. People are pissed."

Junior Westfield turned to glare at Chester White.

16

"What the hell is the problem?"

The vendor leisurely finished his cigarette and snuffed it. He took a long pull from the iced steel tumbler and then fixed his stare at Westfield.

"We've already covered this ground, Johnny. You need another pool table in this place. That one's already over-loaded with money. Are you going to speak to your old man, or am I?"

Again, at the mere mention of his father's name, Junior Westfield's demeanor and diction changed.

"I'll spa, spa, spa speak to my father. You just take care of your business!"

Chester White stood up.

He gathered what was necessary from the dolly and started towards the pool table.

As the vendor crossed the crowded room in Carver's, the jukebox was pulsating The Four Seasons current hit, "Walk Like a Man."

Standing around the pool table were four young men. They looked to be in their early twenties.

The nearby floor tables were filled with boisterous students and empty pitchers of beer thirsting for replenishment.

Chester White immediately took note of the rows of unevenly stacked coins lining the perimeter of the pool table.

One of the table players, sporting a varsity football jacket and brandishing a pool stick, approached Chester White.

"Hey, are you the Mr. Fix It guy? Cause if you are, get your ass in gear!" he demanded. "We're playing for blood over here!"

Chester White walked by the Carver's patron, without acknowledging the pool player's presence.

He inserted a master key into the metallic slide of the table and began emptying coins into a burlap bag.

After securing the money bag, the vendor recalibrated the mechanism to accept only the newly increased price to play.

As Chester White stood up, the college kid got in his face.

"What the hell did you just do?"

"I fixed the machine so you can continue to play," answered the vendor.

"My ass! You just raised the price on us, didn't you, asshole!"

Chester White took stock of the young man for the first time.

He was tall, well built, and looked like a preppy.

"Yea, I did raise the price. Just for you, asshole."

The vendor turned to walk away.

"Hey, my money was already on the table. The old rate should still be good," insisted the now pissed off pool player.

Chester White stopped and looked over his shoulder.

"Little boy, if you're going to play a man's game, learn the rules."

The vendor continued his way back to the bar.

Suddenly, Chester White felt a sharp pain in his lower back. He turned to see the irate young man pointing a pool stick, at him.

"Don't ever let me catch you on the street alone! Because if I do, your ass is mine!" he vowed, with vengeance.

Abruptly, the barroom fell silent.

Instinctively, Chester White dropped the two bags he was holding and started towards his adversary.

Without warning, a vice-like grip grabbed the vendor's right shoulder stopping him in his tracks.

"Not in here, not now."

The words did not resonate a barroom threat. Instead, they were more a thoughtful admonition.

Chester White spun around to confront the faceless force.

Paul Hunter, the bouncer at Carver's Bar and Grill, looked at him and smiled.

"Chet, you've got too much to lose to be getting into it with a jerk like that."

The vendor weighed the scale of his emotions. This time, reason prevailed.

"Get him the hell out of my sight before I change my mind."

"Done," promised Paul Hunter.

Chester White picked up the two bags and resumed his walk back to the bar.

The bouncer turned to face the pool stick wielding collegian.

"Your visit to Carver's is over. I don't want to see you in here for the rest of the evening."

Paul "Bounty" Hunter did not get an argument.

# CHAPTER FIVE

"That was not exactly the best way to encourage future pool table business, Chet," said Johnny Westfield.

Chester White was seated at the bar in Carver's busily pouring coins into his new machine and manually recording its automatic totals in a loose-leaf binder.

"The guy was acting like a jerk," he replied, without bothering to look up.

Junior Westfield was standing behind the bar sipping another Seven and Seven and enjoying the ever-increasing amount of eye candy walking through the front door of Carver's Bar and Grill.

"True, but what about the customer always being right?"

Chester White completed his paperwork. He put the pencil down and picked up the iced tumbler of Jack Daniels. He looked at Johnny Westfield.

"The customer is always right up until he tries to screw with me. After that, the customer is always wrong," explained the vendor.

"You've always had a different perspective on things, Chet," admitted Junior Westfield.

Chester White reached into his pant pocket and pulled out an impressively thick wad of bills.

Carefully, he peeled off the correct number of Jacksons and placed them in front of Johnny Westfield.

"There, that's the House's take for the week."

Junior Westfield looked at the sum of money on the bar in disbelief.

"Are you sure this is the right amount?"

"Absolutely," confirmed the vendor. "J.J., do you think I'm trying to cheat you?" asked Chester White.

"Chet, I don't think that for a minute. It's just that if this is 10% of gross that means you're taking home," his voice trailed off in envious mental calculation.

Chester White smiled knowingly, as he polished off the last of his cocktail.

"Johnny, I've got to run."

With that, the vendor stood up, repacked his dolly, and headed for the kitchen door.

Chester White exited the rear door of Carver's and crossed the parking lot, in the descending darkness of an early evening. He reached his van and opened its back door.

The assailants jumped the vendor from behind. They were all over him!

However, their initial assault had failed to knock Chester White to the ground.

With a strength summoned from an anguished mind, the vendor managed to wrest his right arm free.

He propelled his right elbow in a backward direction. The violent hit landed on its intended target. The nose of one the attackers splintered and cracked with a loud pop. He quickly went down on the graveled parking lot.

With fluid motion, Chester White pivoted and thrust his left knee into the second assailant's groin while simultaneously grabbing the back of his head and smashing it into his right knee. The man limply crumpled to the ground.

The vendor did a catlike three-sixty to determine how many more might be lurking. Seeing none, he immediately turned his attention to the last man standing.

It was the jerk who had given him trouble earlier in the bar!

"Well, you got your wish, pool player. You've caught me on the street and all alone. Now come make my ass yours!" he taunted, with a guttural laugh of malevolence.

Several people, while leaving Carver's, had witnessed the entire incident and retreated back inside the bar for sanctuary and to notify authorities.

The young man, who had once brandished a cocky smile and still sported the varsity football jacket, was frozen with fear. Unable to either run or fight, he simply stood there, helplessly staring into the face he now recognized as unmitigated evil.

With poised deliberation, Chester White approached his would-be assailant.

He grabbed the college kid by the neck and pinned him against the back of his van. After three quick, well placed body blows, the vendor released the neck allowing his attacker to slowly collapse onto the parking lot surface.

There he remained, on hands and knees, gasping for breath.

"Have you learned anything here this evening, Mr. Pool Player?" asked Chester White.

The vendor was talking more, to himself, than his now vanquished adversary.

"I mean, are you beginning to understand how the game is really meant to be played?"

Chester White stood over the helpless young man.

"You want to know something super star? After careful thought, I don't think you have."

With that, the vendor lifted his steel-toed work boot and began to stomp on the two out stretched hands of the student until they were smashed, bloodied, and almost indistinguishable from the parking lot gravel. During the ordeal, the kid let out a non-stop high-pitched scream of agony. After the brutality ceased the scream became a low, pathetic whimper.

"There, the next time you decide to pick up a pool stick you'll think of me and remember how the game is supposed to be played," smiled the vendor.

The sound of approaching sirens could be heard in the distance.

Chester White lit a cigarette, leaned against his van, and waited for the police to arrive.

A patrol car raced into the parking lot of Carver's Bar and Grill with emergency lights flashing. It fishtailed to a stop next to Chester White's van, spewing gravel and dust in its wake.

A Sheriff and his Deputy climbed out of the squad car and approached the vendor.

Sheriff Rick Johnson was a man in his middle forties. His height was average but in recent years the Sheriff had added considerable girth to an already stocky frame.

The Deputy, Kenny Wilson, was tall and lanky. He had been in Chester White's class during high school which made him about twenty-seven years of age.

Wilson was totally into being a cop. Wearing the badge, carrying the gun, and walking with the authority that went with them sometimes made Kenny Wilson a very difficult person to deal with, whether he was on the job or not.

Sheriff Johnson quickly assessed the three broken individuals strewn across the parking lot of Carver's. He motioned to his Deputy.

"Kenny, get the paramedics here pronto," he ordered crisply, but without undue emotion.

"Yes, sir!"

The Deputy walked briskly back to the squad car and placed the dispatch.

Sheriff Johnson took another look at the three fallen men. He idly kicked some gravel and then ambled over to the vendor.

"What the hell happened here, Chester?"

White was still leaning up against the van. He finished his cigarette, dropped it on the parking lot gravel, and rubbed it out with his steel-toed boot.

"Evening, Sheriff."

"I asked you a question," persisted the police officer.

Chester White looked directly into the eyes of Sheriff Johnson and smiled.

"I waited here so I could tell you exactly what happened."

"Go on," prodded the officer.

Chester White straightened his posture and took one step towards Sheriff Johnson.

"After I finished my business in Carver's, I loaded up my equipment. I walked through the kitchen and left through the back door. I walked across the parking lot to my van. As I started to open the van's rear door, those three jumped me from behind," attested the vendor.

"You ever see them before?"

"Hell, yes! They were in Carver's the entire time I was there emptying my machines."

"Do you have any witnesses?" asked the Sheriff.

"Do I have any witnesses? Sheriff, they jumped me! I was too busy defending my life and property to be looking around for witnesses," explained the vendor.

"That makes sense," agreed the police officer.

The sound of EMT sirens could be heard approaching.

Deputy Kenny Wilson returned and joined the conversation.

"Hey, Chet, are you going to be pressing charges against these scumbags?"

The vendor surveyed the now quiet battlefield.

"No, I don't think so, Kenny."

"Why the hell not?" asked the Deputy.

"Because I believe these boys have already learned a very valuable lesson here tonight "said Chester White.

"And what's that?" asked the Deputy.

"To always play by the rules of the game," confirmed the vendor.

"Amen to that!" agreed Deputy Kenny Wilson.

Chester White turned his attention to Sheriff Rick Johnson.

"If there's nothing else, may I take off? I'm running late and I know the old lady is already tapping her foot!"

"You're free to go," said the Sheriff.

Chester White climbed into his van and started out on the short ride home.

The only person who had witnessed the entire episode finished his cigarette and re-entered the front door of the bar.

Paul "Bounty" Hunter was ready to resume his duties, as the bouncer of Carver's Bar and Grill.

# CHAPTER SIX

"I don't know where the hell he is!" yelled Shirley White into the receiver of the phone. Mary, I'll call you when the jerk gets home!"

She slammed the phone onto its cradle and once again glared at the clock. It was nearly eight.

Shirley White stormed across the kitchen. She poured herself another glass of wine, lit a cigarette, and then went to stand at a window where she could see the street and driveway.

"This is supposed to be my special night!" she screamed and angrily stomped her high-heels on the kitchen floor.

Shirley was referring to an evening out with the girls.

The woman she had spoken to on the phone was her old friend from high school, Mary Peterson.

Ironically, it had been a double date with Mary that had ultimately led to Shirley being pressured into marrying Chester White.

The two girls had met while they were candy stripers at Rutland General Hospital.

After graduating high school, Mary Peterson had attended a local state university where she received a degree in nursing. She was currently working full-time as an R.N. at Rutland General.

During that same period of time, Shirley had been forced to drop out of high school, get married, and have her baby.

In the beginning, the newness of motherhood and the responsibilities that went along with it were enough to keep Shirley preoccupied.

However, as time had passed, her resentment towards the unwanted situation, in general, and her growing disdain for her husband, in particular, had made Shirley White a very unhappy young woman.

The constant, never ending obligation of parenthood was a daily reminder to Shirley of the youth she felt had been unjustly stolen from her.

It was for these reasons Shirley had sought an outside release as soon as practically feasible. Her escape had presented itself in the form of Rutland General.

She enrolled in the nurses' aide training program then being offered at the hospital. Upon course completion, she was assigned duties on the night shift.

"*This is perfect!*" she had thought, to herself. "*Chester won't be able to bitch about me interfering with his work schedule. And I'll be out of the house the minute he gets home and free!*"

Shirley viewed it as the perfect solution to a marriage of infernal unhappiness.

"Mommy, why are you yelling?"

It was Patricia Anne who had come downstairs and was now standing next to her mother in the kitchen. She was in her long white cotton nightgown and yawning.

Shirley White looked at her daughter with the frown of parental enforcement.

"Aren't you supposed to be in bed, young lady?"

The eleven-year-old ignored her mother's question.

"Mommy, you look pretty."

The mother's stern facial expression instantly melted into a glowing smile of self-approval.

"Do you really think so, Patty Cakes?"

"Yup," nodded the child.

Shirley White abandoned her window watch.

With wine glass in one hand, and cigarette in the other, she sashayed out of the kitchen. Shirley came to a stop in front of the foyer mirror for one more look.

"*Patty Cakes is right,*" she thought, to herself.

"Mommy, someone is here!" shouted an excited Patricia Anne.

Shirley pulled herself away from the magnet of her image and returned to the kitchen.

She peered out the window and saw the familiar van.

"Patty Cakes, you run upstairs and go to bed. Mommy will be up to tuck you in before she leaves," promised Shirley.

"Okay."

The little girl did as she was told.

Shirley quickly put down the wine glass, picked up the receiver of the kitchen wall phone and dialed.

"He's here," she whispered and hung up.

The kitchen's outside door opened and Chester White walked in carrying two duffel bags filled with that day's proceeds.

Immediately, Shirley went on the attack.

"You're late!" she screeched.

Without breaking stride, Chester walked across the kitchen and into the small adjoining room he had converted into a make-shift office.

He then placed the two duffel bags on top of a small wooden table. Chester glided behind the desk, sat down in an office chair, and swiveled to face a heavy, stand-alone York safety vault.

With agility, his fingers spun the safe's dial until it clicked. He opened the door, deposited the money, and then slammed the vault shut with a re-twist of the dial.

Chester White returned to the kitchen and headed towards the fridge for a beer.

Shirley was standing in the middle of the room with her hands placed defiantly on both hips.

"Why are you so damn late?" she demanded.

Chester White brushed by his wife without a word and took a seat at the kitchen table.

Shirley smelled liquor on her husband's breath.

"You've been out drinking, again. I should have known as much!" she scoffed, in disgust.

"So have you, sugar doll," he said, observing the half emptied wine glass on the table.

"That's different."

"It always is when it comes to you, isn't it?"

Chester White took note of his wife's appearance for the first time that evening.

Her hair was brushed to perfection, her make-up was on, and the champagne colored cocktail dress she was wearing rode just a bit too snugly around a large, shapeless backside.

"What are you dressed up for?" he asked, with disinterest.

"I told you days ago that I was going out with the girls tonight!" she answered, emphatically.

Chester White realized his wife had never mentioned any such thing. Although he rarely listened to her, he always retained every word she said. However, the husband had neither the love nor the patience to pursue his wife's lie.

"Who's the lucky guy this evening?" he asked, mockingly.

Shirley White glared at her husband with heart felt hatred.

"Do you work at being an asshole or does it just come naturally to you?" she hissed.

Chester White stared at his wife, as he drained the last of his beer.

"Neither, actually. I've come to believe it has been a process of osmosis," he concluded.

Shirley White stared blankly at her husband.

"It's been a what, of a what?"

Before Chester White could elaborate, a car horn beeped twice signaling Shirley's ride.

Without thought or hesitation, she grabbed her purse and bounded gleefully towards the foyer and her escape.

"I don't know what time I'll be home, so don't wait up for me!"

The front door slammed and she was gone.

*"Don't worry, I won't,"* he thought, to himself.

Chester White rose from the kitchen table.

He discarded the empty beer and then went to the kitchen cabinet to pour himself a real drink.

# CHAPTER SEVEN

Shirley White climbed into the passenger seat of Mary Peterson's car and closed the door.

"Free, at last!" she shouted, triumphantly.

The two young women broke into spontaneous laughter, just as they had done when they were in high school.

Mary Peterson was born and raised in Rutland, New York.

She was of medium height and weight. Her face was attractive and her blue eyes alert. Mary kept her dirty blonde hair cut shoulder length. She was most often described as "just a really nice person." Peterson was not married.

Their car took off into the night.

"Shirley, what did you tell Chester?" asked Mary Peterson, regaining her composure.

"I told him I was going out with the girls," she answered.

"And he didn't get mad?"

"He's always mad," said Shirley.

"I'm being serious," insisted Mary.

"So am I."

Mary Peterson thought for a moment, before continuing.

"So, you're telling me your husband doesn't care if you go out at nights?"

"Seems that way."

Mary took her eyes of the road to look at her friend.

"Shirley, is that good or bad?"

"Who knows and who cares!"

Shirley White lit a cigarette and rolled down the passenger window.

"Mary, where's Jan?"

"She got tied up at the office and is running late. She's going to meet us."

"What's his name?"

Mary started to laugh. She took the cigarette from Shirley's hand and began to smoke.

"You really do have a one-tracked mind!"

The girls pulled into the parking lot of their destination. The Fontana was a restaurant situated on the outskirts of Rutland Township.

Originally, it had been the private residence of a wealthy turn of the century industrialist. However, the majestic Georgian Manor now served as an ever increasingly popular haunt for the young professionals of Rutland and those of near-by towns.

The Fontana was essentially two establishments in one location. Upon entering its large reception area, guests could choose either the formal dining room for eating or the lounge for drinks, live entertainment, and socializing.

Shirley White and Mary Peterson walked into The Fontana's impressive lobby. The two young women chose the lounge.

"There she is," said Mary, pointing in the direction of a young woman seated alone at a plush circular booth.

They walked across the half-filled room to join their friend.

"Not drinking tonight, Jan?" asked Mary Peterson, as she sat down.

"Thought I'd try to be polite and wait for you two derelicts," she responded.

"Since when have you ever pretended to be polite?" teased Shirley White, as she slid into the booth.

Janet Weiss was the third member of what had been known at Rutland High School as "The Trio".

Janet was short, petite, and spirited. She had cropped black hair, probing brown eyes, and a mind that never quit. She worked as a paralegal for one of Rutland's more prestigious law firms. Janet was also, not married.

"And here I thought I was going to be the late one!" she chastised her two friends, with a smile.

"Blame her," said Mary, affectionately patting Shirley White on the shoulder.

Before Shirley could explain, a solicitous young waiter accosted their booth.

"And what is your pleasure this evening, ladies?"

It was Janet Weiss who answered the call.

"What would you suggest?"

"The Mai Tai's are good and they're twofers tonight," enticed their server.

"Sounds like a winning combination to me," said Janet.

Her two companions readily agreed.

"Coming right up, ladies."

With that, the young man disappeared.

Janet Weiss refocused her attention on her friends.

"Now, why are you two so late?"

"Why else?" spat Shirley White.

"Chester got home later than expected," explained Mary Peterson, diplomatically.

Their waiter returned with the cocktails. He served them and began to leave.

"Hey, it's a little quiet in here this evening, isn't it?" complained Shirley.

The server looked at her and smiled.

"The night is young," he said and departed.

The three women raised their glasses and toasted.

"To a nice evening with good friends!" cheered Mary Peterson.

Janet Weiss looked at Shirley with a face of affectionate concern.

"So, are things any better on the home front?"

Shirley White sipped her drink. She lit a cigarette and smiled at her friend.

"Jan, you're spending too much time around lawyers. You already know the answer to that question. But I'll humor you. Patty seems okay and Chester is still the asshole he'll always be."

Shirley drained the rest of her drink and dangled the emptied glass in the air to get their waiter's attention.

He arrived on cue.

"Are you ready for another one?"

"Oh yes, I'm definitely in the mood for another one," she giggled.

"Coming right up."

Shirley White looked at her friends with a glint in her eye.

"So tell me, how is single life treating the two of you? Have any eligible young professionals come forward to make their intentions honorable? After all, neither of you are getting any younger," she smiled, wryly.

Shirley was alluding to the fact that her two single friends were twenty-seven years of age. In 1963, although not yet considered to be old maids, neither girl was any longer viewed as the spring's newest fashion. Time was at a premium in terms of a "successful" marriage.

Although both Mary and Jan returned their friend's smile, they knew Shirley was not far off the mark.

A four piece band walked onto the small stage and began to set up. Their waiter returned with three drinks.

"I took the initiative. Once the music starts, it tends to get busy in here," he explained.

The lights dimmed and the quartet began to play.

The first song was a melodious instrumental. It filled the room without being too obtrusive. It sounded like something typically played during the first course at a wedding reception.

As if by magic, the room came to life. The people who had been eating in the formal dining room began to fill the tables and crowd the two bars of The Fontana's lounge.

34

Everywhere, people were now co-mingling, laughing, and just flat out enjoying themselves! Shirley White was mesmerized by the scene.

A young man, accompanied by two other young men approached the girls' booth.

"Hi, Janet, I thought that was you."

Dan Hamilton was an attorney at the law firm that employed Janet Weiss as a paralegal. He, like the two guys with him, looked to be around thirty years of age.

"Would you ladies mind if we join you?" he asked.

Janet looked at Mary and Shirley for a decision.

Without words, they both acknowledged their consent.

"We'd be delighted!" beamed Janet Weiss.

The three men piled into the booth.

Dan Hamilton motioned the waiter.

"A round of whatever the ladies are drinking."

"Very good, sir," complied the server.

In the now faintly lit room, the young man seated next to Shirley looked at her and grinned, approvingly.

"If I was to ask, would you dance with me later?"

She studied his face and then smiled, teasingly.

"There's only one way to find out," she laughed and fluttered overly painted eyelashes.

Shirley White silently commended herself. She had taken the liberty of removing her wedding band before entering The Fontana.

# CHAPTER EIGHT

Chester White sat alone in his den watching the television.

*The Jetsons* was his favorite T.V. program. It was an animated series set sometime in the future.

There were two things that attracted him to the show.

The first was the fact it aired in color. That was quite uncommon for U.S. prime-time T.V. in 1963. The second was all the futuristic gadgets featured weekly on the series. Chester's personal favorite was the videophone.

"If it can be done in a cartoon, it can be done in real life," he mused.

While a student, Chester had always enjoyed the science classes. Those subjects had come naturally to him. As a result, he excelled in them. Chester had envisioned himself graduating high school and going on to attend the likes of M.I.T or Cal Tech. That dream had been shattered one fateful night.

*The Jetsons* episode ended. Chester White got up from the sofa and smacked the T.V. off button with the heel of his hand. He walked, a bit unsteadily, towards the kitchen for a refill.

As he stood at the counter replenishing his drink, there was a quick knock on the kitchen's window paned door. Chester glanced over his shoulder to see who it was.

"It's open," he said, with a warm smile.

Kyle Overton entered and stood in the middle of the kitchen with an impish smirk on his face.

"Well, look who's already off to the races," he grinned.

"It's not too late to catch up," challenged Chester White.

"Don't mind if I do."

Chester pulled another glass from the cabinet and made a cocktail for his guest.

The two sat down at the kitchen table.

Chester pulled a pack of Lucky Strikes from his shirt pocket and offered one to Kyle.

"No thanks, I quit."

"I haven't," said Chester and lit up. He tossed the pack on the table.

Kyle Overton had been Chester White's best friend for as long as Chester could remember.

The two had known each other since kindergarten. It was their mutual interest in the sciences that had forged the enduring friendship.

Kyle graduated high school and then matriculated into one of the nation's more respected institutions of higher technological learning. He was, as one of his colligate sponsors described him, "a natural for his chosen field of endeavor."

After his graduation from college, Kyle landed a lucrative position with IBM at their corporate headquarters in Armonk, New York, a mere twenty minutes from his hometown of Rutland. He was assigned a position in their R&D division and had been working happily there ever since.

In most regards, Chester was envious of his lifelong friend.

He knew, by most standards, Kyle was considered to be the better looking and smarter of the two. But the asset Chester most coveted was Kyle's natural ability to have everyone he met take a liking to him. Kyle Overton had never been married.

Chester White stared, affectionately, at his friend.

"So, what brings you knocking here tonight?" he asked, with genuine interest.

Kyle Overton took a long pull from his drink. He shifted awkwardly in his chair, trying to find an emotional comfort zone.

Chester White immediately sensed his friend's uneasiness.

"Kyle, just tell me why the hell you're here," he insisted.

Overton stood up, drained his cocktail and walked to the kitchen counter for reinforcement. He returned to the table and sat down.

"I was at The Fontana tonight," said Kyle Overton.

"Why'd you leave so early?" questioned Chester.

"Because, I wanted to get the hell out of there," he explained.

Chester White remained silent.

Kyle reached for the pack on the table and lit a cigarette.

"I thought you quit," teased Chester.

Kyle Overton ignored his friend's comment.

"I saw Shirley there."

"Did she see you?"

"No, I don't think so. As usual, she was far too absorbed with herself to notice me."

"Who was she with?" asked Chester.

"Mary Peterson and Janet Weiss," informed Overton.

"She mentioned something about going out with the girls," acknowledged the vendor.

As Chester White rose from his chair, he placed a hand on the table to steady himself. The long hours of heavy drinking were beginning to extract their toll on him.

After pouring yet another drink, he managed himself back to the table and sat down. He looked at his friend and grinned a crooked smile.

"You were saying?"

"I wasn't, but I will. The girls weren't alone," revealed Kyle Overton.

Chester White let out a loud laugh of disdain.

"You would've surprised me if you'd told me they were! Who are the fortunate fellows?" chided the vendor.

"I only recognized one of them. His name is Dan Hamilton. He's an attorney."

"An attorney? Now that's what's called poetic justice, my friend! With any luck, they're working on the divorce papers as we speak."

"Shirley wasn't with the lawyer," confessed Kyle Overton.

Although disappointed by the revelation, Chester's interest was piqued for the second time that evening.

"Then who the hell was she with?" he asked.

"I don't know his name. What I do know is that when I left, Shirley was sitting on his lap and bad mouthing you."

Chester White's tone began to change.

"What do you mean, *bad* mouthing me?"

Kyle realized he had struck a nerve. However, he felt it his obligation, as a friend, to tell the truth.

"Shirley was complaining to the guy and anybody else who cared to listen that she had married beneath her station when it comes to you."

Chester White did not respond.

Kyle Overton paused, before continuing.

"Chet, you and I have been best friends, forever. No one in the world knows better than I what that bitch has cost you! She robbed you of the education and future that were rightfully, yours.   And for what? Some kid that doesn't even look like you?"

Chester White had become, hauntingly, removed from the conversation.

Kyle Overton sipped his cocktail and reached for another cigarette.

"Look, I understand how difficult a bad marriage must be to deal with. But still, that doesn't give her the right to publically humiliate you," he continued.

Chester White refocused his attention.

The unblinking eyes of scrutiny began to make Kyle feel uncharacteristically, ill at ease.

"How did she *bad* mouth me?" pressed the vendor.

Overton felt his face begin to flush.

Kyle knew full well that he had, unwisely, entered unsafe territory. He also understood that in order to avoid any possible unpleasantness, he would have to relay the truth and then bid a hasty goodbye.

"Shirley called you **'a stupid little nickel counter with a penny-ante dick'** I believe were her exacts words," winced Overton.

Kyle Overton finished his drink and snuffed his smoke.

"I think it's time for me to go."

"Yes, it is," agreed Chester White, in an eerily monotone voice.

Overton closed the kitchen door behind him.

Chester White's countenance smoldered into the face of cruelty that had so terrified the college kid in the parking lot of Carver's Bar and Grill.

He stood up and careened towards the kitchen counter to pour another drink.

# CHAPTER NINE

"Mommy, is that you?"

Patricia Anne White's sleep had been disturbed by a sudden shard of light.

The little girl sat up in bed rubbing her eyes. She expected it to be her mother, who had promised to come up stairs and tuck her in.

It was not mommy.

Standing in the bedroom's doorway was a menacing silhouette.

It neither moved nor spoke. It simply stood there, staring at the little girl.

Patricia Anne rubbed her eyes, again, trying to get a better look at the hulking shadow that hovered at her bedroom door.

The dark specter remained motionless and silent.

The eleven-year old girl desperately tried to convince herself that she was still sleeping and that the phantom in her bedroom was a dream from which she would soon awaken.

Patricia Anne's nightmare had just begun.

Without warning, the bogeyman of children's lore sprang to life. With ethereal ease it glided across the room and into Patricia Anne's bed. Its face was a twisted evil. Its eyes were the ardent stare of wickedness. And its steamy, intimate breath the very stench of depravity.

The beast's body enveloped the frail frame of Patricia Anne. Its enormous weight literally crushed the air from the little girl's lungs. Suddenly, she felt an unwelcomed intrusion. Discomfort quickly became a searing pain that seemed to travel through her entire body, tearing at the very soul of her existence.

Patricia Anne let out a high-pitched primal scream of agony. Her cries for help were quickly muted by the calloused paw of the beast.

She continued to endure the onslaught in muffled silence. As stinging tears ran down her face, a slow flow of blood began to stain her bed sheets.

Suddenly, the pain stopped. The beast was no longer in her bed. It had returned to the bedroom's doorway and resumed the shape of a silhouette.

"Now, Patricia Anne White, you must never, ever tell anyone what a naughty little girl you've been tonight!"

She did not recognize the voice. The bedroom door closed. The bogeyman was gone.

The little girl sat up and clutched herself with both arms. She began to slowly rock to and fro. Patricia Anne White spent the rest of that night and many more, thereafter, trembling and quietly sobbing, to herself.

# CHAPTER TEN

Shirley White squinted through one eye. With reluctance, she pried the second eye open, only to immediately shut them both. The harsh glare of sobriety was an arduous task to face.

Her head throbbed and her body ached. The cotton-mouth that claimed her throat was a vivid reminder of the previous evening's over-indulgence.

Truth be known, Shirley could remember very little about her night out with the girls. In fact, she could not even recall how or when she had gotten home.

With difficulty, Shirley sat up and swung her legs over the side of the bed. She peered at the clock on the night stand.

"Damn, it's nearly noon!" she muttered, to herself.

Shirley got up and made her way to the bathroom for a shower. Once dressed, she went downstairs to the kitchen. Shirley started a fresh pot of coffee and went to the refrigerator to scavenge something to eat.

She was thankful it was a weekday. Shirley knew that the school bus would have already stopped in front of their house to pick up Patty and drop her off at Rutland Elementary. Mercifully, her husband was already long gone, out busily collecting his precious nickels and dimes.

"At least, I can shake this off without being bothered by those two," she thought.

The phone rang. To Shirley White, it sounded like a three alarm fire. With annoyance, she picked up the receiver.

"Yea?" was her annoyed response.

"Shirley, is that you?"

"No, it's Jackie Kennedy!"

Janet Weiss was on the other end of the phone.

"Are you still among the living, party girl?" she asked, with a good-natured laugh.

"Barely."

"Well, with the way you were going at it last night that doesn't surprise me."

"Then why the hell are bothering me this morning?" grumbled Shirley.

"It's not morning," teased Janet.

"Shove it!"

Shirley White was about to hang up on her high school friend.

"Listen, Shirley. Dan Hamilton just left my desk," said Janet Weiss.

Dan Hamilton was the attorney who worked at Janet's law firm and had initially approached the girl's booth at The Fontana the night before, with his two friends.

"So, why do I give a damn?"

"Because, he told me the guy you were with last night thinks you're the hottest thing going since Marilyn, herself!"

Shirley White's hangover immediately disappeared. It was replaced with the radiant smile of a now rejuvenated beauty.

"Jan, don't leave out a single detail!"

"Well, Dan tells me ..."

Suddenly, Shirley White's attention was distracted.

For the first time, she noticed the two quarters sitting on the kitchen counter. They were Patricia Anne's lunch money.

*"She wouldn't forget her lunch money,"* thought the mother.

An uneasy feeling took hold of Shirley White.

"Jan, I'm going to have to call you back."

She hung up the phone and hurried upstairs.

Patricia Anne's door was closed. Shirley opened it and walked into the bedroom.

The little girl was in bed. She was lying on her side facing the wall.

44

Shirley White approached her daughter.

"Honey, why didn't you get up and go to school this morning?"

The mother sat down on the bed. She immediately felt something damp. Shirley stood up and pulled back the covers, revealing the blood-stained sheets.

"Oh, Patty Cakes, your little friend has arrived!" she exclaimed, with relief. "Now, I understand why you couldn't go to school this morning!"

The mother affectionately stroked her daughter's hair.

"You want to know something, Patty Cakes? Mommy's little friend visited her for the first time when she was just a little older than you are now. So, you have nothing to worry about. Mommy will show you what to do. All of us girls have to learn to live with our little friends."

The child remained motionless in bed, staring at the wall.

# CHAPTER ELEVEN

The months following Patricia Anne's confrontation with the bogeyman witnessed a disturbing change in the little girl's personality. No longer, the out-going and inquisitive child she had always been, Patricia Anne retreated into the withdrawn realm of herself.

There were no violent outbursts or sudden mood swings. Merely the isolation from the world around her. Although the mother noticed a change in her daughter, she had easily convinced herself that it was due to "my pretty little girl becoming a beautiful woman".

The father was spending next to no time at home.

The first one to really take note and become alarmed by the little girl's radical shift in personality was Patricia Anne's fifth-grade teacher, Mr. Tuttle.

"Thank you, for stopping by this afternoon, Mrs. White," said Patricia Anne's teacher. "I must admit, I'm a bit disappointed Mr. White couldn't join us."

"Oh, he's working," explained Shirley.

"I completely understand."

George Tuttle was in his middle forties. He was tall and thin. His short brown hair was neatly parted. He wore tortoise-shelled glasses and sported a tweed jacket.

"Mrs. White, I insisted upon this meeting because I have grown concerned about Patty's fall off in her school work. She rarely participates in classroom discussion anymore and her grades have dropped, sharply."

"It's Shirley," she smiled, fluttering gilded eyelashes.

George Tuttle adjusted his glasses and stared at the parent of his student, with professional demeanor. He continued.

"Mrs. White, has anything recently happened at home that may have caused Patty's sudden change in temperament?"

46

Miffed by what she considered to be the brush off, Shirley White became uncooperative.

"Nothing that I know of," she yawned.

The fifth-grade teacher persevered.

"In that case, would you have any objection if I arranged to have Patty sit down with our school's psychologist? "

Abruptly, Shirley White stood up. She smoothed her tightly fitted dress before answering the teacher's question.

"I'll have to talk that over with my husband."

"Of course, but for Patty's sake, please don't delay that discussion," advised the teacher.

"I wouldn't dream of it. There's no need to see me out, Mr. Tuttle!"

In a huff of resentment, Shirley stormed across the teacher's office and slammed the frosted glassed door behind her.

Once outside the school building, she lit a cigarette and walked across the parking lot to her car and the short drive home.

She pulled into the driveway and came to a stop. Shirley was still out of sorts over the meeting with Mr. Tuttle.

*"School psychologist, my ass!"* she thought, to herself. *"Tuttle's the one that needs to sit down with a psychologist!"* Shirley reassured the reflection in her rearview mirror.

She retrieved the mail and entered the house.

"Patty Cakes, mommy's home," she announced.

After parsing the postal delivery, Shirley tossed the bills on her husband's office desk and crossed the kitchen for a glass of wine.

"It's five o'clock some place," she reasoned.

Shirley climbed the stairs to the second floor and walked down the small hallway towards her bedroom to change clothes.

"Mommy, I don't feel good," complained the voice of Patricia Anne.

"Neither does mommy," she complained, to herself.

Shirley entered her daughter's bedroom. Patricia Anne was not there.

"Mommy, I feel sick," said the unseen little girl.

For the first time, Shirley realized that her daughter's voice was coming from the hallway bathroom.

With a mother's anguish, she rushed to her child.

The eleven-year-old was seated on the tiled floor with her head slumped alongside the toilet bowl.

"Oh my God! What's wrong, Patty Cakes?"

"I don't feel good."

Shirley White knelt next to her daughter and wrapped Patricia Anne in her arms.

"Mommy's here, little one," reassured the mother.

Shirley stared into the toilet bowl to see what her child had vomited. There was nothing visible to the naked eye. However, an ominous stench of sickness had already claimed the room, as its own.

"Come on, I'm going to put you in bed."

Shirley guided her daughter to the bedroom and tucked her under the covers.

"I'll be right back," she promised.

The mother returned with a thermometer and placed it under her daughter's tongue.

"Don't move," she instructed.

Shirley returned to the kitchen picked up the phone and dialed.

"Hello, Mary? It's me. Patty isn't feeling well and I need you here right now!"

"I'll be there as soon as I can," responded the voice on the other end.

Shirley hurried back upstairs to Patricia Anne's bedroom. She removed the thermometer from her daughter's mouth.

"Your temperature is normal, Patty Cakes," she said, with relief.

The front doorbell rang. Shirley retreated into the hallway.

"It's open," she yelled. "We're upstairs."

Mary Peterson, R.N. had arrived at the White's home within fifteen minutes. She entered Patricia Anne's bedroom.

Dressed in a white nurse's uniform and carrying a black leather satchel, she looked the consummate medical professional.

Mary Peterson brushed past Shirley White and sat down on the bed next to the little girl. Her face wore the expression of heart felt concern.

"What's the matter, Patty?" she asked, soothingly.

"I don't feel good."

"Where do you hurt?" asked the nurse.

"I just don't feel good," she repeated.

Gently, Mary Peterson took hold of the little girl's wrist to check her pulse. She looked at Shirley for the first time.

"Have you checked her temperature?"

"Yes, she's not running a fever."

The nurse opened the black leather satchel. She removed several items including a tongue depressor and a stethoscope.

"Patty, can you sit up?"

"Yes."

Mary Peterson, R.N. performed a very basic physical examination. After its completion, the nurse kissed the little girl on the cheek and ordered her patient to stay in bed, under the covers.

She motioned her mother downstairs.

"Shirley, when was Patty's last check-up?"

Shirley White thought for a moment.

"It hasn't been quite a year," she said. "Why, is something wrong?" she asked, with a growing fear in her voice.

Mary Peterson smiled at her long-time friend, with quiet reassurance.

"I didn't find anything that should concern you. I'm just thinking it might be a good idea for me to get a blood sample and urine specimen while I'm here. It can't do any harm. Besides, that will be the first thing the doctor will request next time he sees Patty for whatever reason."

Shirley looked at her friend, warily.

"Are you sure you're telling me everything?"

"Of course, I am."

"Then why isn't she feeling well?" she asked. "My daughter isn't one to complain. So something's definitely not right with her."

Mary Peterson looked at her friend and shrugged.

"Shirley, I honestly don't know. My guess would be a flu bug. One has been making the rounds in the schools, recently."

Shirley mulled her friend's words. The mother relaxed.

"Looks like I panicked and got you over here for nothing," she smiled, apologetically.

"Nonsense, a mother can never be too careful when it comes to her child's health," said the nurse. "And getting the blood and urine for testing is never a wasted trip."

The R.N. went back upstairs to secure the blood and urine. A short time later she descended the staircase. Mary Peterson was ready to leave.

"Shirley, I'm working the night shift this evening. I'll drop these samples off at the lab as soon as I get to the hospital."

"Mary, thanks again," smiled Shirley. "I feel a hundred percent better!"

"Just to be on the safe side, I would keep Patty home from school tomorrow. That will give her Friday and the week-end to rest."

"Yes, I'm going to do that," nodded the mother.

"I'll speak with you in the morning," waved the departing nurse.

Shirley White closed the front door. She walked into the kitchen and retrieved her impatiently waiting glass of wine.

# CHAPTER TWELVE

After leaving Shirley and her daughter, Mary Peterson drove directly to Rutland General Hospital.

She parked in the reserved area of the lot and entered the building through a Personnel Only entrance.

Her first stop was the hospital's diagnostic laboratory facility.

"Hi Mary, what brings a beautiful nurse like you to Igor's drab lab this evening?" grinned the young man seated behind the reception desk.

"Not you, Igor," she disappointed, with a smile.

Matt Gilmore was a med student who spent most of his nights in the hospital's diagnostic lab helping to defray his mounting tuition bills.

He was fairly handsome, good-natured, and quite bright. Unfortunately, he was also the same age as Mary, twenty-seven. In her mind, that meant only two things; more schooling and more tuition.

*"Too young for hunting,"* the nurse thought, wistfully.

Mary Peterson removed the two samples from her black leather satchel. She placed them on the counter with the required paperwork.

"Matt, I'm working the graveyard tonight. I'd appreciate it if you could have the results before I leave in the morning," she said.

"Anything exotic?" he asked, hopefully.

"I highly doubt it," she responded.

"Any chance you might join me for breakfast tomorrow morning?" he pursued, in earnest.

She looked at him and smirked, teasingly.

"I highly doubt it."

Matt Gilmore looked at Mary Peterson and laughed, good-naturedly.

"In spite of your poor judgment, the results will be waiting for you."

Mary's shift ended at five a.m.

Before leaving the hospital she stopped at the diagnostic lab to retrieve Patty White's test results.

Matt Gilmore was no longer on duty. Mary Peterson was almost disappointed by his absence.

After exchanging the required forms, she tucked a manila envelope in her black satchel and headed for the parking lot and the twenty-minute ride home.

Once in her apartment, Mary culled the always nearly empty refrigerator. She took a long, hot shower and then piled into bed for well-deserved oblivion.

It started as either the beginning or the end of an annoying dream. Regardless, the noise persisted.

As the sound intensified, Mary relented. Without opening her eyes, she groped for the bedside phone.

"Hello?" she answered, hoarsely.

"It's Friday afternoon. That means it's not too early to be planning for Friday night!" trilled the excited voice.

It was Janet Weiss.

"Jan, what time is it?" Mary asked, with recovering consciousness.

"It's nearly one. But it's not yet too late for a not so early bird to catch the worm!"

Mary Peterson glanced at the bed-side alarm clock to confirm her friend's unwelcomed revelation.

She sat up in bed.

"Jan, tell me what you already have planned for us," she said, with a smile on her face.

"The Four Seasons are playing The Fontana tonight," she laughed." And guess who's got three tickets for both shows?!" she crowed, triumphantly.

"Get out!"

Mary Peterson was now out of bed and excitedly pacing the length of the telephone cord.

"How the hell did you get the tickets?" she asked in amazement.

"The Jersey Boys are coming across the GW Bridge to promote their current single, "Candy Girl". Our law firm is involved with the copyrighting of their new album. Anyway, none of the brilliant brains here have any idea who the hell Frankie Valle is. They were having trouble giving the tickets away!"

Mary Peterson was now fully awake and anticipating an evening never to forget. She dressed and went to the kitchen to start some coffee.

After retrieving the newspaper, she poured a cup and seated herself at the small dinette to scan the headlines.

"I really have to call Shirley and tell her about the tickets," she said, to herself.

It was then she remembered Patty White's blood and urine samples. She got up from the table and pulled the manila envelope from her black leather satchel. Once reseated, she picked up the phone to call Shirley. She began to read Patty's test results.

With a suddenly trembling hand, she placed the phone's receiver back on its cradle. Mary Peterson was crying.

# CHAPTER THIRTEEN

"Jan, I can't do this by myself," pleaded Mary Peterson over the phone.

"I know," said Janet Weiss, empathetically. She thought for a moment.

"Friday afternoons are slow here at the law firm. I'll tell my boss that I'm leaving early to get ready for tonight's show. After all, he gave me the tickets.  I'll pick you up at your place within the hour."

The two young women started the drive to Shirley White's house, without speaking. It was Janet Weiss who broke the silence.

"How are you going to tell her?" she asked.

"I'm simply going to tell her the truth," decided Mary Peterson.

"Yes, but how?" persisted Janet.

"I don't know," admitted Mary. Tears began to roll down her cheeks.

Shirley White was in a very upbeat mood. Just a few hours earlier, Jan had called to let her know that they would be going to The Fontana to see *both* Four Seasons shows!

"It doesn't get any better than that!" she exalted.

Shirley had decided to get the evening's festivities underway with a late afternoon glass of white.

She was surprised when Jan's car pulled to a stop in front of her house at four p.m. Her two best friends walked up the driveway. Shirley White opened the front door to greet them.

"You two are a little early, aren't you?" she beamed, affectionately.

"Shirley, we have to talk to you," said Mary Peterson, with resolve.

"Okay, so let's talk," she laughed.

54

"I would like to sit down," insisted the nurse.

Shirley led them into the kitchen and motioned towards the table.

"Would either of you care to join me in a glass of wine?"

"No, thank you," declined Mary Peterson.

"I'll be more than happy to join you," accepted a nervous Janet Weiss.

Shirley took a glass from the kitchen cabinet and filled it with wine. She did not neglect to replenish her own. She joined her friends at the table.

"So, here's to a fun night!" she said and raised her glass in toast.

Janet Weiss did not join in the celebration.

"Shirley, where's Patty?" asked Mary Peterson.

"Oh, she went to school today."

Mary Peterson looked at her friend with self-contained annoyance.

"Shirley, I thought we agreed that Patty would stay home today," admonished the nurse.

"Yea, we did. But Mary, she was a different girl this morning! Patty told me she felt fine. It was like she couldn't wait to get out of the house. My little Patty Cakes is her old self."

Mary Peterson and Janet Weiss exchanged uneasy glances.

Shirley White continued.

"In fact, after Jan called me about tonight's shows, I phoned my mother and asked her if she wouldn't mind picking Patty up after school and have her spend the night at her place."

Mary Peterson mustered the inner strength that only a best friend can find within, herself.

"Shirley, Patty is pregnant."

Mary's words did not register with Shirley White. She acted as if they had not been spoken or had simply been ignored.

"I'm still deciding on what to wear this evening!" she said, excitedly, with a chilling non-acceptance of the ugly reality that now confronted her.

Mary Peterson suddenly grabbed Shirley's forearm and squeezed. Without realizing it, her nails pierced the skin. Small droplets of blood began to form.

"Your child is carrying a child!" she screamed.

Mary released her grip and broke down in tears. Janet Weiss stood up and went to comfort her sobbing friend.

For the first time that afternoon, the two friends finally had Shirley White's complete attention. The disbelieving mother lashed out.

"That's bullshit!"

Janet Weiss stood by Mary Peterson and stared resolutely into the angry eyes of Shirley White.

"The lab results indicate Patty is pregnant," she said, with strained control.

Shirley looked at her two best friends and made a final lunge to stab and silence the heart of truth.

"How do you know those are Patty's results?" she hissed, with venom. "There could've been a mix-up at the hospital! It happens. I should know. I work there!"

Her friends' prolonged, awkward silence left Shirley White with no convenient avenue of escape.

The depravity of the situation began to take hold of the mother. Her face contorted, as thoughts of the horrific unthinkable seared through her mind and body.

"That sick son of a bitch!" she shrieked. He's going to hang by his balls! Then I'm going to cut them off, stuff them down his throat, and laugh while he chokes to death!" she vowed.

Mary Peterson and Janet Weiss remained silent. Neither one of them knew what to say.

Abruptly, Shirley White's anger vanished. It was replaced with a sudden sense of fear; an immediate awareness that a twisted evil dwelled within the house she lived.

"He can't ever know!" she panicked. "He can't ever find out what I know! God help me and Patty if he does!" Shirley White broke down into self-pitying sobs of despair.

The three best friends held one another. At that moment in time, it was impossible to tell who was giving comfort and who was receiving it.

Janet Weiss was the first to attempt taking charge of a no-win situation.

"Shirley, you've got to make some decisions, and you've got to make them fast," she said, as calmly as her emotions would allow.

Shirley wiped the tears from her face and looked at her friend. She remained silent.

Janet Weiss continued in an oblique monotone, as if discussing a disinterested third party.

"It must first be determined whether or not the child will come to term."

Shirley White shook her head, violently.

"No, that's not happening! My daughter will not be made to suffer the way I have been made to suffer!" she said, emphatically.

"That leaves only one course of action," said Janet Weiss.

Mary Peterson entered the conversation.

"Patty is entering her seventh month of pregnancy.

Shirley White looked wide-eyed at her friend.

"That's not possible! She doesn't even look pregnant!"

Mary Peterson ignored Shirley White's words and continued.

"I know of a doctor who has dealt successfully with this sort of situation in the past," confided the nurse.

Both Shirley and Janet stared at their friend without saying a word. Their silence gave Mary Peterson the strength to continue.

"He's affiliated with Rutland General. However, he has two private practices. One of those practices is quite well respected. The other is a bit more *discreet*."

Shirley White nodded her immediate understanding.

"Make the necessary arrangements," she instructed, without hesitation.

Janet Weiss and Mary Peterson stood up to leave.

Shirley finished her glass of wine. She also rose from the kitchen table.

"I've got to go upstairs and start getting ready," she said.

Janet and Mary looked at her with perplexed expressions.

Shirley White stared back at them and laughed.

"Please, don't tell me you two have forgotten! We're clubbing tonight with The Four Seasons at The Fontana!"

# CHAPTER FOURTEEN

"But Mommy, I don't feel sick!" complained the little girl.

Shirley White gazed at her daughter, with a mother's love.

"Sometimes, Patty Cakes, you have to go see the doctor to make sure you don't feel sick later on," she explained to the child.

"Oh."

The front door bell rang. Shirley glanced out the window and saw Mary Peterson's car parked in the driveway.

"C'mon honey, it's time to leave," instructed the mother.

Patricia Anne ran to the front door and flung it open.

"Hi, Aunt Mary!" she said, with delight.

Mary Peterson looked at the little girl and forced a smile.

"Hey there, Patty, how are you?"

"I'm good."

Mary glanced at Shirley White.

"Are *you* sure you're ready?" she asked, solemnly.

The mother did not answer the question.

The three of them climbed into the front seat of Mary's car. Patricia Anne was nestled in the middle.

Shirley turned to Mary Peterson.

"How far is it to the doctor's office?"

"It's on the other side of town. About twenty minutes," she replied.

As they neared their destination, Shirley White was heartened by the fact the area was becoming increasingly upscale. Her anguished images of coat hangers began to recede.

Mary pulled into the parking lot of a small red-bricked edifice.

"We're here," she said and parked the car.

They entered the front door of the one-storied professional building.

The room was unoccupied except for a woman seated behind a reception desk.

She rose to greet and verify.

"You must be the Whites. We've been expecting you," she said, with unsmiling professional nonchalance.

Beatrice Strickland was tall and slender. Her face was angular and the eyes hawkish. The starched white nurse's uniform only reinforced her sterility. Beatrice Strickland was a mirthless woman of middle-age.

She eyed both the young women, warily.

"Which of you is the mother?"

"I am," acknowledged Shirley White.

Beatrice Strickland stared at her with the cold calculation of indifference.

"You'll need to complete some paper work and, of course, the necessary payment," she directed.

Shirley complied with both requests.

"Now, can we see the doctor?' asked Shirley, naively.

Beatrice Strickland looked at the mother and shook her head.

"No, *you* can't, but your daughter can," informed the woman.

Shirley White was about to object. Beatrice Strickland glared at Mary Peterson.

"Nurse, didn't you explain to the mother how this appointment is conducted?" she asked, impatiently.

Mary Peterson felt her face begin to flush. She had not found it, within herself, to fully inform Shirley about the impersonal nature of the unsavory procedure.

Before Mary could answer, Beatrice Strickland took charge of the little girl.

"Come with me, Patty. It's time for you to see the nice doctor. He's been looking forward to meeting you."

Beatrice Strickland guided Patricia Anne across the room. She opened a door, ushered her through, and then quickly closed it behind them. It was a brightly lit room. The nurse quickly covered the child's face with a moistened cloth.

Patricia Anne started to become dizzy. She felt like she was falling asleep. She looked up and saw a dark figure staring down at her. It looked like the same bogeyman who had invaded her bedroom that awful night! She feebly tried to struggle. It was no use. Once again, she succumbed to a will that was not her own.

Shirley White and Mary Peterson sat next to one another in the reception room, waiting.

Shirley was too scared to be angry with her friend. But, had to ask the question, anyway.

"Mary, why didn't you tell me I wasn't going to meet the doctor before the…"

Mary Peterson looked at her close friend with an uncharacteristically harsh glare.

"Instead of questioning me, you should be thanking me for being able to arrange a safe resolution to *your* problem!" she snapped. Mary's eyes began to moisten with tears of self-reproach.

Shirley White began to cry. Her tears of self-pity were finally interrupted by the reappearance of Beatrice Strickland and a still groggy, Patricia Anne.

"She's going to be just fine," reassured the nurse. "Just make certain that she stays in bed and rests for at least twelve hours. The doctor has already authorized the necessary medication to ensure that."

Beatrice Strickland handed the prescription to Shirley.

"Mary, please take Patty out to the car. I'll be there in a minute," said Shirley.

Once they were alone, Shirley White turned to face Beatrice Strickland.

"I have to know," she said, in a quivering voice.

The nurse knew immediately what the mother's question was. Again, she looked at her with professional indifference.

"It would have been a girl."

# CHAPTER FIFTEEN

Doctor Henry Spence was in a jocular mood.

After loading the car with everything that was required, he closed and locked the front door of his red-bricked professional building.

The ride from the small Rutland medical facility to his house was a short one. As he traveled north on the Boston Post Road, he turned on the radio.

Henry spun the knob until he found an oldies station to his liking. It was not long before the doctor was drumming his fingers on the steering wheel to the beat of Glenn Miller's immortal tune, "In the Mood".

He crossed the New York state line into his home town of Water's Edge, Connecticut.

Water's Edge was considered to be, in some social circles, the ultimate statement of status. It was a mere stone's throw from the financial mecca of Manhattan.

Water's Edge was littered with countless numbers of impressively priced homes yearning to be bestowed the title of estate. It offered a number of exclusive country clubs whose only membership requirement was that one was already deemed to be a member before formal application

But of utmost importance was the fact that Water's Edge was inhabited exclusively by what its residents always referred to as, "our kind of people".

For Doctor Henry Spence, Water's Edge, Connecticut was simply the town he had grown up in as a kid.

He pulled to a stop in the driveway of his comparatively modest home.

The fifty-eight year old physician entered the house through its kitchen door.

He put his medical bag on a counter and placed the basket he was carrying on the kitchen table.

"Henry, is that you?" called out a voice from an adjoining room.

Mildred Spence walked into the kitchen to greet her husband.

"You're home early dear," she said, with mild surprise.

Mildred was in her early fifties. She was of average height and weight. Her face was attractive and her personality pleasant. She kept her graying brown hair cut above the shoulders.

Mildred eyed the basket sitting on the kitchen table.

"I know why you're home so early. You've planned a picnic for us this afternoon, you rascal!" she gushed, enthusiastically.

"I do know how much you enjoy picnics," he smiled.

"Let me take a peek at the goodies in store for us!" she said, eagerly.

Mildred Spence pulled open the basket's blanket.

Her eyes widened and her mouth dropped in astonishment.

Staring up at her were the striking blue eyes of a tiny baby boy.

"My God, he's beautiful!" she stammered, with mesmerized wonderment. "Henry, whose is he?"

Doctor Henry Spence put an arm around his wife.

"Millie, he's yours," he said, with misting eyes.

Mildred Spence did not say a word. She carefully picked up the infant and cradled him lovingly against her breast. She gazed at her husband and smiled tears of joy.

Henry and Mildred Spence had been married for nearly thirty years. Although the marriage had been a happy one, to their dismay they had been unable to conceive a child. For Mildred Spence, the unexpected arrival of this baby was a literal dream come true!

She looked at her husband and glowed with the happiness of new motherhood.

"I'm going to name him Logan! That was my grandfather's name. They have the same deep blue eyes!"

Doctor Henry Spence started towards the kitchen door.

64

"Hank, where are you going?" she asked, distractedly.

"To bring in everything I could think of that you may need to properly care for our son," he said, with adoring affection.

After completing his self-appointed tasks, Henry sat down at the kitchen table to join his wife. She was busily bottle-feeding the infant.

"You know, Millie, our little Logan here is quite the lady's man," he grinned.

"Would you expect anything less from our son?" she asked, with good-natured motherly pride.

"I'm quite serious, dear. I've kept a diligent eye on him from the very first day he arrived on the maternity ward at Rutland General nearly six weeks ago. The little pink caps came and went but not a one without expressing her displeasure about having to leave our Logan!"

The new mother feigned preoccupation with the child's feeding. In truth, Mildred Spence hung on her husband's every word.

The doctor continued.

"Logan was a bit of a preemie."

For the first time during the conversation, Mildred's eyes drifted from the baby to her husband. Without saying a word, her expression implored clarification.

The husband immediately sensed his wife's concern. He smiled, knowingly.

"Preemie is just a fancy way of saying Logan came into this world a little sooner than expected," he said, reassuringly.

Her fears assuaged, Mildred returned undivided attention to the precious little darling she held so lovingly in her arms.

Seeing that his wife's apprehension had disappeared, Henry Spence resumed.

"What impressed me about Logan from the moment I saw him was his absolute commitment to Life. There was never a doubt in my mind that the little guy was going to survive and thrive!" he laughed.

Mildred Spence stared at her husband, absently.

"Henry, how did Logan become ours?" she asked, without really caring to hear his explanation.

Doctor Henry Spence shifted in his chair. He wrestled with a fleeting moment of uncertainty before responding.

"Millie, when I found out that the pre-arranged adoption agreement for Logan had fallen apart, I decided to take matters into my own hands. I refused to allow that increasingly muddled situation to jeopardize this child's future. He is now legally ours!" he exclaimed, with uncharacteristic emotion.

Mildred Spence looked quietly at her husband before speaking.

"Give me your solemn word that nobody will ever try to take my baby from me."

Doctor Henry Spence did not hesitate in his response.

"I would not let the Devil, Himself, try to take that child from your loving arms!" he vowed.

# CHAPTER SIXTEEN

For, Logan Spence, growing up in Water's Edge, Connecticut had always been a troubling paradox.

Although he had lived in the affluent town his entire life, Logan never felt that he truly belonged. It was as if he had mistakenly been cast in a role for which he was not suited.

Most of Logan's feelings of isolation in Water's Edge were the result of his family's financial position. In short, his parents were not wealthy. The Spence family lived a comfortable life. They lacked for nothing in terms of the necessities. But rich, they were not and would never be.

Doctor Henry Spence was a well-meaning and able physician. However, he was inept when it came to the matters of finance. This was due in good measure to the fact he had never been interested in money.

The house the Spence family occupied was the one Henry had grown up in and, subsequently, inherited from his parents. If not for this fact, they could never have afforded to live there in the first place.

As the years passed, Logan had grown increasingly aware of his family's economic contrast to the rest of the Water's Edge community. It was a disparity that no one ever mentioned or even consciously recognized. Rather, for Logan, it was a reality that reared its ugly head every time a social event took center stage.

Logan's family did not belong to a Waters Edge country club. As such, whenever his friends decided to spend a summer's day poolside, Logan would tag along as someone's "guest". During school recesses it was Logan who was the invitee to someone's Vermont ski house or Caribbean condo.

This ongoing status as the permanent guest began to make Logan feel like the always welcomed outsider; invariably present, but never truly part of the social strata that treated him so graciously.

These abstract feelings of displacement became a harsh reality during the summer of 1977. He was fourteen.

"So, Spence, where're you prepping this fall?"

The question was asked by Mark Campbell, Logan's best friend.

Mark's family was from London, England. His father's business had mandated a re-location from London to the States nearly a decade earlier. The Campbell's had been living in Water's Edge ever since.

Although he was Logan's age, Mark Campbell had already weathered the ravages of puberty. He was nearly six feet in height and towered over Logan who had yet to experience an adolescent growth spurt.

The young Brit was razor thin and possessed a wit that was equally as sharp.

Campbell's facial features were familiarly British; dark inquisitive eyes, auburn hair, and a thin regal nose. His complexion was wan and vulnerable. Mark employed a cockney accent only when it suited his fancy or need.

The two had bonded almost immediately while they were attending Eastern Middle School in Water's Edge.

It was not so much out of fondness or affinity but rather as the result of a mutual awareness that neither of them really felt comfortable with their surroundings in Water's Edge. They were rebels united by a shared sense of isolation.

"I'm going to Water's Edge High School, aren't you?" Logan Spence asked, naively.

"Absolutely not!" exclaimed the now offended young Brit. "I've asked for and been granted an acceptance at Cornwall", he crowed, in his British accent.

Cornwall was an elite private boarding school. It was molded in the staid Northeastern tradition of what a proper secondary institution was meant to be; a salve for those families itching for the Ivy.

Mark Campbell looked at Logan Spence, skeptically.

"Spence, you can't be serious about attending Water's Edge High. After all, you'll be the only one from our crowd that goes that route," he said, dismissively.

Logan Spence had no response.

The two friends entered Mark's home through a small greenhouse that abutted the basement.

Mark had seen fit to commandeer the lower level of the house for his bedroom. It afforded him privacy. More importantly, a short flight of stairs provided direct access to the kitchen and his parent's liquor cabinet.

"I'll be right back," said Campbell, as he disappeared up the staircase.

Logan Spence went over to Mark's impressive stereo system and flipped the ON switch. The tuner was already set on the radio station of his choice.

It was a Friday afternoon. That meant the legendary disc jockey, Scott Muni, would be broadcasting his "Things from England" format on WNEW-FM.

True to his word, Mark Campbell returned with two glasses in his hand. He handed one to Logan.

"Here's to Elvis Costello!" he shouted, with enthusiasm.

Campbell was referring to a then relatively unknown British rocker whose first album Scott Muni was debuting in its entirety that afternoon.

"What did you make us?" asked Logan Spence inspecting the drink.

"It's Beefeater and tonic, old man. What the hell did you expect?"

"By any chance did you happen to forget the tonic?" inquired a smiling Logan Spence.

"I daresay I did not!" insisted the now indignant host.

"That's a pity, *old man*," mimicked Logan Spence.

The two young friends broke into laughter as they clinked glasses and settled into an afternoon of Costello's first album, *My Aim Is True*.

After the first side of the album was over, Muni went into a rare commercial break vowing to return with the second side.

Mark Campbell drained the last of his drink and stood up.

"Would you care for an encore?" he asked Logan Spence.

"By all means," he said and handed over his empty glass.

Halfway up the staircase, Mark Campbell stopped and turned to face his friend.

"Spence, has it ever occurred to you that we are the only ones in our crowd that even know who the hell Elvis Costello is?"

Logan Spence smirked, wryly.

"Campbell, has it ever occurred to you that is the *only* reason we do?"

This time, it was Mark Campbell that had no response.

# CHAPTER SEVENTEEN

During the late August of 1977, Logan Spence spent a good deal of time watching his friends' departures.

He looked on as they crammed personal possessions into their parents' station wagons and then headed off to the various boarding schools of destination.

It was that summer, Logan learned the nuance in the meanings of the words farewell and "goodbye".

Water's Edge High School's student population consisted of the town's three middle schools. In addition to Eastern where Logan had been a student, there was Central and Western Middle Schools.

Eastern Middle was the smallest of the three. Moreover, only a small number of its graduating students went on to attend the public high school opting instead for private institutions. That meant Eastern Middle represented a very small percentage of Water's Edge High's over-all population.

The kids from Central and Western had two things in common walking through the front doors of Water's Edge High School. The first was they already knew each other because of the proximities of their neighborhoods and respective middle schools. The second was their mutual disdain for anyone from Eastern.

Their animus stemmed from the perception that anyone from Eastern Middle attending Waters Edge High was simply a spoiled rich kid who was too stupid to be accepted into one of those fancy private schools. These rejects were, therefore, 'fair game' for the rest of the students to torment, at will.

It did not take long for Logan Spence to come face to face with this ingrained resentment. The matter started with an incident that took place during Orientation Week in the high school's cafeteria.

Logan Spence emerged from the lunch line with tray in hand. He spotted an empty seat at a nearby table and sat down.

"Hey, asshole, that seat is already taken," said a formidable looking guy standing behind the now seated freshman.

There was another empty seat at the same table. Logan Spence silently stood up and moved to sit down at the unoccupied space.

"Don't bother. That seat is also taken," menaced the same young man.

Logan Spence surveyed the cafeteria and saw an empty seat at a table on the other side of the room. He walked over to it and sat down.

"What the hell do you think you're doing?" scowled another ready-made bully who was already seated. "You can't sit here. This seat is reserved. Get lost, loser!"

At the age of fourteen, Logan Spence stood five feet three inches tall. His slight frame presented no possible threat to the menaces of adolescent insecurity.

Logan Spence calmly sipped his soda. He then stood up with tray in one hand and soda in the other. He stared at his tormentor.

"You're right, I don't belong here."

He then dumped the soda and lunch tray on top of his antagonist's head. Spence started to walk away.

The high school junior's shock was quickly replaced by indignant outrage.

"Why you little mother…!"

He jumped out of his seat and charged towards Logan Spence.

Water's Edge High School policy mandated that male faculty members always be present during open cafeteria hours.

Quickly, two teachers grabbed the incensed student before he reached the object of his rage. A third instructor collared Logan Spence. He began to escort the freshman out of the cafeteria to the Principal's office, as much for protection as punishment.

"Your ass is mine today at The Wall! Do you hear me you little asshole! Today, at The Wall!" screamed the furious upper-classman.

72

Logan Spence spent the rest of the school session sitting in a room that adjoined the Principal's office. He did not meet the head honcho that day.

Exactly one hour after the final dismal bell rang a secretary entered the room.

"You may go now. Have a nice day," she smiled.

As his footsteps echoed down the now deserted school corridor, a girl approached him. Although Logan had never met her, he had seen her at Eastern Middle School and knew she was a good friend of Mark Campbell's older sister.

Kate Harmon was sixteen years old and a junior. She had lived in Water's Edge her entire life. After graduating from Eastern Middle School she had been enrolled in an exclusive all girls boarding school.

Unfortunately, her father's business had taken an unexpected downturn half way through her sophomore year. Kate had been attending Water's Edge High ever since.

"I heard about what happened today in the lunch room," she said. Kate stood a good two inches taller than Spence.

"So?" asked Logan.

"So, I intentionally stayed late so I could give you a lift home."

"I'm not going home."

They pushed through a side door and emerged into the sunshine of an early September afternoon.

Kate Harmon looked at Logan Spence understanding full well his meaning and intention. She was determined to see to it that he accepted her offer for safe passage home.

"Logan, do you even know what The Wall is?"

"I've heard of it," he said, with uncertainty.

"Well, let me tell what it is" she hissed, with derision. "The Wall is nothing more than an afterschool hang-out for juniors and seniors. They smoke cigarettes, drink alcohol, and do whatever else. When they get bored with that, they amuse themselves by kicking the crap out people stupid enough to go near the place that they don't like!"

"Just my luck," the freshman smiled, resignedly.

Kate Harmon looked at Logan Spence with a concerned annoyance.

"Do you have any idea who you messed with in the lunch room, today?"

"No."

"His name is Jimmy Kelly. He's one of the Kelly brothers. His brother is named Johnny. They are bad asses. Both of them are waiting for you at The Wall. They do everything together."

Logan Spence looked at her as if he had not heard a word she had said.

"Which way is The Wall?"

Kate shook her head in disgust.

"If you think showing up at The Wall this afternoon to get your ass kicked makes you brave or macho or something, you're a bigger jerk than the people waiting there to do it!"

"I asked you a question."

She motioned towards the football field.

"It's behind the home team's grandstand. Just off school property," she answered.

Logan Spence started out in that direction.

In a last-ditch effort to dissuade him, Kate played what she thought might be her trump card.

"Hey, Logan, if it were Mark Campbell in your situation, he'd be smart enough to stay away from The Wall this afternoon."

The diminutive freshman spun around to confront the voice of admonition.

Kate Harmon was startled by the expression on Logan Spence's face. In particular, the stare of his dark blue eyes caught her off guard. She suddenly felt a sense of uneasiness.

"I'm not Mark Campbell," he said in an eerily detached monotone voice.

With that, Logan Spence turned and marched towards his impending fate.

# CHAPTER EIGHTEEN

Logan Spence walked across the high school's football field. He passed the home team's grandstand and entered a small patch of woods. He began to hear music blaring from boom boxes. As he drew closer to his destination, he could discern the happy voices of people enjoying themselves.

He emerged from the wooded thicket and found himself standing in a small clearing. Logan Spence stood staring at The Wall.

It was exactly what its name conveyed. The Wall was a classic New England stone edifice roughly forty feet in length and about three feet high. Its well-crafted masonry afforded comfortable seating. The Wall was shaded by one huge elm tree. The overly treaded ground surrounding The Wall was dirt. It was littered with cigarette butts, pieces of glass, and other vestiges of parties past.

There were approximately thirty Water's Edge High School students there that afternoon. They were fairly evenly divided between male and female.

Spence spotted Jimmy Kelly. He was sitting on The Wall. To his right was seated a guy who looked to be his older brother. On his left was a girl Logan presumed to be his girlfriend.

Logan walked closer to The Wall and stopped. He stared at Jimmy Kelly.

"You said you wanted to see me."

Suddenly, the voices grew silent. The boom boxes went dead.

Jimmy Kelly nudged his older brother and smiled.

"This is the asshole I was telling you about!"

Johnny Kelly eyed Spence and looked at his brother.

"This shouldn't take too long," he said matter-of-factly.

Although the Kelly brothers were only of average height, both were powerfully built.

Johnny, the elder of the two was a senior. He had already enlisted in the United States Army with the intention of becoming a Green Beret. Jimmy had one more year of high school before graduating. He planned on following in his older brother's footsteps.

Jimmy Kelly stood up. He walked several paces towards the freshman and stopped.

"I'm surprised you even showed up. I didn't think you had it in you!" he scoffed.

Logan Spence looked at Jimmy Kelly and smiled.

"You didn't *think* because most assholes are dumb."

Spence's words ignited the younger Kelly brother. His face reddened with anger. He charged Logan Spence and threw a wild round-house punch that missed its target.

Spence got off his first and last punch. It was a shot to the midsection that landed with accuracy.

Suddenly, Logan was knocked down from behind. Immediately, both Kelly brothers were all over him.

Ironically, it was the girls present at The Wall that afternoon that stopped the carnage. Whether it was out of pity for the pathetic freshman or merely boredom with the inevitable outcome of the event, they started to walk away from the scene. As is generally the case, it did not take long before the guys followed them.

Left with no audience to impress, the Kelly brothers also lost interest. As they departed, the siblings laughed and slapped each other on the back for a job, well done.

Logan Spence remained on his back staring up at the large elm tree. A gentle breeze rustling its leaves was the only sound audible at the now deserted Wall.

Logan lifted a hand to probe his mouth for missing teeth. There were none.

Unexpectedly, Spence heard a lone muffled clapping of applause. With pain he sat up to see where it was coming from. Leaning against The Wall was a guy Logan had never seen before. Spence struggled to his feet. He advanced, unsteadily, towards the stranger.

"I had to see it for myself to believe it," said the young man.

"See what?" asked the bloodied freshman.

"See you come here knowing you were going to get your ass kicked."

"Well, at least I didn't disappoint you."

The stranger continued as though he had not heard Logan's words.

"I ran into Kate Harmon in the parking lot. She told me about what you were going to do. She wanted me to get involved. Of course, I couldn't. Not my fight. But I wanted to see it, anyway."

Carmine "The Cat" Delfino was a seventeen year old junior at Water's Edge High. He was tall and exuded a sinewy, agile strength. His wet, jet black hair was combed straight back. The complexion was olive and the eyes intense. He sported a black tee shirt and matching black jeans. Carmine had graduated from Western, the nastiest of the three middle schools in Water's Edge.

"So, why were you so interested in watching me get my ass kicked?" asked Spence.

Carmine Delfino unfurled his left sleeve to retrieve a pack of Marlboros. He opened the flip box and extracted a cigarette for himself. He then extended the pack towards Logan. Although Spence had never smoked before, instinctively, he took one. Carmine brandished an ornate Zippo lighter and struck a flame.

Logan Spence inhaled and immediately began to cough.

"The Cat" lit his cigarette and continued.

"It wasn't so much watching you get your ass kicked, as it was seeing a kid from Eastern at The Wall. This is my third year here and you're the first."

Logan Spence took another drag of his cigarette. Again, he started to cough.

Carmine Delfino continued.

"You got beat up, today. But you didn't get busted up. Do you know the difference?"

Logan Spence thought for a moment, before responding.

"No, but I do know that I don't want to find out!"

Logan laughed for the first time since arriving at Water's Edge High. His ribs were killing him.

"You didn't get busted up because you showed guts," asserted Carmine.

Spence took another hit off the cigarette and, again, he began to hack.

Carmine looked at Logan and smiled for the first.

"You think you're hurting, today? Let me tell you something. If you hadn't shown up at The Wall this afternoon, a year from now, ten years from now, shit for the rest of your life, you'd be hurting a hell of a lot more than you are right now! That sort of pain never goes away."

Carmine finished his cigarette and tossed it onto the grassless turf of The Wall. He stared at Logan with eyes that knew no fear.

"You've got balls, kid. No school, no instructor, not anything can teach you that! You're either born with them or you're not. Today, should be the proudest day of your life!"

With that, Carmine "The Cat" Delfino walked off, without saying another word.

Logan Spence watched him disappear. He finished the cigarette and ground the butt into the top of The Wall. He was no longer coughing.

# CHAPTER NINETEEN

"My goodness, what happened to you?" asked the concerned woman.

"I got into a fight, mom," answered her facially bruised and battered son.

"You sit down right here!" she commanded and pulled a chair from the kitchen table to accommodate her order.

The young man dutifully complied with his mother's mandate.

"I'll be right back!"

The woman quickly bustled out of the room and even more rapidly returned with a small black satchel in hand. She placed it on the kitchen table.

"Lean your head back so I can get a better look," she instructed.

Again, the adolescent did as he was told.

"These lacerations don't look too deep. I rather doubt any permanent scar tissue," was her initial assessment.

She opened the leather bag and began the process of healing.

Mildred Spence was a former registered nurse at Rutland General. It was there she had met her eventual husband, Doctor Henry Spence.

Although Millie was touching seventy years of age, she was still spry and feisty. Her iron grey hair belied a spirit that maintained an unusually young approach to being alive. In short, she was hell bent on keeping up with the dearest thing in her life, a fourteen-year-old son.

At first, Mildred Spence remained silent. Lovingly, she quietly went about the business of tending to the wounds of youth. However, a mother's curiosity finally got the better of her.

"Logan, do you want to tell me what happened?" she asked, soothingly.

"No!"

Although not surprised by her son's response, Mildred Spence became a bit annoyed.

"You should be thankful it's me asking you that question and not your father!"

"He'd never ask that question," responded Logan.

"And why is that, young man?"

"Because he wouldn't notice anything different in the first place."

The former nurse poured more anti-septic onto the gauze pad. She then placed it on the deepest cut and let it linger.

Logan Spence winced, with pain.

"Are you listening to me?" she asked in a tone of voice that only a mother can invoke with impunity.

"Yes, Mom."

She lifted the gauze pad.

"Your father loves you very much. However, he is also a doctor. That means a lot of people rely upon him to be with them at their times of medical need. He cannot control when those needs may arise. Do you understand?"

"Yes, Mom."

Mildred Spence resumed tending to her beaten-up warrior.

Doctor Henry Spence was well over seventy years of age. Although he refused to admit it, to himself, his practice was winding down.

For quite some time, the younger physicians associated with his medical group had stopped referring new patients to him. That left Doctor Spence with the elderly who knew and trusted him and the memories of those who were no longer among the living.

For Logan Spence, his father had always been a benign figure hovering in the background, but never really an active participant in his life.

Logan had realized early on that his dad was almost twice the age of all his friends' fathers. Although he did not hold that against him, it had always made Logan feel that something was not quite right.

Doctor Henry Spence was more of a grandfather figure to Logan. Someone who was there when convenient for the old guy, but gone when he had more important things to do.

It was for this reason that Logan had not just a love for his mother, but a genuine friendship. He felt comfortable with her. She was someone he could always talk to without the fear of reprisal or shame.

"They're from Central Middle," he offered, without prompting.

"Who are they?" asked Mildred Spence, caught off guard.

"The guys who kicked my ass this afternoon."

Before the mother could respond, the kitchen door opened. It was Doctor Henry Spence.

"Hello, dear. Sorry I'm running a little late. I got backed up at the office. What's for dinner?" he asked, as he dutifully kissed his wife on the cheek.

"One of your favorites, Hank," she answered, while closing the black satchel. "I've got chicken and dumplings baking in the oven."

Doctor Henry Spence looked at Logan and smiled, benignly.

"What the heck happened to you?"

"I bumped into a wall," he said.

Henry Spence shook his head, disapprovingly.

"Son, you've got to learn to be more aware of what's going on around you," he scolded.

"Yes, I know, Dad."

The doctor refocused his attention.

"Mother, I'm going upstairs to shower and change. I've got evening rounds at Rutland General tonight."

With that, Doctor Henry Spence was gone.

Mildred Spence left the kitchen to stow the black satchel. Upon her return, she went to the oven and checked on the chicken and dumplings.

"I'm never going to let this happen to me again," vowed Logan Spence, with pledged conviction.

The mother closed the oven door and turned to face her son. What she saw in his face was an expression that she had never seen before. More disturbingly, his always intense eyes were near tears. Millie Spence could not remember the last time she had seen her son even close to crying. The moment tugged at her soul.

"And how do you plan on making sure of that?" she asked, with difficult control.

Logan Spence stared at the floor and shook his head.

"I don't know," he said, quietly.

The mother looked, intently, at her son.

"Well, I do," she said in the cold calculating voice of a lioness protecting her cub.

Logan gazed up at his mother, expectantly.

She stared back at him and shook her head with resolve.

"I'll place a phone call. Now, go get your father. It's time for dinner."

# CHAPTER TWENTY

The phone call Mildred Spence made was to her sister. Several years earlier, she had told Millie of the trouble one of her grandsons had been having with bullies at school. Mildred was calling to found out how that situation had been resolved.

"My son sent him to a martial arts school to learn self-defense," was her answer.

"Did it work?" asked Millie.

"That's hard to say," responded the sister. "Shortly after that episode, my son moved his family out of Manhattan to a town in Bergen County, New Jersey. He's been commuting ever since."

Mildred Spence thought for a moment. She concluded that she had no other viable options.

"Sis, can you get me the name and phone number of that school?"

There was a pause on the other end of the phone.

"Millie, is Logan having problems at school?" she asked, with concern.

"Yes," was the terse response to her sister's question.

"I'll get right back to you!"

Mildred Spence enrolled her son in a well-known and respected martial-arts school. The dojo was located in mid-town Manhattan.

"Logan, your first class is this coming Saturday morning."

"Does Dad know about this, Mom?"

"No."

Logan looked at his mother. He said nothing.

The mother sensed her son's uneasiness.

"Logan, your father's answer to human relations is quite simple. He believes that if you are nice to people, eventually, those people will be nice to you."

"You don't believe that?" he asked.

"No."

Logan hesitated before asking his next question.

"Mom, what do you believe?"

Mildred Spence looked at her son with eyes of inner resignation.

"I believe that being nice to people is a virtue. However, I also believe that circumstances exist where being nice is never enough. In those situations, it is vital that you are always stronger than the people that are not being nice to you."

Although it was within walking distance of their house, the following Saturday morning Mildred Spence drove Logan to the Water's Edge train station.

"Logan, you have the address and directions?"

"Yes, Mom."

"Okay, if you need me to pick you up this afternoon, just call," she said, with maternal concern.

"I won't."

Logan Spence entered the station house and purchased a round trip ticket to New York City. He emerged from the building and stood on the platform waiting for the train.

It arrived on schedule. Logan boarded and sat down in a nearly empty car. The ride from Water's Edge to Manhattan was less than an hour.

Logan emerged from Grand Central Station onto Lexington Avenue. With duffel bag in hand, he began to walk uptown. After several blocks he spotted the building of his destination. He crossed the street and entered the front door of the dojo.

Although Logan did not know it, his mother had boarded the same train to Manhattan.

After seeing him safely inside the school, Millie turned and started her lonely walk back to Grand Central Station. There were tears in her eyes. She knew, instinctively, that the next time she saw her son he would no longer be the little boy she had followed that morning to the martial arts school. Mildred Spence spent the train ride back to Water's Edge doing battle with the ambivalence of motherhood.

Logan Spence marched up a steep flight of stairs. He found himself standing in front of a reception desk. Seated behind it was a young, attractive Japanese woman. She appeared to be in her twenties.

"Hello, my name is Miku. May I help you?" She spoke English, with no discernible accent.

"I'm here for a lesson," he answered.

"What is your name?"

"Spence."

She scanned her roster.

"Logan?" she smiled.

"Yes."

"The men's changing room is over there," she pointed. "You'll find a locker with your name on it. Once you're properly dressed, return to this desk," she directed.

Logan Spence returned to the reception desk. He was clad in the traditional gi. A white belt was knotted around his waist.

The young woman stood up. She was also wearing a gi. Her belt, however, was brown. The color denoted a ranking of impressive martial arts expertise.

"Your instructor is Sensei Hidaka. Follow me. I'll introduce you to him."

Before stepping onto the large training mat, the young woman clasped her hands together and bowed. Logan Spence did not.

They approached six boys standing in a circle. They all looked to be Logan's age or slightly older. A man stood in the center of the circle. He was giving instruction through body motions.

Sensei Hidaka was best described as a very intense young man from Japan. His height was only five feet, nine inches tall.

However, his body was one solid mass of impenetrable strength. The dark eyes were fierce and the facial expression stoic.

"Suwaru!" commanded Sensei Hidaka.

Immediately, all six youths sat down on the mat and crossed their legs waiting for further instruction.

The young woman spoke.

"Sensei Hidaka, this is Logan Spence," she introduced, in Japanese. Sensei Hidaka spoke little to no English.

He looked past her to apprise his newest student.

"Naze desu anata kokode?" he asked.

"He wants to know why you are here," interpreted the receptionist.

"I'm here for a lesson," responded Logan.

"No, that's not what he's asking you. He wants to know *why* you're here for the lesson?" explained the girl.

"Oh, tell him I'm here to learn how to hurt people before they hurt me," said Logan.

The woman relayed Spence's answer to the Sensei.

"Shinai, manabu baransu!" responded Hidaka.

"He says you're wrong. You must first learn balance," she explained.

"Tell him I've got all the balance I need," insisted Logan.

The woman dutifully complied.

After understanding Logan's words, the veins in Sensei Hidaka's neck became visible. He stared at Spence.

"**Duck walk!**" he commanded.

Logan Spence looked at the female receptionist and shrugged his shoulders. He had no idea what "duck walk" meant.

"Look over there," she pointed.

A young black kid about Logan's age was in a squatting position. His feet were pigeon-toed. He was dutifully walking the perimeter of the large mat, by himself.

"**Duck walk!**" commanded the Sensei for, the second time.

Logan Spence's first thought was to bolt the class. However, instinct convinced him that would be a bad move. With reluctance, he walked across the mat, squatted, and began to duck walk behind the black kid.

"Am I glad you're here!" he said.

"Why's, that?" asked Logan.

"I've been duck walking for nearly ten minutes. My thighs are about to bust! Duck walk ahead of me," he urged.

"Why?"

"So I can put my hands on your shoulders and take some weight off my legs."

Without knowing why, Logan Spence complied with the request. They started duck-walking in tandem.

"Is this your first class?" asked Logan.

"Yes," he responded.

The two boys continued duck-walking.

"So, why's he making you do the duck walk, man?" asked the black kid.

"Gave the wrong answer to the guy's question," answered Logan.

"Was that question, 'why are you here'?"

"Yup."

"Did you tell him to learn to kick some ass?"

"Yup."

"Me, too."

The two kids broke into laughter as they continued to duck walk around the practice mat.

Their amusement drew the attention and ire of Sensei Hidaka. The instructor motioned the two boys to return to the class. As they approached, Sensei Hidaka ordered the six other students to sit. He looked at the two new students

"Kogeki!" he commanded.

The brown belt receptionist returned to the mat.

"He's ordering you two to attack him," she explained.

The boys looked at one another, shrugged, and then charged towards the instructor.

Effortlessly, he dispatched them both to the mat. They got up and ran at him once more. Again, the Sensei threw them to the mat, with ease. Although they were learning quickly that all future attacks would end in the same result, the two new students refused to quit.

The rest of the class sat watching in spell-bound silence.

Finally, the forays ceased. Both youths were too exhausted to stand.

As they sat on the mat catching their breath, the Sensei walked over and stood directly over them.

"Baransu!" he insisted.

"He's telling you, balance," explained the receptionist. "Balance is the cornerstone of your future advancement and success in this dojo. Without learning it, you're wasting your time here," she said.

Sensei Hidaka had made his point.

After class, the two boys walked to the locker room, together.

"I'm Dwight, Dwight Jefferson," said the black kid, extending his hand.

"Logan Spence."

"Are you coming back or calling it quits?" asked Dwight.

"I'll be here next week," confirmed Logan, with resolve.

"Good! Then I'll be here too," promised Dwight.

The following Saturday morning, Logan Spence was on the train from Water's Edge to Grand Central Station. Once again, he walked up Lexington Avenue, entered the dojo, and climbed the steep flight of stairs.

As Logan emerged from the locker room, the same female receptionist approached him.

"I want to introduce you to your instructor for today's class," she smiled.

Before stepping onto the mat, the brown belt dutifully clasped her hands and bowed. Spence did not.

"Logan Spence, this is Sensei Oshiro," she said.

Logan looked at the instructor and shook his head.

"This isn't my Sensei!" he objected.

Although caught off guard by his surprising outburst, the young woman maintained her composure.

"He will be for this lesson," she informed him.

"No, he will not be!" hollered the now angered young man. "And if he is, I'm out of here! I also want my money back!" he yelled, at the top of his lungs. "Hidaka is my sensei!"

Hearing the commotion, Sensei Hidaka suddenly appeared out of nowhere.

The young woman explained the situation to him in Japanese.

Hidaka looked at Logan Spence. His dark eyes were ablaze and the veins in his neck, popping.

"**Duck walk!**" he commanded, with supreme authority.

Logan Spence stared at his instructor. Without a word, he obediently traversed the large mat, squatted, and began the arduous task of duck walking its perimeter.

Dwight Jefferson had witnessed the entire scene. He looked intently at Sensei Hidaka. Saying nothing, he walked across the mat, squatted, and started duck walking behind Logan Spence.

As Sensei Hidaka watched his two newest and most difficult students duck walking, he recalled their tenacity from the week before. He appreciated the loyalty they had for him as *their* Sensei. A small, almost perceptible smile crossed his stoic face.

From that day forward, Sensei Hidaka made certain that he was on the mat whenever those two were scheduled for class.

Something quite special also took place that fateful Saturday morning. Dwight Jefferson and Logan Spence bonded. Without consciously trying or even meaning to, they had become comrades in arms. More importantly, they were now friends.

.

90

# CHAPTER TWENTY-ONE

Logan Spence became passionate about his martial arts classes. After the initial sixteen-week course had ended, he enrolled in the intermediate level program. This mandated that he ride the train from Water's Edge to Manhattan twice a week to comply with that course's requirements.

Dwight Jefferson had been with Logan Spence every step of the way. Although he did not share Logan's passion for the martial arts classes, he relished the time spent with someone he now considered a friend. Dwight Jefferson did not have many friends.

The Jefferson family lived in Harlem. Dwight's father was a professor at Columbia University. He was a man of high ideals and noble principal. As such, he insisted the family reside in the neighborhood where he had been born. Unfortunately for Dwight, those lofty ideals did not extend as far as a public-school education.

Dwight had always attended exclusive New York City private schools. This disparity had not gone unnoticed by the other kids in his neighborhood. In many aspects, Dwight Jefferson was as much an outsider in Harlem, as Logan Spence was an outsider in Water's Edge.

It was the Saturday morning of their graduation from the intermediate level of skill, at the dojo. Dutifully, the students lined up to receive their newly colored belts of distinction.

After the ceremony Dwight Jefferson approached his friend.

"So, Logan, what are you going to do now?" he asked.

Before Spence had the opportunity to respond, Sensei Hidaka grabbed the two boys by the collars of their gis and pulled them away from the other graduating students. The same female receptionist stood by his side.

He stared at the two youths with the inscrutable expression of a martial arts master.

"Kogeki", he said.

Logan Spence and Dwight Jefferson looked at their Sensei. They had not understood the meaning of what he had just said to them. They then turned to the brown belt for an explanation.

"The Sensei says that it is now time for the two of you to learn how to attack and disable those who might try to inflict bodily harm upon you," she translated. "Both of you should understand that this invitation for advancement is a very high honor," she added.

Without hesitation, Logan Spence stepped towards his Sensei. He looked him in the eyes.

"I'm in", he nodded, in affirmation.

Dwight Jefferson backed Spence's play.

The two boys left the dojo together that afternoon. Once on the street, Dwight was the first to speak.

"Hey, man, we've got to celebrate! Let's get a couple of slices and then we'll go to my place and shoot some hoops," he insisted, enthusiastically.

Although Logan was eager for the pizza, he was less than thrilled about the idea of paying a visit to Harlem. Not wanting to disappoint his friend, Logan acquiesced.

The subway ride uptown confirmed Logan's initial concerns. The closer they got to their destination of 125th Street, the darker the complexion of their fellow riders. Although the stares of the other passengers were directed at the white kid, ironically, their resentment for his presence was focused squarely in the direction of the black kid.

Dwight Jefferson seemed to be benignly oblivious to the mounting tension that was beginning to boil underneath the streets of upper Manhattan.

The Jefferson's home was an impressive brownstone located near the Columbia University campus. As the two boys entered its front door, they were met by Dwight's mother and two older sisters.

It was immediately apparent to Logan that he was not the "friend" Dwight's mother and sisters had anticipated.

92

The mother politely introduced herself and then quietly disappeared. The two older sisters were not as socially decorous. Abruptly, they yanked their younger brother into an adjoining room of the house, for reprisal.

Logan Spence stood awkwardly in the foyer of the brownstone listening to his friend being berated for bringing "a white guy" home.

Dwight Jefferson returned to the foyer. He was smiling and holding a basketball at his side.

"C'mon, let's go shoot some hoops," he said, good-naturedly.

The two boys hit the streets of Harlem. As they walked towards the basketball courts, Logan Spence looked at his friend.

"Do you have a problem because of me?" he asked, with genuine concern.

Without breaking stride, Dwight Jefferson answered his friend's question.

"They're the ones with the problem," he said.

"What do you mean?"

"I mean the whole race thing. They just won't let it go!" he said, irritably.

Logan Spence mulled his friend's words before speaking.

"So, you're telling me that because you brought a white kid home they're pissed at you?"

Suddenly, Dwight Jefferson stopped walking. He turned to face his friend.

"What I'm telling you is the only thing that matters to me is that you and I have some fun this afternoon. We've earned it!"

The two youths entered an outdoor basketball complex. It was enclosed by a tall chain-linked fence. There were eight backstops, four on each side of a large cement court.

Two things immediately grabbed Logan Spence's attention. The first was the throngs of kids, of all ages, either playing or waiting to play. The second was the fact there was no netting underneath any of the eight baskets.

*"Hoops,"* he thought, to himself, understanding it's meaning for the very first time.

Naively, Logan had assumed when Dwight said they were going to play some ball, he had meant just the two of them. When it became apparent this was not going to be the format, Logan started getting cold feet.

His level of concern heightened when they were approached by a small group of would-be opponents.

"Hey, Dewey, who's your new friend?" asked one in the group, sizing the white kid up as an easy mark.

"He's a good man," answered Dwight Jefferson.

"Really? Then let's find out just how good he is!" challenged the resentful young man.

Logan Spence was only there because he was an invited guest. As such, during the duration of his stay he would be treated with cool indifference. However, all that would change the moment he stepped onto the basketball court. At that point, all bets would be off!

Spence understood this, intuitively. He had no intention of leaving Harlem that afternoon with anything remotely resembling a broken nose, cracked ribs, or shattered teeth. Besides, he was a lousy basketball player to begin with.

Logan looked at Dwight.

"I think I'll start by watching you guys for a while."

Jefferson stared at Spence and shook his head, in disbelief.

"Suit, yourself," he shrugged and walked onto the court.

Logan Spence stood off to the side watching the action. At the end of the first game, Dwight approached him. Several of the other guys followed.

"Logan, you ready to play now?" he asked, ingenuously.

"Yea, 'good man', you ready to show us your stuff?" asked the same black kid, with attitude.

Spence looked at them and smiled.

"I've been watching how good you guys play. You're way out of my league. Besides, I've got to get going."

Dwight Jefferson was genuinely disappointed. But even the bellicose "brother" was hard pressed to dis the compliment.

"You know how you're getting out of here?" asked Dwight.

Logan Spence nodded his head.

"I think so."

Dwight Jefferson thought for a moment.

"Hell, I've played long enough. I'll walk with you to the station."

The two friends paced the Harlem streets in relative silence. They arrived at the 125th street station. Spence began to descend the stairs to the subway.

"Hey, Logan, if you never planned on playing, why'd you come all the way up here in the first place?" asked a perplexed Dwight Jefferson.

"To hang with you," he said.

Dwight grinned.

"That's it? Then it's official. You're one strange white dude!"

"I have to be. I'm a friend of yours!"

Both boys broke into laughter.

On the train ride back to Water's Edge, Logan Spence struggled with the concept of racism.

"It's a hard word to define, but an easy one to recognize," he concluded, to himself.

# CHAPTER TWENTY-TWO

During the remainder of his freshman year and the first half of his sophomore year at Water's Edge High School, Logan Spence devoted more time and attention to advancing his skill in the martial arts than he did to his school work. It did not take long for his report card to reflect the order of priorities.

Two important things took place during Logan's sophomore year at Water's Edge High School that would change his life, forever.

The first was that he, at long last, experienced his growing spurt. The one-time diminutive five-foot three inch freshman now stood nearly a foot taller. His physique had also developed. Although not overly muscular his frame now carried a quietly imposing strength.

The second event was Logan's growing friendship with Carmine Delfino. After Logan's encounter at The Wall, the now eighteen-year old senior from Western Middle School had taken Spence under his wing. Once it was known throughout Water's Edge High School that Logan was a friend of Carmine's, no one dared to hassle him in the hallways or any place else.

Logan's high school social life revolved around Carmine and his friends. When he was not in Manhattan honing his skills on the mat, Spence was hanging out with Delfino's crowd.

It was in the company of Carmine that Logan first experienced street drugs. Pot and Blow were, by far, the most popular. However, Ups and Downs occasionally wandered into the mix. Interestingly, Smack was strictly taboo in that circle of users.

It was under the tutelage of Carmine Delfino that Logan Spence "met" girls for the first time. Although he enjoyed each of their company, Logan thought it best not to bring any one of them home to meet mom.

It was against this back-drop that Spence had his first real fight with his mother.

Logan descended the hallway stairs. He crossed the kitchen to leave the house. He had an LP tucked under his arm.

His mother called out to him.

"Logan, I want to speak with you," she said, with an insistent tone of voice and walked into the kitchen.

Mildred Spence was now touching seventy years of age. However, she was in fine physical shape and as spry, as ever. The only concession to her years was the lines of concern in her face. She came right to the point.

"Logan, your grades are not acceptable! Do you realize that you're on the verge of flunking out of high school?" she asked, with a trembling anger.

Spence remained silent.

She continued.

"I'm beginning to think that sending you to that martial arts school in Manhattan was a bad idea. In fact, I know it was!" she seethed. "What is it now? Three times a week you travel in there?"

The mother stopped within inches of the son who now towered over her.

"I can only be thankful for the fact that your father knows nothing about that or this!" she yelled, waving the failing report card in her hand.

Logan spoke for the first time.

"It wasn't a mistake," he said, quietly.

"What wasn't a mistake," asked the mother.

"Allowing me to attend the dojo," he replied.

"And why the hell is that?" she spat out in frustration.

Suddenly, Logan Spence's expression changed. His eyes were now something Mildred Spence was uncomfortable with.

"Because, I've learned more there than my father could ever have taught me here!" he shouted, defiantly.

His words were poison to her ears. Reflexively, the mother slapped her son across the face.

"Don't ever speak disrespectfully about your father, again!" screamed the mother. Mildred Spence began to cry.

Logan Spence looked at his mother, stoically. Although her tears hurt him far more than the slap of rebuke, he was in no mood for further conversation. Logan turned to leave.

"Where do you think you're going? I'm not finished with you young ...."

Her words were silenced by the slam of the kitchen door.

Logan walked the back route towards his destination. He lit a cigarette and tried to sort out, in his own mind, what had just taken place. He knew his mother was right about the poor grades. However, he was also convinced that the long hours he was spending in the Manhattan dojo were an investment in his future.

"Someday, they'll pay off," he convinced, himself.

Logan opened the door to the familiar greenhouse and dropped down into the basement Mark Campbell called home.

"Spence, how the hell have you been?" smiled the lanky Brit from London.

"Top form," smirked Logan, in an affected British accent.

The long-time friends shook hands.

Two things startled Mark Campbell about Logan Spence's outward appearance. The first was the fact Logan was now markedly taller than he was. The second was Spence's shoulder length hair.

"Care for a cocktail, old man?"

"Thought you'd never ask," answered Logan. He was no longer smiling.

Mark Campbell disappeared up the basement's staircase headed for his parent's liquor cabinet.

Mark was back at home in Water's Edge on a two week break from Cornwall, the prestigious Connecticut prep school he attended.

He returned brandishing two water glasses filled with anything but. The two friends toasted.

"Where are your parents?" asked Logan.

"Out for the evening."

"How convenient."

"Quite."

Mark Campbell glided over to his impressive stereo system and cued up a record.

"I'll bet you haven't hear these guys yet," he challenged, with confidence.

It was The Police's debut album, *Outlandos d` Amour*. Although Spence had heard the bootleg weeks before, he feigned surprise.

"You preppies are always ahead of the rest of us common folk," he smiled.

"Indeed," agreed his host.

As the music began to envelop the room, the two friends settled in for an evening of catching up and indulgence.

"So, how's Water's Edge High treating you?" Campbell asked, with genuine concern.

"Other than the fact I'm flunking out, not too bad," answered Logan.

Mark Campbell eyed his friend with skepticism.

"You can't be serious."

"*Quite,*" mimicked Logan Spence.

Campbell shook his head, dubiously.

"So you're chucking the whole idea of college?"

"At this point, college isn't even in the picture," admitted Logan.

Mark Campbell thought for a moment. After careful consideration, he looked his friend squarely in the eye.

"You know, Spence, if you were to attend a prep school like Cornwall, or the like, college would not only be in the picture, it would be part of your future," he declared.

Logan Spence stared at his host and began to laugh.

"Mark, for starters, my grades are failing. Besides, even if I was to get into a school like Cornwall, I don't know if my parents could afford the tuition," he said, glumly.

Undaunted, Mark Campbell pursued his train of thought.

"You know, schools like Cornwall are rabid about their sports programs. They take them quite seriously. If you are exceptional at a sport the school wishes to excel in, *you're* in!" he stated, enthusiastically.

Mark Campbell had Logan Spence's undivided attention.

"For example," he continued, "our Director of Admissions at Cornwall is keen on the wrestling program. If an outstanding wrestler walks into his office, the guy will have a real good shot at being accepted."

"What's the Director of Admissions name?" asked Logan.

"Hensley, Mr. Robert Hensley," informed Campbell.

With that, Mark Campbell stood-up. He rescued Logan's emptied glass and disappeared upstairs for refills. Upon his return, he cued up the second side of The Police album and then looked, at Logan.

"Spence, have you ever smoked weed?" he asked, nonchalantly.

"On occasion," replied Logan.

"Feel like getting high, now?" pressed Campbell.

"Why not?" responded Spence.

Excitedly, Mark Campbell produced a joint and started towards the walk-through window leading to the greenhouse.

"This stuff is primo! A guy on campus gets it from New Haven and distributes," bragged the host.

Mark Campbell lit the bone. He took a few hits and handed it to Spence.

Just by the texture of the joint, Logan knew he was in for disappointment. He took a couple of perfunctory pulls and then handed it back to Campbell.

"I'll be inside," he said.

Mark Campbell took a couple more quick hits, snuffed the joint, and followed Logan. He sat down in his customary chair and stared at his friend.

"So, what do you think?" he asked, with a goofy smile plastered across his face.

Logan sipped his cocktail.

"I think the stuff sucks, no pun intended," was Spence's objective appraisal.

The goofy smile disappeared. Campbell's initial disappointment quickly morphed into resentment.

"And I suppose you have something better?" he challenged.

Logan Spence smiled, serenely.

"As a matter of fact, I do."

He pulled from his pocket a very thin joint. However, it was recently imported, "in-season" ganja. It had a very different texture, taste, and high than the typical street weed being peddled on the streets of America in the late Seventies.

"Now, that *does* look impressive," mocked the now wounded Campbell.

"C'mon, let's go outside," beckoned Spence.

Once in the greenhouse, Spence lit the joint, took two deep hits, and then passed it.

"The rest is yours. But, be warned, a little dab will do you."

Logan returned to the basement. The Police album had finished. He retrieved the record he had brought with him. He put on *Excitable Boy*, Warren Zevon's breakthrough album.

Several songs elapsed. Campbell still had not returned from outside. Logan decided to go find his friend. Campbell was quietly standing in the greenhouse.

"Mark, what the hell are you doing?"

"Whoa," he said in a slow, deliberate monotone.

"Did you finish the rest of that joint?" Spence asked, with concern.

"I think so."

"C'mon, let's go back inside."

Logan guided his friend to his usual chair in the basement.

"Whoa," repeated Campbell.

"Mark, are you going to be alright?"

"I think so."

As Logan left Mark Campbell to contemplate the cosmos, "Werewolves of London" was blasting on the stereo.

"*How appropriate*," thought Spence, as he started the walk back to his house.

# Chapter Twenty-Three

Logan Spence thought long and hard about what Mark Campbell had told him regarding Cornwall's Director of Admissions.

"If Robert Hensley is into wrestling, I might just find my way into Cornwall," he concluded, to himself.

He was also mulling the fight with his mother the night before. Those were the two things on his mind as he descended the stairs the next morning.

Mildred Spence was seated at the kitchen table. She was sipping coffee and reading the New York Times. She did not look up. As usual, his father was nowhere in sight.

Without speaking, Logan crossed the kitchen and poured himself some orange juice. He seated himself at the table directly facing his mother.

"I've been thinking about what you said last night," began Logan.

His mother did not look up from her paper.

He sipped the orange juice and continued.

"You're right, if things don't change, I will flunk out of high school. I don't want that to happen. I've decided I want to go on to college. That's why I'm going to apply to The Cornwall School," he said, with finality.

This last statement quickly grabbed his mother's attention. She put her reading glasses on the newspaper and stared into the eyes of her son.

"Cornwall? Logan, I rather doubt your grades merit admission there," she dismissed. "Besides, I don't know if your father and I could even afford the tuition!"

Logan pressed on as if he had not heard his mother's words.

"I went to Mark Campbell's house last night. He goes to Cornwall. He tells me that grades are not the only thing they consider when it comes to admission there. They also look at standardized test results. Mark says the personal interview is very important," concluded Logan.

For the first time that morning, Mildred Spence's face, softened. She was encouraged by her son's newly found sense of direction. The tone in her voice returned to that of maternal love and concern.

"Okay, Logan, you register yourself for whatever test is required. After that is taken care of I'll try to arrange a personal interview," she said with commitment.

The drive from Water's Edge to Cornwall was just over an hour. Logan sat in the passenger seat as his mother drove. His father's scheduled rounds at the hospital prevented him from joining them that afternoon.

Cornwall was located in Sheffield, Connecticut. The downtown was a typical, past its prime New England mill town. However, the campus of Cornwall was a world unto itself.

Its quaint streets were lined with majestic trees. The large, impressively constructed stone buildings resonated a rich tradition of academic excellence. And the expansive athletic fields were well equipped and manicured.

They pulled to a stop in the visitor's parking lot. After asking directions, Logan and his mother started the walk to the Administration Building.

Mildred Spence was dressed in a well-tailored, gray two-piece suit. She looked all business. Logan was wearing a blue blazer, black knit tie, and khakis. His hair was pulled back in a tight pony tail.

As they entered the front door of the Administration Building, they were greeted by a young woman seated behind a reception desk.

"We're here to see Mr. Hensley," informed Mildred Spence.

"Of course, his office is up those stairs and at the end of the hall," she replied, politely.

Once upstairs, they walked to the end of the hall. An older woman stood up from behind a desk.

"Good afternoon, Mrs. Spence," as she extended her hand, smiling. "My name is Louise. And you must be Logan," she said warmly. "Mr. Hensley is expecting you." She opened the door to afford entry and then quietly closed it behind them.

The office was large and sumptuously furnished. Its most striking feature was the huge bay window that afforded views of athletic fields and an indoor sports complex in the distance.

A man stood up from behind a formidable desk and came forward to greet them. He looked to be around forty years of age. He was of medium height and build. His brown hair was parted neatly to the side. He was wearing a dark, well-tailored suit. His horned-rimmed glasses complimented a pleasant face.

"Hello, I'm Bob Hensley," he smiled and extended his hand towards Logan's mother.

"Mildred Spence," she nodded, agreeably. "And this is my son, Logan." The two shook hands.

Suddenly, the smile disappeared from the man's face. There was an awkward moment of silence.

"Is there something wrong Mr. Hensley?" asked Mildred Spence.

"Well, truth be told, I'm a little disappointed Mr. Spence isn't here. I generally like to meet both parents on the initial interview."

"Unfortunately, *Doctor* Spence's hospital schedule precluded his presence this afternoon," explained the mother.

"*Doctor* Spence. Well, that does explain things," he agreed. His awkwardness quickly disappeared.

"Let's sit down, shall we?" as he motioned to a small circular table located next to the bay window. He adeptly removed what would have been an unoccupied fourth chair.

There was a file folder placed in front of Mr. Hensley's seat. For the first time, his undivided attention was focused on the applicant.

"Logan, I've reviewed your transcripts. Quite frankly, I'm less than impressed with your grades."

He let the gravity of his words linger before continuing.

"On a more positive note, your test results in math were better than acceptable. However, you're markedly weak on the verbal end of the spectrum."

Robert Hensley looked at his two guests.

"May I offer either of you something to drink?" he asked with perfunctory politeness.

Both declined.

"Well then, Logan, that leaves me with only one question. Why would you and Cornwall be a good fit?"

Logan Spence stared directly into the eyes of the Director of Admissions.

"Because it would be mutually beneficial for both of us," he stated with unwavering confidence.

Robert Hensley smiled benignly, almost condescendingly.

"And how's that, Logan?"

"Cornwall could help me get better at reading and writing. And I could improve Cornwall's already impressive wrestling program."

Hensley's facial expression turned to one of surprise.

"You didn't mention anything about wrestling on your application!" he said, without having to re-examine it.

"That's because the application only asked about school athletics. My wrestling training has been off campus at a private facility," he explained.

The entire dynamics of the interview changed on a dime. Mr. Robert Hensley was now evaluating Logan Spence from a whole new perspective.

"Logan, what's your weight class?" he asked with keen interest.

"I can wrestle at 160lbs, 167lbs, or 174lbs depending upon what the coach and team might need at the time."

106

Although Hensley's head was spinning with the possibilities, he willed himself back to solid ground.

"Logan, just how good a wrestler are you?" he asked, anticipating the usual self-promotion.

Spence looked at the Director of Admissions and shrugged.

"There's only one way to answer that question, Sir; on the mats."

# CHAPTER-TWENTY-FOUR

The young man's answer caught Cornwall's Director of Admissions by surprise. He looked long and hard at Logan. His fingers unconsciously drummed the applicant's file folder. Clearly, Robert Hensley was at the crossroad of decision.

He looked directly at Logan's mother for the first time since the three of them had sat down at the circular table.

"Mrs. Spence, after the time we have spent together this afternoon, I think Logan merits a second interview of consideration. At such a meeting we would discuss, in length, how a possible enrollment here at Cornwall might best serve his future academic pursuits," suggested Hensley. "Also, it would give you and Logan the opportunity to tour our entire campus."

The Director of Admissions opened his appointment book.

"Let's see, today is Wednesday. Might we say this coming Monday morning around ten a.m.?"

Mildred Spence thought for a moment before speaking.

"Well, I don't see any reason why we couldn't," she agreed, tentatively.

Immediately, Logan shook his head.

"Mother, have you forgotten? We're visiting Bardsville this coming Monday," he reminded.

Bardsville was a very prestigious northeastern private secondary school. According to Mark Campbell, it was Cornwall's arch rival and had been for generations. This was especially true when it came to athletic competitions between the two schools.

Logan's pronouncement came as a surprise to his mother. This was because they had no upcoming appointment with Bardsville. However, Mildred Spence did not miss a beat.

"Oh, that's right, dear. I completely forgot." She looked at the director. "I'm terribly sorry, Mr. Hensley, but this Monday will simply not be possible," she said, apologetically.

108

This sudden turn of events had inwardly flustered Robert Hensley. Cornwall's Director of Admissions was having disquieting visions of Logan Spence single-handedly dismantling the entire Cornwall wrestling team at their next match with Bardsville. This simply would not do!

He looked anxiously at Mildred Spence.

"Mrs. Spence, might your schedule this afternoon permit Logan time enough to visit our sports complex; in particular, our wrestling facilities?"

"I suppose so," answered Logan's mother with a hint of feigned impatience. The old gal had caught on real fast!

"Very good."

With that, Hensley picked-up the receiver of a phone located on the circular table.

"Louise, get me Coach Hubbard." He hung up.

Robert Hensley looked at his two guests.

"Coach Hubbard is in charge of Cornwall's entire sports complex in addition to running the wrestling program," he explained.

Several moments later Hensley's phone rang.

"Hi, Coach. Would you have several minutes for me? I'd like you to meet an interesting young man." He listened to the other end of the phone and then glanced at his watch. "Say twenty minutes? Great!"

The Director of Admissions refocused his attention on Logan Spence.

"We're in luck. Not only are you going to meet the coach, but the wrestling team is holding a practice today, so you'll meet some of the guys, as well."

A sudden cloud crossed Robert Hensley's face. He turned to face Logan's mother.

"Mrs. Spence, in the excitement of the moment I neglected to take into consideration the fact that the men's athletic training facilities do not permit women," he admitted, sheepishly.

"Oh, don't give it a second thought, Mr. Hensley," she said, graciously. "I'll be fine."

"Wait, I have a thought," he smiled and picked up the phone. "Louise, will you come in here, please?"

The office door opened and the woman entered. She appeared to be about Mildred Spence's age.

"Louise, Logan and I are going to meet with Coach Hubbard. I thought it a good idea if you would give Mrs. Spence an abbreviated campus tour."

"I'd love to," she beamed and looked at Logan's mother. "Would you like to start with the library or our campus theater?"

"Oh, the theater!" exclaimed Mildred Spence, enthusiastically.

"We should be about an hour," informed the head of admissions.

The two women disappeared, closing the door behind them.

Once they were gone, Hensley walked across the office and opened a closet door. He removed his suit jacket and tie replacing them with a blue windbreaker. He picked up a pair of sneakers and sat down to change shoes.

"C'mon, we'll go out the back."

Once outside they climbed into a golf cart and started towards the sports facility.

"You're my last appointment of the day," he said, explaining his change of attire.

They pulled to a stop in front of an entrance located on the side of the large domed building.

"This is the wrestling wing of the complex," informed Hensley.

He opened the door and ushered Logan inside. They found themselves standing in a long room. On either side were rows of steel meshed lockers accompanied by two long, padded benches. Immediately to the right was a room with a saddle door, the upper half of which was open. An old man was inside leaning against its top counter observing the new arrivals.

110

"That's the equipment room. The gentleman standing there is the equipment manager. Anything you might require along those lines, see him," Hensley instructed.

"Hi, Gus," he greeted without breaking stride to chat.

"Mr. Hensley," was the deferential response.

The Director of Admissions continued the guided tour.

"Over there," he motioned to the left, "are the showers and bathrooms. The steam and sauna rooms are also located in that area. Through that door on the right is a completely equipped gym. Unfortunately, today's time constraints won't permit a full inspection."

As they continued to walk, voices could now be heard coming from the other side of an approaching closed door.

"That is the trainer's room," said Hensley pointing to what looked like a small infirmary.

As they pushed through the closed door, they were met by the loud noise of a wrestling practice in progress. The room was a large barren square. Its floor was one seamless mat.

There were forty or so people clad in sweats busy with various drills, maneuvers, and instruction. Three coaches were supervising the session.

Robert Hensley stopped at the mat's edge.

"This is where the Jay-V's and wannabes practice," he shouted over the din. "The Varsity is in the next room."

He started across the mat. Suddenly, he stopped and turned.

"Logan, take off your ..."

Spence was already barefooted and holding his loafers in one hand.

The plaque above the low open doorway read "The Pit". Three steps led down to a smaller version of the first room. The only difference was a high rectangular window that spanned the outside wall.

A man stood in the center of the mat. The sixteen members of the Cornwall varsity team were standing in a semi-circle listening to his words.

The two outsiders were immediately noticed.

"Coach, do you have a minute?" called Robert Hensley.

The man glanced over in their direction. After finishing whatever he had to say to his team, he blew the gold whistle that hung from his neck. Led by their two co-captains the team walked to the far end of the room and commenced warm-up exercises.

Frank "The Tank" Hubbard was a force to be reckoned with. Standing over six feet in height, he was a powerfully built man. Although touching nearly sixty years in age, not even the baggy sweat suit he was wearing could camouflage a still impressive physique. His gray hair was cropped military short. His jaw was fully squared. And the intense eyes were seemingly no longer capable of any form of surprise.

"Coach, this is Logan Spence," introduced Hensley.

Hubbard stared at Logan as if appraising the worthiness of a race horse.

"How much do you weigh?" were his first words to Logan.

"Around one-sixty."

"But Logan says he can wrestle more than one weight class," interjected Hensley.

Coach Hubbard addressed the head of admissions without taking his eyes off the new prospect.

"I don't give a damn what *Logan* has to say! Mr. Spence, get your ass upstairs and suit-up!"

# CHAPTER-TWENTY-FIVE

Logan walked back to the locker room and stood in front of the equipment room's saddle door.

"Here to suit-up?" asked Gus with a smile that revealed a long hiatus between dental visits.

"Yes."

"That's always a good sign. What's your size?"

"Large."

The equipment manager gathered the necessary gear and placed it in a neat pile on top of the counter.

"What's your shoe size?"

"Twelve."

Gus disappeared momentarily. When he returned, he handed a pair of white leather wrestling shoes to Logan. The old man then looked at him with distant eyes.

"I know black is the color everyone is wearing these days, but these babies have been around. They don't make them anymore. But, they won't ever let you down. Just make sure you never let them down."

Suddenly, Gus returned from wherever far-away place he had just been.

"That's your locker, over there," he pointed.

Logan suited-up quickly and returned to "The Pit". The team was still going through warm-up exercises. Coach Hubbard and Robert Hensley were off to the side in conversation. Spence approached the two men.

"So, Spence, you ready to wrestle?" asked Coach Hubbard.

"I'm always ready to wrestle, Coach," responded Logan.

"We're about to see about that. You want to warm up?"

"No need."

With that, Coach Hubbard walked across the mat towards his team. He motioned to one particular individual. The two of them returned to where Logan and Hensley were standing. The wrestling team continued its work-out.

"Logan Spence, meet Carlos Acosta," introduced the coach.

The two soon to be combatants shook hands.

Although several inches shorter than Spence, Acosta had a weight advantage that looked to be between ten and fifteen pounds. His body build was muscular with no excess bulk. Carlos was in his senior year at Cornwall. He had recently placed third in his weight class at the Connecticut State Finals. Expectations were growing for an impressive showing at the upcoming New England Regionals. His short dark hair and light-olive complexion accented his Argentinian heritage.

"This match is going to be strictly regulation; three two-minute periods. The wrestler behind on points at the end of the first period will start the second on top," instructed Coach Hubbard.

Hubbard walked to the large encircled golden "C" in the center of the mat. The two young men put on and adjusted their respective head gear and followed him to the center. They shook hands. The whistle blew. The match was on.

Both wrestlers started in a standing position. The two circled each other warily, each looking for an opening.

Acosta's standing position was unique. The entire body was in constant motion. His head bobbed to and fro. Both arms were raised to eye level with each hand continually flipping inward to outward. His legs were slightly crouched with both feet pigeon-toed and rhythmically thumping the mat to a silent South American drum beat. It was a scorpion war dance!

With surprising quickness, Acosta took Spence down, gaining the advantage and scoring his first points of the match. Unfortunately for Carlos, those would prove to be his last.

The rest of the Cornwall varsity team was now standing still and watching the event in captivated silence.

Acosta spent most of the first period desperately trying to make short work of the unknown walk-on. His efforts expended needless energy. Towards the end of the period, Spence reversed his opponent. Additionally, he scored a near pin as the whistle blew.

Behind on points, Acosta started the second period on top. Again, he went for the kill but was rebuffed. Halfway through the period Spence reversed Acosta and finished it by quietly adding to his point total.

The third period started with Spence on top. He was comfortably ahead on points. Acosta had grown tired and frustrated. Halfway through the final period, Logan knew he could pin his opponent, at will. He chose not to. He was there to make the team, not enemies. He figured a resounding decision would serve his purposes more effectively than an in your face pin.

The final whistle blew. The match was over. The two contestants shook hands.

"You're good. You're very good!" said Acosta, graciously.

Coach Hubbard approached the two gladiators.

"Spence, you hit the showers. Acosta, you rejoin your team," he ordered.

Logan started toward the stairs leading out of "The Pit".

"Hey, Johnny White Shoes, don't ever let me catch you and your ponytail without a chaperon," challenged a member of the team.

Instinctively, Logan turned and started towards his antagonist. Without hesitation, Coach Hubbard stepped in front of him to block his path.

"Spence, I told you to hit the showers," he said in a mollifying tone of voice.

The two stared at each other. Neither had fear in their eyes. Without a word, Logan turned to leave the room.

"Thompson, you know the drill!" shouted Hubbard.

Without further prompting, the heckler hit the deck and started doing push-ups. The sharp chirp of the coach's whistle refocused everyone's attention on the practice in progress.

Logan climbed the short set of stairs and pushed his way through the doorway that was still crowded with "Jay-V's and wannabes" who had gathered to watch the show. As he entered the locker room, Gus was waiting for him. He fell into stride with Spence.

"So, why didn't you?" he asked.

"Why didn't I what?" replied Logan.

"Why didn't you pin his ass when you could," persisted the equipment manager.

Spence made no response.

"Hell, it doesn't matter anyhow. If I know you could've pinned him, Coach knows you could've pinned him," rationalized the old man.

Logan Spence showered and dressed quickly. He walked over to the equipment room. He threw the sweats in the laundry hamper and placed the white wrestling shoes on the counter of the saddle door.

"Thanks for your help, Gus."

The old man looked at Logan Spence.

"These are yours now," he said tapping the shoes. "You earned them. They'll be waiting for you when you come back."

"How do you know I *will* be back?"

"Oh, you'll be back alright," predicted the equipment manager.

Robert Hensley was positively giddy on the golf cart ride back.

"I think Coach Hubbard was impressed with you today. I know I was!" gushed the Director of Admissions.

As they came to a stop in front of the Administration Building, Logan's mother and Hensley's secretary, Louise, were just returning from their quick tour of the campus.

"What perfect timing," smiled Mildred Spence. "I can't tell you what a pleasure it has been meeting the two of you."

She turned to face her son.

"Logan, are you ready to go?"

Before he could respond, Robert Hensley broke in.

"Mrs. Spence, I think it important that we return to my office. It will only take a couple of minutes," he insisted.

Once they were settled in his office, Robert Hensley was the first to speak.

"Mrs. Spence, allow me to come directly to the point. After spending the afternoon with the two of you, I have come to the conclusion that Logan would be an ideal fit for Cornwall," he stated emphatically.

Mildred Spence shifted uneasily in her chair as she formulated a response.

"Mr. Hensley, allow me to come right to the point. I'm not at all certain that Dr. Spence and I are currently in a financial position to send Logan to Cornwall."

Robert Hensley remained undaunted.

"Mrs. Spence, as Director of Admissions I have a certain amount of, shall we say, latitude when it comes to the financial arrangements pertaining to tuition. In Logan's case, I'm quite confident we will be able to arrive at a figure that all parties concerned will be comfortable with," he smiled assuredly.

Before the mother could respond, Hensley looked in her son's direction.

"Logan, one of the first things you told me was that you want to improve your reading and writing skills. I can think of no better way to achieve that goal than by having you assigned a mentor. In fact, the tutor I have in mind is currently teaching here as a requirement in completing Yale's PhD. Program in English Literature."

Mildred Spence was hooked. She looked at Mr. Hensley with moistness in her eyes.

"Oh, that would be wonderful!" she half whispered.

"No, I think Logan and Pat will work very effectively together," concluded the Director of Admissions.

"And what is his last name?" asked Mildred Spence.

"Oh, Pat is not a he. Pat is a she," he corrected with a smile. "But to answer to your question, her name is Ms. Patricia White."

# CHAPTER TWENTY-SIX

"So, Patty, are you going to this thing or not?" asked Kate Whitson.

Patricia White looked at her closest friend and shrugged, with resignation.

"I suppose I really don't have much choice, do I?"

"Not if you want to remain within the ranks of the politically correct," cautioned Kate, smiling.

"Who would ever have guessed that politics would rear its ugly head in the pristine world of academia," grinned Patty, sarcastically.

Both young women started to laugh.

Patricia White and Katherine Whitson had been best friends since they were eleven years old. The two had met on the first day of sixth grade when they attended Spenser Academy. The spelling of their last names had placed them at adjacent desks. Spenser was a prestigious private day school serving girls in grades Pre-K through the twelfth. It was located in Water's Edge, Connecticut.

Every other girl in that sixth-grade class had been attending Spenser for years. The sudden arrival of two new "outsiders" was met with unanimous resentment. It was the mutual feeling of non-acceptance that had immediately bonded Patty White and Kate Whitson.

Kate and her mother had moved from New York City to Water's Edge earlier that summer. Although Dina Whitson remained married to her husband, he had not made the move with his wife and daughter.

After Patty completed the fifth grade, Shirley White, unexpectedly, removed her from Rutland Elementary School and made arrangements to have her attend Spenser Academy. It was the mother's thought that a change of schools might improve Patty's then slumping grades and attitude.

Besides finding common ground as the new "outsiders", the two young girls shared a mutual love of books. For both Pat and Kate, reading had become far more than a pleasurable past-time. Books provided each of them a safe haven; a place where they were sheltered from menacing forces that always seemed a little too close, at hand.

To the surprise of those who knew both women, Dina Whitson and Shirley White became good friends. This puzzlement stemmed from the fact that they came from different worlds and had, seemingly, nothing in common.

Dina Whitson was born into money and then married into more money. She had been educated at the most exclusive of schools during her years as a student. Fashionably attractive, upon her arrival in Water's Edge, Dina effortlessly glided to the top of that town's highest social stratum.

By contrast, Shirley White was a high school drop-out from Rutland, New York who still lived in Rutland, New York. Although not unattractive, she sorely lacked the pedigree credentials and social grace of her newly found friend. Despite the disparity in backgrounds, their friendship was genuine and enduring.

It was for this reason it came as no surprise to anyone that when Dina Whitson decided to transfer Kate out of Spenser Academy at the end of her eighth-grade year, Shirley White followed suit with Patty's simultaneous departure.

The new institution of choice was the private and well-regarded secondary school, Angelica Hall. Several years earlier, Angelica Hall had relocated from Water's Edge to Sheffield, Connecticut to become the sister school of Cornwall. Henceforth, the institution was known as Cornwall Angelica Hall.

Upon graduating Cornwall Angelica Hall, Patty and Kate applied to and were accepted at Vassar College in Poughkeepsie, New York. After completing their undergraduate studies there, both girls decided to pursue their eventual, PhD's at Yale. A curriculum requirement had brought Pat and Kate back to Cornwall Angelica Hall to teach at their alma mater.

120

As these years had passed, people who knew both girls were not at all surprised by their impressive academic accomplishments. Furthermore, the curiosity surrounding the friendship between Dina Whitson and Shirley White had long since run its course.

However, whenever the White and Whitson names became a topic of conversation at Water's Edge cocktail parties, one question inevitably reared its ugly head: "How in the world does a loser like Chester White afford those exorbitant tuitions year in and year out?"

"So, Patty, you're definitely going to the faculty reception party this evening," confirmed Kate Whitson.

"Yes," replied Pat White. "What time does it start?"

"Six o' clock in the drawing room of the Cornwall library."

"I'll meet you downstairs in the lobby at seven o' clock," decided Patricia White.

Kate looked at her friend, disapprovingly.

"So, you want to be fashionably late, is that it?" she chided.

"No, just late," corrected Pat.

"I'll be waiting for you downstairs at 6:30," finalized Kate, as she closed the door behind her. She headed back to her apartment located in the other wing of the girls' dorm, to dress.

The two twenty-seven year old women started their walk towards the Cornwall library. Both campuses were nearly deserted on that late August evening. However, that would change the following week when students started arriving for the fall term.

Both were dressed in conservatively cut cocktail dresses, low-heeled shoes, and wearing very little make-up. Neither wanted to run the risk of agitating any of the faculty wives. However, despite this low-key approach, their physical attractiveness was self-evident.

Katherine Whitson was a bit taller than average, with a well-proportioned figure. Her blonde hair and blue eyes were ideally matched to a pleasant looking face. She was widely regarded as "pretty". Kate was definitely her mother's daughter.

Patty White was taller and more slender than Kate. Although never described as "pretty", Patricia White was a hauntingly attractive young woman.

"You know, Patty, I've heard Tom Wilkerson might have eyes for you," related Kate.

"Lucky me."

"He seems like a nice enough guy," she continued. "He's a history teacher."

"Then why don't you go find out just how nice he is, for yourself?" suggested Patty.

"If he's here tonight, I just might."

As they entered Cornwall's library, the staid voices of festivity could be heard emanating from the far end of the hall. The room itself was awash in tweed jackets and floral maxi dresses. A three-piece combo played, unobtrusively, in the background.

"Well, I for one am going to the bar," decided Patty. "Kate, why don't you go find Tom what's his name," she suggested, with a trouble maker's smile.

"Shove it, White!"

They each secured a glass of wine from the bar and moved to an unoccupied pub table, to place their drinks. Immediately, Robert Hensley, the Cornwall Director of Admissions approached them.

"Good evening, ladies. I was beginning to fear you might not be joining us tonight," he smiled.

"No such luck, Bob," bantered Kate Whitson, with a grin.

He was holding a manila file folder in one hand, and a scotch on the rocks in the other.

"Pat, may I have a quick word with you about an incoming student?" he asked.

Such a request was not unusual at faculty gatherings. In fact, it was encouraged. The rational being that if "school business" was being discussed the amount of alcohol consumed that evening was merely "all in the line of duty".

"Why, of course, Bob," agreed Patricia White.

Robert Hensley placed the manila folder on the table. In one adept motion he drained the remainder of his cocktail and motioned a near-by waiter for a refill.

"The student's name is Logan Spence. And his situation is that he has to make up a lot of ground in the areas of reading comprehension, writing, and word command in preparation for the SAT's, explained Hensley.

Pat thought for a moment before responding.

"Why, me?"

"Because I think you are the best suited both in terms of educational credentials and teaching temperament to be his most effective mentor," explained Hensley.

"What's in the folder, Bob?" asked Pat.

"His application for admission and standardized test results"

"May I see?"

"That's why I brought it."

Patricia White quickly scanned the results and then closed the folder, keeping it in front of her.

"How can someone score so well on math and so poorly on verbal?" she mused, aloud.

"That's now for you to find out," smiled the Director of Admissions.

The waiter returned with Hensley's cocktail.

"Where's this kid from, Bob?" asked Patty.

"Water's Edge." He answered.

"Another typical preppie from Water's Edge. Come to think of it, that happens to be Kate's particular area of expertise!" laughed Patty White.

Kate Whitson opted to sip rather than bite.

Robert Hensley chose to ignore White's obvious play on words. He tipped his scotch and stared at Patricia White.

"I've only spent several hours with the young man, but I'm quite certain of one thing."

"And what's that, Bob?" she asked, with growing disinterest.

"Logan Spence is no typical preppie from Water's Edge."

# CHAPTER TWENTY-SEVEN

"So, when's the next time you're going to be coming in?" asked Dwight Jefferson.

"Probably sometime around Thanksgiving," answered Logan Spence. "I think that's the first school break."

"Thanksgiving? Hell, I don't know if I'll even recognize you by then!" laughed the good-natured sixteen-year-old.

"Oh, I'll make sure you remember who the hell I am," vowed Logan, with a smile.

Spence had made the trip into Manhattan that Friday morning to clean out his locker at the Dojo and pay his respects to the instructors. He had also called Dwight to let him know what time he would be there.

"So, how are you getting along with your Uptown brothers?" asked Spence with genuine concern.

"These days, it's more like how are *they* getting along with me," corrected Jefferson. He was not smiling.

Logan Spence believed his friend's words. Dwight Jefferson now stood six feet-five inches tall. He was impressively muscular yet remained surprisingly agile; and above all else, trained to inflict damage when necessary.

The two young men were chatting near the Dojo's training mat. Sensei Hidaka came off the mat and walked towards them. Miku, the English-speaking receptionist was at his side. Logan immediately noticed her recent advancement from brown to black belt.

The Sensei stopped in front of Logan and bowed. Spence returned the gesture of respect. Hidaka then opened a clenched fist revealing a silver necklace.

"The Sensei is offering you a gift of esteem," explained Miku. "The amulet symbolizes 'calm strength.' Lower your head so that he may place it around your neck."

Logan Spence did as he was instructed. Hidaka then turned to the receptionist and asked her a question in Japanese.

"He wants to know when you will be returning."

"Tell him this November," responded Logan.

Miku relayed his answer. The Sensei stared into Logan's eyes. His face almost betrayed a smile. He then bowed and returned to his awaiting class on the mat. Miku followed behind him.

Logan and Dwight were standing on the street just outside the Dojo.

"You got time to grab a slice?" asked Jefferson.

"No, I don't," said Spence. "I've got to get back and clean out my school locker. It's going to be a zoo; non-returning students clearing out and incoming freshmen going through orientation," explained Logan. "But listen, as soon as I'm settled, I'll give you a number you can reach me at," he promised.

Dwight Jefferson studied his friend with a look of uneasiness.

"Watch your ass up there, man," he said with cryptic concern.

Logan Spence shook his head and laughed.

"What, you afraid that a couple of rich preppies are going to bust me up or something?"

"I don't know about that. But I do know you're walking into a new world; a place you don't know and a place that doesn't know you. Just watch yourself."

With that, the two friends embraced and then went their separate ways.

On the train ride back to Water's Edge, Logan studied the necklace Sensei Hidaka had given him. He also tried to make sense of Dwight Jefferson's parting words of warning. However, as the train came to a stop at his station, Logan's thoughts shifted from the events of that morning to the task now before him.

With duffel bag in hand, Spence walked directly to Water's Edge High School. He entered the main building. As he had expected, the hallways were jammed with shuffling students and filled with noise. He got to his locker, cleaned it out, and bolted for the nearest side door.

Logan was relieved to be outside in the relative quiet of the parking lot. As he started the walk home, a car horn beeped causing him to turn.

Several cars were parked at the far end of the parking lot next to the football field. One of them belonged to Carmine Delfino. It was he who had honked. Spence approached his friend who was sitting in his top-down convertible, by himself.

"I was hoping I'd catch you here," smiled Carmine. "Are you still going away to that preppie place?"

"Yea, I figure it's my only shot at getting into a college," answered Logan.

Carmine Delfino looked at his friend and shook his head.

"You know, I kind of wish I'd been thinking like that a couple of years ago," he said whimsically. "Anyway, I wasn't, so here I am. Guess I'm lucky just to be graduating from this place."

"What are you going to do now?" asked Logan.

"Well, I've got three older brothers. Two of them own a pretty profitable auto body shop just outside town. They've offered me a job there."

"I know the place," nodded Spence.

Carmine Delfino continued.

"And my third brother is in sales."

"What kind of sales?" questioned, Logan.

"Commodities."

Logan Spence had a pretty good idea what his friend meant by "commodities" but chose not to pursue any specifics.

Suddenly, Carmine stood up and sprang over the driver's side door. Standing next to Logan, he pulled out a pack of cigarettes. The two lit up.

"Anyway, I'm not here to talk about me," revealed Carmine. "You've always liked this baby, haven't you?" he said, affectionately patting the dark blue 1968 Buick GS.

"You know I do!" admitted Logan, enthusiastically.

"Well, I'll tell you what. Meet me at my brothers' shop tomorrow at noon with two-hundred dollars cash, and this baby's yours. Call it a belated sixteenth birthday present," offered "The Cat".

"I'll be there!" committed Logan without hesitation.

A young kid walking across the parking lot suddenly stopped in front them.

"Can you tell me where The Wall is?" asked the frail looking freshman.

"Walk across the football field and through those trees. You can't miss it," instructed Carmine.

"Thanks," he said and continued walking.

Carmine looked at Logan.

"You know him?"

"No, should I?" asked Spence.

"I heard Jimmy Kelly got into it with someone from Eastern Middle School in the lunchroom today. He must be the one," reasoned Delfino.

Logan Spence said nothing.

"In fact, Jimmy's older brother, Johnny is home on leave this weekend. How much you wanna bet I can tell you where they both are right now?" wagered "The Cat".

Logan continued to watch the kid in silence until the freshman disappeared between the trees. Spence finished his cigarette, picked up his duffel bag, and looked at Delfino.

"Tomorrow, twelve o'clock at your brothers' shop," he confirmed.

Logan Spence started walking across the football field.

Delfino had no doubt where his former protégé was headed. He waited until Logan had nearly reached the trees before signaling the occupants in the other car. Carmine and his friends then started towards The Wall.

"*Just in case,*" thought "The Cat," to himself.

As Logan neared the thicket of trees, he could hear music blaring from boom boxes and the shrill of people enjoying themselves. The smells of tobacco and pot began to infiltrate the air. Suddenly, with eerie abruptness the sounds of revelry fell silent.

"*He's arrived,*" thought Logan as he continued walking.

Spence stopped at the edge of the clearing to take in the scene. Gathered around The Wall were about forty young men and women. Sitting on the edifice itself, in the midst of the crowd, were the Kelly brothers; Jimmy, the graduating senior and Johnny, the new army recruit. Both were holding cans of beer. The crowd was silent.

The lone freshman stood motionlessly in the center of the clearing waiting to see what was going to happen next.

After finishing their beers, the two brothers stood up and started advancing towards their target. Logan Spence emerged from the trees and walked towards the freshman. Seeing Spence approach, the Kelly's momentarily halted half way between The Wall and their intended mark. Logan stopped once he was standing next to the kid.

"What's your name?" asked Spence.

A fragile looking face stared up at him.

"Elwin."

"*Elwin?*" smiled Logan. "What the hell do your friends call you?"

"I don't have any," admitted the kid.

Spence shook his head with cold resolve.

"Well, Elwin, you do now." Logan let his duffel bag drop to the ground. "Wait here," he instructed.

Spence walked up to the two Kelly brothers, stopping when he was within three feet of them and smiled.

"I'd forgotten how small you two assholes really are," he laughed good-naturedly.

His nonchalance took them by surprise. Both Jim and John Kelly stood dumbstruck; stunned that he had the nerve to cop an attitude with them!

Logan continued.

"Now, listen up. I'm only going to say this once. Elwin is a good friend of mine. That means anyone who messes with him is messing with me. And anyone messing with me is going to get busted up real bad. Do you two assholes understand? Good. Now be nice little boys and go back to those two ugly sluts you call girlfriends. You're dismissed."

With that, Logan turned and started walking back towards Elwin. He got about half way there. Spence did not need to see the panic in the freshman's face to know what was happening. Both Kelly brothers were coming straight at him. Logan Spence had anticipated their reaction. Indeed, he had *prayed* for it.

Turning with practiced agility, Spence stopped Johnny Kelly in his tracks with two vicious blows to the windpipe. With both hands he then grabbed the back of Kelly's head and slammed Johnny's face into a waiting knee. The impact broke the nose and shattered most of the upper teeth. The older Kelly brother crumpled helplessly to the ground, desperately clawing at his throat for air.

Spence's sudden movement had caused the younger Kelly to overshoot his intended target. Now, seeing his brother writhing in pain, he charged wildly looking to end it with one punch. Smiling, Spence easily sidestepped the advance. He then secured Jimmy Kelly's right wrist and elbow and violently slammed the forearm into his raised thigh. The impact fractured the ulna. The rupture ripped through the flesh, spewing blood and exposing raw bone. Spence then wheeled to Kelly's left side and with two well-placed kicks shattered the kneecap. The second Kelly brother collapsed.

The whole thing was over in a matter of seconds. Horrified by what they had just witnessed, the girls hanging at The Wall that afternoon began to flee. Most of the guys were right behind them.

Carmine and company had arrived in time to catch most of the action. They stood off to the side. There was no need for their intervention.

With slow deliberation, Logan walked to The Wall. The guys who had stayed stood motionlessly, saying absolutely nothing.

"Anyone else want to hassle my friend? Now is your chance!" challenged Spence.

There were no takers.

Without another word, Spence turned to leave, stopping only to retrieve his duffle bag. He then quietly disappeared into the trees. Logan Spence never returned to The Wall.

# CHAPTER TWENTY-EIGHT

"I'm going to get another drink," said Kate Whitson. "Would you like one?"

Patty White, without looking up, handed her empty wine glass to Kate indicating the affirmative. Pat was reviewing the file on Logan Spence that Robert Hensley had given her a little while earlier. Kate returned with two replenished vessels. Pat closed the folder and shook her head.

"What's wrong?" asked Kate.

"I don't get it."

"What don't you get, Patty?"

"How this kid Spence ever got accepted to Cornwall," she said, picking up her glass.

Kate Whitson sipped her wine and smiled.

"Okay, I'll take the bait. What's so wrong with his application for admission?"

"Everything!" exclaimed White. "His grades are terrible and his test scores are below average."

"Wait a minute. I thought both you and Hensley said his math scores were pretty good," interrupted Kate Whitson.

Patty White hesitated, momentarily, before responding.

"Granted, his math scores are acceptable. However, he's obviously incapable of putting that aptitude to work in the classroom," she concluded.

Patricia sipped from her glass and continued.

"What's more, Spence has absolutely no extra-curricular school activities or hobbies. Hell, he didn't even complete the personal essay section of the application. That's unheard of!"

"Well, Patty, maybe his grandfather donated the money for Cornwall's new library," laughed Kate. "You never know."

"I do know, and grandpa didn't!" hissed Patty White.

"What makes you so sure?" asked Kate, with surprise.

"Because according to the file, he's been approved for financial aid towards tuition."

Whitson looked at her friend and shrugged.

"Well, at least let me see what this mystery student looks like," she insisted. Her curiosity was now piqued.

"That's another thing. There is no photograph! Kate, it's like this kid came walking in off the street and was immediately accepted at Cornwall. He then receives money for his trouble. Not only that, he gets his own private tutor, me!" she complained, with a rising tone in her voice.

"Ladies, I hope we're not interrupting anything," said the young man, good-naturedly.

"As a matter of fact, Scott, you are," laughed Kate Whitson. "And for that, I shall be forever grateful!"

Scott Abrams was a history teacher at Cornwall. He and Kate had become somewhat friendly during the prior term. Abrams looked to be around thirty. He was on the shorter side with a medium build. The hair was black. His most impressive physical attribute was a pair of piercing brown eyes that were in no way muted by the omnipresent wire rims.

"Kate, this is Tom Wilkerson. And please don't prejudge him because he happens to be a friend of mine," laughed Scott Abrams.

Wilkerson was also in the Cornwall History Department. He appeared to be about the same age as Scott Abrams, although taller and carrying less weight. He had sandy brown hair and a face that was best described as innocuous.

"Scott, you know my friend, Patty White," motioned Kate.

"Of course."

"Tom Wilkerson, say hello to Pat White," introduced Kate.

"Hello, Pat White," he smiled, awkwardly.

*"Well, this explains Tom Wilkerson,"* she thought, wearily, and beamed her social best.

133

"We were hoping you girls might let us buy you a drink," ventured Scott Abrams.

"That's big of you sport, considering this is an open bar," scolded Kate Whitson, in jest.

"No smart girl. Tom and I were thinking about going into town to the Oak Tree Tavern for pizza and beer. We were hoping you two might join us," explained Scott Abrams. "That is, if you can tear yourselves away from the new Cornwall library."

"I'm not a big beer drinker," demurred Patty White.

"Oh, the Oak Tree has a full bar!" gushed Tom Wilkerson, not picking up on Pat's tacit refusal.

Before Pat could respond, Kate chimed in.

"That sounds like fun doesn't it, Patty?" she committed. "I'll tell you what. Give us a chance to change into something more comfortable. Meet us in the lobby of our building in say, an hour. Is that okay with you?"

"It sounds great!" laughed Scott Abrams. "In an hour, then."

The two men returned to the bar to replenish their cocktails and hopes.

"Kate, why the hell did you do that?" snapped Pat White, on their walk back to the girls' dormitory.

"Oh, lighten up, Patty. It's not going to be that bad. Besides, what the hell else would we be doing tonight?" she challenged. "We'd be sitting in front of the T.V. watching *The Love Boat* and *Fantasy Island*," she said, answering her own question.

"Right now, that sounds better to me than hanging out in some townie bar trying to make small talk with the likes of Scott Abrams and Tom Wilkerson," sighed Pat White.

"Listen, Patty, the kids are returning tomorrow for Fall Term. God only knows the next time we'll be able to get out for an evening. Besides, you might actually enjoy yourself. Hell, you might even end up thanking me," grinned Kate.

"You want to bet?" she finally smiled and headed off to her apartment to change.

The ride from the Cornwall Angelica Hall campus to downtown Sheffield was ten minutes. Scott Abrams parked his car. The two couples entered the Oak Tree Tavern.

To the left was a long, well-stocked bar. On the right were six cushioned booths. A four-foot high wooden railing stood in front of the bar and ran its length. The structure served two purposes; it accommodated any over flow of bar patronage and it effectively partitioned the dining area.

The Oak Tree was doing a fairly brisk Saturday night business. The bar was crowded but not boisterous. A jukebox located at the far end of the room was playing the 1979 Donna Summer hit "Bad Girls" at a reasonable volume. All but one of the booths were occupied.

"Must be our lucky night," observed Scott Abrams, as they went to sit down.

"Must be," said Patricia White.

The girls sat down facing one another. Tom Wilkerson slid into the booth next to Patty. Scott Abrams sat down next to Kate. A waitress came over to the table with menus.

"Can I get anyone anything from the bar?" she asked, with weathered habit.

"Yes, we'll start with a pitcher of your house beer," said Scott Abrams.

"How many glasses?" asked the woman.

Abrams hesitated.

"Two, I guess."

"Make that three," chimed Kate, agreeably.

"I'll have beer, as well," decided Pat.

Tom Wilkerson looked at Patricia White with a face of concern.

"Pat, you said you don't like beer. Please, order anything you like from the bar," he insisted.

"I said that I'm not a big beer drinker. That wasn't meant to suggest I don't drink the stuff," she smiled. "Besides, it feels like a beer kind of night."

The waitress returned with the pitcher and glasses.

"You folks ready to order?"

The two men looked across the booth's table waiting for a response from the ladies. Kate Whitson spoke first.

"I was under the impression you guys brought us here for pizza and beer. Please don't tell me you lured us under false pretenses!" she laughed.

"Really!" added Pat, with mocked disgust.

Scott Abrams looked at the waitress.

"The ladies have spoken! One large pie," he said, good-naturedly.

"Anything on it?" she asked.

Abrams deferred to the girls. They both shook their heads, no.

"Plain will be fine" he instructed.

"It'll be right out."

Tom Wilkerson filled the four glasses and then raised his to toast.

"To a new school year!"

Glasses clinked and well-wishes exchanged.

"So, what do you girls have planned for the Fall Term that's new and exciting?" asked Scott Abrams.

"Well, Patty is going to be mentoring a new student," volunteered Kate Whitson.

"Oh really, what's she like?" asked Tom Wilkerson.

"Actually, *she* is a he," corrected Pat.

"A Cornwall student?" interjected Scott Abrams. "Pat, you best be on your guard. You know us Cornwall boys!" he laughed.

"Indeed, I do," she smiled, with discreet contempt.

Patty felt a sudden kick from underneath the table. Kate Whitson shot her a glare of silent disapproval.

The pizza arrived and the conversation drifted, elsewhere. After the pie was finished and the second pitcher nearly empty, Tom Wilkerson stood up.

"If you'll excuse me, I'm going to visit the little boys' room," he said and left their table.

As soon as he disappeared, a man who had been drinking at the bar slid into the booth next to Patty White and smiled, lewdly. He looked to be in his mid-twenties. Although not overly big, his body pulsated negative energy. His face was mean and old before its time. He looked like trouble trying to find a home.

His two companions lurked just to the right shoulder of Scott Abrams.

"I've been thinking about that gorgeous ass of yours since you walked in this place," he grinned, exposing a mouthful of nicotine stained teeth. "What do you say we go outside for a little fun?"

"Get lost, asshole," said Pat White, without turning her head in his direction.

"The beautiful ones always play hard to get even though they're the ones who want it the most!" he chuckled.

Tom Wilkerson returned from the men's room. He stood silently in front of the booth not sure exactly what was going on or what to do about it.

"Hey, it's the nutty professor! You're a smart guy. Can you figure out why this piece of tail wants me more than you?" asked the bar thug.

Before the teacher could respond, a man slapped the booth's table with a loud whack. He looked to be in his fifties. He was barrel-chested and what gray hair remained was combed straight back. He wore blue jeans, a black tee-shirt, and sported a white apron around his waist.

"Billy, if you and your two friends don't get lost now, I'm going to cut you off, permanently! Not only that, I'm going to make some phone calls around town. Next time you want a drink, it's going to be out of a brown paper bag on some street corner!"

That was one threat the man was not about to challenge. Reluctantly, he got up from the booth. He stared long and hard at Tom Wilkerson. He then turned to face Pat White.

"The next time you're in the mood for a real man, come around and ask for Billy, Billy the Kid," he smiled and walked away.

"I'm sorry about that folks," said the older man. "My name is Sal, Sal Fusco, owner-operator. Please, don't let that one jerk keep you from coming back to the Oak Tree or any other establishment here, in town. All us merchants really appreciate your school's business," he said, apologetically.

Scott Abrams was the first to speak.

"Well, thank you, Sal. And yes, of course you'll see us again. But right now, I think we'll take a check and call it a night.

"Check? What check? Tonight is on the house! In fact, the next time the four of you come back that will be on the house, too," he promised.

The short ride from town back to the Cornwall Angelica Hall campus was ridden in comparative silence. Kate Whitson's "there's an asshole in every bar" was met with only muted nods of agreement. Scott pulled to a stop in front of the girls' dorm. Brief goodbyes were exchanged. The two men drove off.

Pat and Kate entered the lobby of their building.

"Well, that was fun," said Patty, shaking her head.

"I thought the evening was going just fine until that loser showed up," allowed Kate.

"I'm glad you think so."

"Patty, you've got to admit that both Scott and Tom are very nice guys," she insisted.

"I suppose they have to be, don't they?" said Pat, cynically.

Kate Whitson stared at her friend, before responding.

"Patty, if you're suggesting Scott and Tom are any less men for choosing not to mix it up with those bar bullies, I think you're way off base," she asserted. "In fact, I would have thought less of them if they gotten into a fight with those jerks!"

"That's your opinion," shrugged Pat.

"And it's not yours?"

138

"Hey, Kate, it wasn't you that lunatic was hitting on, now was it?"

Instead of answering the question, Kate tried to diffuse the growing friction.

"Well anyway, everything worked out for the best in the end," she said, lamely.

"Yes, it *did*," said Pat White, with finality.

Although she did not pursue it, Kate Whitson knew exactly what her best friend's last word had meant.

# CHAPTER TWENTY-NINE

"Logan, I expect you to take full advantage of all the academic resources that Cornwall has been gracious enough to afford you," admonished his mother.

"That's why I applied there, mom," he said, curtly.

"Don't get snippy with me young man," warned Mildred Spence.

Logan's mother was behind the wheel of her car driving towards Sheffield, Connecticut, the home of Cornwall Angelica Hall.

"I want you to know how proud your acceptance to Cornwall has made your father," continued his mother.

"Yea, he's so proud he just couldn't find the time to be with us, today," challenged her son.

The normally feisty Mildred Spence hesitated, before speaking.

"Logan, I don't have to explain to you how much time your father's medical practice requires," she defended.

"It has nothing to do with him being a doctor. It all has to do with him not being comfortable around me. He never has been, never will be," he said, with disquieting dispassion.

"Logan, there are things you and I must talk about," she said, quietly.

"Well, it won't be today!" he responded in a dismissive voice.

Their car entered the Cornwall Angelica Hall campus. Mildred Spence pulled to a stop in front of the administration building.

"I'll drop you off, find a parking space, and then meet you inside," instructed Mildred Spence.

"And then do what? Go with me to my room and make the bed? Not happening. I am getting out of the car and you are gone!" he said, dismissively.

140

The emotionally drained mother did not argue. Without another word, she drove away with tears in her eyes and sadness in her heart.

Logan entered the administration building carrying a suit case in one hand and his duffel bag in the other.

Four portable tables had been placed in the reception alcove. Each was adorned with a banner displaying the eventual graduation year of the incoming students. The room was empty except for a young man seated behind the table brandishing the numerals 1982.

"You must be Spence," he said, with a smile and stood up to extend his hand. "I'm Reed, Jack Reed."

"How'd you know?" asked Logan, returning the clasp.

"Well, for starters, you're the last one here today," informed Reed. "Besides, Campbell described you pretty accurately."

"You're a friend of Mark's?" asked Spence, with sudden interest.

"I don't know if I'd call him a friend," he laughed, good-naturedly. "But he's been my roommate for the last two years."

"So, you're Mr. Music!" said Logan and nodded approving recognition.

"Music has always been my passion," revealed Reed. "I play piano and sax. I'm also a D.J. at the campus radio station. You should come up one night when I'm on the air," he invited.

Jack Reed was short and on the chubby side. His curly red hair was a natural match for the sun shy white complexion that sported freckles. Jack was a friendly sort.

"You're rooming in Squire House. C'mon, I'll take you there," he offered.

"I don't want to put you out."

"You won't be," assured Jack Reed.

"And why's that?" asked Spence.

"Because, that's where I'm living," he smiled.

The two young men exited the administration building and started their walk across the Cornwall campus.

"You travel light," observed Reed, motioning towards Spence's suitcase and duffel bag.

"I wasn't really sure what to bring," admitted Logan, with a shrug.

"Well, right now you've got a bed with linen and a desk with a chair," informed Jack.

"That's it?"

"No, you also have a roommate," advised Reed.

"Do you know him?" asked Logan.

"Yes. His name is Pete Ellison. He's a pretty good guy," said Reed.

"Is this his first year at Cornwall?"

"No, Pete's been here for two years," answered Jack Reed.

"Then why doesn't he already have a roommate?"

"Because his former roommate isn't returning to Cornwall," explained Reed. "He flunked out."

As they neared Squire House, Logan Spence immediately noticed the convergence of station wagons. Mothers and fathers were busily helping their sons unload the vehicles of those possessions that would soon be furnishing their rooms.

Logan Spence looked at Jack Reed.

"Is Campbell already here?"

"Come and gone. He's out to dinner with his folks. It's a Cornwall tradition," informed Reed.

"Then why aren't you out with yours?" asked Spence, curiously.

"For starters, they live in Seattle. Besides, I had to wait around for your sorry late ass," he laughed.

Squire House was a wooden two-storied Victorian that had been built in the 1930's. It boasted a wrap-around porch. The large downstairs common room was furnished with well- worn couches and a large RCA color T.V.

142

"C'mon, you're on the second floor," said Jack Reed.

They proceeded up the stairs and down a hallway.

"That's yours," motioned Reed, as he disappeared into the adjacent room.

The door was open. There were three people already inside the room.

"Hi, I'm Pete Ellison."

A young man strode across the room with an offering hand and a smile. He was tall and thin. His hair was brown and his face friendly. He gave the impression of a gracious host welcoming an unwanted guest.

"Logan Spence," said the new arrival, as he returned the handshake.

Pete Ellison motioned towards the other two people in the room.

"Logan, these are my parents, Steve and Barbara Ellison," he introduced, with practiced polish.

Mr. and Mrs. Ellison appeared to be in their mid-forties. They were both attractive, well-groomed, and exuded the comfortable social air of those accustomed to wealth and position. After the requisite exchange of pleasantries, Steve Ellison got down to business.

"Logan, we were just leaving for dinner. We would be thrilled if you would join us," he offered.

Intuitively, Spence knew that it was a polite invitation that would have been impolite to accept.

"Thanks, Mr. Ellison. But, I really have to unpack and get myself set-up here," he responded.

"Maybe next time," smiled Steve Ellison.

"Maybe," nodded Logan Spence.

And with that, the Ellison family departed the room, bound for an afternoon of Cornwall tradition.

# CHAPTER THIRTY

Logan Spence quickly unpacked. Already feeling the familiar role of miscast, he decided to walk the fifteen minutes into downtown Sheffield. He took a seat on a street bench facing a row of retail shops. It was the liquor store he was eyeing. Spence had a cigarette in his hand and vodka on his mind. He was in a dark mood.

A young man emerged from one of the stores trying to juggle a large package of Pampers diapers in one hand and a case of baby formula in the other. Suddenly, the package of diapers was knocked out of his hands. It fell to the sidewalk.

"Hey, Roger the Dodger, juggling two kids can be tough!" laughed the man who had intentionally dislodged the package of diapers from the young father's arms.

The two men who accompanied the thug looked on with smiles of amusement.

On impulse, Logan Spence rose from the street bench and approached the assailant. With his left elbow, he nailed the solar plexus of the attacker. With his right fist, he pile hammered the nose. The erstwhile bully fell to the cement pavement gasping for breath and, for the first time, tasting his own blood.

Spence quickly pivoted towards the other two young men.

"Which one of you is next?" he asked, with an unnerving calmness in his voice.

Both shook their heads.

"Then pick his ass up and get lost."

The two guys complied with Spence's mandate. They gathered their crumpled comrade and disappeared.

"Hey, man, thanks," said the young father, as he retrieved his package of diapers. "I'm Roger Kaminski."

"Logan Spence."

Roger Kaminski was in his early twenties. His height was medium and his frame frail. He sported a scraggly goatee. He reminded Spence of Shaggy Rogers, the cartoon character in the *Scooby-Doo* series.

"Hey, Logan, if there is anything I can ever do for you, just let me know, man," and nodded his appreciation.

"Roger, as a matter of fact there is. You can go into that package store and buy me a bottle of Absolut," replied Spence, as he dug into his jean pocket for cash. "And buy something for yourself while you're in there," he offered.

"Sure, I'll be glad to do it! Personally, I'm not much of a drinker. But, my wife loves her Grand Marnier! Only, it's kind of expensive."

"Get her the Grand Marnier," insisted Spence.

Roger Kaminski emerged from the package store with two brown bags in hand.

"Hey, Logan, do you get high?" he asked, tentatively.

"Only when the product is good," responded Spence and smiled, reassuringly.

"Then why don't you come over to my place and sample the weed for yourself? Besides, my wife is going to want to meet the dude who bought her the Grand Marnier," urged Roger Kaminski.

"Why not?" responded Logan Spence.

The Kaminski's lived in a small two-storied row house located within a short walking distance of downtown Sheffield. It was clean and affordable.

"Hey, Beth, I want you to meet someone," announced Roger Kaminski, as they entered the house's front door.

A young woman descended a flight of stairs and stood in the tiny foyer. She looked at her husband.

"They're both *finally* asleep" she said, with weariness in her voice.

Beth Kaminski was also in her early twenties. She was not unattractive. However, the premature lines in her face reflected the weight of responsibility that goes with mothering two kids under the age of three.

"Honey, this is Logan Spence," introduced Roger Kaminski. "He just kicked Billy the Kid's ass," Roger added for good measure.

Beth Kaminski eyed Logan Spence with sudden interest.

"Billy's been a jerk for as long as I can remember. I think I like you Logan Spence," she said, approvingly.

"That's not all, Beth. Look at the present Logan brought for you," smiled her husband.

He removed the bottle of Grand Marnier from its brown paper bag and handed it to her.

"Now, I *know* I like you, Logan Spence!" she laughed, appreciatively.

Spence pulled the bottle of Absolut from its wrapper. Without prompting, Beth Kaminski seized the vodka and headed towards the kitchen.

"How do you drink your Absolut, Logan?" she asked, with a new easiness in her voice.

"On the rocks generally works for me," he responded.

"Beth, we'll be in the den," said Roger. "C'mon, I'll twist one up for us. This stuff you're going to like," promised the host.

The den was a small room. It was furnished with a sofa and cocktail table. A television and stereo system sat on a long wooden bench. Roger walked towards an impressive stack of record albums.

"What would you like to hear?" he asked.

"Surprise me."

Roger selected ELO's 1979 hit album *Discovery*. He cued it up and then sat down on the sofa next to Logan to roll a joint. Beth returned with Logan's Absolut on ice and a glass of Grand Marnier. She sat down on the sofa nestling between the two men.

"So, Logan, why'd you kick Billy's ass?" she asked, with keen interest and a smirk.

146

"Because, like you said he's a jerk," responded Spence, as he took a long sip of the chilled vodka.

Beth Kaminski studied the face of Logan Spence, before asking her next question.

"How come I know you're a Cornwall student but don't look or act like one?"

Before Logan could respond, Roger lit the joint. After two hearty tokes, he passed it to his wife. She took a hit and then gave it to their guest. Logan took a long drag and then handed back to Beth. The song "Shine A Little Love" was now enveloping the small room. Spence drained the remainder of his cocktail.

"Logan, can I get you a refill?" offered Beth Kaminski, as she passed the joint back to her husband.

"I'd be mad if you didn't," smiled Spence.

With that, Beth stood up and retreated to the kitchen with two empty glasses.

"So, what do you think of this shit?" asked a grinning Roger Kaminski.

"It's definitely primo," agreed Spence, not wanting to be rude. The inferior quality of the weed reminded Logan of Mark Campbell's crap.

"I knew you'd be impressed. Any time you want more, you know where to come."

"Yes, I do," nodded Logan.

Beth Kaminski returned with two replenished cocktails. She handed Logan his drink and then re-seated herself between the two guys. Logan was the first to resume the conversation.

"Roger, I need some things for my room," informed Spence.

"What kind of things, man?" he asked, while snuffing the roach into an ashtray.

"Desk lamp, reading chair, stuff like that."

Roger Kaminski nodded his head and winked.

"Logan, it's your lucky day. My aunt owns a used furniture store here in town. You just let me know when and I'll take you there," he offered. Kaminski jotted his phone number and handed it to Logan.

"Thanks."

Spence finished his drink and stood to leave.

"I've got to get back to Cornwall. It was great meeting you guys," he said, sincerely.

"You want a ride?" asked Roger.

"No, I'd better walk this one off," smiled Logan.

"Oh, man, I totally hear you," smiled Roger Kaminski.

"Hey, Logan, do you want to take your bottle of Absolut?" reminded Beth.

Spence looked at the young mother of two and shook his head.

"You keep it safe until my next visit," he instructed.

Beth Kaminski stared at her now departing house guest, with the affectionate feeling of newly found friendship.

"You can count on it."

# CHAPTER THIRTY-ONE

Logan Spence left the Kaminski's house. He lit a cigarette and started the fifteen-minute walk back to the Cornwall campus. Nearing Squire House, he noticed that the once pervasive throng of paternal station wagons had departed.

"The dependents are now, independently, dependent," he laughed.

Spence entered the front door of Squire House. He walked through the T.V. room and up the stairs. As he made his way down the hallway he saw that his room's door was open. He entered to see his roommate, Pete Ellison busily hooking up a stereo system. His friend, Mark Campbell was slouched in Ellison's reading chair.

"There you are!" smiled Mark Campbell. "We were starting to get worried. Thought you might have lost your way in the big city of Sheffield."

"No such luck, Campbell," grinned Logan, as he extended his hand. "How was dinner with your folks?"

"Dinner with the folks," dismissed Mark, with a shrug. "The good news is the next one won't be until Thanksgiving."

Pete Ellison, momentarily, stopped his work in progress and turned towards Spence.

"Hey, Logan, you had a visitor while you were gone," informed his new roommate.

Spence looked at Ellison.

"Who was it?" he asked, not having a clue.

"A piece of ass, that's who!" interjected Mark Campbell, nodding his male appreciation.

Pete Ellison stared at Mark and shook his head.

"Campbell, try to keep it in your pants," he lectured and then answered Logan's question.

"It was Patricia White. She is a teacher at Angelica Hall. She left an envelope addressed to you downstairs. I brought it up when I got back from dinner. It's on your desk."

"How the hell do you know her?" asked Mark Campbell.

"I don't," responded Spence.

"Then why the hell is she leaving you love notes?" persisted Campbell.

Logan Spence looked at his friend from Water's Edge and smiled.

"You know, Mark, you really should be trying to get a little bit more of what you're obviously not getting enough of," he chided.

"Screw you, Spence," said Campbell, defensively.

"That's not what I had in mind, old chap," laughed Logan. Pete Ellison entered the fray.

"No really, Logan, what's your connection with her?" he asked.

"She's going to be my tutor in English.

"Why?"

"To improve my SAT scores," he revealed.

"How'd you pull that off?" asked Ellison.

"I didn't," admitted Spence.

"Who did?" pressed his roommate.

"The Director of Admissions."

"Hensley arranged it? You must be a wrestler," concluded Pete Ellison.

"That's the rumor," corroborated Spence.

Logan walked over to his desk. He picked up the envelope and opened it:

"Dear Mr. Spence, I would ask that you stop by my office tomorrow afternoon after your orientation. At that time, I will outline this term's curriculum and provide you with all required study materials. Sincerely, Ms. Patricia White"

Logan tossed the note back on his desk. He looked at Pete Ellison.

150

"What's the deal with orientation?" he asked.

"It's a bunch of crap!" was Mark Campbell's unsolicited response.

Pete Ellison ignored Campbell's outburst.

"It's basically a campus tour and then class assignments," he explained. "It ends with lunch in the main dining room."

The following morning, all students residing in Squire House dutifully assembled in the T.V. room. The meeting's purpose was to be read the house rules by the two faculty members charged with the responsibility of overseeing the comings and goings of Squire House's inhabitants when classes were not in session.

Alan and Susan Tompkins were a married couple in their middle thirties. He was a math teacher at Cornwall. She was a guidance-counselor at Angelica Hall. They had no children. The couple lived in a self-sufficient apartment located on the first floor of Squire House. The Tompkins we're benignly academic.

The morning's orientation moved on to Summit House. It was there that the new students were segregated from the repeat offenders and dutifully given a campus walk around to familiarize themselves with the various classroom buildings.

Once back at Summit House, class schedules were assigned. From there it was on to the campus book store. Mailboxes were allotted and textbooks purchased.

Logan Spence, armed with an arsenal of hardcovers, got back to his room at Squire House just before noon. Pete Ellison was nowhere in sight. He dumped the books on his desk and started the walk back to the main dining room.

Logan got on the cafeteria line. After moving down the metallic aisle he entered the eating facility.

Cornwall's main dining room was impressively large. Its size easily accommodated students, faculty, and sundry guests at one sitting. The sixty round wooden tables seated twelve, at each. The room's walls were lushly paneled between streaming windows. The floor was oak. The massive room was partitioned in the middle by an impressive two-way fireplace.

Logan Spence sat down at the first available seat he saw.

"You can't sit here," said a guy already seated at the table. "You're not allowed!" he confirmed, authoritatively.

Logan surveyed the nearly empty table and then looked at the speaker.

"And why's that?"

"Because this is the Afro-American table!" he stated, with belligerence.

"I didn't notice," responded Logan.

"Well, now you're on notice," he warned.

Before Spence had a chance to react, Carlos Acosta was suddenly on the scene. Acosta was the senior Logan had wrestled during his first visit to Cornwall.

"Spence, follow me. There's an empty chair at our table," he instructed.

Without another word, Logan stood up and gathered his tray. He stared at his antagonist, permanently, committing the face to memory.

*"High school lunchrooms are all the same,"* he thought, to himself.

# CHAPTER THIRTY-TWO

Logan Spence pushed through the door of Cornwall's main dining room and started the walk back to Squire House. He entered his room to find Pete Ellison staring out the window. His new roommate looked troubled.

"What's the matter, Pete?" asked Logan.

Ellison turned his attention from the window. Without answering Logan's question, he walked across the room and plopped himself into his reading chair. He looked at Logan and shook his head, forlornly.

"Spence, you have no idea the pressure I'm under," he revealed.

"What kind of pressure, Pete?"

"Family pressure," answered Ellison.

"I'm not following you," confessed Logan.

Pete Ellison looked at Logan Spence, impatiently.

"The kind of pressure you probably won't understand," he said.

"Try me."

"Spence, my older brother applied to Stanford. He was accepted."

"Good for him," replied Logan.

Ellison pressed on.

"My father also attended Stanford".

"Good for him, too."

Pete Ellison looked at Logan. He continued to explain his dire situation.

To make matters worse, my grandfather went to Stanford. Not only that, granddad is currently on Stanford's Board of Governors! Now, can you begin to see the kind of pressure I'm facing regarding acceptance at Palo Alto?" he asked, looking for sympathy.

"Pete, I can only imagine that kind of pressure," commiserated Spence, cynically.

Logan walked to his desk. He picked up the note from Patricia White and headed for the door.

"Where are you off to?" asked Pete Ellison.

"Angelica Hall."

Logan left the future Cardinal to, naively, agonize over what Spence already knew was going to be his new roommate's inevitable alma mater.

He crossed the grounds of Cornwall and entered Angelica Hall's campus. Logan stopped at a four-way sidewalk intersection not knowing which path to take.

"Are you lost?" asked an Angelica Hall co-ed.

"More times than not," he admitted, with a smile.

"Well, you've found the right place!" she said and laughed a disarming charm of welcome. "What's your port of call, sailor?"

"I'm looking for Ms. Patricia White's office."

"Patty's office is in the admin building. C'mon, I'm heading in that direction," she offered.

Logan fell into lock-step with his impromptu campus guide.

"I'm Glynn."

"Logan."

Logan was fascinated. Glynn was the first girl he had ever met that immediately attracted him, without a thought to her appearance. She was definitely pretty. However, the way she spoke and carried herself made physical beauty take a back seat to a personality that Logan found, utterly, alluring.

"So, is it my pleasure or bane to have met you, Logan?" she asked, with an impish grin.

"That depends," responded Spence.

"On what?" challenged Glynn.

154

"My mood."

They approached a large brick building of obnoxious self-importance.

"Her office is in there," she motioned and continued walking.

"Glynn!" shouted Logan.

She stopped and turned.

"Do you have a last name?"

"That depends."

"On what?" he asked.

"My mood," she smiled and proceeded on her way.

Logan Spence entered Angelica Hall's administration building.

He walked up to the reception desk. The older woman seated behind the station eyed him, with wary suspicion.

"I'm looking for Ms. Patricia White's office."

"And who are you?" she asked, curtly.

Logan did not answer. Instead, he pulled the letter out of his pocket and handed it to the receptionist.

She read it with pedantic deliberation. The gate-keeper picked-up the receiver of her desk phone.

"He's here."

She listened and then put the receiver back on its cradle.

"Ms. White's office is up the stairs and down the hallway on the left`," she motioned.

Logan walked down a corridor that echoed his footsteps. He stopped at the designated door and knocked.

"Enter," was the response.

Spence opened the door and walked into the office. He closed the door behind him.

"So, you're Logan Spence," said the woman seated behind an impressive desk.

"Yeah, I'm Logan Spence.

She looked at him, dismissively.

"It's not *yeah*, Mr. Spence. It's, **yes**, I am Logan Spence," she corrected, with stringent authority.

"**Yes**, I am Logan Spence," he repeated.

"Be seated, Mr. Spence," she said, with no room for nonsense.

Logan sat down in a chair situated in front of her desk. He studied Ms. Patricia White, for the first time. He saw an unusually attractive young woman.

Their eyes locked in mutual gaze. It was not a magical moment. He felt something was not quite right. Uncharacteristically, Logan Spence felt unsure of, himself.

"What are you staring at, Mr. Spence?" she asked, with impatience.

"You", he replied, lamely.

"And why is that, Mr. Spence?" she demanded.

"I guess it's because you don't look like what I thought a teacher from Angelica Hall is supposed to look like," he struggled.

Patricia White glared at Logan.

"Well, if it's any consolation, you most certainly do not look like what a Cornwall student is supposed to look like, as far as I am concerned!" she countered, defiantly.

Abruptly, Logan stood up. He looked at Ms. Patricia White.

"I don't think this was such a good idea," he said and started towards the door.

"Sit down, Mr. Spence!" she commanded.

Normally, Logan would have simply slammed the door behind him. However, there was just something about the tone of her voice that made him reconsider. Obediently, he sat back down.

Patricia White looked at Logan Spence. Her face softened. She almost smiled.

"Let's get down to work, shall we?"

The teacher opened a desk drawer and removed a rectangular blue box and two books. She handed them to Logan.

156

"These are your study materials for this term. The box contains one thousand vocabulary cards. The words are arranged alphabetically. Their definitions and pronunciations are printed on the back of each card. I expect you to master fifteen new words daily," she instructed.

Logan looked at Ms. Patricia White and objected.

"Ms. White, I have other classes. Fifteen new words a day is too many! I'll do five."

The teacher looked at her new charge, with dispassion.

"Your other courses are not my responsibility, Mr. Spence."

The two stared at each other in a silent showdown.

"**Ten**" they agreed in spontaneous unison.

Ms. Patricia White pointed to the smaller of the two books. It was *A Portrait of the Artist as a Young Man.*

"That is a novel. It was written by James Joyce. Have you heard of him?"

"No."

"Joyce is considered to be one of the most influential writers of the twentieth century. His writing style is challenging. However, for those who can learn to familiarize themselves with his technique, it is also one the most fulfilling," she explained.

Ms. White nodded towards the second, larger book.

"That is biography on James Joyce. Its author is Richard Ellmann. The book is widely regarded as the best James Joyce biography ever written. It is vital that you read it in tandem with the novel. Besides being a good read, it will help you more quickly understand the writings of Joyce."

She looked at Logan.

"Are you with me, thus far, Mr. Spence?"

"Yeah"

He quickly corrected himself. "**Yes**, Ms. White."

She continued.

"We shall meet once a week in this office for one hour. The day and time will be determined by what best accommodates our respective schedules. At those meetings, we will review your vocabulary cards and monitor your reading progress. Furthermore, you will provide me with two paragraphs of writing."

"What kind of writing?" he shrugged.

"Anything of your choosing.

Patricia White looked at her watch.

"Do you have any questions?"

"No."

"Then, that will be all for today, Mr. Spence."

# CHAPTER THIRTY-THREE

"That's the price. Take it or leave it," said the man seated behind the desk.

The younger man stared across the table. Without saying a word, he stood up and reached into his coat pocket. He pulled out an envelope and tossed it on the desktop.

"It's all there," he said.

"Oh, I don't doubt that," smiled the older man, with confident malice. He nodded towards a package on the desk. "Go on, take it."

The younger man picked up the package and started to leave.

"Hey, kid, your customers won't be disappointed with the product," reassured the older man. "Close the door behind you."

Just to be sure, the man seated behind the desk picked up the envelope and counted its contents. Satisfied, he swiveled his chair to face an impressive floor safe. He deposited the envelope inside the vault and re-locked its door.

Chester White stood up and walked to his office bar. He selected a tall water glass and filled it with ice. He poured a generous portion of Jack Daniels. After stirring the drink, he took a long pull. He lit a Lucky Strike and exhaled a blue plume of self-satisfaction.

At the age of sixteen, circumstances had dictated Chester assume ownership of a then dying vending business. With hard work and an uncanny sense for knowing future markets of profitability, before the herd, he had built an impressive business.

What had once been a lone van delivering candy and nuts to various local businesses was now a fleet of vehicles delivering a wide variety of products to a large number of area establishments. In addition to cigarette machines, pool tables, and jukeboxes, video games were now being installed.

Chester White had possessed the foresight to secure the exclusive distribution rights to Atari in the local area. The trend towards video games had started with *Pong*. In the current year of 1979, the rage was *Space Invaders*.

The small room in his house that had once served as his office had long since been abandoned. His business headquarters was now a spacious loft overlooking an impressive warehouse. The large building was located on three prime acres in Rutland, New York. He owned the property and structure free and clear.

However, in spite of his business success, Chester White was still a bitter man. His long-time ambition to secure a liquor license and share in the lucrative spoils of liquid indulgence had been, continuously, obstructed by the local political power brokers. In particular "Big John "Westfield had been a pain in his ass.

"If I can't be *legally* illegal, I'll just be illegal," he had finally decided.

Chester White entered the underground business of selling marijuana.

He had calculated that the structure of his existing vending business to bars was a perfect fit for the product's sale. Initially, it had been a one-man operation. However, as the vending business grew, so did the means by which the pot was distributed. Trusted van drivers now handled the transfer of product from warehouse to the various points of sale along the vending routes.

As pot consumption increased, the volume of liquor sold in bars declined. However, the bar owners were more than compensated by their cut in the invisible revenue generated by the drug sales. The only ones getting screwed on the deal were the political fat cats who had underestimated, Chester White.

There was a knock on Chester White's office door.

"Enter."

It was Paul "Bounty" Hunter. He was a Viet Nam vet. After returning to the States, Hunter had initially made his living as a barroom bouncer at Carver's Bar and Grill. That was where he met Chester White. The two men became friendly.

In Paul Hunter, Chester saw a potential business asset. In Chester White, Paul had seen a path for career advancement. So, when Chester White offered him a job in the vending business, Hunter jumped at the opportunity. He was now Chester's second in command.

"We have to talk," stated Hunter, as he made his way to the office bar.

Chester White remained silent. He waited until Hunter had filled a glass with ice and Dewar's and seated himself in front of the desk. Paul "Bounty" Hunter sipped his cocktail and spoke.

"We have an issue," he said, in a business-like tone of voice.

"What kind of issue?" asked Chester White.

"Someone is selling product on our turf," responded the former bouncer.

"Where?" demanded Chester White with growing anger.

Paul Hunter took a slow pull from his glass before answering.

"Carvers."

Chester White looked at Paul Hunter, in utter disbelief.

"Carvers?!" he asked, shaking his head. "Who'd be that damn stupid?"

"Some college kid out of New Haven," answered the second in command.

"That answers my question," said Chester. He rose from his chair and returned to the bar for a refill.

"Paul, how do I know what you are telling me is accurate?"

"I got the call from Junior. He cut the kid some slack last night. Problem is, he's back tonight trying to build a nest."

Chester White stirred his cocktail.

"Well, all baby birds have to be pushed out of their nests," he said. White drained the drink with one massive chug.

"C'mon, let's go."

The ride from Chester White's building to Carver's Bar and Grill was twenty minutes. Paul Hunter was behind the wheel.

"While I was on the phone with Junior, I instructed him to have someone from his camp score some weed from the college kid. I figured with a reference, things will go a lot smoother when we make our move," he explained.

Chester White nodded his head, approvingly.

"I've always liked the way you conduct business, he smiled."

Paul Hunter pulled into the graveled parking lot. The two men entered the rear entrance and walked through the kitchen. The busy employees immediately recognized both men and continued about their business. Chester White and Paul Hunter pushed through a door and stood standing next to the impressive mahogany bar.

The large room was packed with patrons. The high volume of noise was an equal combination of human din and jukebox music. As usual, townies crowded the bar. The tables, booths, and gaming machines were flooded with students. A man standing behind the bar spotted White and Hunter. He ambled towards them. Without saying a word, he began mixing two cocktails.

Johnny "Junior" Westfield was the manager of Carver's Bar and Grill. His father, "Big John" Westfield was its owner. Johnny and Chester White had known each other as classmates during their time at Rutland High School. Through the years, they had remained friendly.

"The kid is still here," said Johnny Westfield, as he placed the two drinks on the bar. He started making one for himself.

Chester White looked at his one-time school mate.

"Thanks, for the heads-up, Johnny."

Westfield looked at White with irritation.

"I've got skin in this game, too!" he reminded Chester.

Johnny "Junior" Westfield had spent his entire life dwelling timidly in the shadow of a powerful and over-bearing parent. Getting involved in Chester White's drug business had been the first major decision he had ever made, without the knowledge or consent of his father.

As the money he netted from the drug trade increased, so had his confidence. He cherished his newly found financial independence. "Junior" no longer stuttered.

"Johnny, who copped from the college kid?" asked Chester White.

"Eddie," he responded.

Chester White thought for a moment.

"Okay, this is how we are going to play it." Chester looked at Junior Westfield. "Johnny, tell Eddie to let the kid know he's got a buyer. Make sure Eddie lets him know that I'm cool. Then have Eddie lead him out the front door. I'll be waiting there."

Chester White looked at Hunter.

"Paul, ten minutes after Eddie re-enters the front door leave through the kitchen. I'll meet you at our car."

Chester White then turned his attention back to Westfield.

"Johnny, stay by the phone. You'll hear from me fifteen minutes after Paul, leaves. Got it?"

Both men nodded their understanding. With that, he exited through Carver's kitchen.

Chester White was standing in the parking lot of Carver's. The bar's front door opened. Two silhouettes emerged and started walking towards him.

"This is the guy," said Eddie, to a young man. With that, Eddie turned and walked back inside.

"Thanks, Eddie," smiled Chester White.

The college kid looked at him.

"Eddie tells me you're interested in product."

"More than interested," reassured Chester White.

The seller produced a plastic bag.

"It's a lid. It'll cost you thirty," he said, in a matter of fact tone of voice.

Chester White feigned disappointment.

"Is that all you've got? I was hoping to buy a little more than that."

"It's all I've got on me. Don't want to be hassling intent to distribute," explained the kid. "How much more were you looking to buy?"

"As much as you have," answered Chester White, pulling out an impressive wad of bills.

The kid's already dilated eyes grew wider.

"I've got six more ounces in my car," he said, with self-serving eagerness.

"Where's your car?"

"Over there," he pointed.

"C'mon, let's go. I don't have all night," demanded the now impatient buyer.

The two walked across the parking lot. The kid pulled out a set of car keys and opened the trunk door. He leaned inside and began to extract plastic bags of pot.

Without warning, Chester White violently slammed the trunk door on top of the hunched over figure. With malice, he banged it several more times before lifting the kicking legs, to stuff them inside the trunk. He took the car keys and then closed the trunk door. He wiped the keys and tossed them underneath the car.

White could hear muffled whimpers of pain coming from the trunk. He lit a cigarette and walked towards his car. Paul Hunter was already seated behind the wheel. Chester climbed into the passenger seat and closed the door.

"Find the nearest payphone," he ordered.

After leaving Carver's parking lot, Hunter pulled the car to a stop in front of a phone booth. White got out and placed the call.

"Johnny, it's me. I want you to call the cops. Tell them there's a 72' green Ford LTD that's been parked at your place all night. Tell them you're suspicious and want them to check it out. I'll be in touch." He hung up the phone and got back into his car.

"So, how bad did you bust him up?" asked Paul "Bounty" Hunter.

"Not bad enough to keep his ass out of jail tonight," smiled Chester White.

# CHAPTER THIRTY-FOUR

"So, how's the student prince progressing?" asked Kate Whitson, with a smug smile.

Patricia White paused before answering her best friend's question. Her hesitation was due to the fact she did not know what to make of Logan Spence. The teacher still had no clue what made the young man tick.

The one constant she had noted was the preparedness he exhibited at every one of their weekly tutorials. It was this obvious dedication to her curriculum that Ms. Patricia White found most intriguing about the enigmatic student. He had captured her interest.

"Actually, Kate, I'm quite surprised at the progress Logan has made thus far this term, answered Pat White."

A statement like that coming from her life-long friend could have almost been taken as a compliment. Patricia White rarely bestowed such praise on *any* student. This caught Kate Whitson, unaware.

"Tell me about this progress," she insisted.

"Well, for starters, Logan has aced every vocabulary test I've given him. His writing is showing noticeable improvement, and his conversational syntax is night and day."

Kate looked at Patty and laughed.

"I think the progress you describe has a lot more to do with you than your student. You should be proud of yourself. And if his test scores reflect your efforts, Mr. Spence is going to be a real plus on your resume," she concluded.

Patricia White continued as if oblivious to her friend's words.

"However, the most interesting thing to me is how he's actually beginning to assimilate Joyce! He's starting to understand and appreciate *Portrait*. At first, it was a slow go, but...."

Kate abruptly stood up and headed for the kitchen in Patty's apartment.

"I'm going to have a glass of wine. Are you joining me?"

"Of course."

Kate returned with two glasses. She handed one to Patty and then reseated herself on the sofa.

"Today is Saturday," she said.

"Well, thank you for that information, Kate," smiled Patty White.

"I'm just reminding you about your commitment for this evening," she explained.

Patty sipped her wine.

"I haven't forgotten," she said, unenthusiastically.

The commitment Kate had mentioned was a double date slated for that evening. It was to be Kate and her now boyfriend, Scott Abrams, and Patty and her would-be suitor, Tom Wilkerson. The itinerary was a faculty cocktail party followed by an off-campus dinner for the two couples.

Kate looked at Patty and shook her head.

"I don't understand why you always have to be so difficult!" she said, with exasperation.

"And I don't understand why you always insist upon trying to hook me up with Tom Wilkerson!" retaliated, Patty.

"Tom is a wonderful guy. He's quite bright and by all standards not bad looking. Besides, he adores you!"

"That's his problem!"

Kate Whitson was undeterred.

"You know, Patty, Tom has been very patient as far the two of you furthering your relationship together, if you know what I mean."

"I know exactly what you mean!" Patricia paused, before continuing. "That gives me an idea. Why don't you and Scott concentrate your efforts on finding Tom a girl who won't try his patience as much as I do! That way, all concerned will be a lot happier," snapped Patty White.

"You're impossible!"

Kate finished her wine. She stood up and headed for the door.

"The guys are meeting us in the lobby at six. I'll stop by here so we can go down together."

Kate Whitson closed the door behind her.

# CHAPTER THIRTY-FIVE

Logan Spence was in his room at Squire House. He was seated in a recliner he had bought at Roger Kaminski's aunt's used furniture store, at the beginning of the term.

In addition to the leather chair, Spence had purchased a standing floor reading lamp. However, the piece of furniture that had caught Logan's fancy was a book case mounted atop a wooden cabinet. What had drawn him to it was the cabinet's secret interior panel. Once opened, the clandestine space was ideal for housing items of discretion.

After Roger told his aunt about their encounter with Billy the Kid, she had made a good price even better. She also loaned Roger a truck to transport the furniture back to Logan's room.

Spence was reading Richard Ellmann's biography on James Joyce. Not only was the book helping him better understand *Portrait*, it was turning out to be a fun read for the kid who had rarely picked up a book, before attending Cornwall.

The interesting thing was he did not consider what he was reading to be homework. It was something he wanted to do. In his mind, it was as much for Ms. Patricia White as it was, for himself. He knew that the better he did with her curriculum, the better it would be for her. For reasons he did not understand, that was very important to him.

The door to the room burst open. In walked Logan's roommate, Pete Ellison and his Water's Edge friend, Mark Campbell.

"How was the movie, guys?" asked Spence and put the book down.

"Logan, man, it was awesome!" extolled Ellison.

"Yea, it was all of that and then some!" agreed Mark Campbell." Spence, you really should've come."

Every Saturday night a feature movie played at the campus theater. That week's film had been *Star Trek: The Motion Picture*.

Logan had never been a big *Star Trek* fan. So, he figured he had not missed too much. However, he was definitely taking in the following week's movie. He thought Francis Ford Coppola's, *Apocalypse Now* would be far more to his liking.

"So, how are you two renegades occupying yourselves for the rest of the night?" smiled Spence.

"Jack is working at the radio station tonight," said Mark. "We thought we'd head over there and hang out."

Jack Reed was Mark Campbell's roommate and the guy who had greeted Logan upon his arrival at Cornwall.

"But first, we thought it might be a good idea to put ourselves in a more musical frame of mind," laughed Pete Ellison.

"Never a bad idea," agreed Logan.

"You care to join us, Spence?" asked Mark Campbell.

The thought of Campbell's mediocre weed did not thrill him, but getting out of the room did.

"Sure."

"Logan, we'll be in Mark's room rolling a couple of bad boys for the road. Meet us there," said Pete Ellison.

They closed the door behind them and headed across the hall.

Logan stood up and put on a jacket. He then went over to his cabinet. Opening its door, he removed the false panel. Spence pulled out a bottle of Absolut and a flask. After filling the flask, he took a pull from the bottle and then put it back in its hiding place.

Logan checked his coat pocket for smokes and then shut the door, as he walked over to Campbell's room. He knocked on the door.

"Spence, is that you?" barked Campbell.

"Yes."

Without waiting for further response, Logan entered the room and closed the door behind him. Mark was seated at his desk rolling the second of two joints. Pete Ellison was strumming through Jack Reed's impressive collection of record albums.

Finished, Campbell stood.

"You chaps ready to rock and roll?"

The trio left Squire House. They took the "scenic" route across the soccer fields allowing them the opportunity to light a joint. Logan pulled out his flask. He took a swig and passed it on.

The radio station was located in a small classroom building on a street facing the campus quad. Its front door was always locked after class hours. However, Jack Reed had provided his roommate with a key. Mark Campbell opened the door. Logan and Pete Ellison followed him up two flights of stairs. The radio station was situated at the far end of a hallway.

Logan had never been to the campus radio station. He was immediately impressed. A large WCAH banner hung-over its entrance. To the left of the front door was a large Plexiglas window. It afforded a view of the entire inside of the station. The neon ON AIR sign was illuminated, indicating broadcasting in progress.

A buzzer sounded unlocking the front door. A student Logan recognized but did not know greeted them.

"Jack told me you guys might be dropping by tonight," he said, good-naturedly.

Charlie Davenport was the studio engineer for that night's shift. He immediately turned his attention to Logan.

"You're Spence, right?"

"Yes."

"Charlie," he said extending his hand.

"Logan."

"You seem a little surprised, Logan," observed Davenport.

Actually, Spence was overwhelmed by the vast array of audio equipment that occupied the room. There were even in-house speakers situated throughout the studio. The Clash's album *London Calling* was currently playing.

"I guess you weren't expecting a real radio station," surmised Charlie.

"I guess not," admitted Logan.

"Actually, we have enough wattage to reach most of southern Connecticut," he boasted.

In the next room, also separated by Plexiglas, Logan could see Jack Reed seated behind a microphone. The desk was crowded with turntables, reel to reels, and several telephones.

Logan reached into his pocket and pulled out a cigarette. He lit it.

"Hey, Logan, you're not supposed to be smoking in here! That said, can I bum one?" laughed Charlie Davenport.

Spence tossed him the pack.

"Hey, Charlie, what's that room used for?" asked Logan pointing to a separate area that housed a round table and several chairs. It was also separated by Plexiglas.

"That's where we conduct interviews," explained Davenport, returning Logan's pack.

"Hey, I've got an idea," offered Mark Campbell, obviously feeling no pain.

"And what's that, Mark?" asked the studio engineer.

"Why don't we do a live interview tonight?"

Charlie Davenport looked at a prominent wall clock and then focused on Mark Campbell.

"We go to commercial break in less than five minutes. When Jack comes out, you talk to him about it," suggested Charlie.

"I'll do that," agreed Campbell.

As soon as the ON AIR light went off, Jack Reed left his seat at the mike and joined the others. He spoke first to Mark Campbell.

"Did you remember what I asked you to do?"

"Would I forget my favorite roommate?" asked Campbell, with feigned chagrin.

"In a heartbeat!" laughed Jack Reed.

Mark handed his friend a joint. Jack lit it, took a couple of hits, and then passed it to Charlie.

"Jack, we think it would be fun to do a live interview tonight," offered Pete Ellison.

"And who the hell am I going to interview, Pete?"

172

Ellison thought for a moment.

"We'll make it some sort of spoof. Something funny."

"And what are we going to do for material, Pete?" asked Reed, glancing at the studio clock.

"I have an idea," ventured Logan Spence.

Spence had everyone's attention.

"Jack, you'll do an exclusive interview with a student from Sheffield High. The purpose of the interview will be simple. By giving him a chance to have his say, you might be able to ease the ongoing hostility between the students at Sheffield High and Cornwall," suggested Spence.

"And where am I going to find that student?" pressed Reed.

"You're looking at him, Jack," smiled Logan.

Charlie Davenport was the first to speak.

"It's not a bad idea, Jack. If nothing else, it'll be different!"

Reed looked at Davenport.

"Is the interview room wired for sound?"

"Absolutely!" confirmed the studio engineer.

Jack Reed thought for a moment. He made his decision.

"What the hell, let's do it!"

Jack Reed, Logan Spence and Mark Campbell entered the interview room. Jack and Logan sat down at the circular table. Each had a microphone in front of him. Campbell sat off to the side. Charlie Davenport and Pete Ellison were at the main console in the next room.

The radio station's ON AIR neon flashed red.

**"This is Jack Reed THE VOICE of WCAH coming to you, LIVE from our Cornwall studios!"**

"Tonight, I have a very special guest with me. He is currently a senior at Sheffield High School and anxious to have his voice heard."

"What is your name, sir?" asked the radio host.

Logan broke into an accent located somewhere between Brooklyn, New York and Boston, Massachusetts.

"Joe."

"Do you have a last name Joe?"

*Joe* thought for a moment.

"Townie, Joe Townie."

"And Joe Townie why did you request this air time?" asked the commentator.

"To, ah, set you people straight."

"By *you people*, I assume you mean the students at Cornwall."

"Yeah, that's what I mean."

"Well, Joe, the microphone is all yours!"

Spence lit a cigarette and settled into his seat. He felt quite comfortable in the role he was now playing.

"Well, it's pretty simple. You guys from Cornwall think us guys from Sheffield are dog crap. But that's okay. Cause we think that's kind of funny."

"Well, Joe, I'm not suggesting what you're saying is true. But, if it was, why would you and your friends from Sheffield High find that humorous?" asked the radio host.

"Cause you Cornwall hand jobs ain't gettin the joke!"

"And what is that joke, Joe?" smiled the commentator.

*Joe* paused before answering the question.

"I'll bet a lot of you corn holes listening tonight are wonderin why you ain't getting enough of that fine Angelica Hall tail. Well, I'm here to tell you why."

"And why would that be, Joe?" pressed the radio host.

"Cause those pretty young things are already getting more than they can handle without it hurtin thanks to me and my friends at Sheffield High, that's why!"

Mark Campbell had been quietly seated to the side. He was now bent over laughing, desperately trying not to make any noise.

174

"Quite frankly, Joe, I find that rather difficult to believe," balked the show's host.

"There's nothing difficult about it, man. See, those gorgeous fillies from Angelica Hall spent all their lives having to hang out with dull preppy wimps like who go to Cornwall. They come up to Sheffield and for the first time meet some real men! Guys who play hard on the field and even harder between the sheets, if you know what I mean! I know you ladies listening tonight know exactly what **Big** Joe's talking!"

At his point, Jack Reed, the consummate radio professional was having difficulty keeping his act together, without breaking into laughter.

"So, Joe, are you suggesting that the guys from Sheffield High are more macho than the guys from Cornwall?"

"Suggesting it? No, man, I'm proving it! You name one corn hole who would have the guts to go to Sheffield High alone and do what I'm doing here tonight!"

"Well, Joe, I can honestly say that not one Cornwall student would go to Sheffield High and do what you are doing here, tonight. But that's only because your school doesn't have a radio station!" smirked the host.

Suddenly, *Joe* lurched out of his chair.

"See! That's the attitude I'm talking!"

"Joe, it was only meant as a little ON AIR humor. Now, please, sit back down!" implored Jack Reed.

"I'm not finding that funny. I'm not finding that funny, at all! You keep that up and I'm going to bust your face wide open! You hear me, Wolf Jack dude!"

Pete Ellison was standing at the Plexiglas window with a wide grin. He was holding up the telephone console. The lights were lit. The phone lines were on fire!

*Joe* reseated, himself. The radio host continued.

"Joe, your claim that the guys from Sheffield High are somehow more manly than the students at Cornwall is only your opinion. You have absolutely no proof of that."

"You want proof? I'll give you proof! Let me make a couple of phone calls. I'll get five of my friends over here. You come up with twelve guys from Cornwall who got the balls to meet us on the Quad. We'll go two on one. Take us two minutes to kick their asses! And you ladies from Angelica Hall are welcomed to come and watch the show!"

"Well, I don't know about that, Joe. But I do know it's time for a commercial break. When we return, we'll start taking your phone calls. Maybe you'll be lucky enough to go mano a mano with Joe Townie!

**"This is Jack Reed, The Voice of WCAH saying we'll be right back."**

"Logan, you were terrific!" beamed Jack Reed, as he removed his head set.

"Sterling performance, Spence," agreed Mark Campbell.

Charlie Davenport suddenly rapped on the Plexiglas window. He motioned Jack Reed into the other room. The studio engineer was not a happy camper. Logan and Mark Campbell followed Reed out.

"Jack, we've got problems."

"What kind of problems, Charlie?"

"Take a look out that window," motioned Davenport.

Reed looked down to see a throng of Cornwall varsity football players milling around the front door of the building.

"What is it Jack?" asked Logan.

"What is it? It's half the varsity football team looking to kick Joe Townie's ass, that's what it is!" screamed Jack Reed.

"Jack, be cool. I'll go downstairs and explain it was all a goof," reassured Spence.

"It's not going to be that simple, Logan," said Charlie Davenport, as he nodded towards the room's other window.

Jack Reed and Logan crossed the room to take a look. Down below, cars full of Sheffield High students were beginning to line the curbside.

Jack Reed went into full panic mode.

176

"Spence, what the hell have you done?! There's going to be a damn rumble down there and I'm going to be blamed for it! Oh, I'm toast! I'm a dead DJ walking!"

Jack Reed started to hyperventilate anxiety. He managed to compose himself long enough to bark orders.

"You three assholes are out of here, now! And never even think about coming to this station, again!"

Mark Chapman, Pete Ellison, and Logan Spence started to leave the radio station. Suddenly, Logan stopped and turned.

"Jack, does this mean *Joe* won't be taking any phone calls tonight?" he grinned.

"Get out!"

The three exited the building through a little used side door. As they crossed the soccer fields on their way back to Squire House, the sounds of approaching police sirens could be heard descending upon WCAH.

# CHAPTER THIRTY-SIX

"A special meeting of the radio station's Board of Governors is in session, as we speak," said Mark Campbell. "That's all I know."

He was speaking to Logan Spence and Pete Ellison in their dorm room at Squire House. It was the Monday afternoon following the now infamous and much talked about radio broadcast of, "An Evening with Joe Townie".

"I only hope they don't kick his ass off the air," continued Campbell, in a rare display of heartfelt concern. "Music is his life. If they pull his show it will kill him."

The room's door opened without a knock. Standing in front of them was Jack Reed. His face was oddly expressionless. Suddenly, he broke into a mile-wide smile.

"Gentlemen, pay due homage to WCAH's newly appointed Program Director."

The tension in the room vanished. It was replaced by the awed bewilderment of his three friends. Mark Campbell was the first to speak.

"What the hell are you talking about, Jack?" he asked.

Reed plopped himself down in Pete Ellison's reading chair. The smile was gone. His face now reflected weariness. The preceding thirty-six hours had obviously drained him both physically and emotionally.

"The weekend sweeps came out this morning," he began.

He was referring to the tracking numbers that station executives monitor during broadcast cycles.

"Anyway, my Saturday night show broke all school records in terms of the number of listeners. In fact, WCAH was holding its own with some of the more popular Rock stations out of New Haven and Waterbury!"

"Congratulations, old man!" beamed Mark Campbell.

"Yea, really Jack, that's unbelievable!" agreed Pete Ellison.

"But do you know what really saved my ass?" He was now looking directly at Logan Spence.

"Might it be new advertising sponsors, Wolf Jack dude?" smiled Spence, as he stood up and walked towards his desk.

"Bingo! The phone has been ringing off the charts this morning! The Board is really excited about the potential increase in ad revenue for the station."

Logan picked up a small stack of books off his desk and headed for the door.

"Reed, I'm glad everything worked out for you," said Spence, as he closed the door behind him.

"Hey, Jack, what are you going to do for an encore?" asked Pete Ellison.

"I have no idea," admitted the Dee Jay.

Logan was on his way to an economics class at Angelica Hall. As he entered the tiered lecture room, he took a seat in the back row. Spence was hoping this would preclude anyone from sitting too near him. He could then continue to prep for Ms. Patricia White's tutorial that immediately followed.

When someone decided to sit down right beside him, his annoyance was instantaneous. He did not even bother to glance up from his notes.

"I hope this seat wasn't reserved for anyone, in particular," said the voice of the intruder.

Logan's anger immediately, vanished. He looked up smiling.

"If it had been, it would've been for you," he laughed.

The "intruder" was Glynn Benamure, the girl he had met during his first visit to Angelica Hall, at the beginning of the term. During the ensuing months, the two had become very good friends.

Glynn continued to fascinate Logan. She was the most appealing girl he had ever met. The two had not had sex. In some strange way, the absence of physical intimacy had been replaced by an even more magnetic closeness, one of unencumbered friendship.

"So, are you planning to cause another disturbance during today's lecture?" she needled, with mischievous intent.

"Only if you insist upon behaving yourself," he countered, affectionately.

Glynn was alluding to an argument that Logan had ignited with the economics professor over the stupidity of not including food and energy in the Consumer Price Index equation.

"Do you have a date for tomorrow night's dance?" she asked, already knowing the answer to her question.

"No."

"Well, you do now," she said, with confident self-satisfaction.

"How thoughtful of you," said Spence. He shook his head in silent disapproval.

Logan knew Glynn was not referring, to herself. That was because she had been seeing the same guy for well over a year.

Bradley Stevens was a senior at Cornwall. Bradley's Pre-Ivy resume included president of the student council and captain of the varsity lacrosse team. He was most often described as just a really nice guy. Spence had never liked nor trusted "nice guys".

"Who's the girl?" he asked, disinterestedly.

"Blair Sumner."

Logan looked towards the ceiling.

"Glynn, I have absolutely no interest in her."

"And why not?" was her immediate question.

"For starters, I don't think she's capable of slinging together two coherent sentences," answered Logan. "The girl is dumb as a stump."

"But, she has a great face and body," smiled Glynn, with ironic mirth in her eyes.

"Not impressed."

Benamure's eyes narrowed in quiet resentment.

"Do you have any idea what most guys would give to be set up with Blair Sumner?"

180

"I don't give a damn."

"Well, I do! Besides, she likes you. Anyway, I want you to meet Blair, myself, and Bradley in front of the girl's dorm tomorrow night before the dance."

"And what makes you think I'm going to show up?"

Glynn Benamure stared at Logan Spence before responding.

"Because, I told her you'd be there," she confided.

"I'll consider it."

As the economics class commenced, Logan returned his attention to Ms. Patricia White's study materials.

Noticing her friend's preoccupation, Glynn leaned over and whispered in his ear.

"I'll take notes for both of us."

The walk from the economics class to the Angelica Hall Administration Building was a short one. Logan Spence knocked on the office door of Ms. Patricia White.

"Come in."

Logan entered the room. He closed the door behind him. Ms. Patricia White was seated behind her desk. Logan sat down in the chair facing her. He placed his pile of books on the floor.

Patricia White silently studied the young man seated in front of her. The Fall Term was coming to an end.

"Mr. Spence, James Joyce's written narrative is most frequently referred to as 'stream of consciousness'. In a few words, define 'stream of consciousness' as it pertains to his novel, *A Portrait of an Artist as a Young Man*. Logan did not hesitate with his response.

"Joyce's 'stream of consciousness' manifests itself in "*Portrait*" every time he goes to bed at night and wets it," answered Spence.

His succinct, yet ironically accurate, answer startled Patricia White. The instructor searched the face of her student trying to determine whether he was being sincere or merely a wise ass. His expression did not tip his hand.

Logan immediately sensed her uneasiness. He altered the course of conversation.

"I used to do that," he laughed, without a trace of self-consciousness. He was referring to bed-wetting.

Before thought or hesitation, Patty White responded.

"So did, I."

Her unanticipated and candid admission caught Logan by surprise. He suddenly felt awkward. Student and teacher stared at one another, in a wordless showdown. Teacher won. Logan averted his eyes to the floor. When he finally looked up, his ears were tinged with the red of embarrassment. He shook his head.

"Girls don't do that kind of stuff," he smiled, sheepishly.

"Some do," she stated with unvarnished veracity.

Logan Spence was rendered speechless.

This was the first hint of emotional vulnerability she had ever seen in the young man. Her initial impulse was to seize the opportunity and establish a dominant role in their teacher-student relationship. However, for some reason she could not find it, within herself, to shatter the pane of frailty now so nakedly exposed in front of her. Patty made her decision.

"That will be all for today, Mr. Spence. You may go."

Logan was still reeling from what had just taken place. Awkwardly, he picked up his pile of books from the floor. He stood and headed for the door.

"Mr. Spence."

He stopped and turned around. Patricia White rose from her chair. She started walking towards him. She was smiling. It was the first time she had ever smiled at him. It was the most beautiful smile Logan had ever seen. It made him feel warm. It made him feel welcomed. It was a smile that made him feel safe.

"If I don't see you, have a wonderful Thanksgiving, Logan." Patricia White offered Logan Spence her hand.

# CHAPTER THIRTY-SEVEN

*"She called me Logan. She smiled at me and called me Logan!"* he exalted, to himself.

Spence had just left the office of Patricia White. He was still basking in the glow of the first-time friendliness she had shown him moments earlier. The young man was tripping the light fantastic.

All the hours of study he had dedicated to her tutorial had been worth that wonderful smile of acceptance she had, finally, bestowed upon him. For reasons he did not try understand, pleasing her was very important to him. He vowed to never disappoint Ms. Patricia White.

Logan was on his way to the Cornwall Sports Complex. The coach of the varsity wrestling team had scheduled an "optional" preliminary work-out before the Thanksgiving recess. Although Spence had only met Coach Hubbard once, he was certain about one thing. There was nothing "optional" about the son of a bitch.

Logan entered the wrestling team's locker room.

"I told you you'd be back."

It was Gus the equipment manager. He was sitting in his usual position behind the half-opened saddle door. He was smiling.

"I have something for you," he said.

The old man disappeared. When he returned, he placed a pair of wrestling shoes on the door's counter.

"They'll never be new, but I patched them up the best I could. They're fit for duty."

They were the white wrestling shoes Gus had loaned Spence for his varsity try-out.

"Thanks, Gus."

"Your sweats, jock, socks, and towels are already waiting for you, inside your locker."

Logan knew, immediately, that Gus was giving him preferential treatment. Before he had a chance to speak, the old man answered Spence's unasked question.

"You're the first kid I've seen walk in here in a long, long time who actually earned his way."

Logan quickly suited up and headed for the mats. He walked through the larger training room where the wrestling wannabes were busily grunting and groaning their way into obscurity. He descended the three short steps and entered "The Pit".

"How nice of you to fit us into your schedule, Spence," glared Coach Hubbard.

The coach was standing in the middle of the mat on the golden "C". The entire Cornwall varsity wrestling team was standing abreast at the far end of the room. Obviously, Spence had been the last to arrive.

Coach Hubbard looked, dubiously, at Spence's white shoes.

"This year's official wrestling uniform mandates black shoes, Mr. Spence."

Logan stared at the venerable coach with a quiet self-assuredness that gave the older man reason to pause.

"Coach, I feel comfortable wearing these shoes."

Frank "The Tank" Hubbard took closer note of the white wrestling shoes Spence was wearing. They were the very same ones he, himself, had worn many years earlier. He refocused his attention on Spence.

"They're yours until you lose," he said, brusquely.

Coach Hubbard walked off the mat to join his two assistants. That left Logan standing, by himself, facing the rest of the Cornwall varsity wrestling team. It was obvious they resented his pre-arranged membership into their exclusive club. The tense stand-off was suddenly broken by a member of their own ranks.

Carlos Acosta, the guy Logan had wrestled during his first visit to Cornwall and who had helped him out in the lunch room walked across the mat. He now stood next to Spence. He did so because of the natural bond that is formed between two athletes who have competed against one another and then walked away, with mutual respect.

Acosta looked at Spence.

"You're going to be one pain in the ass," he smiled.

Spence ignored Acosta's words.

"Let's settle this thing. I'll take out those two," he said, loudly enough for all present to hear. Spence pointed at the team's co-captains. "You handle everybody else."

Logan started moving forward. Acosta grabbed him by the shoulder.

"I have a better idea. I'll take out those two and *you* handle everybody else," he said, with a legitimate commitment that impressed Spence.

"I can deal with that. Let's do it!"

Their forward march was quickly halted by the sharp bark of Coach Hubbard's whistle. He walked back onto the mat.

"Acosta, Spence, hit the showers! The rest of you hit the mat! Fifty sit-ups, twenty-five push-ups, and then ladies, we'll start this afternoon's warm-up!"

As he watched the now two exiled wrestlers leave The Pit, Frank "The Tank" Hubbard smiled, to himself. The coach knew, at long last, he finally had the nucleus of a championship wrestling team.

Gus had witnessed the entire episode. As he walked back through the locker room, to assume his traditional seat behind the saddle door, the old man shook his head.

"It's starting to feel like old times around here," he mumbled to no one, in particular.

Logan quickly dressed and exited the Cornwall Sports Complex. As he walked back to Squire House, Spence's thoughts shifted from what had just taken place at the wrestling practice to his earlier encounters with Glynn Benamure and Patricia White.

"*It's been one strange afternoon,*" he thought, to himself, as he entered the dorm.

Logan climbed the stairs and walked down the hall. The door to his room was ajar. As he entered, the music of Pink Floyd's album

*The Wall* greeted him. His roommate, Pete Ellison, was propped on his bed. Mark Campbell was slouched in Ellison's reading chair.

Logan dumped the books and papers he had been carrying onto his desk. He then sat down in the recliner he had purchased from Roger Kaminski's aunt.

Pete Ellison looked at his roommate.

"So, how was your first wrestling practice?"

"Didn't even break a sweat," replied Logan.

Mark Campbell nodded "hello" to Spence. He then returned his attention back to Ellison and their prior conversation.

"So, Pete, are we going tomorrow night or not?" He was referring to the traditional "End of Fall Dance" hosted by Angelica Hall.

"Mark, I really haven't decided." Ellison then looked at his roommate.

"Logan, are you going?"

Before Spence could respond, Mark Campbell chimed in.

"Logan, definitely go! The three of us will first get properly lubricated and then take the dance by storm!" encouraged Campbell. "Hell, we might even get lucky."

Spence looked at his friend from Water's Edge and shook his head.

"If I go, I already have a date."

This bit of information caught Mark Campbell completely by surprise.

"And who might that lucky girl be?" he smiled, skeptically.

"Blair Sumner."

This bit of news rocked Campbell.

"How the hell did you hook yourself up with that piece of tail?" he asked, with envy.

Before Logan could respond, Pete Ellison entered the fray.

186

"I bet I know," he nodded. "It was Logan's little Angelica Hall friend, Glynn Benamure who set him up."

"Benamure!" exclaimed Campbell. "That's one little minx who has it all working in her own right!" he said, approvingly.

Logan remained silent. Mark Campbell continued.

"Logan, why the hell would you even think twice about not going out with Blair Sumner?"

"Because I've spoken to her," he answered. "As far as I'm concerned, she's a blank page."

"What do you mean?"

"The girl has no substance," responded Spence. "She has absolutely nothing to say. Blair Sumner would bore the crap out of me."

Mark Campbell looked at his friend from Water's Edge, with condescending reproach.

"Well then, old man, you'll simply have to skip the small talk and get down to matters of greater importance," he grinned. "Besides, Blair Sumner is an absolute doll!"

"One with less on her mind than Chatty Cathy," dismissed Spence.

"Well, she can pull my string any time she likes," laughed Campbell.

"Assuming, of course, you're not already pulling that string, yourself," smiled Logan.

Pete Ellison erupted into a convolution of laughter.

"Go to hell, Spence!" shouted the now wounded would be ladies' man.

Mark Campbell stood up.

"I'm going to dinner. Pete, are you coming?"

The still recovering Ellison rose from his bed. He looked at Spence.

"Logan, are you going to dinner?"

Spence looked at his roommate and shook his head.

"Save me a seat at the table. I'll catch up. I have to hit the head."

After his two friends closed the door behind them, Logan got up from his recliner and walked to the mini-fridge. He threw ice cubes in a glass and then opened his private cache. He poured some vodka and then sat back down.

Spence reflected upon that day's events. He could not make complete sense of everything that had taken place. However, as he drained the last of his cocktail and rose for dinner he arrived at one firm conclusion.

"I think I will go to the dance tomorrow night."

# CHAPTER THIRTY-EIGHT

A Cornwall jitney pulled to a stop at the Sheffield train station. The students emptied the bus and walked to the platform to await the train bound for New Haven, Connecticut. From that major terminal each would board different trains headed for their particular point of destination to celebrate the Thanksgiving Day Weekend.

Logan Spence and Mark Campbell were standing on a platform waiting for the southbound train to New York City. One of its stops was Water's Edge, Connecticut.

Their train arrived. The two friends boarded. Although the cars were crowded on that Wednesday afternoon before Thanksgiving, they managed to secure two seats next to one another. They stowed their bags and settled in for the ride home.

"So, did you score?" Mark Campbell asked, with keen interest.

He was referring to Logan's date with Blair Sumner the night before. Spence thought for a moment before answering Campbell's question.

"That's none of your business," he responded.

Mark Campbell nodded to his friend and smiled, conclusively.

"That means you didn't get down her pants."

"Blair was wearing a dress last night."

Mark stared at Logan. He did not understand his friend's obvious evasiveness.

"Spence, either you nailed the babe or you didn't. No big deal either way," he said.

Logan looked long and hard at Campbell, before responding.

"Mark, you've been going to Cornwall Angelica Hall two years longer than I have. How fast does news travel there?"

"Real fast."

Logan paused before continuing.

"I've learned that kiss and tell kind of guys usually end up not getting kissed. I'm not going to let you or anybody else interfere with my kisses. Understand, old chap?"

Mark Campbell did not, immediately, respond. The usual Brit Wit was stalled in momentary reflection. When, at last he spoke, it was with sincerity.

"I've never viewed the whole thing in that light," he admitted, with a self-effacing candor Logan had never seen before in his friend.

As their train pulled into the Water's Edge station, Spence and Campbell gathered their belongings. Once on the station platform, the two friends looked at one another and shook hands.

"I'll call you tomorrow after gobble, gobble time," promised Campbell.

"Make sure that you do. Anything to get me out of the house," nodded Spence.

The two walked their separate ways. Campbell started off towards his home on Club Lane. Spence lit a cigarette and began his walk to the other side of the tracks.

Logan dreaded going home. He never felt comfortable there. From an early age, he had sensed his father's tacit unacceptance, at his very presence. That was something Logan had never understood.

As he grew older, Logan had become acutely aware of the constant strain his mother was under trying to navigate the untenable situation. Oddly, with the passing of those years, Logan had grown to dislike his mother's efforts at placation as much as he did his father's resentment for him being there in the first place. It was a depressing scene.

"Logan, how wonderful to see you!" beamed Mildred Spence, as she hugged her son. "Your father's hospital rounds have him running a little late this evening, which is why he is not here to greet you," she explained.

"I understand."

Logan's seventeenth birthday happened to fall on that Thanksgiving Day. He considered it a God send.

*"Two family celebrations knocked off at one seating. Who could ask for anything more?"* he thought, to himself, and sat down to a Thanksgiving dinner table of three.

True to his word, Mark Campbell called. For Logan, it was a governor's stay of execution. Spence was out the door.

The following morning Logan was up early. He dressed, ate, and then started a long walk's destination. As he stood in front of Delfino's Automotive, Logan was impressed. The one-time small auto body shop had grown into a corporate operation to be reckoned with.

The new building was huge. In addition to body work, the company now had a full-service department. The Delfino's had purchased adjacent lots and were now operating new and used car divisions. It was a thriving enterprise.

Logan entered the front door and approached the reception desk.

"Can I help you?" asked the young woman.

"I'm here to see Carmine."

The receptionist looked at him, warily.

"Is Mr. Delfino expecting you?" she asked.

"I don't have a scheduled appointment if that's what you mean," admitted the young man.

She stared, skeptically.

"Are you a salesman?"

Logan started to laugh.

"No, just an old friend of *Mr. Delfino's.*

His answer prompted her to pick-up the phone.

"Carmine, I mean Mr. Delfino, there's someone here that wants to see you," she said, with tension in her voice.

She listened into the receiver and then looked at the young man standing in front of her.

"What's your name?"

"Spence."

"He says his name is Spence."

The young woman nodded and hung up the phone. She was now looking at Logan with different eyes and attitude.

"Carmine, I mean Mr. Delfino, will be right down," she said in a relieved tone of voice. "Can I get you a cup of coffee?"

"Never touch the stuff."

*Mr. Delfino* descended the staircase.

"So, you here to pick her up?" he asked, with a smile.

"No, just to check her out."

Logan Spence and Carmine "The Cat" Delfino shook hands and then embraced.

The "her" Carmine had referred to was the 1968 Buick GS he had sold Spence for the more than reasonable price of $200, before Logan's Cornwall departure.

"So, how's preppie world treating you?"

"Like a Dublin pauper."

Although Carmine did not recognize Logan's specific reference, he fully understood what his friend had just told him. Spence was still the outsider, looking in.

"Let's take her for a ride," suggested Delfino.

Logan was behind the wheel of the Buick GS, as they pulled to a stop in front of a convenience store.

"What kind of beer do you want?" asked Carmine.

"Your call," deferred Spence.

"I'll be right back," he said and disappeared inside the store.

Logan glided to a halt at the far end of Sheffield High's now empty parking lot. Carmine popped a can of Pabst Blue Ribbon and handed it to Spence. He opened one for himself and then lit a cigarette. Delfino came right to the point.

"I am now working with my brother. The one who deals in commodities."

"And how's that panning out for you?" asked Logan, as he lit a cigarette.

"So far, so good," answered Carmine. "But we're always looking to increase our share of the market."

"And what market is that?" he asked.

"Pot," answered Delfino.

Spence quietly sipped his beer and smoked his cigarette. "The Cat" continued.

"Do people smoke weed at your school?"

"Of course."

"What's the general quality of product?"

"Crap."

Carmine flicked his finished cigarette out the window and opened another beer.

"If you had a far superior product to sell there could you develop a consistent demand for that product?" he asked.

Spence finished his beer. Without prompting, Delfino handed him another. Logan tossed his cigarette.

He was now beginning to understand the overly generous price for the car.

"That depends," answered Spence.

"And what does it depend on?" asked Carmine.

"Quality and price."

Delfino smiled.

"You just told me the quality of the stuff floating around your school is crap. That's because the product currently being sold in this part of the country *is* crap. The weed you'd be offering would consistently have two to three times the THC level of anything currently on the street."

"And the price?" continued Spence.

"$1500 a pound. I don't deal with less than pounds these days."

Logan stared at his high school mentor and shook his head.

"Cat, I don't have that kind of money."

"I'll front you."

"And why the hell would you do that?" demanded Spence.

Carmine "The Cat" Delfino opened the last two cans of beer. He handed one to Logan. He then lit another cigarette and studied his friend.

"The first time I saw you was the day you went to The Wall and faced the Kelly brothers. You knew before you got there that you were going to get your ass kicked. But you went anyway. Not many guys would do that. You're a different breed. From where you're coming from, ripping me off would be like ripping yourself off. Only worse," he smiled.

It burned Spence that Carmine knew him, so well.

"Pop the trunk. I want to show you something," instructed "The Cat".

They got out of the car and looked inside.

"Take out the spare," instructed Delfino.

Logan removed the tire.

"See that button?" he pointed.

"Yes."

"Push it."

Logan did as he was told. A small panel gave way to a hidden compartment space. It reminded Spence of his secret cache in the bookcase at school.

"Very convenient for transporting things of value," nodded Carmine.

They were on their way back to Delfino's Automotive.

"So, when do you have to know?" asked Logan.

"Know what?" replied "The Cat".

"How many pounds I'm taking."

"*Pounds?*" responded Carmine, in a voice that betrayed his surprise.

Logan Spence looked at his friend with earnest conviction.

"If I'm going to get into the game, I plan on being an impact player."

Carmine Delfino did not back off.

"When do you head back to school?"

"I'll be picking the car up Sunday morning," confirmed Logan.

"Call me Saturday night with the amount of your order. You know where it will be waiting for you," said Carmine.

It took only a handshake to seal the deal.

# CHAPTER THIRTY-NINE

The next day Logan boarded a train from the Water's Edge bound for New York City. He was going to meet Dwight Jefferson at the mid-town dojo.

As he walked up Lexington Avenue, Logan thought it only appropriate to bring Sensei Hidaka a gift of respect. He stopped into a neighborhood food mart. Spence stood in the beer aisle torn between the Kirin and the Sapporo. Unable to decide, he bought a six-pack of each without being proofed.

Logan entered the dojo and walked up the flight of stairs. Miku, the beautiful black belt was seated behind the reception desk.

"It's good to see you, Logan," she smiled, with the warmth of an Eastern sun rising.

"It's better to see *you*," he said, grinning mocked lewdness.

"Hey, watch that Buster! Don't make me have to embarrass you on the mat," she threatened, kiddingly.

Spence laughed.

"These are for Sensei Hidaka," said Logan, as he placed the two six-packs on the counter. "I didn't know which brand he'd prefer."

"Neither will go to waste," she reassured him. "The Sensei is now teaching a class so he won't be able to say…"

Before Miku could finish her sentence, Sensei Hidaka left the mat and approached the reception desk. He stared at Logan Spence. Miku began speaking in Japanese to the Sensei. Hidaka did not pay any heed. His eyes remained fixed on Spence.

Logan already knew what was on the Sensei's mind. He opened his shirt collar. It revealed the silver necklace that Sensei Hidaka had bestowed upon him, during his graduation ceremony. Satisfied, the Sensei returned to the mat and his class.

"He likes you," confirmed Miku.

"Well that's a relief," smiled Logan, in only half jest, as he watched Hidaka's departure.

Spence returned his attention to the black belt.

"I'm meeting Jefferson here," he informed the receptionist. Miku looked at him and shook her head.

"No, you're not. He called earlier and said he couldn't make it. But he wants you to call him."

Spence turned to leave.

"Logan, speak to him here," insisted Miku. She punched the numbers and handed Spence the phone.

Logan hopped an uptown subway bound for Harlem. He got off at the 125th street station and walked the stairs to daylight. Dwight Jefferson was waiting for him. The two friends hugged.

"I'm sorry I couldn't meet you at the dojo," apologized Jefferson. "Family crap."

"Say no more," said Spence, with an understanding wave of the hand.

Dwight looked at his friend.

"So, what do you want to do?"

"Talk."

"About what?" asked Jefferson.

"Business" replied Spence. "Do you know a place close by where we can get a couple beers?"

Jefferson looked at his friend. He shook his head with impatience.

"Of course, I do. Let's go."

They started to walk. Once on a sparsely populated side street, Spence lit a small joint. Carmine had given him product to sample. Initially, he did not share it with his friend.

"Are you going to let me smoke some of that or is your real name Bogart?" he laughed.

"Here, have the rest," offered Logan.

"You didn't leave me much," grumbled Jefferson.

"Wasn't much there to start with."

197

They arrived at the bar of destination. As Dwight opened the door, he turned to look at Spence.

"Damn, this shit is good!"

They entered the establishment. The regulars turned to size up the newcomers. Once satisfied they were not there to hassle them, the patrons returned to their drinks and conversation.

A bartender approached the new arrivals.

"What'll it be?" he asked, with practiced indifference and tossed two coasters.

Dwight Jefferson deferred to Spence.

"Bud", ordered Logan and slapped a twenty on the bar.

"Make that two," nodded Jefferson.

The bartender returned with the two beers and change. He departed.

"So, what kind of business are you talking about, Logan?" asked Dwight, with a stoned smile.

"You just smoked it," answered Spence.

Dwight Jefferson looked at his friend and shook his head.

"I'm not catching your drift."

Logan took a pull from his long-neck. He looked at his friend.

"What's the quality of weed around here these days?"

Dwight sipped his beer.

"Nothing like what we just smoked," he grinned. "Around here the quality is hit or miss. Recently, it's been mostly miss."

Spence lit a cigarette.

"If you had to sell what we just smoked could you build a customer base around here?" he asked, bluntly.

Jefferson chugged the remainder of his beer. He placed the emptied bottle on the bar just loud enough for the bartender to hear. Logan Spence followed suit. The man behind the bar returned with two more beers. He began to pick-up the cash already on the counter.

"No!" objected Dwight.

The six-foot-five inch Jefferson stood up. He dug into his pocket and placed a twenty on the bar.

"These are on me."

Dwight stared at his friend.

"To answer your question Logan, like everything else in Life, it depends upon the cost."

"$1500 a pound," informed Spence.

Jefferson looked at Logan and frowned.

"That's one heavy lift, man."

Spence persevered.

"True, but this is exceptional pot. That means we can carve it up in exceptional ways. We'll sell it in smaller quantities for usual prices. In the world of street drugs, quality *always* conquers quantity."

Dwight looked at his friend, apologetically.

"Logan, even if I was interested, I don't have that kind of bread," he admitted.

"I'll cover your first pound. You just make damn sure you get me back the $1500. Anything over the $1500 you collect will be profit. We'll split that profit 50/50," he said in a business-like tone of voice.

Jefferson pensively sipped his beer. He then swiveled his bar stool to stare at Spence.

"And what stops me from just taking that pound and ripping your ass off?"

Logan Spence looked at Jefferson and shrugged his shoulders.

"To be honest with you, Dewey, that particular possibility never even crossed my mind."

Logan's candid admission touched the big fellow. The bartender brought another round of beers on the house. Dwight Jefferson sat quietly pondering the conversation that had just taken place. After several minutes, he hoisted his bottle of beer and stared into the eyes of Logan Spence.

"I'm in," he toasted.

The two friends emerged from the bar laughing and pleasantly, high.

 And as the imposing looking black dude and the crazy white kid duck-walked shoulder to shoulder down 125th Street, on that particular Harlem afternoon, no one saw any good reason to ask any questions.

# CHAPTER FORTY

"Are you quite certain you have a ride back to Cornwall?" asked Mildred Spence. Her face was a countenance of maternal concern.

"Yes, mom," assured her son. "We're meeting at the Campbell's house. Mark's father will be taking us from there," he lied.

"Well, that is good news, Millie!" exclaimed Doctor Henry Spence. "Saves you the long drive up and back from Sheffield," and smiled his approval.

"I suppose," she said in a tone of voice laced with a mother's caution.

After the dutiful goodbyes and well wishes, Logan picked up his duffel bag and a carry-all. He closed the door behind him. Spence started the thirty minute walk to Delfino's Automotive.

"Nice to see you again, Mr. Spence," greeted the same vacuous receptionist. "I'll tell Carmine, I mean, Mr. Delfino, you're here. He's been expecting you."

Without further instruction, the young woman picked up the desk phone and placed the call. She listened into the receiver and then returned it to its cradle.

"He'll be right down," she smiled.

Carmine "The Cat" Delfino entered the room. He was all business.

"Your car loan has been approved," he said. "The Buick GS is waiting for you in the parking lot out front. It has a full tank of gas."

"That's good news," replied Spence. "Say, do you have a place where I might change?" he asked, lifting the carry-all.

"Of course, right over there," nodded the salesman and pointed to a rest room area.

Once inside, Spence shed his leather jacket, black tee shirt, and blue jeans. When he emerged from the men's room, he was clad in blue blazer, white shirt, and gray flannels. The tie was black knit.

"Are you going to a wedding?" asked the now surprised receptionist.

"No."

"A funeral?" she persisted.

Carmine Delfino cut the interrogation short, before Spence could answer her question.

"C'mon, I'll walk you to your car," he said, dangling the keys.

Once outside, Carmine looked at Spence.

"My business partners are more than a little concerned about the amount of product I've fronted you without any cash outlay on your end," he said, with self-preservation in mind.

"I can understand their concern," nodded Logan.

Carmine stared at Spence.

"When can I expect our money?" he asked, tensely.

"I'll be home for Christmas break. You'll get your money plus interest," assured Spence.

Carmine "The Cat" Defino tossed Logan the keys to the Buick GS. Spence started towards the car and then stopped. He turned.

"Carmine, you have my **word**," was all he said.

Logan Spence climbed into the Buick GS and started the engine. He drove out of the dealership parking lot without looking back.

Delfino walked back into the office building.

"Hey, Carmine, in the mood for a little bob knob?" asked the receptionist, with a dirty smile.

"No!"

As he trudged the staircase back to his office, Carmine "The Cat" Delfino had only one thing on his mind.

*"What the hell have I gotten myself into?"*

202

Although Sheffield, Connecticut was due north, Spence drove his car due south. His destination was Harlem. His rendezvous was with Dwight Jefferson.

"You said one pound, man!" objected the big guy.

"A change in corporate mission," explained Spence.

"Two pounds is a lot of weed!"

Logan Spence looked at his best friend.

"Dewey, it's the best stuff this part of the country has to offer. And as I have told you, primo product will always have buyers at primo prices," he said, reassuringly.

"So, now I owe you $3000 plus profit," stated Jefferson, with business-like formality.

Logan shook his head and smiled.

"No, you owe me $2800 plus profit."

"How's, that?"

"Volume discount."

Dwight Jefferson studied his friend before speaking.

"You're playing for keeps," he said, in a solemn tone of voice.

"Do you know any other way to play?" challenged Spence.

Dwight Jefferson remained silent. He accepted delivery.

Logan Spence left Harlem. He headed north. Once in Connecticut, he got off I-95. He opted for the Old Boston Post Road. Although a longer and slower route, Logan thought it best to reduce the chance of a run-in with the always hard-ass Connecticut State Troopers. His change of clothing had been in case of just such an occurrence.

Spence entered the town of Sheffield. He pulled to a stop in the driveway of a familiar row house. His arrival was unexpected. He knocked on the front door with duffel bag in hand.

"Logan, good to see you," smiled Roger Kaminski, as he opened the front door.

"You have time for a bone?" asked Spence.

"Always."

Logan stepped inside the small hallway. He handed his host a joint. Kaminski looked at the small size of the twist and shook his head with polite disappointment.

"Thanks."

"When you finish that one come find me for more," offered Spence, smiling. "Where's Beth?"

"She's in the kitchen. You want to hear anything in particular?" he asked and walked towards the den.

"Whatever you feel like playing," nodded Spence and headed for the kitchen.

Roger selected Zeppelin's *In Through the Out Door*.

"Logan, this is a pleasant surprise!" smiled Beth Kaminski, with genuine welcome.

"I hope this is too," he grinned. Spence pulled a bottle of Grand Marnier from the duffel bag and placed it on the kitchen counter. He put the duffel bag on the floor.

"You're going to spoil me, Logan Spence!" she laughed.

"If any one deserves being spoiled, it's you," he said.

"You're usual?"

"Please."

Beth Kaminski removed two glasses from a kitchen cabinet. She walked to the refrigerator and opened the freezer door. She pulled out Logan's bottle of vodka. Beth poured two drinks. She handed Logan his glass and then hoisted her Grand Marnier.

"To friendship."

They toasted.

"Where're the kids?" asked Spence.

"With my mom for the weekend," said the young mother, with a sigh of relief. "Where's Roger?" she asked.

"He's in the den sampling the weed I brought," answered Logan.

"He couldn't wait for us?"

"Don't worry about that right now."

Logan Spence stared at Beth Kaminski.

"Beth, I have a favor to ask and then a question to pose."

"What's the favor?"

"Would it be alright if I keep my car here?"

"Of course, it would be!" she responded, without a moment's hesitation.

 She then looked at Spence.

"What's your question, Logan?"

He came right to the point.

"Would you consider joining me in a business venture?"

She stared at him, in stunned surprise.

"What kind of business venture?"

"The marijuana business," answered Spence.

Beth Kaminski paused.

"Logan, I think that's something you should be discussing with Roger," she said.

Spence ignored her words.

"Beth, who handles the household finances here?"

"I do!" she said, with authority. "Roger couldn't balance a checkbook with three hands," she laughed.

"That's exactly why I approached you first," explained Logan.

"Go on," she nodded.

Spence took a sip of vodka and continued.

"The way I envision it is, Roger would handle the point of sale. He knows the local marketplace for weed. You would be responsible for everything else".

"And what does 'everything else' entail?" she asked, with growing interest.

"Once I've established the proper price to quantity ratio, you'd be in charge of the amount of product going out and the amount of money coming in for that product. You would handle all cash at all times. Furthermore, you'd be responsible for maintaining a book of transaction."

The young mother looked at Spence.

"I was a business major in college before...." her voice trailed off, without completing the sentence.

Logan looked at his friend and smiled.

"Mind if I have a cigarette?"

"Of course not."

Logan finished outlining his business plan.

"All profits will be split 50/50."

Beth Kaminski looked at Logan Spence. She had only one question regarding the proposed arrangement.

"How good is the weed?"

Spence pulled a joint from his jacket. He handed it to Beth.

"I think it's time we join Roger," she smiled.

As they entered the tiny den, the room was filled with Zeppelin's, "All of My Love". Roger was seated on the sofa. He was totally absorbed in the song. Beth went over to the stereo and lowered the volume.

"Roger, there's something we have to discuss."

"*Wow*", was all he could muster in a slow, self-absorbed monotone.

Beth looked at Logan and then at the joint he had given her. Spence shook his head.

"I really can't, Beth. I've got to get back to Cornwall."

Beth Kaminski tossed the unlit joint into an ashtray.

"I'll walk you out. Roger, I'll be right back."

"*Wow*."

Once back in the kitchen, Beth turned and faced Logan.

"Well, I guess you've answered that question," she grinned.

Logan reached into his duffel bag. He removed three plastic wrapped bundles and handed them, to Beth.

"Please, keep these in a very safe place until my next visit," he instructed.

"Done."

He then handed her the keys to his car.

"Feel free to use it anytime you like," he smiled.

"I appreciate that, Logan," and returned his smile.

As he started to leave, Spence stopped.

"Beth, I hope I didn't give you the impression that I don't trust Roger. Actually, I think he's a great guy."

Beth Kaminski stared at Logan with an expression of seriousness he had never seen in the young woman's face before.

"Business is business," was all she said.

# CHAPTER FORTY-ONE

"So, are you going back upstairs?" asked Paul "Bounty" Hunter.

"Yes," responded Chester White.

The two men were seated in Hunter's idling car outside Chester's warehouse. They had just returned from Carver's Bar and Grill. Earlier that evening, a phone call from the Carver's manger had informed them that a college student from New Haven was selling product on their turf. Chester White had taken immediate action.

"Do you think the cops have found the kid in the trunk, yet?" smiled Hunter.

"Who cares?" responded White.

Paul Hunter yawned. He looked at his watch.

"I think I'm going to call it a night."

Chester White climbed out of the passenger seat.

"I'll see you tomorrow morning," he said and closed the car door. He watched Hunter's car disappear.

Chester White entered his building. The night security guard was seated behind his desk monitoring security cameras.

"Good evening, Mr. White," he said, politely.

Chester White nodded as he walked past the man and climbed the stairs towards his office. As he approached the closed door, something caught his attention in the darkened hallway. There was a light on in his office. Chester was certain he had closed all the lights before departing for Carver's Bar and Grill. Instinctively, his right hand moved for the stiletto inside his jacket, as the left hand turned the door knob.

"There you are! I was beginning to think you were going to be a no show," exclaimed a smiling Kyle Overton. He was seated at the small conference table.

Chester White relaxed. Kyle Overton was his life-long best friend. Kyle was an already risen star in the R&D division at IBM's headquarters in Armonk, New York.

"The security guy didn't tell me you were here," said Chester, making a mental note of the guard's breach.

"Oh, don't blame Harry. He knows me. Besides, I wanted my visit to be a surprise. I hope you don't mind that I've already helped myself to some gin and tonic."

"Not in the least," said Chester White as he made his to the office bar to pour himself a drink.

Chester sat down in a chair facing Kyle Overton.

"To the good old days," he grinned and raised his glass to toast.

"And to better days to come," clinked Overton.

Kyle Overton looked at his friend with a face of uneasiness.

"Chet, I'm seriously considering picking up and moving."

Chester White was stunned. He quietly sipped his drink, before speaking.

"Where to?" he asked.

"Silicon Valley," replied Overton.

"Where?" responded Chester White not recognizing the name.

"The San Francisco Bay area of California."

"Why?" pressed Chester White.

Kyle Overton drained his drink. He stood up and ambled towards the office bar.

"My life is technology. In my opinion, the future of technology is unfolding out there, in real time, as we speak. To be anywhere else would place me behind the information curve and at an insurmountable career disadvantage."

Kyle Overton returned to his seat at the table and stared at Chester White.

"Chet, the year is 1979 and a brand new decade is just around the corner. In Silicon Valley, they're already patenting things you and I only fantasized about as kids!"

Chester White sat, glumly, in his chair. Kyle Overton quickly changed the topic of conversation.

"So, how's your business treating you?" he asked, with genuine interest.

"Which one?" responded Chester and stood to replenish his glass.

"The pot business."

"With respect," assured Chester White, as he re-seated himself.

Chester pulled a pack of cigarettes from his pocket and lit one. He tossed the pack on the table.

"Mind if I steal one?" asked Overton.

"I thought you were trying to quit."

"I've been trying to quit smoking from the day I started smoking!" he laughed.

Chester White stared at his friend.

"I know where you're coming from in that regard," nodded Chester.

Kyle Overton sipped his gin and tonic.

"So, is the weed business still profitable?" he asked.

"Quite."

Overton narrowed his gaze.

"You know, Chet, when you realized a liquor license wasn't in your future, the move into pot demonstrated true foresight," he acknowledged.

Chester White looked at his friend, warily.

"What are you trying to say?" he asked, bluntly.

Kyle patiently sipped his cocktail before answering.

"What I'm saying now is what I said earlier, a new decade is upon us. And with that new decade I believe cocaine will become the recreational drug of the 80's."

Overton was not telling Chester anything he did not already know. Truth be told, a year earlier White had added cocaine to his drug distribution operation.

"The only problem with the Peruvian Lady is she's fickle. You never know who the hell she's hanging out with," said Chester.

Kyle snuffed his cigarette.

"True, but the players who gain control of the cocaine market will, ultimately, run the pot business. And weed will never go out of style."

Chester White knew his friend was speaking the truth.

Kyle Overton became quiet. He was grappling with the right way to phrase what he wanted to say next. A gut-wrenching honesty won the day.

"Chet, why the hell do you stay married to that worthless, self-serving bitch? All she's ever done is torment you!" he said, with heart felt conviction.

Chester White grew pensive. The more pensive he became the more alcohol he consumed. With his glass once again emptied, Chester started towards the bar. His gait was no longer steady. A long day's drunk had begun to take its toll. He reloaded and leaned against the bar for support. White stared at Kyle Overton. He became belligerent.

"Look around you! Everything you see is mine! This building is mine! All these vehicles are mine! The inventory is mine! The property next door is mine! And I won't split any of it with that worthless bitch!"

Kyle Overton was familiar with Chester White's emotional outbursts. He sat, quietly, listening to his friend's tirade. He waited for the storm to pass. When he thought the coast was clear, Kyle spoke.

"Chet, no one appreciates what you have done on your own to become successful more than I do. Hell, I've watched you every step of the way! However, there comes a point when you should cut your losses and move on," he said.

Chester White stared at Kyle Overton.

"That whore's throat will be the first thing I cut," he said, with a calm ruthlessness that unnerved even Overton.

Sensing that the storm was just beginning, Kyle Overton opted for a hasty retreat. He finished his drink and then looked at his watch.

"Time for me to be on my way," he said, sheepishly.

Chester White grinned at Kyle Overton. He walked towards his friend with arm extended. The two shook hands. It was a clasp that quickly became a far more intimate embrace.

# CHAPTER-FORTY-TWO

"I know something you don't know!" she said in the sing-song glee of a school girl.

Patricia White looked up at Kate Whitson and shook her head, with affectionate annoyance. She was seated at the desk of her Angelica Hall apartment grading term papers.

Kate continued.

"I'll tell you, but only for a price," she teased.

"And what's your ransom?" asked the now smiling Patty White.

"A glass of white."

"I don't have to tell you where that it is," she laughed and returned her attention to the term papers.

Whitson disappeared into the kitchen. When she returned, it was with two glasses of wine. Kate handed one to her closest friend.

"To help you through those miserable attempts at serious writing," she said, empathetically.

The two friends touched glasses. Kate settled herself on the near-by sofa. She then stared at Patty White.

"I know why your student prince was admitted to Cornwall," she said, with the wry smile of gossip plastered all over her face.

Whitson was referring to Logan Spence. Suddenly, Kate now had her best friend's complete attention.

"Go on," insisted Patty.

Whitson slowly sipped her wine. She was, selfishly, relishing the bouquet of the moment.

"Well, according to what Scott tells me, Logan is a student at Cornwall only because he's a professional jock. Supposedly, Spence is some kind of hot shot wrestler."

Patty stared at her friend, silently, parsing her words.

"So, you're telling me Logan is a student-athlete?" she asked, in a surprised voice. "He doesn't look like any jock I've ever seen before!"

Kate Whitson polished off her wine. She smiled at her friend.

"It does seem a bit incongruous. But, then again, some dumb jock trying to read James Joyce is a hoot in itself. It doesn't get any richer than that!" she laughed and stood up for a kitchen refill.

With emotion she could not control, Patty lashed out at Kate.

"Logan Spence doesn't *try* to read James Joyce. He actually understands and appreciates James Joyce! And that's more than I can say for ninety percent of the assholes that populate these two campuses!" she shouted, with a vehemence that caught her friend off-guard.

Kate Whitson postponed her trip to the kitchen. Still reeling from Patty's sudden outburst, she attempted to re-establish a more comfortable ground for dialogue.

"Patty, I wasn't trying to belittle Spence's academic efforts. It's just that, well, the whole situation is a little unusual, that's all."

Patricia White eyed her friend with the slow deliberation of a judge rendering a final verdict.

"If Logan takes his athletics as seriously as he takes James Joyce, he'll be a force to be reckoned with!"

Kate Whitson was anxious to change the subject.

"Seth and Tom want to go out to dinner tonight. They still have the free dinner vouchers the owner of the Oak Tree gave us the last time we were there. You interested?"

"Not really," answered Patty.

Kate looked at her with a face of emoted disappointment.

"For me?" she pouted, unabashedly groveling.

Pat White looked at her friend and finally smiled.

"*Only*, for you."

The two couples were in Seth Abrams' car for the short ride from the Cornwall Angelica Hall campus to downtown Sheffield.

"I hope you guys enjoyed the Thanksgiving recess," said Seth to no one, in particular. "I can't believe the Winter Term is already here," he continued, in an attempt to make conversation.

"Well it is," replied Patricia White, effectively stifling any further talk.

Abrams parked the car. The two couples walked to the restaurant. As they entered, "Billy the Kid" and his two cohorts were just leaving the Oak Tree.

"Well, I knew it was only a matter of time before you came looking for me," laughed Billy and leered, hungrily, at Patty White.

"Get lost, loser," she hissed.

Billy continued, undaunted.

"But what I don't understand is why you brought along the nutty professor. He can only wind up getting himself hurt."

Tom Wilkerson and Seth Abrams remained, awkwardly, silent.

The lewd smile suddenly disappeared from Billy's face. His attention was now focused, elsewhere.

Standing a half block behind the four teachers was Logan Spence. He had just left Roger and Beth Kaminski's house and was on his way back to the Cornwall campus. He now stood with duffel bag in one hand and a cigarette in the other, silently, observing the confrontation that was unfolding in front of him.

Billy's decision was a quick one. He wanted no part of Spence. Abruptly, Billy and his two cronies crossed the street and went on their unsavory way.

Kate Whitson looked at her best friend and grinned.

"You see, Patty, I was right! Taking the moral high ground always wins out in the end," she said and rested her head, affectionately, against the shoulder of her white knight, Seth Abrams.

But as the two couples entered The Oak Tree Tavern, Patricia White had her doubts about that.

# CHAPTER FORTY-THREE

"I was surprised that you weren't in the car with Mark when his father dropped him off earlier today," admitted Logan's roommate, Pete Ellison.

"They were leaving Water's Edge too early for me to join them," explained Logan.

"Not early enough for either one of them," said Ellison, shaking his head.

"Pete, what do you mean?" asked Logan.

"I mean, Mark couldn't wait to get out of the car and Mr. Campbell couldn't wait to be on his way back to Water's Edge. So much for Happy Thanksgiving!" smiled Ellison.

Spence looked at his roommate and grinned.

"Well, the good news is Merry Christmas is right around the corner!"

The two now friends cracked-up in laughter.

"Is our Limey friend in his room?" asked Logan.

"No, he's at the radio station. Jack is doing the evening show tonight. In fact, I'm on my way over there now. You want to come?"

Logan shook his head.

"No, I can't. I've got a tutorial with Ms. White tomorrow afternoon that I haven't started studying for."

"Say, no more."

Ellison knew how much the Angelica Hall teacher's sessions meant to his roommate. Without another word, he picked up his jacket and closed the door behind him.

After Pete's departure, Spence tossed the duffel bag next to his reading chair. He grabbed a glass and some ice from the mini-fridge and sat down. He opened the recessed panel of the bookcase and pulled out a bottle of Absolut. He poured a drink

216

and returned the bottle. Logan savored the success of a long day's trek. He then went to work.

Spence extracted product, a box of plastic baggies, and a small scale from the duffel bag. He began to weigh quantity to price and profit margin. Once satisfied with his calculations, he stowed the contraband in its designated hiding place inside the bookcase, save for a small joint. He poured another drink and called it a night.

The first day of the Winter Term at Cornwall Angelica Hall was always, uneventful. Everyone already knew their assigned classes and schedules. There were very few inter-term newcomers. For the most part it was a half-day for students and faculty, alike. The first afternoon of the Winter Term was a time to be spent getting organized and mentally prepared for the longest term of the school year.

After lunch, Logan walked directly to the Angelica Hall campus. He entered the administrative building and knocked on the office door of Ms. Patricia White.

"Come in, Logan."

Spence closed the door behind him. He sat down facing Ms. Patricia White. Logan placed the book he had been carrying on the floor. He looked at her with a question.

"How did you know it was me?"

She smiled.

"Because you and I are probably the only people around here who have anything scheduled for this afternoon," she laughed, good-naturedly.

Patricia White paused before continuing. She was no longer smiling.

"Logan, I want you to know how pleased I was with your progress last term," she said. "Your improvement in vocabulary, reading comprehension, and form writing exceeded all my expectations," she revealed, with an unexpected sincerity that deeply touched Logan Spence.

Patricia White stared at Logan. For the first time since he had met her, she seemed unsure of herself. It was as if she did not know what to say next. Spence remained silent.

"Truth be told, Logan, your progress last term was so surprising to me that I haven't yet been able to decide upon a curriculum for this term that I feel comfortable with." Her words were almost that of an apology.

"Well, I've decided upon one!" he said, with a decisiveness that both surprised and comforted her, at the same time.

Spence picked up the rather thick book from the floor and placed it on the desk in front of Patricia White. It was James Joyce's novel, *Ulysses*.

Patty looked at the book and thought for a moment. She then focused on the young man seated across from her.

"Logan, *Ulysses* is a college level semester course all by itself," she started to explain.

Spence cut her short.

"I've made up my mind. Besides, I've already started the book."

"But, Logan, any curriculum we undertake has to be approved by the heads of the English Department. And *Ulysses* is going to be a very tough sell," she explained.

Spence looked at Patty White and smiled.

*Ulysses* is going to be a hell of a lot easier to sell than what you've currently got planned for me."

Patty broke into that rare, but wonderfully infectious laugh of hers.

"That, I can't argue with!" she admitted still shaking her head.

Spence stared at his tutor.

"Then it's agreed. *Ulysses* will be my Winter Term's curriculum unless you decide, otherwise."

He extended his hand for confirmation. She accepted it. Merely touching the hand of Patricia White sent torrents of excitement racing through Logan's entire body. Spence picked up the book and stood to leave.

"Thursday afternoons are still good for me", she smiled.

"Me, too," he nodded.

Spence started towards the door.

"Logan," she called out. He stopped and turned. "It's been brought to my attention that you are a highly regarded student-athlete. Good luck with your wrestling endeavors."

Spence looked at his tutor, weighing her well-intentioned words.

"Luck will have nothing to do with it," was all he said and quietly closed the door behind him.

Logan walked back to Squire House. He made a quick call on the pay phone located on the dorm's first floor. He then headed upstairs. His roommate, Pete Ellison, was nowhere in sight.

Spence quickly tossed *Ulysses* on the desk and retrieved his duffel bag. He opened the recessed panel of the bookcase and removed the scale and half of the plastic bags he had prepared the night before. He placed them in an inside pocket of the duffel bag and zipped it. He was out the door.

"That was fast," commented Beth Kaminski, as she opened the front door and kissed Logan Spence on the cheek. "Roger is on his way."

"Where are the kids?" he asked. before entering the Kaminski home.

"They're both upstairs sleeping. Its afternoon nappy time," she said, with a young mother's gratefulness.

Spence entered the house and proceeded down the small hallway to the kitchen. Beth Kaminski followed. Logan placed the duffel bag on the floor.

"You want a drink?" she asked.

"Yes."

Beth Kaminski plucked two glasses from a cabinet. She then retrieved a bottle of Absolut from the freezer and a bottle of Grand Marnier from a side cupboard. Beth poured two drinks and handed Logan his glass.

"To good friends," she toasted.

They hoisted, clinked, and indulged.

"Have you spoken to Roger about my business proposition?" asked Spence.

Beth Kaminski took another pull from her glass and eyed Logan with the tone of business defining her response.

"I already told you. Roger is on his way."

Before Logan could respond, the voice of Roger Kaminski could be heard from the front hallway.

"Beth, I'm home. Where the hell are you?"

"In the kitchen, Roger."

The twenty-one-year old father of two entered the kitchen. He had a record album tucked under his arm and a smile on his face.

"I should've known you two rummies would be in here getting loaded!" he laughed, with kindness in his heart.

Logan Spence embraced Roger Kaminski with genuine affection.

"How the hell are you high flight?" he grinned.

"Not high enough!"

"Let's see if I can't do something about that," offered Logan.

Spence reached into his duffel bag and tossed Roger Kaminski a plastic bag.

"Roll one for the three of us," he instructed.

Roger looked at the bag and then at Spence.

"Same shit?"

"Yes."

Roger Kaminski started, happily, towards the small den to cue his new album and roll a joint.

"Wait till you guys here this!"

"Roger, not too loud. The kids are sleeping," warned the mother.

Spence looked at his hostess.

220

"Beth, are you guys really in?"

"Yes."

"Then it's time to join Roger in the den."

As they entered the room, Queen's latest album *Live Killers* was thumping the floor boards. Beth lowered the volume to a reasonable level and then sat down next to her husband on the room's lone couch. Logan remained standing.

Roger lit the joint and started smoking. He then passed it to his wife. She took a long drag and handed the bone to Logan. Spence took two quick hits and then snuffed the joint in an ashtray.

"Hey, what the hell are you doing, man?" objected Roger.

Spence ignored Roger's question. He stared at him. As was his custom, Logan came right to the point.

"Do you think you can establish an ongoing demand for weed of this quality around here?"

"That depends upon the price," responded Kaminski.

"Forty bucks for the bag I just gave you," answered Spence.

Roger Kaminski thought for a moment, before speaking. He then stared at Logan with an incisiveness that surprised Spence.

"Look, I'm not saying the bag isn't worth forty bucks. I think it is. The rub is going to be getting people accustomed to the trade-off between quantity and *quality*. Around here, forty bucks buys a nearly full bag," he explained.

"Yes, a bag full of crap!" countered Spence.

This time it was Roger Kaminski who ignored Logan's words.

"Initially, effective long-term marketing is going to require a few loss leaders," deduced Roger.

"Meaning what?" asked Spence.

"Meaning, some free samples to spread the good word," explained Kaminski.

Spence looked at Roger, warily.

"And can you accomplish that without giving away the store?" pressed Logan.

"Absolutely," reassured Roger and eyed the now dead joint in the ashtray, with eager anticipation.

"Then start spreading the good word," authorized Spence.

Suddenly, a question sprang into Kaminski's head.

"Say, Logan, what are you doing to market this stuff at Cornwall Angelica Hall? There's a lot of bread on those campuses."

Spence shook his head.

"Yes, there's a lot of money to be made there, but also a lot of loose mouths. Any on campus drug sales transacted by me would become school knowledge in a matter of hours," he explained and drained the rest of his vodka.

Beth Kaminski spoke for the first time.

"I think I may have a way to safely tap into that market," she smiled and finished her Grand Marnier. "C'mon Logan, I'll explain my idea over a second round."

Beth stood up and headed for the kitchen. Logan followed her. Roger picked up the dormant joint and relit it. He then rousted himself from the sofa and ambled towards the stereo to turn up the volume on Queen's "Keep Yourself Alive".

# CHAPTER FORTY-FOUR

"My kid sister is a day student at Cornwall Angelica Hall," Beth told Logan, as she handed him his drink. She then replenished her Grand Marnier.

Spence stood quietly, waiting for Beth to say what was on her mind.

"My sister's name is Val, Valerie Larsen. Larsen is my maiden name," revealed Beth. "Anyway, she's a senior there."

Logan recognized the name but could not place the face. He sipped his drink and said nothing. Beth looked at Logan and continued.

"I think Val might be able to help us establish a market for our product with the students at Cornwall Angelica Hall," she said, confidently."

Instinctively, Spence felt uneasy about such a potential arrangement. However, he had grown to respect Beth Kaminski far too much not to hear her out.

"Go on," he nodded.

Beth took a swallow from her glass and spoke her mind.

"Val already has a sort of network going on there," she explained.

"What kind of network?"

Beth Kaminski finished her drink. Her first instinct was to reload. She deferred.

"Val has become a quiet conduit between the ladies of Angelica Hall and the town of Sheffield," stated Beth.

Although Logan could already guess what his friend was alluding to, he wanted to hear it from Beth in her own words.

"What kind of conduit?" he asked.

Beth Kaminski smiled at Logan.

"Nothing as big as what you have in mind."

Logan pulled a pack of cigarettes from his inside pocket. He lit two. Spence handed one to Beth.

"You haven't answered my question," he said, patiently.

Beth Kaminski blew a plume of blue towards the kitchen ceiling and then got down to business.

"To answer your question, Val affords the ladies of Angelica Hall the luxury of remaining *ladies*. By that I mean, my kid sister provides the girls attending that venerable institution all the things they want without having to risk the uncertainty and possible indignity of going off campus to obtain them."

"Things like what?" asked a now interested Logan Spence.

Beth Kaminski took a drag on her cigarette. She continued.

"Oh, the usual suspects," replied Beth, laughing. "Alcohol, cigarettes, lousy pot, and on occasion, discreet male companionship."

"So, Joe Townie is alive and well?" asked Logan, smirking with amusement.

"Who?" she asked not having a clue as to what he was talking about.

"No one you'd know," dismissed Spence, smiling.

Beth Kaminski stared at Logan Spence and shook her head, in exasperation.

"You're not taking me seriously! In fact, you can't even appreciate the merit of what I'm suggesting. But then, again, you're not thinking like an outlaw!"

This last declaration caught Logan, totally, off guard. His smile was gone. Kaminski now had Spence's complete attention.

"Go on."

Beth took a final drag on her cigarette and snuffed it. She stared at Logan.

"The quality of weed we have to sell is unprecedented in this area. So, when it first makes its presence felt on the campuses of Cornwall Angelica Hall, the natural assumption will be its origin is the doings of the young men from Cornwall. The *innocent* young ladies of Angelica Hall would never even be considered capable of initiating such a totally *male* undertaking! After all, this is 1979," she sneered.

Logan drained his drink and extinguished the cigarette. Without prompting, Beth picked up his emptied glass and started towards the refrigerator.

"So, essentially, everyone will be looking to put out a fire where none exists, only smoke. Pun intended," she laughed.

Beth handed Logan his cocktail. He was already mentally calculating the potential downsides to what Kaminski had put forth, as a marketing plan. As always, Logan Spence came right to the point.

"How bright is your kid sister?"

Beth Kaminski answered, without hesitation.

"Bright enough to follow my instructions."

Logan said nothing. He studied the face of Beth Kaminski. She returned his gaze. A silent stand-off was underway. It was the young mother who flinched, first.

"Logan, I messed up a couple of years ago. I think you know what I'm talking about. That doesn't mean I don't love my babies and my husband. I cherish my family! But, I short-changed myself as an individual along the way. It's a very empty feeling."

Beth Kaminski picked up her glass. She then placed it back on the counter, without drinking. She stared at Logan.

"Since you left here yesterday, all I've been able to think about is the opportunity for a decent financial future for my family and redemption, for myself. Yes, I know drug dealing is totally illegal and very risky. But, it's also the only chance I'm ever going to get at personal salvation," she said, with searing conviction.

Spence sipped his vodka and said nothing. Beth Kaminski's eyes began to mist.

"Look, Logan, I don't expect you to fully understand my motivations. But I *demand* that you appreciate two things. The first is, I'm real good at whatever I set out to do. And the second is that when it comes to our business relationship, my first loyalty will always be to you. I'll be one of the very few you'll be able to turn your back on, without ever having to look over your shoulder."

Without saying a word, Spence reached into his duffel bag. He placed the scale and sample plastic bags of pot on the kitchen counter.

"These are the proper weight," he instructed.

Beth looked at the bags and then at Logan.

"They may be the proper weight, but not the proper price. For this kind of quality weed, I can get us fifty not forty bucks a bag at Angelica Hall," she said, confidently.

Her tears had disappeared. Beth Kaminski was, once again, all business.

# CHAPTER FORTY-FIVE

"So, Mr. Spence, what are you tipping the scales at this week?" asked Coach Hubbard.

"One sixty-five Coach," answered Logan, as he entered "The Pit" for that afternoon's varsity wrestling practice.

Coach Hubbard motioned Spence towards him.

"Do you think you can drop a few pounds by Saturday's match with Hartfield?" It was more a directive than a question.

Spence looked Hubbard in the eye.

"I told you the first time we met that I would wrestle at whatever weight class you needed me for," reminded Logan.

"Well, I need you at one-sixty on Saturday," ordered the coach and waved his dismissal.

Logan lingered.

"Something on your mind, Spence?" barked Hubbard.

"What's Dixon going to say?"

Kevin Dixon was a senior. He had held the one sixty-pound weight class on the varsity squad for the past two seasons. He was a very capable wrestler.

"If he wants to remain on my varsity team, he'll say nothing and do what I tell him to do!"

Spence held his ground. Coach Hubbard realized he was not going to escape without an explanation.

"Look, Logan, Dixon has wrestled this guy from Hartfield twice. Both times Kevin's gotten his ass pinned in the first period. There's nothing telling me that if Dixon wrestles him, again, the outcome will be any different."

Hubbard paused, to carefully choose his words, before continuing. "Spence, this kid from Hartfield is good. He's real good and even cockier. He went deep in last year's regionals. He's the odds-on favorite to win it all this time around."

Logan looked at his coach and shrugged.

"What makes you think I'm going do any better against this guy?"

"I don't know if you will. But, I do know you can't do any worse. Besides, Dixon can handle the Hartfield wrestler at the one seventy-pound slot. So, even if you lose but don't get pinned, the team benefits."

As Logan walked onto the mat to join his teammates, he knew the news of the coach's decision was going to stir up even more antagonism towards him. But, then again, they already resented his presence on the varsity squad. Spence figured that if he was destined to have only two friends on the team one of them might as well be the coach.

The official wrestling schedule did not kick in until after the Christmas recess. However, the preseason scrimmage between Cornwall and Hartfield had become a tradition that both schools took very seriously. It was always held on the Saturday afternoon before the winter break.

 The contest provided the coaches from both teams a real time opportunity to make final assessments about the talent they were working with going into the new season. Just as importantly, it whetted the appetite of loyal wrestling fans thirsty for action and victory. Hartfield was hosting that year.

In the upper academic echelons of the prep school world, Hartfield Academy was considered a "B" school. However, its athletic program was universally respected. Every year, an impressive number of Hartfield senior student athletes were matriculated into some of the country's finest collegiate sports programs. The town of Hartfield took its high school sports very seriously. It was a tail-gating kind of community.

When Logan Spence walked onto the wrestling mat that Saturday afternoon, the Hartfield crowd had grown quietly restless. The team score between Cornwall and Hartfield was too close for their characteristic comfort zone of victory. However, their collective spirits perked up when a local legend took center stage.

Lou "The Jewel" Jasko was eager to please his home town fans. He was tautly muscular and nimble on his feet. In Jasko's mind,

228

the opponent he was now staring down was a mere inconvenience between himself and the forthcoming adulation he had grown to covet, from the people who always came to cheer his victories.

"Say, those are the sweetest little white things I ever did see!" he yelled, pointing to Logan's wrestling shoes.

The crowd roared its approval.

"I think you might be in the wrong place, lady! Hartfield doesn't come to see ballet shows!" he taunted and slapped Spence across the side of his headgear.

Again, the town faithful erupted with cheers. "The Jewel" was putting on quite a performance.

Quickly sensing a situation potentially getting out of hand, the referee sprinted towards the scoring table.

"Award one point to the Cornwall wrestler resulting from an illegal hit by the Hartfield wrestler," he instructed.

There was a loud and prolonged chorus of jeers as the referee's decision was announced over the loud speaker.

"I think he should be given at least two points!" screamed Jasko. "At least, make it a fair contest!"

The Hartfield fans began their familiar chant: "Jewel! Jewel! Jewel!"

The wrestling match between Jasko and Spence, finally, got underway. The Hartfield wrestler quickly took Spence down scoring two points. He spent the remainder of the first two minute period riding Spence looking for an opening and an easy pin. None was forthcoming.

The second two minute period began with Jasko ahead on points. He started in advantage position. Again, he broke Spence down and scored more points. For his part, Logan was concentrating on Jasko's moves. He was getting to know his opponent's shifts in body weight and balance.

Spence was also listening to the abusive heckling that was coming from the crowd. A couple who were obviously Jasko's parents we're particularly obnoxious.

"Hey, pussy boy, those fancy white shoes are about to be shoved up your ass!" yelled the proud front row father.

"Yea, that's a good place for them!" shouted the mother of Spence's opponent.

The crowd was loudly enjoying their native son's easy ride to victory.

As the third and final two-minute period was about to begin, Logan could feel his opponent beginning to tire. Jasko's overly aggressive pin and win tactics had taken their toll. Spence was on top in advantage position.

As the referee's whistle blew, Spence's left arm simultaneously crossed his opponent's face securing the right forearm. The quick move "by chance" broke The Jewel's nose. Once Jasko's right arm was securely pinned underneath the entire weight of his own body, Spence used his right hand to force his opponent's head into the mat. He then began to push Jasko's face across the mat towards his now stunned parents. A trail of blood followed Hartfield's favorite son's impending arrival. Every move Spence had used was technically legal.

The home crowd was appalled into silence. Just before the out of bounds line Spence halted the face grinding assault.

He looked up at Jasko's parents and laughed.

"Should I put Jewel out of his misery here or drag him back to my side of the world?"

The parents were too mortified to respond. However, the subdued home town crowd sprang to life.

"You sick freak!" shouted someone from the stands.

"Yea, I'll shove those white shoes up your ass!" yelled another, to thunderous approval.

Spence glared at the hostile throng. Without another word, he easily flipped his now helpless opponent onto his back to make it official. The referee counted three and blew whistle. It was over.

Logan's arm was raised in victory. The Hartfield trainers immediately started tending to Lou "The Jewel". Instead of returning to his team's bench, Spence walked from the center circle of the mat towards the Hartfield stands. He had unfinished

230

business. The referee was now in hot pursuit. He grabbed Spence by the arm trying to slow his destination.

"You're real close to having me disqualify you and your points!" he threatened.

Spence brushed the referee aside. He now stood alone facing the angry home town crowd.

"Anyone who thinks they can shove these white shoes up my ass, now's your chance!" he challenged, menacingly.

As a small contingent of fans started to make their way towards the wrestling mat, the referee scampered to the scorer's table to make the disqualification official, in an attempt to restore order.

And then, something even stranger took place on that Saturday afternoon at Hartfield. The entire Cornwall wrestling team emptied their bench. Led by Carlos Acosta, they surrounded Spence waiting to join him in any fight that might take place. The Hartfield team was instructed to remain seated. They did so.

Coach Frank "The Tank" Hubbard stood on the side lines with his arms crossed, serenely taking in the entire scene.

The announcement blared over the field house's loudspeakers.

Logan Spence had been disqualified for disobeying the referee's instructions. His victory was nullified. More importantly, the entire Cornwall wrestling team had been disqualified for unsportsmanlike conduct, thereby, awarding the match to Hartfield. The news was received by the home town crowd with muted ambivalence. They began to disperse.

Immediately, the Cornwall assistant coaches angrily confronted Coach Hubbard.

"Frank, Spence just cost us the entire match! What the hell are you going to do about it?!" they complained, in unison.

Hubbard looked at his assistants and shook his head.

"Not a goddamn thing!" he smiled.

The bus ride back to Sheffield felt like a victory party. The members of the Cornwall varsity wrestling team interacted with one another like never before. The young men aboard that bus were now fellow soldiers on a common mission. They did not view their disqualification at Hartfield as a loss. In their minds, it was a badge of honor; one to be worn with pride. They were no longer merely a varsity athletic squad. They were now a family to be reckoned with.

Coach Frank Hubbard sat in the front of the bus. His eyes were closed. However, he was quietly savoring everything that was going on around him. He now knew that his instincts had been correct. That year's group had the nucleus of a championship wrestling team. And that was most appropriate. It was to be Frank "The Tank" Hubbard's final season, as head coach at Cornwall.

Logan Spence sat in the back of the bus. He was, by himself. A small overhead light illuminated the book he was reading. It was James Joyce's, *Ulysses*.

# CHAPTER FORTY-SIX

The news of the wrestling team's disqualification at Hartfield consumed the entire Cornwall campus during the final few days leading up to the Christmas recess.

It was a rare occurrence to have a Cornwall athlete disqualified for inappropriate behavior. However, having an entire team disqualified for unsportsmanlike conduct was unprecedented in the school's history. Both students and faculty, alike, were anxiously waiting for heads to roll. To the morbid disappointment of some, none were forthcoming. However, advance ticket sales for the wrestling team's home opener were selling at record pace.

Logan Spence finished packing his duffel bag. He departed Squire House and started the walk to downtown Sheffield. He knocked on the door of his destination.

"C'mon in, Logan, its open," answered Beth Kaminski.

Spence entered the house and proceeded through the small foyer towards the kitchen. To his surprise and uneasiness, Beth was not alone. Standing next to her was Valerie Larsen, Beth's younger sister.

"I don't believe you two have ever been formally introduced," smiled Beth Kaminski. "Logan, this is Val. Val, this is Logan," she said, with contrived nonchalance.

Valerie Larsen was a seventeen-year old woman of unmistakable presence. Oddly, Valerie bore little resemblance to Beth. She was taller than her older sister. Her figure was firm and her face magnetic. The long brunette hair complimented steel blue eyes; eyes that immediately pierced through any semblance of bullshit. Valerie was a player. She was also responsible for the discreetly robust sale of product currently taking place on the Cornwall Angelica Hall campus. Logan Spence was impressed.

"I like your taste in cars," said Valerie Larsen referring to Logan's 1968 Buick GS that was parked in the driveway.

"I like the way you conduct business," responded Spence.

The two stood silently apprising one another. It was Beth Kaminski that broke the stalemate.

"Logan, would you like a drink?"

"Beth, you read my mind," he smiled.

"I hope you read mine too, Sis," laughed Valerie.

Beth Kaminski pulled three glasses from a kitchen cabinet and placed them on the counter. She then retrieved Logan's Absolut from the freezer and a bottle of Grand Marnier from a cupboard. She poured a glass of vodka and handed it to Spence.

"Val, what are you drinking this afternoon?" asked the older sister.

"Absolut," she responded, without hesitation. Her steel blue eyes remained fixed on Logan Spence.

"To friends and bright futures," toasted Beth. She then turned her attention to money. "It's all there," nodded Beth Kaminski.

Three stacks of cash were neatly assembled on the kitchen table; one mound noticeably taller than the other two.

"The largest pile is the money owed for product. The other two are our respective profits," explained Beth.

Logan picked up the largest stack and began counting. He did so more to ensure accuracy than honesty. He trusted Beth Kaminski. Satisfied, he stowed the cash in one of the duffel bag's inner pockets. Spence eyed the two remaining piles of cash.

"What was the profit margin?" he asked.

"Fifty percent," answered Beth.

"That's not a bad rate of return," he smiled, approvingly.

Logan Spence scooped one of the piles of profit and neatly tucked it into another inner pocket of his duffel bag. This time he did not bother counting. Spence drained his drink. He turned to leave.

"Logan, you're forgetting something," admonished Beth Kaminski.

She pointed to the remaining stack of cash on the kitchen table.

"I want you to take that with you," she instructed.

"Why?"

"Reinvestment."

Logan Spence eyed the young mother, with uncertainty.

"Beth, are you sure you want to do that?"

"Quite," she said, without pause. "If you can deliver the same quality product, I can deliver the same profit margin. But this time, hopefully, it will be on larger volume."

Spence immediately realized she had left him no choice. Without another word, he picked up the cash and deposited it in his duffel bag.

"Logan, here are the keys to your car," smiled Beth. "It has a full tank of gas.

Spence took the keys and headed towards the door.

"I'll see you out," volunteered Valerie Larsen.

Once in the driveway, Logan popped the trunk of the Buick GS. He removed the panel of the clandestine storage compartment and stowed the duffel bag.

Valerie Larsen stood watching the procedure in progress.

"Do you have a girlfriend?" she asked.

"No."

"Why not?"

"Who knows?" he answered, distractedly.

Once the panel was back in place, Spence shed his leather jacket and tee-shirt. He put on an Oxford button-down and began to knot a tie.

"Do you have a boyfriend?" he asked, trying to make conversation.

The young woman thought for a moment.

"I haven't decided yet," she said.

"Well, when you do, let me know who the lucky guy is," he laughed and donned the blue blazer.

"You'll be the very first to know," she promised.

Logan got behind the wheel of the Buick and started its engine. Valerie Larsen leaned into the driver's side window.

"Spence, watch your ass!" she said, in the barely audible voice of concern.

Carrying only a small amount of weed, Spence opted for I-95 over the Boston Post Road for the trip home. The faster highway route would better suit his time schedule. He passed the Water's Edge exit and entered New York State. He was bound for The City and a pre-arranged meeting with Dwight Jefferson.

Logan parked the Buick in front of the same Harlem bar he and Dwight had frequented in the past. He was early. Spence entered the establishment and walked directly to the bar.

"I'll have a double Absolut on the rocks."

The bartender eyed Spence with suspicion. The two had never met before.

"You have ID?" he asked the white kid. He did so more to placate the bar regulars than an adherence to the law.

"As a matter of fact, I do, sir," responded Spence.

Logan fished into his pocket and pulled out a twenty-dollar bill. He placed it on the bar.

"I would appreciate a double Absolut on the rocks," he repeated. "Please, sir, keep the change."

The bartender ignored the money. He studied the face of Logan Spence. At length, he pulled a glass from the overhead rack, scooped some ice, and poured a generous portion of Absolut. He tossed a coaster in front of Spence and placed the drink. He then picked up a shot glass from the bar and threw it in the air. With dexterity, he landed the jigger face down on the twenty-dollar bill.

"Your next one's with me," he said, loudly enough for everyone in the place to hear. Barroom volume returned to normal.

Spence sipped the drink. He lit a cigarette. As he reached for his cocktail, Logan's right wrist was suddenly clasped. The glass shattered on the bar. With practiced precision he jerked his right wrist down-ward in the direction of the assailant's thumb. The

236

hand was now free. Simultaneously, he pivoted to his left to confront the attacker. The barroom fell silent.

Standing in front of him was the six foot five-inch Dwight Jefferson. He was grinning ear to ear.

"For a preppie, you're pretty fast!" he laughed.

"You're an asshole! Do you realize how much vodka you just wasted?" chided Logan, with a smile.

The two friends embraced, warmly. The barroom patrons resumed conversation. The bartender was already on the scene cleaning up the mess called friendship.

"Bartender, I'll have a Tanqueray and tonic. Go lightly on the tonic," instructed Jefferson. "And back up my friend with whatever he's drinking."

"Your friend is already backed up. Go fish," replied the keeper of the spirits.

Jefferson dug into his pocket and pulled out a Jackson. He slapped it on the bar. He stared at the bartender.

"Go fetch!" Jefferson was no longer smiling.

The man behind the bar returned with their drink orders. He then quietly moved on without taking any money off the table. Dwight raised his glass.

"To us," he said, simply.

"To us," toasted Spence.

"C'mon, let's grab a booth," he motioned. Jefferson walked with a newly found swagger.

The two young men sat down facing one another. Before a word was spoken, Spence felt a light tap on his left knee. Dwight Jefferson looked into the eyes of Logan Spence.

"It's the money you fronted me for product. It's all there," he said, quietly.

Spence discreetly took the envelope and tucked it inside the right pocket of his blazer. He had no doubt that the count was accurate. Logan then felt a light tap on his right knee.

"That's your half of our profit," Jefferson nodded, without taking his eyes off his friend.

Spence accepted it and deposited the second envelope inside the left pocket of his jacket.

"What's our profit margin?" inquired Logan.

"It's about forty percent. It could've been a lot more if I knew what the hell I was doing from the start," admitted Jefferson, with a sheepish grin.

"Still, not a bad take," acknowledged Logan.

Spence felt a third tap. This time he sat, motionlessly, staring at Dwight Jefferson.

"What's that?" asked Logan.

"It's my half of our split. I want to buy more of the same."

Spence quietly sipped his drink. He lit a cigarette and tossed the pack on the table. Logan studied the face of Dwight Jefferson.

"Dewey, are you sure?"

"I've never been surer of anything in my life, man."

Spence pocketed Jefferson's money.

Dwight drained his cocktail and motioned the bartender for another round. Once refueled, Jefferson continued.

"Logan, I've met this girl. She's a freshman at Columbia. Bria is going to be a music major. She plays several different instruments with very impressive talent."

"Are you one of them?" asked Logan, smiling.

"Screw you, Spence!" snapped Jefferson, as he pawed at the pack of cigarettes Logan had left on the booth's counter top.

"Dewey, I thought you quit," observed Logan.

"I've quit quitting!" he growled and lit up. Jefferson continued. "Bria is into the downtown music scene. She has friends and connections at CBGB and the Mudd Club. With their money to burn and our quality shit we can make a fortune!" he boasted.

"I know CBGB but I've never heard of the Mudd Club," admitted Spence.

"Mudd just opened last year," informed Jefferson.

As if on cue, Bria Cummings entered the bar. She made a beeline towards their booth. In old school tradition, both young men rose to greet her. Bria kissed Dwight on the lips. She then turned to face Spence.

"You must be Logan. I've been looking forward to meeting you. Dwight tells me you're different," she smiled and extended her hand.

Bria Cummings was tall and slender. Her face was attractive and her smile radiant. As he accepted her handshake, Spence's thoughts drifted to Dwight's mother and sisters. He could not help but puzzle over what they thought of Dewey's new girlfriend. Logan began to wonder if they had even met her. After all, Bria Cummings was a white girl.

# CHAPTER FORTY-SEVEN

Logan Spence was on I-95 heading north towards Water's Edge, Connecticut. He had just left the Harlem bar where he had hooked up with Dwight Jefferson. The thruway traffic was light. He would be on time for his next scheduled appointment.

As he drove, Spence assessed his current business situation. The sales results had been good. The fact that Dwight Jefferson was eager to reinvest in more product did not surprise him given Dewey's circumstances. Besides, New York City was a big pond.

However, Beth Kaminski's insistence on reinvestment had caught him, by surprise. As a mother of two little ones and of limited financial means, Logan had assumed she would have taken her profit and run.

*"She's an enterprising young woman,"* he thought, to himself.

Spence pulled into the parking lot of Delfino Automotive. He popped the trunk of his Buick GS and got out of the car. After stowing the cash in his duffel bag, Logan entered the front door of the building. The same receptionist was seated behind the arrival desk.

"They're waiting for you upstairs, Mr. Spence", she said and rose from her chair. "Please, follow me." The young woman was acting the consummate corporate employee on that particular afternoon.

Spence followed the receptionist up a flight of stairs to the second floor. She nodded to a closed door.

"They're in there."

Without another word, she turned and descended the staircase to reseat herself at the reception desk. Spence knocked on the closed door.

"C'mon in, Logan," responded a muffled voice. It was a voice Spence had never heard, before.

Logan opened the door and quickly closed it behind him. He found himself standing in a large conference room. A wall of glass overlooked the Delfino Automotive parking lot. Two men were seated at an impressive table. One of them was Logan's good friend, Carmine Delfino. Surprisingly, it was the unfamiliar voice that rose to greet him.

"I've got to admit it. I'm impressed!" he said, while extending his hand. "I thought for sure I'd have to come looking for your ass!" smiled the now visible, unfamiliar voice.

"Thought I'd save you the trouble," responded Spence, while accepting the man's handshake.

Angelo "The Angel" Delfino was the older brother of Carmine. His trade was commodities. He was in his late twenties. Angelo was of medium height and stocky build. He wore a dark business suit and a predatory smile. "The Angel" was a no-nonsense kind of guy.

"Logan, join us at the table," motioned Angelo, as he sat back down.

Spence dropped his duffel bag on the floor and took a seat.

"So, when my kid brother here tells me he fronted you five pounds of weed with no down payment and no track record, I'm thinking I should kick his ass!" laughed Angelo.

Logan did not respond. Instead, he sat studying the man seated across the table from him. As a general rule, Spence determined whether or not he liked an individual within the first thirty seconds of meeting that person. The jury was still out on "The Angel".

Angelo Delfino returned Logan's stare of assessment. He was undecided about the kid sitting across from him. The host politely broke the silence.

"So, what are you drinking?" asked Angelo.

"Absolut on the rocks."

"Carmine, you heard the man! Get him an Absolut on the rocks! And while you're at it, get me a Chivas and an ashtray!"

"The Cat" sprang from his seat to comply with his older brother's commands. It was the first time Logan had seen Carmine Delfino take orders from *anyone*. He made a mental note.

Carmine returned with the drink orders and an ashtray. He reseated himself. "The Cat" had not poured himself a cocktail. Spence notched another mental note.

Angelo lit a menthol cigarette and took a pull from the whisky filled glass. He settled back in his chair. His attention was, once again, focused on Spence.

"So, how'd you make out for us?" he asked, in a voice laced with calculated suspicion.

Spence did not touch the drink in front of him. Instead, he swiveled his seat towards the duffel bag. He plucked a neatly wadded stack of bills and placed it on the conference table.

"That's your return on investment," he said, curtly.

Angelo Delfino eyed the stack of money on the table and then Logan Spence.

"Is it all there?"

"If it isn't, you're doing business with the wrong guy," dismissed Spence, with a smile.

Logan sipped his cocktail. He then lit a smoke and sat back to see what was coming next.

Angelo Delfino did not hesitate. He picked up the money and tossed it to his younger brother.

"Carmine, make sure it's all there," he instructed.

Without a word, "The Cat" stood up and went to the side bar to count the cash. Angelo's eyes zeroed in on Logan Spence.

"And how much did you make on this deal?" he demanded.

Spence drained the rest his drink and snuffed the smoke. He reached into the duffel bag and pulled out a second wad of bills. He placed it on the conference table. It was the money he, Dwight Jefferson, and Beth Kaminski had netted on the deal. Logan had bundled the cash to ensure that their involvement was not known.

"A little over forty-five percent," answered Spence.

"Forty-five percent?!" yelled Angelo Delfino, in frustrated disbelief. "With the quality shit you were handling that number should've been more like fifty-five percent!" he scoffed.

"I know that now," admitted Spence. "I'll do better next time."

Angelo Delfino sipped his cocktail. "The Angel's" eyes narrowed.

"And what makes you think there's going to be a next time?" he asked, in a low tone of intimidation.

Logan returned "The Angel's" stare. He pointed to the cash on the table that was his profit.

"Because, I'm going to reinvest that money in more weed," stated Logan, confidently.

Carmine Delfino returned to the table. He stood in front of his older brother.

"It's all there," he said, in a voice of obvious relief.

Angelo Delfino finished his drink and doused his cigarette. He glared at Logan Spence.

"It's not quite that easy, kid," advised "The Angel". "You want another drink?"

"Why not?"

Without prompting, Carmine went to the side bar for another round. This time he returned with three glasses and sat down at the table to join the discussion. Angelo continued.

"Logan, the commodities business is changing like the decade is changing. The recreational drug of the 80's is going to be cocaine. Pot will always sell. However, to ensure top quality weed I've got to move top quality blow. Capisce?"

Spence understood, all too well. He was not overly anxious about getting involved in the business of selling coke.

Cocaine had spawned an entirely new generation of recreational drug user in the late '70's. It attracted a different breed of player and adhered to a different set of rules than that of marijuana. In short, blow was a different world; a world that Spence was very reluctant to enter. He lit another cigarette and looked at Angelo Delfino.

"So, what does that have to do with me buying weed?" he asked, already knowing the answer.

"The Angel" sat back in his chair. He appeared to relax for the first time during the meeting.

"It's really quite simple, Logan. If you want to continue buying the weed you're going to have to buy the coke. It's all or nothing. Does that answer your question?" he smiled.

Spence's first inclination was to take the money off the table and walk. However, his thoughts shifted to Beth Kaminski and Dwight Jefferson. They were expecting him to deliver more quality pot. Hell, they were depending upon it! Logan sipped his drink. He made up his mind.

"So, what's the bottom line, Angelo?" he asked, with resolve.

"The Angel" pointed to the stack of cash on the table.

"You use that money to buy the coke," he explained, pointing to Logan's profit pile. "And I'll front you another five pounds of weed," he said, authoritatively.

Suddenly, "The Angel's" facial expression changed.

"Say, you want to taste some of your new product line?"

"Not during business hours," declined Spence.

Angelo Delfino looked at Logan and laughed.

"Say, I like that answer. I like that approach!" He had just made up his mind about what he thought of Logan Spence. "So, we have a deal," he said and stood up to leave.

"Not yet we don't," objected Spence.

He stared at "The Angel".

"I'll use the money on the table to buy the coke. You'll front me **ten** pounds of weed. As you said earlier, it's all or nothing."

Angelo Delfino glared at Logan Spence. He thought for a moment and then turned to his brother.

"Do it!" he said and walked out of the room. "The Angel" was no longer smiling.

244

Carmine sat across the table from Logan and grinned.

"You've got balls! I knew that the first time I met you."

"I hope I just didn't cut them off!" laughed Logan.

"Hey, as long as you deliver, all is forgiven around here," reassured "The Cat".

Spence finished his drink. He got up to leave.

"Carmine, I'll be leaving my car here," informed Spence.

"It'll be ready for you. Just let me know the date and time," he instructed. "Do you need a lift?"

"No, but I do need some samples of my new product line."

"Done."

The two young men left the conference room and descended the stairs to the reception area.

"Have a nice day, Mr. Spence," smiled the same young woman seated behind the desk.

Logan turned to face Carmine.

"*Mr.* Spence?" he shrugged.

"Hey, what can I say? You're moving up in the world, kid," he laughed.

Logan pushed through the front door and started his walk homeward. Carmine Delfino lingered at the window watching his friend's departure. Angelo Delfino came to stand next to his younger brother.

"So, what's your take on the kid?" asked "The Angel".

"I think he's growing up real fast," answered "The Cat".

# CHAPTER FORTY-EIGHT

"I know he's cheating on me!" declared Shirley White and slammed her now emptied glass on the table. "And if I can prove it, I'll be able to divorce his ass and collect half of what is rightfully mine without having to put up with his crap, anymore!" Shirley had been drinking since early afternoon.

Her two closest friends sat silently digesting Shirley's words. Janet Weiss was the first to speak.

"Who's the lucky lady?" she smiled, sarcastically.

Shirley eyed her friend.

"Jan, I don't think it's a girl he's messing around with!"

This last revelation rocked the normally steadfast Janet Weiss. Shirley White continued.

"I think Chester White is a homo. There, I said it!"

"Well, even if your accusations are true, marital infidelity is always a tricky thing to prove in a court of law," responded the now recovering friend from high school days.

Janet Weiss was never married. She had chosen career over children. After graduating college, Janet went to work for the most prestigious law firm in her hometown of Rutland, New York, as a para-legal. During the ensuing years, Janet attended night school to obtain a law degree. She had been successful in that endeavor. Now, after years of perseverance and numerous court case successes, Janet was in line to become that law firm's first female partner. No small feat for a woman in the year 1979.

The other woman seated at their table now voiced her opinion on the matter, at hand.

"Shirley, even if your suspicions are right, playing with Chester White is playing with fire! You of all people should know that!" warned Mary Peterson, shaking her head.

From its inception, the marriage of Chester and Shirley White had been one in name only. The couple did not share the same

246

bedroom. They actually hated one another. Not, coincidently, their respective work schedules kept their face time to a minimum.

Chester's vending business had him out of the house early in the morning and not home till early in the evening. As a nurses' aide at Rutland General Hospital, Shirley's night shift usually got her out of the house in the nick of time. On the rare occasions they were together, the couple fought. And the more each drank during those confrontations the uglier the situation became.

Sadly, the only true victim of this unseemly situation had been the couple's only child, Patricia Anne White. Mercifully, for the little girl, she spent the majority of time staying at her grandmother's house. Shirley's mom lived just across town. Nonetheless, Patricia Anne White had been doomed to a nightmare from which she would never fully awaken.

Only two things had kept Shirley from abandoning the marriage. The first was money. To her pleasant surprise, Chester always seemed to have an endless supply of cash available for her to spend. And even as her spending habits increased, he never once questioned nor complained. It was only in recent years she had grown suspicious of that leniency.

The second reason she had never tried to end the marriage was out of pure and simple fear. Shirley was frightened of Chester and what he might do to her if she ever dared to file for divorce and disrupt his thriving business.

"So, who's the lucky guy?" smiled a now fully recovered Janet Weiss.

"His name is Kyle Overton," answered Shirley White.

"And how long have Chester White and Kyle Overton been *friends*?" asked Janet, with the mocked tone of attorney in her voice and a smile on her face.

"According to Chester, since they were kids," responded Shirley.

Her answer quickly erased the smile from Janet's face.

"Shirley, I attended Rutland public K-12 and don't remember even hearing the name Kyle Overton," she said and looked at Mary Peterson for confirmation.

"I don't either," shrugged Mary.

Shirley White looked at her two friends and shook her head, with a knowing smile.

"That's because Kyle Overton only attended fancy schmancy private schools," she explained.

"Shirley, what's this guy like?" asked a now very interested Mary Peterson.

"I wouldn't know."

"And how's that?" persisted Mary.

"Because I've never met him," admitted Shirley. "For obvious reasons," she added.

Janet Weiss narrowed her eyes and stared at her friend.

"Shirley, what exactly do you know about Kyle Overton?" she asked.

Shirley thought for a moment.

"I know he works for IBM right over here in Armonk," she said.

"Do you know what he does at IBM?" pressed the attorney.

"He's some kind of whiz in their research and development division," responded Shirley.

"How do you know that?" demanded Janet Weiss.

"Because, every time Chester gets a load on, which is all the time, he throws **that** in my face!"

Janet's expression softened. She looked at her friend and smiled.

"What do you mean by **that**?" she asked, quietly.

"I mean, Chester still blames me for getting pregnant in the first place. He thinks the whole thing was my fault! In fact, he's convinced himself that I got knocked-up on purpose. How sick is that? Anyway, in his mind, if it wasn't for me he'd have finished high school, gone on to some big-name college, and now be working along-side his faggot friend."

Janet Weiss stared at her friend.

"Shirley, does you're your husband abuse you?"

"Not physically," she admitted. "But in every other way, yes!"

Weiss sat, silently, considering an appropriate course of action. She looked at Shirley.

"Tomorrow, I'll have my office initiate a preliminary background check on one Kyle Overton. Then we'll ...."

Shirley cut her short. She was shaking her head, no.

"Jan, if Chester was to even suspect something like that ..." she did not complete her sentence.

Shirley's hand was now shaking, as she reached into her purse for a cigarette. Janet gently placed her hand on top of her friend's and looked her in the eyes.

"Shirley, the process is very discreet. We do it all the time. Overton himself won't be aware that it's even taking place, let alone, Chester White. Shirley, you have to trust me on this one."

Although not completely reassured, Shirley agreed to the background check.

All the while, Mary Petersen had been studying the face of Shirley White. Something was bothering her.

"Shirley, let's forget Kyle Overton for a moment. You've known for years that Chester White is a despicable human being. And yet, you've stayed married to him all this time. You also know what the bastard is capable of doing. Now, all of a sudden, you're hot to trot for a divorce. Why?"

Before Shirley could answer the question, a young waiter accosted their table.

"Ladies, the show will be starting in about ten minutes. I would strongly suggest you place your drink orders now. You know how busy it gets around here after the music starts."

Shirley White beamed at the young man, fluttering overly laden eyelashes.

"Do you have any specials tonight?" she smiled.

"The Sea Breezes are twofers."

"They any good?" she asked.

"They'll blow you away," responded the waiter, in a voice of tired repetition.

"That sounds good to me!" exclaimed Shirley.

"I'll second the motion," nodded Janet Weiss.

The waiter looked at Mary Petersen.

"I'll pass," decided Mary.

As the room's lights dimmed, the waiter returned with their drink orders and disappeared. Not another word was spoken about Kyle Overton, Chester White, or Shirley's over-all situation. After all, it was Ladies Nite at The Fontana.

# CHAPTER FORTY-NINE

"Patty, why don't you reconsider?" urged Kate Whitson. "Not even you can convince me that you'd rather spend Christmas break grading papers than skiing at Killington!"

Without looking up from her desk, Patricia White pointed towards the kitchen. It was a tacit request for wine. Kate needed no further prompting. She returned with two glasses of white and stood patiently while her friend finished the paper she was reading. Moments later, Patty placed her reading glasses on the desk and stood up to accept a glass. She was laughing.

"What's so funny?" asked Kate, as glasses clinked.

"Logan Spence."

Kate Whitson stared at Patty and shook her head, dubiously.

"I don't find anything humorous about Logan Spence other than the fact he's got a big-time crush on you! Now that, I find funny."

Patricia White continued on as if she had not heard a word her best friend had just said.

"Kate, Logan wrote his entire final term paper on *Portrait* in Joyce's 'stream of consciousness' narrative mode. It's really quite an impressive effort!"

"I bet."

Patty suddenly realized Kate's disinterest. She sipped her wine and tactfully changed the topic of conversation.

"So, when are you guys leaving for Vermont?" she asked.

"Tomorrow morning."

"How many are going?"

"I think the final count is going to be around a dozen," answered Kate. "Patty, I really wish you'd change your mind and join us."

Patty thought for a moment before answering.

"I assume you're going up there with Scott, right?" she asked.

"Yes."

Patricia White sipped her wine and said nothing. She knew that if Scott Abrams was going, his best friend, Tom Wilkerson would be along for the ride to Killington. It was a potentially awkward situation for Patty that she was determined to avoid. Her dilemma was a simple one. Tom Wilkerson was in love with her. She did not share those same feelings towards him.

Patty realized that Tom was a nice guy. In fact, during the course of that Fall Term she had developed a genuine affection towards him. However, fondness was as far as her emotional feelings could carry her when it came to Tom Wilkerson.

Kate Whitson looked at her friend. She shook her head, with patient reproach.

"Patty, isn't it about time you got over your lousy childhood? After all, I've managed to get over what my asshole father did to me!"

"I'm not you!" hissed Patricia White.

The two young women glared at each other with an anger reserved, solely, for best friends.

It was Kate who broke the silence. Her words were softly conciliatory.

"Should you decide to join us, you'll be sharing a room with me."

Patty looked at Kate and broke into laughter.

"And what's Scott going to say about that?"

"Not a damn thing."

This time it was Pat White who retreated to the kitchen. When she returned it was with two replenished glasses of wine. Kate had nestled herself on the living room sofa. Patty sat down next to her friend.

"What are you telling me, Kate?"

Whitson sipped the wine and shrugged her shoulders.

252

"I'm saying that whether you go or not, Scott and I will be staying in separate rooms."

Patty looked at Kate with a face filled with bemusement.

"And why the hell is that?"

Kate hesitated before responding.

"Actually, it was Scott's decision," she smiled.

"And what prompted that decision?" pressed Patty.

Kate shifted her position on the sofa to better face her best friend.

"Career considerations," she replied, in a somber tone of voice.

Pat looked at Kate and grinned.

"I hate to break the news to you, but your relationship with Scott is not exactly the Manhattan Project here on campus!" she smirked, good-naturedly.

Kate looked at Pat and nodded her agreement.

"You're right. However, dating is one thing. Giving everyone a visual by shacking up together at Killington is an entirely different matter. Doing that might come back to haunt both of us given the political crap that flies around this place!"

"Enough said!" conceded Patty White.

Kate sipped her wine and smiled at Pat.

"So, have I changed your mind about coming?"

Patricia White thought for a moment, before answering. She then nodded her head.

"Well, you're right about one thing. Killington will be a lot more fun than grading papers. What time do we leave tomorrow?"

The two best friends hugged one another. Both had tears in their eyes.

# CHAPTER FIFTY

Logan Spence was in his Buick GS heading south on I-95. He was on his way to meet Dwight Jefferson in Manhattan. The Christmas school break had come to an end.

Earlier that day, Spence had walked to Delfino Automotive with duffel bag in hand to pick up his car. The recessed compartment in the trunk now housed ten pounds of pot and five ounces of cocaine. As was his custom when transporting product, Logan was wearing a blue blazer, charcoal gray slacks, and a conservative tie.

Although carefully maintaining the thruway's speed limit, Spence's mind was racing. He had realized from the moment "The Angel" insisted upon including coke in any pot transactions that things were quicly going to become more complicated.

Logan knew that trying to sell cocaine on the campus of Cornwall Angelica Hall, even by third party, was not an option. For starters, "The Angel" had been true to his word. The blow was primo. It topped anything Logan Spence had ever had before. That alone would make selling the product on campus a suicide mission.

Great pot is always a nice option for the recreational smoker. However, great cocaine can rapidly become an unmanageable situation for its user. Spence knew that scenario, played out on the stage of Cornwall Angelica Hall, would quickly lead to his ruination.

That left Logan with New York City as his only viable point of distribution for the blow. And his point man in the city was Dwight Jefferson.

Dwight had no idea about the stipulation of coke in the recent pot transaction. Logan had no feel for what his friend's reaction was going to be about having to sell coke in order to sell pot. He was about to find out.

Spence pulled to a stop in front of the Harlem bar that he and Dwight had come to in the past. Spence parked the car and entered the room. Logan immediately spotted Dwight and his girlfriend, Bria Cummings, seated at a booth. They had not seen him.

Spence walked to the bar. The man behind it was the same guy who had accepted Logan as a patron on his last visit to the place. Spence extended his hand.

"I'm Logan."

The bartender studied the young man. He was trying to decide whether he liked him or not. He accepted the handshake.

"I'm Floyd."

"What are my two friends at the booth drinking?" motioned Spence.

"The lady is having Chardonnay. Bobo Brazil over there is drinking Tanqueray and tonic. He likes the tonic light. He gets it light only if I'm in a good mood."

"I'll take two of those and a...."

"Double Absolut on the rocks," finished the bartender.

Logan looked at the man and laughed.

"You've got a pretty good memory."

The man shook his head.

"It's got nothing to do with memory, man. Not too many white boys walk into this place," he said and smiled for the first time.

The bartender returned with the drinks. Logan placed a twenty on the bar.

"The rest is yours, Floyd."

As he started towards the booth, a young male bar patron intentionally bumped into Spence causing him to spill the three drinks. Logan dropped the glasses on the floor and turned to confront his adversary. The barroom fell silent. Before any words were exchanged, Floyd vaulted the bar to intercede. He now stood between the two would be combatants. He stared down the young bar patron.

"If you **ever** pull that crap, again, on my shift, I'll kick your nigger ass! Now get lost!"

The young man bid a hasty retreat out the door. The barroom noise level returned to normal. Floyd turned to face Spence.

"Logan, I'll personally bring the cocktails to your table. Go join your friends."

As Spence approached the booth, the six-five Dwight Jefferson rose to greet him. He had a grin on his face and was shaking his head.

"I can't take you anywhere without you getting your ass into some kind of trouble!" he laughed.

The two friends embraced and sat down in the booth.

True to his word, Floyd the bartender returned with their drinks. He first handed Bria Cummings her Chardonnay. He then set Spence's Absolut in front of him. As he was placing Dwight's Tanqueray and tonic down, Floyd looked at Logan and smiled.

"I'm in a good mood." He winked and departed.

The three friends raised their glasses and toasted. Suddenly, Dwight Jefferson started to gag. Bria Cummings became alarmed.

"Baby, what's wrong?"

"I don't think there's any damn tonic in this drink!" he coughed.

Logan Spence looked across the table at his two friends.

"Floyd's, obviously, in a very good mood," he grinned.

A now recovered Dwight Jefferson peered into the eyes of Logan Spence.

"So, did you come with the product?"

"Yes."

"Well, that's good, because we've got a lot of demand for that kind of quality weed here in town."

Logan was now at the cross road he had been dreading since meeting "The Angel".

Spence decided to roll the dice. He reached into his jacket pocket for cigarettes. Simultaneously, he pulled a plastic packet. As he lit a cigarette, underneath the table, Logan gently tapped Bria's thigh. Although quietly startled, she quickly picked up on what he was handing her. She accepted delivery.

Spence looked at Dwight Jefferson.

"Dewey, for us to continue selling the pot, we've got to expand our product line," informed Logan Spence.

A now antsy Bria Cummings broke into the conversation.

"Gentlemen, I hate to interrupt. However, I have to powder my nose," she smiled, coquettishly.

Both young men rose to acknowledge her departure. They reseated themselves.

"So, what kind of product expansion are you talking about?' continued Dwight Jefferson.

"Coke," answered Logan.

Jefferson looked at Spence and shook his head.

"That stuff can get nasty real fast."

"I know."

"How good is it?" asked Jefferson.

Before Logan had a chance to respond, Bria Cummings returned from the ladies' room. She did not sit down.

"I'm in the mood to hear some music!" she shouted.

Cummings picked up her glass of Chardonnay and floated towards the jukebox.

Dwight Jefferson watched his girlfriend waltz towards the music machine. He then turned his attention to Logan Spence.

"You already baited the trap didn't you, you son of a bitch!" he glared.

Spence stared his best friend's anger straight in the face.

"Guilty as charged," he admitted.

The barroom was now filled with Michael Jackson's current hit "Don't Stop Till You Get Enough". Dwight Jefferson cast a protective eye towards his girlfriend. Bria was swaying, rhythmically, in front of the jukebox.

Dwight Jefferson remained silent for a moment. He sipped his Tanqueray and looked at Spence.

"Do I, at least, get a free taste of our new product line?" he smiled.

Logan passed a plastic packet underneath the table. Jefferson was off to the men's room. When he emerged from the bathroom, Dwight did not return to the booth. He was now with Bria in front of the jukebox selecting their next song.

Logan finished his drink and lit a cigarette. Floyd the bartender approached the booth.

"Logan, you guys want another round?"

Spence looked at his two friends who were now dancing in front of the jukebox.

"Floyd, I think another round would be a good idea."

# CHAPTER FIFTY-ONE

Spence was on I-95 heading north. Logan had just left the Harlem bar where he had met Dwight Jefferson and his girlfriend, Bria Cummings. Before his departure, Logan entrusted them with four pounds of pot and three ounces of cocaine for retail distribution.

As he drove, Logan's thoughts were all about the huge gamble he had just taken. The four pounds of pot were not a concern. It was the damn cocaine! Three ounces was about eighty-four grams. At one hundred and twenty dollars a gram it amounted to about a ten-thousand dollar street value. And blow was a very difficult beast to keep tamed. Hell, Logan was finding himself getting a little too fond of his new product line.

"Screw it!" he said out loud and began to concentrate on how he was going to handle the next meeting.

Spence got off the thruway at the Rutland exit. He was quite familiar with the last New York town before the southern Connecticut state line. After all, Rutland's legal drinking age was only eighteen.

Logan pulled to a stop in the parking lot of his destination. He got out of the car and walked across a graveled yard. He entered the front door of Carver's Bar and Grill.

The barroom was the usual Rutland tavern scene. Townies were wedged at the bar. Migrant students from Connecticut schools filled the tables, booths, and gaming machines on the other side of the room. It was the first time Logan had been to Carver's.

Spence surveyed the room. He spotted the person he was looking for hunched over the control panel of *Asteroids*, Atari's newest video game. Logan walked across the floor.

"So, are you keeping our world safe?" asked Spence with a smile, as he viewed the video screen.

"You'd better believe it!" answered the young man, without taking his eyes off the game. "So, Spence, how much do you want to buy?" he asked, absently.

Logan remained silent for a moment.

"I didn't come to buy, I came to sell," he answered.

The video player looked up from the screen. His spaceship was instantly vaporized. The world had suddenly become a far more dangerous place.

"What the hell are you talking about?"

"Buy us a round and I'll explain."

The young man hesitated. He thought for a moment, before responding.

"What are you drinking?" he finally asked.

"Absolut on the rocks."

"I'll be right back," he promised and started towards the bar.

"I'll grab us a table."

"Good luck, this place is packed!"

Logan started looking for a place to sit. A young couple was seated in a booth. As he walked by their table, the man maliciously slapped the girl across the face. He was about to do it again. Spence intervened. Deftly, he secured the guy's right hand and eased him out of the booth and onto the floor.

"A gentleman never hits a lady! Do you understand me!" seethed Spence.

Before the young man had a chance to answer, his girlfriend jumped out of her seat and on to the back of Logan Spence. She was now, frantically, trying to claw at his eyes.

"This is none of your goddamn business, asshole!" she screeched.

Logan released the man's hand. He was now defending himself against the onslaught of the recently abused young woman. Quickly, two Carver's bouncers were on the scene. One subdued the girl. The other picked the guy up off the floor.

"We saw everything," said one of the bouncers, to Logan Spence. "You're in the cool."

"But these two aren't!" shouted the other bouncer. "You guys are going to take your fight out of here! Let's move!"

Logan looked at one of the Carver's enforcers.

"May I sit at this booth?"

"It's all yours, man."

Spence sat down. He lit a cigarette. As he was trying to figure out the plight of battered women, the guy he had come to see returned with cocktails. He seated himself across from Spence.

"You clear a table real fast," he laughed.

Glenn Jenkins was a casual friend of Spence's. He was a senior at Water's Edge High School and a year older than Logan. The two had met when Spence was a freshman there. They had bonded, for only one reason. Both were part of a small group of students at Water's Edge High who had attended Eastern Middle School.

The reason Glenn had to attend the public high school was a simple one. His parents had divorced. Although his mother retained ownership of the family's Water's Edge home, Glenn's mom did not have the income to afford tuition for a private prep school.

As far as Logan was concerned, Glenn was a fellow Eastern Middle School outsider. In Spence's mind, that meant he could be trusted until proven, otherwise.

He was also a minor league pot dealer who sold product primarily to keep his own recreational drug use free of charge. Spence was there that evening to determine whether or not Glenn Jenkins had major league potential.

"I heard what you did to the Kelly brothers," smiled Glenn. "God knows they had it coming to them!"

"How are they doing?" asked Spence, without any real concern.

"I've heard they're both on the mend," reported Jenkins.

"That's too bad."

Glenn pulled at his Heineken and stared at Logan.

"So, what are you here to sell me?"

"Blow."

Jenkins nearly choked on his beer, with laughter.

"What did you do, Logan? Mash up some Rice Krispies, throw in a bunch of sugar, and put it in a plastic bag for me to buy?" he grinned.

Suddenly, Glenn Jenkins' smiled disappeared. He felt a tap on his thigh from underneath the table.

"I suggest you taste my Rice Krispies," nodded Spence.

Glenn Jenkins picked up his beer and departed for the men's room. When he returned it was with a second round of cocktails. He sat down. His mood was now euphoric.

"Logan, this shit is primo!" he gushed.

Spence sipped his drink. He looked at Glenn Jenkins.

"So, are you Snap, Crackle, or Pop?"

"All of the above, my friend," he laughed.

Spence narrowed his eyes.

"Glenn, are you in?"

Jenkins' expression, suddenly, turned serious. He returned Logan's stare.

"Damn straight I'm in!"

The two friends finished their drinks and stood up to leave Carver's Bar and Grill.

 A man standing behind the bar had been closely monitoring the interaction between the two young men after Spence's earlier altercation with the fighting couple. His decision was made. He picked up the phone and started punching numbers. Johnny "Junior" Westfield placed the necessary call.

# Chapter Fifty-Two

Logan Spence had just parted company with Glenn Jenkins. He was in his car heading north towards Sheffield, Connecticut. Logan opted for the safer Boston Post Road over the faster route of I-95. That decision had been an easy one for Spence. He knew that legally he was in no shape to be behind the wheel. Besides, thirty-five miles per hour was far more manageable to navigate than sixty-five miles per hour in his current condition.

"*Adapt or perish,*" he mused and lit a cigarette.

Spence had consigned one ounce of cocaine and one pound of pot to Glenn Jenkins. The financial arrangement was the same he had established with Dwight Jefferson and Beth Kaminski.

"Get back the cost of product and any profit will be split fifty-fifty," he had instructed Glenn.

Logan knew full well he had taken a major gamble in dealing with Jenkins. However, he had one big factor in his favor. That was the high quality of both the coke and the weed. Logan figured that Glenn would do his best to maximize profits on his trial delivery to help ensure a larger second shipment of product. If Jenkins was going to try to rip him off, it would be then.

A tired Logan Spence pulled into the Kaminski's driveway and came to a stop. He shut off the car's engine. Logan would have been content to just fall asleep in the car. However, that was not an option. Spence opened the driver's side door and got out. He popped the trunk.

Logan emptied the pockets of his jacket into the duffel bag. As he started to take off the blue blazer, an outside light went on illuminating the driveway. A silhouetted female figure emerged from the house's front door and approached.

"Beth, I'm sorry I didn't call to let you know I'd be coming," he apologized.

"I'm not Beth!"

It was Beth Kaminski's younger sister, Valerie Larsen. She walked up to Spence and studied his face. She shook her head.

"You look like crap! When was the last time you slept?"

"With whom?" he grinned.

Val placed a hand on each hip and stared her disapproval.

"That's not even close to be being funny! Now give me the jacket and the rest of your clothes."

Logan looked at her and smiled.

"I don't undress on the first date."

Valerie Larsen scowled, at Spence.

"This isn't a date! You should be so damn lucky! Now strip!"

Spence was too weary to argue. The driver's side door of the Buick GS was still opened. He sat down facing, outwardly. He kicked off the loafers and shed his shirt, tie, and gray flannels. Meanwhile, Valerie was rummaging through the car's trunk. When she returned, Larsen hurled a pair of jeans and a tee-shirt, at Spence. She then gathered the rest of his clothes and started towards the house.

"Are you going to burn them at the stake?" he laughed.

Valerie Larsen stopped and turned.

"No, I'm going to have the dry cleaners fumigate them tomorrow morning."

"Why?"

"Because they smell like a barroom's armpit!" she hissed and huffed back into the house.

Spence hoisted the jeans and slapped on a black tee shirt. He re-entered his loafers and walked to the  trunk of the car. He donned his leather jacket.

Logan then opened the clandestine panel of the trunk. He placed five pounds of pot into his duffel bag. Spence then reached into the duffel bag and tossed his personal plastic bag into the stowaway to keep the remaining ounce of cocaine, company.

Spence pocketed his cigarettes and lighter. He resealed the compartment and closed the trunk.

Logan was perplexed. He did not understand why Valerie Larsen was so pissed off at him. As far as Spence was concerned, he had done nothing to justify her anger towards him.

"*Women are emotional little creatures,*" he finally concluded, to himself.

With duffel bag in hand, Spence knocked on the front door of the Kaminski home.

"It's open, Logan," chimed Beth Kaminski.

As Spence entered the house, he immediately noticed the absence of loud rock and roll. He walked through the tiny foyer and entered the kitchen. Beth Kaminski rose from her chair at the kitchen table to greet him. Valerie Larsen remained seated.

"Logan, I'm so glad to see you!" she smiled, as the two friends embraced. "Would you like a cocktail?"

"No, but I'll take one anyway," he said and dropped the duffel bag on the floor to sit down at the table.

"Val, do you want a drink?" she asked her younger sister.

"No!"

Beth returned to the kitchen table with an Absolut on the rocks and a glass of Grand Marnier.

"Where's Roger?" asked Spence.

"With his folks," answered Beth Kaminski. "He's helping his mom deal with his dad."

Spence pulled at his drink. He lit a cigarette.

"What's wrong with Roger's father?"

Beth Kaminski sipped her Grand Marnier. Before she had a chance to answer Logan's question, a baby's cry came from the upstairs. Val Larsen sprang out of her chair.

"I'll take care of her, Sis," she volunteered and sprinted out of the kitchen and up the stairs.

Beth Kaminski studied the face of Logan Spence. She frowned.

"You're wired," she said, with calm concern.

"That's the rumor," he admitted and sipped his Absolut.

"What are you on?"

"Coke."

"Why?"

Although Beth Kaminski was only four years his senior, Logan had come to regard the twenty-one-year old mother of two as his maternal mentor. He trusted her. Logan Spence trusted very few people. He owed her the truth.

"Because of this."

Spence reached into his duffel bag and placed five pounds of pot on the kitchen table. Beth Kaminski stared, at him.

"What does pot have to do with cocaine?" she asked, naively.

"Everything," he replied.

Beth Kaminski shook her head.

"Logan, I want nothing to do with cocaine."

Spence pulled at his drink and dragged the cigarette.

"You're out of the loop when it comes to the blow," he reassured her.

Beth Kaminski stood up from the kitchen table.

"Come on, I want to show you where I keep the weed for 'safe keeping,' she smiled."

Spence looked up at Beth.

"What's wrong with Roger's dad," he asked, again.

"Roger's father served in Nam. While he was over there, he came in contact with something called Agent Orange. Anyway, he's not long for this world," she explained.

"War is a whore," agreed Logan Spence, as he snuffed his smoke. He put the pot back into his duffel bag. With drink, in hand, Spence rose from the kitchen table to follow Beth Kaminski.

She led him to the basement and an impressive free standing metallic safe. As she was twisting its dial, Beth told Logan Spence the safe's combination. Its door opened. Logan placed the pot inside the safe and closed it.

"Now, reopen it," she instructed.

He did so.

"Good," she smiled.

Beth looked at Spence. She made up her mind.

"Logan, I think it best if you stay down here tonight," she said and pointed to a bed located in a corner of the basement. "Get some sleep."

Spence did not argue. As Beth Kaminski retreated upstairs, Logan walked to the bed and sat down. He dropped his duffel bag and kicked off the loafers. He did not bother to undress or even get under the covers as he swung his legs onto the bed. He took a sip from his glass and then rested it on his chest. Logan Spence closed his eyes.

"This is where I sleep when I stay at my sister's house!" informed a voice.

Spence opened his eyes to see Valerie Larsen staring down at him.

"Okay, I'll move. I'll sleep on the floor," he said in a tired voice.

Valerie Larsen thought for a moment. She came to a decision.

"We can share the bed but we're not doing anything!"

"Don't worry about that," he said, distantly, and closed his eyes.

Thirty-six hours of no sleep and non-stop substance abuse had caught up to Logan Spence. All he wanted to do was crash.

Valerie Larsen sat down on the bed next to Spence. She was still clad in blue jeans and tank top. She nudged him.

"Logan?"

"What?!" he responded, with annoyance.

"Do you remember what I told you the last time you were here?"

"No," he said wearily, without opening his eyes.

"I told you that you'd be the very first to know," she continued.

Spence began to snore. Valerie Larsen gently removed the glass from his hand and placed it on the night table. She then slid into bed next to him. She whispered in his ear.

"I've decided I do have a boyfriend."

Spence had not heard her words. He was already, long gone.

# CHAPTER FIFTY-THREE

"Logan, are you nervous about sitting for the SAT's?" she asked.

Spence looked at the young woman seated across the desk from him and shook his head.

"Not as nervous as you are," he smirked.

Patty White's facial expression feigned annoyance.

"I could care less how you do on those tests!"

Logan smiled at her, warmly.

"I'll do fine."

The two were in Patty White's office for Logan's weekly tutorial. The Cornwall Angelica Hall Winter Term was reaching its mid-point. During that time, teacher and pupil had bonded in a rather odd way.

Patricia White now respected Logan Spence, as a student. As their weekly tutorials progressed during that winter term, she had become very comfortable with his presence. Ironically, during that same period of time, Patty had become increasingly comfortable with herself, both as a teacher and as a woman.

When student and teacher's conversations drifted from James Joyce, Patty found herself telling Logan things she might not otherwise mention to anyone else. However, that was not her concern. Intuitively, Patty knew that whatever she told Logan Spence would never go any further than the two of them.

What was upsetting her was the fact he was not returning her unguarded candor. Their bed-wetting showdown had been the only time Logan Spence had let his emotional guard down.

For his part, Logan had been enamored with Patricia White from the moment he had set eyes on her. Spence thought she was the most beautiful woman he had ever seen.

However, Logan harbored no delusions nor fantasies. He continued to master her curriculum for only one reason. That was to ensure he would remain a part of her life. Logan was content just being around the young woman, who so intrigued him.

"I've been hearing your wrestling team has a big match coming up this Saturday against Bardsville," commented Patricia White. "Are they as good as everyone is saying?"

Logan looked at his mentor and frowned.

"Since when are you into sports?"

Patty ignored his question.

"So, are they?"

Spence looked at her and shook his head, with disinterest.

"I don't know and I don't care."

Undaunted, Patty continued.

"Jeff Williams tells me you're way good," she smiled.

Williams was a Cornwall faculty member and an assistant coach for the varsity wrestling team. Although Logan knew who he was, he had rarely spoken to him. Spence always dealt directly with head coach, Frank Hubbard.

"What else did he tell you?" asked Logan, with a tinge of annoyance.

"Jeff told me that some of your teammates are starting to emulate you by wearing white wrestling shoes," she answered.

Logan Spence looked at her and shook his head, with a fondness he had never felt before.

"Patricia, it isn't emulation. Its superstition. A lot of athletes are funny that way", he explained.

The winter term was their second together in the roles of teacher and student. Patty White had insisted that they be on a first name basis.

"Please, call me Patty," she had smiled. Spence felt more comfortable with 'Patricia'.

The Cornwall wrestling team was on an undefeated season roll. Following their home opening victory, Carlos Acosta had been the first to chuck his black wrestling shoes for white ones. After the team's second win, one more teammate donned white wrestling shoes. With each subsequent triumph, another Cornwall wrestler would lace up in white.

"So, are you a superstitious athlete?" she asked.

"I'm not an athlete."

Patty White shook her head with a puzzled expression.

"Then, what are you?"

Spence did not immediately respond. He stared down at the floor and became awkwardly, pensive. When he finally looked up it was to stare Patty White in the eyes.

"I don't really know," he admitted, with a soft sincerity that rendered her even more vulnerable than, he.

Patty's immediate instinct was to protect him. This was only the second time Logan had revealed any kind of emotional vulnerability in front of her. The young woman was careful not to break the fragile moment that she now held so delicately in her hands.

"Logan, you and I will figure that one out together," she said, tenderly.

As if snapped out of a trance, Spence stood up.

"Speaking of wrestling, I've got to get to practice."

"Well, good luck on Sat...."

She stopped herself in mid-sentence. Patty looked at Logan.

"I almost forgot. Luck will have nothing to do with it," she laughed.

"No, it won't," he said and closed the office door behind him.

Logan Spence walked from the Angelica Hall campus to the Cornwall sports complex. He entered the door of the wrestling team's locker room.

"Coach gave the guys a day off from practice," informed Gus the equipment manager, from behind his saddle door. "Wants everybody rested and ready for Bardsville."

"Best news I've had all day," grinned Spence and turned to leave.

"But, he wants to see you in his office," added Gus.

"That's not good news," laughed Spence.

Logan tapped on the frosted glass door of Coach Hubbard's office.

"Come in, Spence," barked the coach, from behind his desk.

Logan entered the room and sat down in a chair facing "The Tank".

"You're wrestling at one seventy-two this Saturday against Bardsville," he said, curtly.

"Fine," said Spence and stood up to leave.

"Sit down!" he ordered.

Logan complied. The coach resumed.

"Do you have to drop any weight?" he asked.

"No."

Hubbard looked at Spence.

"Your Saturday's opponent is named Bob Duncan. He's a senior and one of their co-captains. It goes without saying that he's very good. What you should know is that during his three years on the Bardsville varsity team he has never been beaten at home."

"The Tank" paused for effect.

"Duncan lives for and thrives on the cheers of the home crowd fans."

Logan Spence looked at his coach and shrugged.

"Most of them do."

Frank Hubbard stared at Logan and smiled at him for the first time, ever.

"You don't. If anything, it's the hostility of away crowds that seems to motivate you," he said, with a growing respect for the young man.

272

Spence now understood Hubbard's decision to match him against Duncan.

"Will there be anything else, Coach?"

"Yes, there is one more thing." Frank Hubbard hesitated, before continuing. "Logan, I just want you to know what an asset you've become to our team," he said, quietly. "Now, get out of here!"

# CHAPTER FIFTY-FOUR

Logan left the Cornwall sporting complex. He had just finished the meeting with Coach Hubbard. Spence was bound for Squire House. He climbed the stairs and walked the hallway towards his room. Although the door was closed he could hear voices, as he entered.

Roommate Pete Ellison was sitting on his bed. Logan's friend from Water's Edge, Mark Campbell, was slouched in Ellison's reading chair. Their conversation was momentarily halted by the sudden appearance of Spence. Logan dropped the books he was carrying on his desk. He then crossed the room and sat down in his recliner. He looked at his two classmates.

"What have I interrupted?" he asked, smiling.

Mark Campbell was the first to speak.

"Squire House is in crisis mode, old man!" he answered.

"And why's that?"

Pete Ellison answered Spence's question.

"That's because Squire House has run dry. There's not a drop of alcohol in the entire dorm!"

Spence's immediate thought was of his own, always well-stocked cache. Squire House's lack of booze was not one of his problems. Logan picked up James Joyce's *Ulysses* to resume the travails of Leopold Bloom.

To his annoyance, Pete Ellison and Mark Campbell continued their rant about having no cocktails in the house. They were making concentration impossible. Finally, Logan closed his book and looked at the two of them.

"I have a brilliant idea," he said, impatiently. "Why don't you just go into town and find someone to buy you whatever the hell want to drink?"

Pete Ellison and Mark Campbell looked at each other and broke into laughter. Campbell was the first to address Spence's question.

274

"For starters, old man, we're Cornwall students. Most of Sheffield already resents us for just being here. If we were to stroll downtown looking for someone to buy us liquor, illegally, chances are we'd get our asses kicked before we'd get any alcohol. Besides, even if someone said they'd do it, odds are they'd take the money and run. That's happened before."

Pete Ellison chimed in.

"Logan, he's right. You haven't been here long enough to know. Sheffield can be a real nasty town when it comes to Cornwall students."

Spence thought for a moment. He then looked at his two friends.

"Is Squire House thirsty enough to come up with four hundred dollars and a wish list?"

Mark Campbell and Pete Ellison stared at Spence not understanding what he had just asked. Ellison was the first to speak.

"Logan, what the hell are you talking about?"

"A moonshine run," said Spence.

"And what's that?" asked Pete.

Logan looked at his roommate and smiled.

"You come up with the four hundred bucks and I'll take you on one."

Mark Campbell looked at him, skeptically.

"You can pull that off?"

"Yes."

Campbell was convinced. Without another word, he and Pete got up and closed the door behind them, as they went to take liquor orders from the parched residents of Squire House.

Logan stood and walked to the mini-fridge. He tossed ice into a glass and returned to his recliner. He removed the panel of his bookcase's secret compartment and poured vodka. Before resealing it, Spence extracted a small plastic packet.

Within the hour, Campbell and Ellison returned to the room. They were in jovial moods. Spence glanced up from his book.

"Did you guys come up with the four hundred?"

"No," laughed Pete.

"We came up with five hundred, old man!" crowed Mark and handed Logan the cash and a sheet of paper listing the orders for alcohol.

Spence looked at his two friends.

"Okay, this is how we are going to play it. After dinner tonight, you two meet me in the parking lot of the Sheffield Elementary school. We'll go from there," instructed Logan.

The elementary school was a short walk from the Cornwall campus. Both Pete Ellison and Mark Campbell nodded, in silent confirmation.

After leaving the dining hall, Spence started the walk to Roger and Beth Kaminski's house. As he entered the driveway, he could see Beth standing at the kitchen sink. Logan hopped the porch's stairs and stood at the window. The young mother was bathing one of the kids. He gently tapped. Beth looked up and smiled when she saw who it was. She motioned him to come in. Spence shook his head and dangled a spare set of car keys. Beth nodded her understanding and returned to shampooing.

Logan started the engine of the Buick GS and let it idle. Cornwall students were strictly prohibited from having cars on campus. Technically speaking, the Buick GS had never been there.

Spence eased into the parking lot of Sheffield Elementary. Ellison and Campbell were already there. He stopped and flashed the headlights. They got in the car.

"Nice wheels, Logan!" exclaimed Pete Ellison. "Is it yours?"

"I wish. Borrowed it from a guy I know," he lied.

"So, what's our destination, old man?" asked Campbell.

"To fill this order," replied Spence and removed the sheet of paper from a jacket pocket.

Logan eased the car out of the parking lot. He was bound for a small package store located just outside of downtown Sheffield. Spence knew about the place because he had passed it several times while traveling with Roger on the way to Kaminski's aunt's used furniture store.

"Rumor has it that the Nutmeg is customer friendly when it comes to minors buying alcohol," Roger had once commented, to Logan.

Spence was about to find out. He pulled to a stop in the parking lot of the Nutmeg Wine and Spirits Shoppe. He got out of the car and leaned inside the opened window.

"In about fifteen minutes, I want both of you outside the car and leaning against it," he instructed.

Logan unlocked the trunk of the Buick GS and then walked to the front door of the Nutmeg.

There were two men standing behind the store's counter. One was in his fifties and the obvious owner. The other was in his early twenties and ready to enforce the law.

"Well, look at what just walked in," smiled the younger man. "It's a corn hole looking for a six pack. Can I bust him, George?" he asked, eagerly.

"Sure, why not?" shrugged the proprietor.

Spence made no eye contact with the two guys standing behind the counter. He confidently walked down the first aisle of the liquor store. Logan selected four bottles of vodka and returned to place them on the counter. He then went back to claim four bottles of gin. He placed those bottles on the counter.

"Can I bust him now, George?"

"Not yet," decided the older man.

Spence pulled out his liquor list. After review, he proceeded down the aisle of darker spirits. He came back with four bottles of scotch and placed them on the counter. Logan turned to continue shopping. When he returned it was to place four more bottles on the counter.

The liquor store owner looked at Spence.

"Sir, how will you be paying for this evening's purchase?" he inquired.

Spence looked at the two men, as if noticing their presence, for the first time.

"Cash," he said, curtly, and turned to resume his assault on the Nutmeg's liquor shelves.

"Can I bust him now, George?"

"Shut-up, Ned!" hissed the proprietor, under his breath. "Start boxing these bottles," he ordered.

Spence's final selection was a bottle of Grand Marnier. As he placed it on the counter, he looked at the store's owner.

"Might you have a gift box for this?"

"Of course!" beamed the merchant.

Ned finished packing the bottles.

"Are you going to need a hand with these?" asked the owner.

"My car is out in front. My two friends are waiting to help load."

"Ned, get the dolly," instructed the older man.

As Ned was wheeling the cases towards the Buick GS, another car pulled into the parking lot of the Nutmeg. The five men inside the vehicle remained seated to watch what was taking place in front of them.

"With volume discount, your total is four-hundred and ninety dollars," announced the owner.

Logan pulled out the wad of bills and handed it to the merchant.

"Keep the change," he smiled and turned to leave.

George quickly counted the cash.

"You're welcome here, anytime!" he shouted, as Spence exited the establishment.

Logan passed a disappointed Ned wheeling the dolly back to the store, as he walked to the Buick GS. Spence climbed into the driver's seat.

"Well, look who it is!" sneered one of the guys in the idling car. You want to tail him?"

The man sitting behind the wheel thought for a moment.

"No, I've got a better idea. Get his license plate number. I'll have my uncle run it through DMV. I don't think corn holes are allowed to have cars on campus. Especially, cars they drive to local package stores. I think I'll let his own kind handle that asshole," smiled a vengeful Billy the Kid.

Logan Spence pulled into the parking lot of Sheffield Elementary and came to a stop.

"This is as far as I go, gentlemen," he said and got out of the car to pop the trunk.

Pete Ellison and Mark Campbell joined him. Spence eyed his two friends, as they began taking cases of liquor out of the trunk.

"I don't think I have to remind the two of you that if any one finds out about the car and what we did tonight, all three of us are screwed," he said, quietly.

Ellison and Campbell looked at one another. They then stared at Spence.

"What car?" they chimed. Neither was smiling.

Logan was on his way to return the Buick GS. He turned into the Kaminski's driveway. Spence climbed out of the car. The kitchen light was still on. Beth was seated at the table. She was alone. He tapped on the window. Seeing who it was, Beth got up to open the side door.

"Logan, I was getting a little worried about you, she smiled, weakly.

Spence studied the face of his good friend and frowned.

"Beth, what's wrong?"

The young mother pulled no punches.

"Logan, Roger's father is on his death bed. He's over there now, trying to handle that situation and cope with his mother and sister. It's a nightmare," she said and shook her head.

"Where are the kids?" asked Spence.

"My mom picked them up a little while ago," she sighed. "I'm just sitting here waiting for the call."

Logan presented her with the gift-wrapped package.

"This might help your wait," he smiled.

Beth Kaminski knew exactly what he had just given her.

"I hope you'll join me," she laughed, for the first time that evening.

"Cocktails are in order," he agreed.

As Beth busied herself with the drinks, Logan lit two cigarettes. When she reseated herself, he handed her one. Glasses clinked in silence.

"So, how are sales?" he asked, trying to steer the conversation away from Roger's dad.

"Brisk," replied Beth. "Do you want to see the book?"

Spence shook his head.

"No need."

Beth hesitated before her next words.

"Logan, Val likes you," she said, referring to her younger sister.

"I like her too," he smiled.

Beth eyed him with a face of frustration.

"Logan, I mean she *really* likes you!"

Before Spence could respond the phone rang. The two friends stared at one another. Beth rose to answer it. She listened, silently, and then hung up the receiver. Beth looked at Logan.

"Roger's father has passed. It's a God send," she whispered, with a quiet inner strength.

Logan got up from the table and held his friend.

"Do you need a ride?" he asked.

Beth Kaminski shook her head.

"Roger is already on his way to get me. He couldn't wait to get out of that house."

Spence gently kissed Beth on her forehead.

"I've got to be going," he said and started for the door.

Kaminski stared at him.

"Logan, be careful."

# CHAPTER FIFTY-FIVE

The following day Spence was in the main dining room. Friday lunches were his favorites. He particularly enjoyed the fried shrimp and clams. As he was eating, a middle-aged woman who worked in the Cornwall administration building approached.

"May I have a word with you, Mr. Spence?" she asked, without asking.

Logan stood up and followed her to a hallway outside the dining room.

"The Office of the Headmaster has requested your presence this afternoon, after your final class. Shall we say around four o'clock?" she smiled, baring the fangs of comeuppance.

"I'll be there," he nodded.

Logan returned to the dining room and sat down. However, he had lost his appetite. Instinctively, he knew he was being called to the carpet for the previous night's escapades. As Spence sat at the table, his thoughts were not about his own fate. He pretty much knew what that was going to be. Instead, he was already plotting his revenge on the person or persons who had turned him in.

Logan left the dining room and walked back to Squire House. He entered his room to find Pete Ellison busily shoving dirty clothes into a laundry bag. He was heading home that weekend to have mommy do his wash.

"Hey, Logan," he smiled.

Spence stared at his roommate.

"Do you have any idea why the headmaster wants to see me this afternoon?" he asked.

Ellison's smile quickly disappeared. It was replaced with concern and a spirited self-defense.

"Logan, if it has anything to do with last night, it didn't come from me or Mark. I swear to you! Nobody in Squire House even knows you were involved. If anything, Campbell and I are the ones with all the exposure for the liquor run!" he pleaded.

Spence's dilemma was now compounded by the fact he believed his roommate's words.

Logan walked into the Cornwall administration building and climbed the stairs to the second floor. He knocked on the office door of the headmaster.

"Enter," said the stern voice of authority.

Spence found himself in the reception room of the headmaster. A humorless woman with graying hair sat behind a desk.

"I'm Logan Spence. I am here to see the headmaster."

"The headmaster is not in his office. However, he asked me to give you this."

The secretary handed Spence an envelope.

"Open it in front of me, so I can assure the headmaster you were duly received."

Logan tore open the envelope and read it out loud:

**"Mr. Spence, a special meeting of the Cornwall Disciplinary Committee has been scheduled for tomorrow, Saturday at nine a.m. Your attendance is mandatory."**

Logan looked at the woman seated behind the desk.

"May I go, now?" he asked.

She looked at him and smiled.

"Mr. Spence, I think you're already gone."

Logan walked back to Squire House. As he entered his room, Spence was consoled by the fact Pete Ellison had already left for the weekend. He plopped himself into his recliner and picked up James Joyce's *Ulysses*. He fell asleep with Molly Bloom gently nestled against his chest.

It was raining the following morning, as Logan entered the Cornwall Administration Building. He sat down at a table facing the members of the disciplinary committee.

"Mr. Spence, it has been brought to this committee's attention that you have been harboring a vehicle on campus, in violation of school policy," admonished one of the members seated across from him.

Spence looked at his accuser and shook his head.

"The car has never been on campus," he corrected.

The committee member looked at Logan and shook his head.

"Mr. Spence, whether the car was physically on campus or not is irrelevant. You have clearly transgressed the spirit and intent of our school's regulation!"

Another member of the disciplinary committee made his voice heard.

"Mr. Spence, it has been reported to this committee that your car was seen Thursday evening at a local liquor store. Is that true?"

"Yes."

"And what were you and your car doing at that liquor store?" he demanded.

"Buying liquor," responded Logan.

The lone female panel member spoke for the first time.

"Logan, this committee is aware of the fact that two Cornwall students were with you on Thursday evening at that liquor store. If you provide us the names of those two students, I am quite certain this committee will bend towards leniency when it comes to deciding your punishment," she said, reassuringly.

"*So that's the game,*" thought Spence.

The members of the disciplinary committee knew full well that Logan was on scholarship. They also knew that regardless of whoever the other two students were, it was a safe bet their parents had money. With two quick phone calls and two quicker financial contributions to Cornwall, all would be forgiven and forgotten. As far as Spence was now concerned, the meeting was nothing more than an old-fashioned shakedown.

"So, Logan, who are the other two students?" she coaxed.

"I don't recall."

"How can that possibly be?" she smiled.

"Because I was too drunk at the time to remember."

The head of the disciplinary committee became outraged.

"I've heard enough! Mr. Spence, you wait out in the hallway while this committee decides your Cornwall future!" he ordered. Logan closed the door and sat down on an empty bench to await the committee's verdict.

Suddenly, the administration building's front door opened. Coach Frank Hubbard entered. He walked by Spence without acknowledging his presence and barged into the disciplinary committee's meeting, without the courtesy of a knock. He slammed the door behind him.

Several minutes later, Frank "The Tank" Hubbard re-emerged. Again, he passed Logan without even looking at him. Spence was then summoned back into the meeting room.

"Mr. Spence, this committee has reached its decision," announced the head of the proceedings. "Effective, immediately, you are hereby placed on probation and school bounds for the duration of the winter term. Any violation of school policy on your part during this period of time shall result in your immediate expulsion from Cornwall. Do you understand?"

"Yes."

"You are dismissed!"

Spence walked out of the administration building and into that Saturday morning's drizzle. He sat down in the bleachers overlooking the varsity football field. The seats were empty. He lit a cigarette. Logan realized that any hopes for a scholarship to a top-flight college were now gone. However, he also knew that his decision not to rat was one he could live with, comfortably, for the rest of his life.

*"I'd rather be a clean mongrel than a pedigree with fleas,"* he thought, to himself.

# CHAPTER FIFTY-SIX

Patty White knocked on the door of Kate Whitson's Angelica Hall apartment.

"Come on in, Patty, its open."

Pat walked in to find her best friend standing in front of a hallway mirror applying the final touches of make-up.

"So, where are you off to?" she asked, in a surprised tone of voice.

Kate Whitson did not take her eyes off the mirror.

"Bardsville," she said, distractedly.

"And why are you going to Bardsville?" asked Patty.

"This afternoon's wrestling match. Actually, we're going for the pre-event festivities. Seth has some friends on the Bardsville faculty. There's going to be a party before the contest."

"And why wasn't I included?" demanded Patty White, with resentment.

"For starters, you've got zero interest in sports. Besides, Tom Wilkerson is coming with us. And he's bringing a date. I think he's finally over waiting around for you."

"Then, I'll just tag along as their chaperone," smiled Patty. "I've decided I want to go to Bardsville!"

Kate Whitson pulled her face away from the mirror, for the first time. She stared at her best friend.

"If the only reason you want to go to Bardsville is to see your student prince in action, forget it!" she snapped. "Chances are, he's not even going to be there today!"

Patty looked at Kate and shook her head in bewilderment.

"Why wouldn't Logan be there?" she asked, with growing concern.

Kate Whitson looked at her life-long friend. Her tone softened.

286

"Logan was placed on probation and school bounds earlier this morning," she explained, in a voice just louder than a whisper.

"Why?" demanded Patricia White.

Kate mustered the fortitude to break the news to Patty.

"Apparently, Spence had a car on campus and was using it to supply Cornwall students with alcohol he was purchasing from a local liquor store."

Patty eyed Kate, suspiciously.

"How do you know any of that is true?"

Kate Whitson returned her attention to the mirror.

"Because, Seth called and told me everything a little while ago," she said.

"And how does Abrams know so much?" persisted a skeptical Patty White.

Whitson's eyeliner took a momentary pause. Kate looked at Patty.

"Seth is good friends with Ralph Dooley. Dooley is on the Cornwall Disciplinary Committee. Anyway, it was Dooley who told Seth about the committee's decision regarding Spence."

Kate Whitson paused, in a moment of hesitation. Patty White immediately sensed her friend's uneasiness.

"What aren't you telling me, Kate?"

Whitson was now feeling very uncomfortable with the responsibility that best friendship always demands, the truth. She sighed and then continued.

"According to Ralph Dooley, Spence was extremely uncooperative with the disciplinary committee."

"And how was he uncooperative?" questioned Patty.

Kate Whitson spoke with measured words.

"Dooley told Seth that Spence was not alone at the liquor store this past Thursday evening. Two other Cornwall students were with him," she divulged.

"So?"

"So, all Spence had to do is provide the disciplinary committee with the names of those two Cornwall students and he would have walked away with a slap on the wrist! How stupid is he?"

Patty mulled her friend's words. She stared at Kate.

"So, you're telling me that Logan is on probation and schools bounds because he didn't turn in his friends?" she asked.

"Pretty much."

Patricia White started towards the door.

"Patty, where are you going?" asked Kate.

"To get dressed."

"For what?" smiled Kate.

"Bardsville."

Whitson looked at Patty and shook her head.

"You haven't heard a word I've said, have you?"

Patricia White stopped. She turned towards Kate with a face full of quiet confidence.

"Logan will be there," she said, with a calm certainty that rattled her childhood friend.

Patty closed the door behind her.

# CHAPTER FIFTY-SEVEN

Spence finished his cigarette and flicked the butt. He stood up from the varsity football bleachers and started the walk back to Squire House. As he entered his room, Logan was heartened by the fact Pete Ellison was gone for the weekend. Spence cherished the solitude.

Although it was only eleven in the morning, Logan grabbed a glass and went to the mini fridge for ice. He sat down in his recliner and opened Pandora's Box. Spence filled the glass with vodka and resealed the hidden compartment. He then settled back and picked-up James Joyce's *Ulysses*.

There came a knock on the door.

"Enter."

Terry O'Keefe walked into the room. He closed the door behind him. O'Keefe was one of the two co-captains on the Cornwall varsity wrestling team. Spence and O'Keefe did not like each other. O'Keefe spoke first.

"I heard about what happened this morning," he said.

Logan eyed O'Keefe. He picked up his glass and sipped. He placed it back on the floor.

"You and everyone else in Cornwall Nation I would imagine," smiled Spence.

O'Keefe ignored the words and the glass.

"The team bus leaves at one p.m. I would like to think you'll be on it."

Spence looked at O'Keefe and grinned.

"Oh captain, my captain, my fearful trip is done! I'm officially on bounds for the rest of the term," he dismissed.

O'Keefe reached into his jacket pocket and pulled out an envelope. He handed it to Spence.

"This is a 'get out of jail free card'. It was signed by the headmaster, himself. If you choose to go to Bardsville today, you can."

Spence tossed the envelope on the floor.

"How lucky can one guy get in one day?" he laughed, cynically, and reached for the glass.

O'Keefe looked at Spence and shook his head.

"Spence, just because you let yourself down, doesn't mean you have to let the rest of the team down," he admonished. Without another word, Captain Terry O'Keefe left the room.

Spence sat in his recliner reflecting on that morning's events. As he sipped the vodka, his eyes drifted ambivalently between the mini-fridge and the envelope he had tossed on the floor. He drained the drink and picked up the envelope. Logan had made up his mind.

Spence entered the wrestling team's locker room. The only person still there was Gus, the equipment manager. He was seated in his customary space behind the saddle door.

"I knew you'd show up," he smiled. "Are you *really* going to wrestle today?" he asked, with keen interest.

"I'm here," answered Logan.

"That wasn't my question, son."

Logan looked at the beaten old man sitting behind the saddle door.

"Gus, I don't know," admitted Logan.

"I heard what happened this morning," reported the equipment manager.

Spence looked at the old man and smiled.

"You and everybody else on campus."

"That's always the way it goes around here. Anyway, you made the right decision."

Logan stared at Gus. He paused before speaking.

"How do you know that?"

Gus became pensive. When he spoke next, his eyes were moist with emotion.

"Look at me, Logan".

"I'm looking at you, Gus."

"No! Look at what I am. Look at what I've become!"

Gus reached underneath the saddle door and re-surfaced with a pint of George Dickel. He took a swig.

"You care to join me?" he asked.

"It's a little early for me, Gus."

The old man smiled.

"Why do I doubt that? Anyway, believe it or not, I was once a Cornwall student. In fact, I was caught up in a situation like you had this morning. Only difference is, I bought their line of bullshit. I gave them names."

Gus paused for another pull from one of Tennessee's finest. He continued.

"That was the worst mistake I ever made in my life. I didn't even make it through the rest of that term. I dropped out of Cornwall because I was known as 'The Snitch'. I was despised by everybody. It was brutal".

Logan looked at the equipment manager. He had only one question.

"Gus, then how the hell did you end up back here at Cornwall?"

"One of the guys I named back then was Frank Hubbard. Frankie and I are local boys from Sheffield. Anyway, as the years passed and he saw that I was flushing myself down the toilet, he started to feel sorry for me. So, when he landed the head coaching job at Cornwall, he hired me as his equipment manager. End of story."

Spence looked at the wall clock.

"Gus, I've got to get moving if I'm going to make the bus to Bardsville."

"I already put everything you're going to need in your locker," he said.

Spence walked across the room. He began packing his duffel bag.

"Hey, Logan, I'll be listening to find out if you're *really* wrestling today," grinned Gus, as he tapped an old white plastic Magnavox AM/FM radio he had perched on the saddle door.

"Stay tuned, Gus," laughed Logan and left the locker room.

Actually, Spence had already made up his mind. He was travelling to Bardsville that afternoon to merely go through the motions. He would not let himself get pinned. However, that was going to be the extent of his effort; no more, no less.

Logan boarded the Cornwall travel bus. As he made way down the aisle, his teammates avoided eye contact with him. It was not rejection. Almost everyone on the bus knew what had gone down earlier that morning. They were merely giving him the space and the respect that space deserved.

Logan placed his duffel bag on the back bench of the bus. He pulled out *Ulysses*. He sat down and began to read. His mind quickly drifted from the words on the pages he was reading to that morning's events.

He knew that his chances for scholarship money at a prestigious university were now gone. Spence also realized that his status as a Cornwall student had been reduced to that of an imprisoned inmate. Ironically, none of that really mattered to him, anymore.

As the Cornwall travel bus bumped and jostled its way towards Bardsville, there was only one question troubling Logan Spence.

"What's Patricia going to think?"

# CHAPTER FIFTY-EIGHT

"Wow, this place is humongous!" exclaimed Charlie Davenport, as he entered the Bardsville field house.

"Wait till the crowd rolls in," warned Jack Reed, the voice of WCAH. "You won't believe the noise level."

The disc jockey and studio engineer were setting up to broadcast that afternoon's wrestling match.

"So, what's the deal with Spence?" asked Davenport.

"He's still a Cornwall student from what I heard."

"Is he going to be here, today?"

"I doubt it. The disciplinary committee placed him on probation and bounds," responded Reed.

"That's, too bad. Logan is always very entertaining when he wrestles," lamented a disappointed Davenport.

The Bardsville field house began to fill. The volume of anticipation began to rise with each arriving spectator.

"I told you it was going to get loud, Charlie," laughed a now pumped up Jack Reed.

The match got underway. As expected, it was close. By the time Logan Spence stepped onto the mat, Cornwall was clinging to a small lead. Nonetheless, the Bardsville faithful were not concerned. Their premier wrestlers were waiting on deck.

Bardsville co-captain, Bobby Duncan approached the mat. Spence noticed his opponent was still holding his head gear. Instead of stepping onto the mat, Duncan walked to the Bardsville grandstand. He stopped in front of an attractive young woman seated in the front row. She stood up. Duncan handed her the headgear. She kissed the headgear for good luck and then placed it on his head to the roaring delight of the hometown crowd. Co-captain Bobby Duncan was now equipped and ready to vanquish his opponent.

As the match began, Logan's mind was a million miles away. His thoughts were about the probation and its foreboding consequences. His attention then shifted to his mother. He was now happy she had never come to see him wrestle. But his biggest concern was Patricia White. The thought that she might no longer have anything to do with him depressed Logan Spence.

The second period ended with Bobby Duncan well ahead on points. The home crowd was in a euphoric frenzy. All their hero had to do now was safely ride out the third and final period for the win.

Cornwall co-captain Joe Mancini was seated on the bench. He turned to his fellow co-captain, Terry O'Keefe.

"What the hell is up with Spence?"

"You didn't hear?"

"Hear what?"

"Spence was placed on probation and bounds this morning," explained O'Keefe.

"Why?" asked the surprised, Mancini.

"Having a car on campus and using it to distribute alcohol."

Joe Mancini shook his head.

"Why the hell didn't they just expel him?"

Terry O'Keefe looked at his teammate and smiled.

"Because, Joe, there's no fun in that for the faculty."

"Good point."

The two co-captains laughed, in spite of the increasingly bleak outcome to that day's match, with their arch rivals.

Before the start of the third period, Bardsville co-captain Bobby Duncan did something out of the ordinary. Confident of his victory and intoxicated by the home crowd adulation he approached Spence.

"Now, you be a good boy for one more period and you'll get out of here without me having to *really* hurt you!" he taunted and patted Spence on the head. The crowd erupted in jeering laughter.

Instantly, Spence snapped out of his funk. The condescending insult had hit home. For the first time that afternoon, the Bardsville co-captain had Logan's undivided attention.

For Spence, it was now no longer about a wrestling match. It was no longer about probation. It was no longer about school rivalries. Bobby Duncan had made their current situation a personal matter. And Logan Spence was now determined to handle that matter in a very personal way.

The third period started with Duncan on top, in advantage position. He was now paying more attention to the home crowd than his opponent. Subtly, Spence began to shift his weight and balance. Half way through the third period Logan made his move. Suddenly, Bobby Duncan found himself in mid-air and about to land squarely on his back. Spence knew the match was over. The terror in his opponent's eyes told Logan that Bobby Duncan knew it, too.

The referee dropped to the mat. He saw that both of Bobby Duncan's shoulders were pinned. He counted to three and then blew his whistle. As quickly as that, it was over.

The once raucous Bardsville crowd went eerily, quiet. The only voice that could now be heard in the field house was coming from the Cornwall media table.

    **"In an absolutely stunning turn of events, Logan Spence has just pinned Bardville's co-captain, Bobby Duncan!"** announced Jack Reed.

The two wrestlers stood in the center of the mat. The referee raised Logan's arm in victory. A now defeated Bobby Duncan walked dejectedly towards his team's bench, still trying to figure out what had just happened.

Logan remained standing in the center of the mat, savoring the home crowd's disappointed silence. He then began to walk. However, it was not towards the Cornwall bench.

Spence was now confidently strolling across the mat towards the Bardsville grandstand. He came to a stop directly in front of the young lady who, only moments earlier, had been rooting so ardently for his opponent. He looked at her and smiled. Logan then bowed, graciously. He removed his head gear and gently presented it to her. She took the head gear, in hand, more out of reflex than acceptance. The young woman, like everyone else in the Bardsville field house, was now in a state of shock.

Patty White was transfixed. As she watched the scene that was playing out in front of her, Patty began to experience an emotion she had never felt before. Its ugly name was called jealousy.

Logan lingered in front of the young lady just long enough to let her know how much he appreciated her physical attractiveness. He then turned and started the trek across the large wrestling mat towards the Cornwall bench. The Bardsville field house remained hushed.

After a momentary loss for words, Jack Reed, the voice of WCAH regained stride.

**"Logan Spence has turned this afternoon's wrestling match into a Saturday Broadway Matinee!"**

Spence crossed the mat and stopped directly in front of Carlos Acosta, who was on deck and warming up to wrestle Bardsville's other co-captain. Without warning, Spence slapped Acosta's headgear. The smack reverberated throughout the silent field house. Logan pointed a finger in Acosta's face.

"If you don't kick the shit out of him, I'm going to kick the shit out of you!" he yelled, loudly enough for all to hear.

Acosta was now enraged. His first instinct was to lash out at Spence. However, the Argentine turned his anger towards his Bardsville opponent.

For his part, the other Bardsville co-captain was already unnerved. Besides witnessing what had just taken place during the prior match, his home crowd's silence was a first. So when Carlos Acosta came out doing his patented scorpion war dance, the Bardsville wrestler freaked. The co-captain spent much of that first period running for his life. However, once Acosta got a hold of him, the match was over.

The first thing a victorious Carlos Acosta did when he walked off the mat was embrace his unlikely friend, Logan Spence. The two had done their part that afternoon at Bardsville.

Logan glanced at Coach Frank Hubbard and pointed discreetly to his crotch, indicating the need for a men's room. Hubbard nodded his tacit approval and refocused on the next match that was about to get underway.

Spence walked into the visiting team's locker room and found his jacket. He wedged a red fire extinguisher against an outside door and stepped out into a cold afternoon. He lit a cigarette. His thoughts were all about Patricia White.

*"She's going to have nothing to do with me from now on,"* he lamented, to himself.

Spence yanked his flask from a jacket pocket and took a swallow of self-pity.

*"She's not even going to be mad,"* he thought. *"She's going to be disappointed in me. And that's even worse!"* Logan finished his cigarette and took another pull.

When Spence re-entered the field house, the home crowd was once again rocking. The meeting between Cornwall and Bardsville had come down to the final match. Although Cornwall clung to a four-point lead, the outcome was going to be decided by the heavyweights.

Cornwall's heavyweight was big but soft. He was a nice guy with rosy cheeks and a mild disposition. Bardsville's heavyweight was the defending New England Regional champion. He was big, muscular, and mean. The contest essentially boiled down to a fight between an affectionate Saint Bernard and a nasty Russian Wolf Hound.

*"This thing is over,"* thought Spence, as he contemplated an early exit to the showers.

The two heavyweights walked onto the mat. Suddenly, the rosy cheeks of the Cornwall wrestler disappeared. He had become overwhelmed by both the crowd noise and the menacing face of his opponent. Without warning, the affectionate Saint Bernard bent over and vomited on the wrestling mat.

As officials rushed to clean up the mess, the two head coaches hustled to the scorer's table to determine the consequence of a forfeit. They learned that a forfeit would award Bardsville five points and, thus, the match.

Logan watched Coach Hubbard return to their bench. The resignation of defeat now clouded his eyes. The assistant coaches were now crowded around him, doling out sympathetic support.

Spence had seen enough. He stood up and confronted his coach.

"I'll wrestle for you."

Frank Hubbard looked at Logan Spence and shook his head.

"You don't have to do that, Spence."

"Yes, I do."

"Why?"

"Because, I owe you one for this morning."

The cloud of defeat in the coach's eyes was suddenly replaced with hope. He walked to the scorer's table to confirm Spence's eligibility. When he returned, Hubbard was all business.

"Do you understand that all I need out of you is not to get your ass pinned?" he asked, emotionally.

Logan stared at Frank "The Tank" Hubbard and smiled.

"I know the deal."

Carlos Acosta approached Spence.

"You're going to need this," he said and handed Logan his head gear. Carlos walked away, without another word.

When Spence approached the mat, the Bardsville crowd's noise level subsided. There began a smattering of boos. He stepped onto the mat. His thoughts were about Sensei Tanaka.

"*Baransu.*"

As he shook hands with his larger opponent, Logan's mind drifted to his childhood sports idol, Muhammad Ali.

"*Rope a Dope!*" he laughed, to himself.

Patty White tapped Seth Abrams on his arm.

"Why is Logan wrestling, again?" she asked, with concern in her voice. "What's going on?"

Seth turned towards Patty to answer her question.

"Spence is taking one for the team," he replied. "The kid has guts!"

"I don't understand," persisted Patty White.

Abrams looked at her, impatiently.

"It's really quite simple, Patty. If Spence gets pinned we lose. If he doesn't, we win."

Patty White thought for a moment.

"What are the chances Logan won't get pinned?"

"Slim to none," interrupted Tom Wilkerson, with the jilted smile of unrequited love.

In actuality, given the circumstances of the match, Spence's size disadvantage was basically nullified by the fact he did not have to win. More importantly, he did not even have to try to score any points. All he had to do is ride out the storm. And what a storm it was!

As soon as the ref's whistle blew, the Bardville heavyweight grabbed Spence and lifted him off the mat. To the delighted glee of the home crowd, he held Logan in mid-air and then hurled him to the canvass. Spence was slow to get up. However, he made certain to stay in bounds to keep the time clock running.

*"Keep doing that big boy,"* thought Spence, as he returned to the center of the mat.

The Bardsville heavyweight was relentless in his repeated attempts to quickly pin Spence. However, his foolhardy over-exertion began to take its toll.

By the start of the third and final period, the Bardsville heavyweight was exhausted. Although Logan started in advantage position, he quickly let himself get reversed to gain the safety of better balance.

As the final seconds of third period ticked away, the Bardsville heavyweight had nothing left. The home crowd had grown sullenly silent. It was apparent to all that Logan Spence was not going to be pinned. For a fleeting instant, Logan toyed with the idea of pinning Goliath. He deferred.

With ten seconds left on the clock, Carlos Acosta jumped up from the bench and stood at the mat's edge.

"Nine, eight, seven!" he shouted.

Suddenly, the entire Cornwall wrestling team was on its feet standing beside Acosta.

"Six, five, four!" they chanted, in unison.

And then, an extraordinary thing took place that late afternoon, inside the Bardsville field house. In a display of class and sportsmanship, a majority of the home crowd stood up and joined the chorus.

"Three, two, one!" they conceded, acknowledging Spence's efforts.

Cornwall had won the match. Patricia White grabbed Kate Whitson and hugged her. Patty was crying.

As the Bardsville heavyweight's arm was raised in triumph, his eyes glistened with tears. He knew he had let his team down. The Pyrrhic victory remains one of Life's cruelest ironies.

As the Cornwall wrestling team mobbed Coach Hubbard in celebration, Logan Spence remained alone on the mat. He sat down and began to unlace the white wrestling shoes. He then stood up and walked towards his team's jubilation. Spence stopped in front of Coach Frank Hubbard. Logan handed him the shoes.

"These belong to you. I lost," he said and turned towards the visiting team's locker room.

As he watched Spence walk away, Frank Hubbard's very own words echoed inside his head:

*"They're yours till you lose."*

The coach shook his head, ruefully. He realized that what Spence had just said to him had absolutely nothing to do with wrestling.

Logan quickly showered and dressed. He boarded the team bus and walked to his customary back bench. He pulled *Ulysses* from his duffel bag. He propped the bag as a pillow and lay down to read.

The young woman walked with purpose. She was flanked, on either side, by a girlfriend. She held Logan Spence's headgear in her hand. Their destination was the Cornwall travel bus.

"Where is he?" she demanded. The young lady was not smiling.

Several Cornwall wrestlers were standing idly on the sidewalk. One of them poked his head inside the stairwell of the bus.

"Hey, Logan, you've got company."

Spence sat up and looked out a window. He saw who it was.

Logan emerged from the bus and stood in front of the girl who was holding his headgear.

"I believe this belongs to you!" she said and thrust it into Logan's hand.

Without another word, the three girls turned and walked away. Some mild ribbing took place after the obvious rebuke. However, no one on the Cornwall wrestling team was overly anxious to really piss Spence off.

Logan re-boarded and walked to the back of the bus. As he tossed the headgear into his duffel bag, something caught his eye. Spence retrieved the headgear. On one of its inside flaps, Bobby Duncan's girlfriend had written down a phone number.

# CHAPTER FIFTY-NINE

The wrestling team's travel bus pulled to a stop in front of the Cornwall sports complex. As his teammates piled into several school mini vans to enjoy a victory dinner off campus, Spence started the long walk back to Squire House. The 'get out of jail free' card had expired.

As he entered the dorm room, Logan was surprised to see his roommate.

"Pete, what are you doing back so soon?"

"I just felt like coming back," shrugged Ellison.

Spence knew something was bothering his friend.

"Pete, did you have a fight with your folks?" he asked, with concern.

Ellison looked at Spence and shook his head.

"I wish," he said, wistfully. "Truth is, they're the ones fighting! I don't think they're going to stay married, too much longer. It's not a fun situation."

Suddenly, Pete Ellison changed the subject.

"I hear congratulations are in order!" he smiled.

"You mean the fact I got probation and bounds instead of being expelled?" laughed Logan.

Ellison frowned.

"I heard about that, too," he said, quietly. "No, I'm talking about how you single-handedly dismantled Bardsville this afternoon. That's a job well done!"

Spence sorely wished he gave a damn. Pete Ellison stood up and put on his overcoat.

"Logan, I'm going up to the radio station. You want to come? Jack's doing his Saturday night show."

"Pete, I don't think so," declined Spence.

Ellison looked at him, mischievously.

"I scored some pretty good weed while I was home."

"Pete, I'm tired," confessed Spence.

"I can understand that. I'll see you later," he said and closed the door behind him.

Logan walked to the mini fridge and filled a glass with ice. He sat down on his recliner and opened the secret compartment from hell. He poured vodka. He re-sealed the cache and then sat back to savor the silence.

As if on cue, there was a knock on the door.

"Enter," acknowledged Logan.

The door opened. A woman remained standing in the doorway. It was Susan Tompkins. She and her husband, Alan, were the faculty residents at Squire House.

"Mr. Spence, you have a lady caller asking for you in the television room downstairs," she informed and then hastily closed the door behind her.

Spence had visions of Patricia White standing downstairs with a loaded shot gun just itching to blow out the brains she had spent so much time nurturing over the prior two terms. Logan finished his drink and tucked the glass under the recliner. Reluctantly, he stood up.

*"I might as well just get this over with,"* he thought.

When he entered the room, Logan was surprised to see that it was Glynn Benamure standing there.

"I thought I'd come over and congratulate you, personally. I listened to the whole thing on the radio this afternoon," she smiled and swayed, unevenly, on her feet.

Benamure had been drinking.

"That was nice of you, Glynn."

The young woman stared, unevenly, into Spence's eyes.

"You want to go on a date with me tonight?" she asked, teasingly.

"Glynn, I'd love to. But I'm on bounds, so we wouldn't get very far," he laughed.

"We can go far enough to smoke this."

Benamure unfurled her hand exposing a joint.

"Logan, you've never had pot like this before!" she grinned.

Spence looked at the joint and, silently, cursed himself. He took Benamure by the arm and seated her on one of the foyer's sofas.

"Glynn, you wait here. I'll be right back," he instructed.

Spence entered his room. His intention was to get Glynn back to her dormitory. He donned a coat. Logan pocketed a flask and some smokes. Spence descended the stairs and knocked on the door to the Tompkins' apartment. Susan opened it.

"Mrs. Tompkins, I'm just going to escort my friend back to her dorm. She's been drinking."

"So I noticed!" she said and scowled, her disapproval.

"Mrs. Tompkins, I just want to make sure she gets back to her room, safely. I won't be long."

Susan Tompkins' face softened. Her tone of voice was now almost conciliatory.

"That's very considerate of you, Logan. I'll let Mr. Tompkins know where you are."

"Thank you."

Logan re-entered the foyer to find Glynn Benamure seated on the sofa. Her eyes were fighting off sleep.

"C'mon, party girl, we're out of here," he said and gently got Glynn to her feet.

They walked arm in arm. The crisp evening air revived her. As they neared the Angelica Hall dorm, Glynn suddenly steered Logan off the walkway and into a small patch of woods.

"Did you think I forgot about our date?"

They were now standing in seclusion.

"Can you at least provide a lady with something more comfortable to sit on than pine needles?" she laughed.

304

Logan removed his coat and spread it on the ground. They sat down. Glynn handed him the joint.

"Will you please light this for me?"

Spence fired the joint. He took a sociable hit and then passed it. Glynn looked at him in the moon lit shade.

"You've wanted to have sex with me since the first day we met, haven't you?"

"Yes."

Benamure handed Spence the joint. He snuffed it.

"Well, tonight's your lucky night!"

Glynn wrapped both her arms around Spence's neck and pulled him to the ground. She kissed him with passion.

"Let's do it! It doesn't matter anymore, anyway," she said more, to herself, than to Logan.

Spence abruptly, sat up.

"What's that supposed to mean?" he demanded.

She remained prone and silent. Spence took hold of her shoulders and eased her to a seated position.

"Glynn, what are you saying to me?" he asked, gently.

Benamure began to tremble. She then began to cry. Glynn buried her head in Spence's shoulder.

"Logan, I'm pregnant!"

Her words were iced water being poured down his pants. Spence lit a cigarette.

"So, who's the lucky guy?" he asked, already knowing the answer to his question.

"Bradley," she said, with quiet venom in her voice. "But, he's denying it!"

Spence searched the eyes of his close friend.

"Glynn, are you sure it's Bradley?"

The young woman shook her head, vehemently.

"He's the only man, *boy*, I've ever slept with."

Logan believed her. Benamure's revelation quickly reminded Spence of why he had never liked, nor trusted, "nice guys".

"Glynn, who else knows about your situation?"

"Just my roommate."

"*Which means half the campus*," he thought, cynically, and finished his cigarette.

Benamure read Spence's mind.

"Diane would never betray my trust!"

Logan stood up. He extended a hand to Benamure. She rose. Spence gathered his coat. He draped it around Glynn's shoulders. The young couple walked, hand in hand, back to her dorm.

"Do you know what you're going to do?" he asked her.

"No."

"Would you like an option?"

Benamure remained silent. The young woman knew exactly the option Spence was alluding to. They came to a stop in front of her dorm. Glynn shed Logan's coat and handed it to him. He put it on. Spence then cupped her face with both hands and gently kissed her on the forehead. Without another word, he started walking.

"Logan!"

Spence stopped. Glynn approached him.

"Can you provide me with that option?"

He nodded.

"*Will* you provide me that option?" she now asked, with resolve.

Spence stared into the face of his close friend. Logan had conflicted emotions. He made up his mind.

"Yes," he promised. "I'll call you tomorrow."

This time it was Glynn who held Logan's face in her hands. She kissed him. It was not on the forehead.

"I'll always love you, Logan," she whispered and then quickly walked away, hiding newly found tears.

306

Spence stood in the darkness and watched her safely disappear inside the dorm. Ironically, that was to be the last time he would ever see or hear from Glynn Benamure.

# CHAPTER SIXTY

Logan left Glynn's dorm. He was on his way back to Squire House. Three figures approached walking in the opposite direction. As he passed, one of the Cornwall students intentionally bumped him. It was the jerk who had hassled him for sitting at the Afro-American table his first day at Cornwall. His two cohorts were members of the varsity football team.

"Is this the Afro-American sidewalk?' asked Logan, facetiously.

"It is as far as I'm concerned!" said the young man, with attitude, and continued to walk.

Spence was in no mood. He turned to face them.

"Hey, Little Black Sambo, I have something I want to say to you!" he smiled and started walking towards the now standing threesome.

Spence stopped within five feet. He stared at his antagonist.

"If you ever get in my face, again, I'm going to bust you up into little pieces and mail you home to your Aunt Jemima. Do you understand me, asshole?" he said, with a disquieting nonchalance.

The young man flew into a rage. He started towards Spence, assuming his two friends would back his play. Logan stood grinning with eager anticipation. Suddenly, one of the football players grabbed "Sambo" by the collar to restrain him.

Spence stood waiting for their next move. He was very disappointed when they turned and walked away, without another word.

Logan lit a cigarette and continued the walk to his dorm. His best friend, Dwight Jefferson, came to mind.

*"If Dewey had been here tonight, he would have gone ahead and kicked ass out of sheer principle,"* mused Spence.

Logan entered his room. He was surprised to see Pete Ellison back, so early, from the radio station.

"Jack run out of songs to play?" smiled Spence.

Ellison looked at him and shook his head.

"I guess I'm just not in party mode tonight."

Spence looked at his roommate.

"Pete, I need a favor."

"Anything, Logan," he said.

"I have to go into town tonight. So, I want you to cover my ass in case there's a room check."

Ellison looked at Spence. He was not enthusiastic.

"Logan, you're on probation and bounds. The entire faculty is just waiting for the chance to throw your ass out of here!" he reminded him.

Spence ignored his roommate's words.

"Do I have your word you'll cover me?"

Pete Ellison did not need a moment, to even think about it.

"Yes."

Spence was out the door and bound for the Kaminski house. He knocked on the front door. Roger opened it.

"Logan, Beth didn't tell me you'd be stopping by tonight."

"That's because she didn't know," he explained.

Spence then looked at Kaminski.

"Roger, I'm sorry about your dad."

Kaminski returned Logan's gaze.

"Don't be. Actually, his passing was a blessing for the entire family, himself, included. He was in real bad shape his last few months. Anyway, it's over." "Logan, you got time for a bone?"

"No, I'll be out of here in a couple of minutes."

"Beth's in the kitchen," he motioned and walked back into the small den where Queen's "Crazy Little Thing Called Love" was playing, at a reasonable volume.

Spence entered the kitchen to find Beth and her younger sister, Valerie Larsen seated at the table.

"Logan, what a pleasant surprise!" smiled Beth and stood up to greet him with a hug and kiss. "Can I get you a drink?"

"Yes.'

Beth retrieved a glass and then went to the freezer for ice and Absolut. She was careful not to neglect her own emptied glass.

"Val, can I get you something?" asked the older sister.

"No," she said.

Valerie was troubled by Logan's unexpected visit. She knew about the Cornwall Disciplinary Committee's decision to place him on probation and bounds, earlier that morning. She had not told her older sister.

Beth sat back down. Before she could say another word, Logan Spence came right to the point.

"Beth, I need your help."

"Of course, Logan. Anything I can do."

Spence sipped his drink. He looked into the eyes of Beth Kaminski.

"A good friend of mine is pregnant. She doesn't want to be. Can you provide her with a safe option?"

Beth returned Logan's stare. Her face remained expressionless.

"Are you the father?"

"No."

Kaminski's eyes did not waver from Logan's.

"Tell me you're not the father," she insisted.

"Beth, I'm not the father!" he shrugged.

Beth Kaminski took him at his word.

"Then, Logan, why the hell are you getting yourself involved in that mess? You can only lose."

Spence tilted his glass and lit a smoke.

"Because, she's a friend of mine," he said.

Beth looked at him with a 'been there, done that' stare of disapproval.

"Logan, just because she's a friend doesn't mean you have to get tangled up in her personal nightmare. I've learned. And, I've got lots of friends."

"I don't."

His quiet revelation struck a chord. Beth Kaminski sat, silently, trying to make up her mind. Emotion vanquished common sense.

"There is a physician here in town who happens to specialize in your friend's current situation. He's quite competent and discreet. However, he's very expensive."

"That's not my problem," dismissed Spence.

Beth rose from the table. When she returned it was with a slip of paper, in hand. She gave it to Logan and re-seated herself.

"That's the name, address, and telephone number of the doctor. However, I need some information from you."

"What sort of information?" asked Spence.

"Your friend's name," responded Beth.

"Why?" he demanded.

"Because this doctor requires trusted referrals," she explained and took a sip of Grand Marnier.

Logan thought for a moment. He quickly realized he had no choice.

"Benamure, Glynn Benamure."

*"Benamure!"* thought Valerie Larsen. Her heart sank. Although her friendship with Logan, up to that point, had been platonic, Val's feelings for him ran far deeper. She had never told Logan how she truly felt. Her hope had been the relationship she desired would have evolved on its own. It had not.

Larsen was aware of the persistent rumors regarding Spence's "friendship" with Benamure. Although that thought did not sit well with her, she also realized it was none of her business. What was gnawing at Valerie was the possibility Logan had lied to her and Beth about not being the father. That would be something she could never forgive nor forget. Val had to know the truth. And she had to know it that night.

"Logan, I'll contact the doctor's office Monday morning," said Beth Kaminski. "They'll be expecting her phone call."

"Thank you, Beth," was all he said.

Spence finished his drink and rubbed out the cigarette. He stood up to leave.

"I've got to be going."

"Why so soon, Logan?" asked a surprised Beth Kaminski.

"Circumstances," was his explanation.

Val Larsen jumped up from the table.

"I'll see you out, Logan." It was more a command than a courtesy.

Once outside, Val stopped. She looked at Logan.

"I heard about what happened today," she said.

Spence shook his head.

"I'm beginning to wish they'd just expelled me."

"I'm not talking about that. What you did at Bardsville was something special."

Spence frowned.

"Valerie, that's ancient history."

The couple stared at each other, in awkward silence. Larsen was the first to speak.

"Have you ever had sex with Glynn Benamure?"

Spence got annoyed.

"I don't see how that's any of your damn business!"

Val Larsen turned and started walking back towards the house. She was holding back tears.

"No!" he suddenly, volunteered.

Larsen stopped and turned.

"No, I've never had sex with Glynn, to answer your question," continued Spence.

"And why not?" asked Valerie, with a quivering defiance.

Logan paused a long moment, before answering.

312

"Because, when I thought I wanted to, she didn't. And when she thought she wanted to, I didn't. It's as simple as that."

"Then why are you putting your ass on the line for her?"

Logan Spence did not hesitate.

"Glynn is a close friend of mine! Besides, I'm the only one she knows who might be able to help her right now."

Without another word, Spence started the walk back to Cornwall.

As she re-entered her sister's house, Valerie's tears had disappeared. She was, once again, confident she had fallen in love with the right guy.

# CHAPTER SIXTY-ONE

Pete Ellison sat in his dorm room with the door ajar. Saturday nights were notorious for room checks by faculty members. With the door opened, he would be able to hear anyone climbing the stairs to the second floor. He was anxiously awaiting the return of his roommate, Logan Spence.

Suddenly, his worst fears became reality. He could hear the voices of Alan and Susan Tompkins, the faculty residents of Squire House, bidding all a good night. They were now climbing the stairs to the second floor.

"*Shit!*" he panicked.

Quickly, Ellison closed the door. He undressed and threw on a bath robe. Pete was now standing in the hallway, leaning against the now closed door. Alan and Susan Tompkins approached.

"Mr. Ellison, what are you doing standing out here in the hallway?" asked Alan Tompkins.

"Just standing, sir."

"Why?"

"I feel comfortable standing in the hallway, sir."

Alan Tompkins scrutinized the face of Pete Ellison. He now had questions.

"And where's Mr. Spence?"

"He's in the room, sir."

"Well, I suppose you'll have no objections if I pop my head into the room to wish him a good night."

"He's busy, sir."

Alan Tompkins' years of proctoring, at prep schools, told him something was awry.

"And what is Mr. Spence busily doing in the room?" he pressed, with suspicion now in his voice.

Pete Ellison looked at Alan Tompkins. He then looked at Susan Tompkins. Pete lowered his head. When he looked up Ellison, obliquely stared into space.

"He's masturbating."

"Oh, my word!" gasped Mrs. Tompkins, as she clasped both hands across her mouth.

Alan Tompkins immediately took charge of the situation, at hand. He, gently, put his arm around his wife.

"Susan, now don't be alarmed. Such behavior from a male adolescent Spence's age is to be expected. This is nothing unusual," he reassured his wife. "I think this concludes our evening rounds, dear."

Alan Tompkins then turned his attention to Pete Ellison.

"Mr. Ellison, I think it a good idea if you accompany us downstairs to the television room."

"I think you're right, sir."

As he settled into a chair, Pete watched the Tompkins' disappear inside their apartment. His mind was not focused on the television. Several minutes later, Ellison heard a tap on one of the room's windows. It was Spence.

*"Thank God!"*

After making sure the coast was clear, Ellison motioned Spence, inside. The two roommates quietly ascended the stairs towards their room. Ellison closed the door behind them.

"Is everything cool?" asked Logan Spence.

"Pretty much," replied Pete Ellison.

Logan looked at his roommate.

"What does 'pretty much' mean," he asked, with an instinct for trouble.

Pete Ellison related the events of earlier that evening in graphic detail.

"You told them what?!" demanded a now enraged Logan Spence. He started towards Ellison.

Pete had never seen the anger of Logan Spence. Instinctively, he held up both hands in self-defense and back-peddled.

"Logan, your instructions to me were to cover your ass! I did what I had to do!"

Immediately, Spence realized his roommate was right. He backed off. Logan walked across the room and stood in front of the window. He was, painfully, aware of the fact that Beth Kaminski's words of warning were already coming back to bite him in the ass.

Pete Ellison pulled a bottle of Dewar's from his closet. He looked at Logan.

"You want to join me?" he asked, hopefully.

As a general rule, Spence never drank scotch. That night, he made an exception.

The following morning Logan left a message for Glynn Benamure at her dorm's reception desk. She was to meet him, that afternoon, on the bleachers of the varsity football field. The pretense was to compare notes on the economics class they both attended.

Glynn was late. That was not like her. As Logan sat on the bleachers, he began to wonder if she had even gotten his message. Suddenly, Spence saw a girl approaching. It was Glynn's roommate.

Diane Wexford was a snooty little prep who fancied herself as being far more attractive than the open market would otherwise suggest. When she sat down on the bleacher bench, it was a prophylactic distance from Logan Spence.

"Do you have what I came for?" she asked, with imperial impatience.

Spence looked at Diane Wexford, with humorous disdain.

"Diane, I'm not sure I know exactly what made you come," he smiled.

Once she picked up on the double entente, the princess of primp became incensed.

"I can't believe Glynn jeopardized her wonderful relationship with Bradley for a vulgar little person like you!" she seethed.

Her obvious insinuation that Logan was responsible for Glynn's current circumstance fell on deaf ears.

Spence said nothing. He handed her a slip of paper, with all the necessary information.

Diane Wexford rose and started to walk. She came to a halt and turned.

"If Glynn has any questions, I assume she knows how to contact you, with *discretion?*"

Logan now looked at Diane Wexford with total indifference.

"If Glynn has any questions, I suggest she contacts Bradley Stevens, with *discretion,*" was all he said.

Benamure's roommate departed in a huff. Spence lit a cigarette. As he looked out across the empty football field, Logan realized his days at Cornwall were, most likely, numbered. It was a concern. However, his biggest fear was that Patricia White had already shut him out of her life. He started the walk back to his dorm.

Spence was surprised to see Carlos Acosta seated in the television room of Squire House.

"Carlos, what brings you to my humble hacienda?" he smiled.

Acosta stood up. He was in a somber mood. He looked at Spence.

"The seniors on the team held a meeting this afternoon to select next year's captain. You were our unanimous choice. The coaches then informed us that because of your probation you're not eligible. Another vote was taken and we all selected you, again. I just thought you should know that," he said, quietly.

Acosta started to leave.

"So, Carlos, who's next year's captain?" asked Logan.

Acosta glanced over his shoulder and shrugged.

"Who cares? The coaches are now going to make that decision."

# CHAPTER SIXTY-TWO

Logan Spence had been dreading Thursday afternoon. His scheduled tutorial with Patty White would be his first contact with her since the probation. He was assuming the worst.

"*Might as well just get this over with,*" he thought, and started the walk to Angelica Hall.

Spence paused at the four-way sidewalk intersection, where he had first met Glynn Benamure. For Logan, that chance encounter was now something out of a past life.

He entered the Angelica Hall administration building. Spence did not bother stopping at the reception desk, to be formally announced. The woman seated behind the desk picked up the phone. She knew who he was going to see. However, as the receptionist watched the dejected young man trudge the staircase, she gently placed the receiver back on its cradle.

Spence knocked on Patty White's closed door.

"Come in, Logan."

Spence entered the office and closed the door, behind him. He was surprised to see Patricia standing in front of the window and not seated behind her desk. Her back was towards him.

Truth be told, she had been anxiously waiting to see whether or not he was even going to show up that afternoon. Patty White was pleased, by his arrival. She turned and smiled.

"Sit down, Logan," she said, with a disarming ease that caught the young man by surprise.

Spence complied. Instead of assuming her usual seat behind the desk, Patty sat down in the chair next to Spence. She had never done that before. Logan's mind was now swimming in the uncertainty of unchartered waters.

"You didn't bring any study materials with you, today," she observed, indifferently.

"I haven't done much studying this week," he admitted.

Patty looked at Logan and smiled.

"Oh, I can understand *that*," she laughed, with an uncanny empathy.

Her amiable acceptance of his academic truancy only intensified Logan's uneasiness. He was now just waiting for the axe to fall.

Patty White's smile was quickly replaced by a disappointed frown.

*"Here it comes!"* thought Logan and braced for the guillotine.

"Logan Spence, you have not been completely honest with me!" she chided.

Suddenly, Logan was no longer uptight. He was now confused. The one thing he had always been with Patricia White was truthful. Spence's confusion quickly morphed into anger.

"I have no idea what the hell you're talking about!"

Patty shook her head and grinned.

"You told me that you're not a student-athlete. I don't think that's the truth. I was at Bardsville this past Saturday."

Her revelation surprised Logan. He knew Patty White was not into sports.

"And what were you doing at Bardsville?" he asked, with annoyance creeping into his voice.

"I was there to see you," she admitted, candidly.

Logan stared at Patricia but said nothing. Her eyes did not stray from his, as she continued.

"Logan, you made me very proud on Saturday. Do you know why?" she asked, in a soothing tone.

Spence shrugged. He had no clue what she was talking about.

"Because, I helped the team win?" he answered, lamely.

"No, that's not it."

Logan shook his head.

"Then, I have no idea."

Patricia looked at him with an expression he had never seen from her before.

"I'm proud of you for what you *didn't* do on Saturday," she explained.

Logan was now, completely, in the dark.

"Patricia, I don't understand where you're coming from."

"I'm talking about the fact you chose not to humiliate the Bardsville heavyweight by pinning him in front of his home crowd."

Spence was stunned! He found it hard to believe she knew he was toying with the idea of pinning Goliath during the end of their match. Not another soul in the Bardsville field house on that Saturday afternoon would have even guessed.

"You don't even know if I could have pinned him," he said, objectively.

"I know you could have! You know you could have! The fact you didn't, makes you a special person, as far as I'm concerned," she smiled.

Spence became uneasy. Logan was unfamiliar with people knowing him as well as Patricia did. He stood up to leave.

"Sit down, Logan! Our session is not over," instructed Patty White.

Spence sat down. He, defiantly, pulled a cigarette from his pocket.

"I do not permit smoking in my office," she admonished.

Logan ignored her words. He lit up.

Sensing his mood swing, Patty opened a desk drawer and placed an ashtray in front him. She then shifted gears.

"So, do you like her?" continued Patty White.

"To *whom* do you allude?" he asked, with an insolence that dated back to their initial tutorial on proper grammatical English.

Patty White's face flushed with anger. She felt like smacking Logan Spence across the mouth. She decided not to give him that satisfaction.

"I'm *alluding* to the young lady from Bardsville."

320

"They're a lot of young ladies from Bardsville," he said, with a smirk.

"I'm talking about the one you felt compelled to introduce yourself to in front of an entire school!" she reminded him.

The emotion in her voice betrayed hidden feelings she had for the young man.

This time, it was Spence who sensed a mood swing. He immediately extinguished the cigarette. Logan looked at Patty White.

"Patricia, anything I did that afternoon at Bardsville was done only to help my team win. After all, I'm a student-athlete," he laughed.

Patty White ignored his words.

"That girl likes you. She'll be in touch, if she hasn't been already."

Again, Spence was jarred by Patricia's seeming omniscience. Without another word, he stood up and started towards the door.

"Logan?"

Spence stopped and turned.

"Yes?"

"Do you have a girlfriend?" questioned Patricia White.

"No."

"Why not?" she asked, with gentle concern.

Spence stood in awkward silence, trying figure that one out, for himself. He looked at Patricia White.

"I guess it's just the way the cards are being dealt right now," he said, and closed the door behind him.

Patty rose from her chair. She walked to the window. The young teacher watched Logan Spence until he disappeared out of sight. As she had done most her life, Patricia White was now quietly crying, by herself.

# CHAPTER SIXTY-THREE

"Glynn Benamure has left Angelica Hall," was all she said.

Logan Spence looked at Valerie Larsen. They were sitting together on the varsity football bleachers. It was the first time either of them had mentioned Benamure's name since that fateful evening.

"What do you mean, left?" asked Logan.

"She dropped out," responded Valerie.

Spence hesitated before asking his next question. He looked Valerie in the eyes.

"Did she use the option I provided her?"

"Yes."

Logan Spence was perplexed.

"Then why did she drop out?"

This time it was Valerie who paused, before speaking.

"She probably didn't want to be around that jerk, Bradley Stevens," conjectured Larsen.

"I can understand that," agreed Logan.

Valerie Larsen diverted her eyes to the empty football field. Something else was on her mind. She was hesitant to speak her thoughts.

Spence sensed her emotional divide.

"Just say it, Valerie!"

Larsen returned her gaze, towards Spence.

"I think the real reason Glynn dropped out of Angelica Hall is because she never wants to see you again," she said, with a bluntness that stung.

Logan shook his head. He was now, totally, baffled.

"Why wouldn't she want to see me, again?"

Valerie Larsen looked at him with a quiet patience.

"Because Glynn is a woman."

Logan Spence needed no further clarification. He was quickly learning, that grappling with the heavyweights of the wrestling world was a far easier task than dealing with the emotions of beautiful girls.

Valerie Larsen stood up to leave. Logan also rose. As they walked off the football field, Spence suddenly stopped.

"What's wrong, Logan?" she asked.

Spence looked at her. And then, he stared at the ground. Uncharacteristically, Logan was unsure, of himself.

"I get off probation and bounds at the end of this term. I was thinking, maybe, we could go out together after that," he smiled.

Valerie shook her head.

"Logan, I don't know," she said, non-committedly.

Her tacit rejection immediately returned Logan Spence to the familiar turf of being a solo act.

"So, you have a boyfriend," he concluded.

"Yes, I do."

"Well, I don't want to interfere with that," he said and turned towards the future.

"Logan!"

He stopped.

"What?"

"Ask me."

"Ask you, what?"

"Ask me to go out with you."

Logan looked at her and began to laugh.

"Valerie, you already have a boyfriend. Let him ask you out."

Larsen walked up to Spence, within kissing distance.

"Ask me," she whispered.

Spence was now confused.

"Valerie, I don't want to cause any trouble between you and your boyfriend."

"Don't worry about that. I can handle him," she said, confidently.

"Ask me!"

Logan Spence looked into the face of Valerie Larsen. He liked what he saw.

"Valerie, will you go on a date with me?" he asked, with a vulnerable sincerity reserved for the very few.

Valerie stared back at Logan and smiled.

**"I'll think about it!"** she said and walked away, without another word.

As he watched her departure, Logan laughed. One of only two consolations about his probation that winter term at Cornwall had been his emerging friendship with Valerie Larsen. Although a day student at Angelica Hall, she had been spending more time on campus.

For Spence, Valerie's increased presence had, magically, filled a void created by Glynn Benamure's sudden absence. Ironically, Valerie was only the second girl Logan had ever met whose mind turned him on more than her body. Not so ironically, Larsen's body ran a very close second place.

Spence entered Cornwall's main building. He proceeded to the school kitchen. The terms of his probation required Logan to spend a specified number of hours on KP duty. Unexpectedly, the time spent in the school kitchen had been his second consolation about being placed on probation and bounds.

During that winter term, Spence had gotten to know the people who truly made the campus run. He was now on a first name basis with the kitchen staff, the maintenance crew, and the campus security guards. In an odd sort of way, Logan felt more comfortable with them than he did around his fellow classmates.

For their part, the employees of Cornwall Angelica Hall had gradually come to accept Logan Spence. They no longer viewed him as a "corn hole". He was now considered a friend. Spence was both liked and, more importantly, trusted by the employees of Cornwall Angelica Hall. On that particular campus, trust was a very rare commodity.

As they sat eating in the employee's dining room, the head of campus security suddenly stood up and approached Logan Spence.

Jerry Tasker was in his late twenties. Jerry was of medium height and build. Spence sensed a quiet intensity about him.

"I have an announcement to make," said Tasker, to the now attentive crowd.

He looked at Logan Spence with the friendly eyes of respect.

"Logan, you are now an honorary member of the Campus Key Club," he smiled and handed Spence a key. "It's the key to the kitchen. From now on, if you ever get hungry at any hour of the day or night the kitchen will always be open for you."

Jerry Tasker then looked at Logan Spence and winked.

"I should also tell you that this key happens to be a master."

Spence stared at Tasker and shrugged.

"What does that mean?"

"It means that besides the kitchen, you can open up pretty much any other door on campus," he smiled.

Logan thought for a moment.

"Jerry, what are you going to do if you catch me in a room I shouldn't be in?"

The head of campus security did not hesitate.

"I guess I'll have no choice but to look the other way," he laughed, to the approval of the other Cornwall Angelica Hall employees present that afternoon.

Everyone in the room knew Spence was on probation for not ratting out his friends. They also knew what that decision had cost him. They also knew that was the only reason he was now a trusted friend.

As he walked back to Squire House, Logan Spence found himself in a comparatively good mood. The fact that he was restricted to school bounds but could now roam the campus more freely than any Cornwall Angelica Hall faculty member, amused him.

# CHAPTER SIXTY-FOUR

It was the last Saturday of the winter term. The impending Monday was a holiday. The three-day weekend was a welcomed excuse for both students and faculty to render the campus of Cornwall Angelica Hall a ghost town. The following Tuesday was the start of the spring term and the end of Logan Spence's probation and bounds.

Spence sat alone in his room at Squire House. He was reading. It was late in the afternoon. There was an unexpected knock on the door.

"It's open."

Jerry Tasker, the head of campus security stood in the doorway.

"Logan, mind if I come in?"

Spence put his book down. He looked at Tasker and smiled.

"Jerry, have you already decided to revoke my membership as a Campus Key Club member?"

"No, nothing like that," he laughed.

The security chief immediately noticed the glass on the floor next to Logan's recliner.

"Spence, what are you drinking?"

"Vodka. You want some?"

The officer hesitated. Logan pulled a bottle of Absolut from underneath the recliner and tossed it to Jerry Tasker.

"The glasses are on the window sill and the ice is in the freezer."

"I think I will have a drink," decided the campus guard.

Jerry Tasker interested Spence. The man was, obviously, working a job that did not match his potential nor talent. Spence wanted to know, why.

"Jerry, what are you doing at Cornwall Angelica Hall?" he asked.

Tasker sipped his drink. He looked at Spence and shook his head.

"Logan, that's a long story."

"Jerry, I've got the rest of the weekend to kill."

Spence lit a cigarette and tossed the pack to the head of campus security.

"Logan, I've been trying to quit."

"Jerry, everyone is," laughed Spence.

Tasker stoked one.

"To answer your question, when I was a sophomore at Williams College, a co-ed approached me at a party. She started hitting on me heavy time. I wasn't interested."

"Why not?" asked Spence.

Tasker sipped his drink, in reminiscence. He looked at Logan.

"She was a nasty little bitch. That's why not!" Tasker angrily drained his drink.

"Jerry, have another," insisted Logan.

Tasker's annoyance disappeared.

"Logan, I don't want to drink you dry," he smiled.

The host looked at his guest.

"Jerry, that's one thing you'll never have to worry about," he said.

The head of campus security poured another cocktail and resumed.

"Anyway, she got so pissed off by my rejection, she went to her father and convinced him that I had tried to rape her. Turned out daddy was an associate dean at the school."

"So, Jerry, what happened after that?"

Tasker sat in silence. His mind was now conflicted with unpleasant memories. After a long pause, he continued.

"I was pressured into dropping out. No criminal charges were ever filed. I applied to other colleges. They all wanted to know why I dropped out of Williams. When they found out the reason, none of them wanted to risk an accused rapist being on their campus."

Tasker took a long pull of vodka. Without asking, he lit another cigarette and stared at Spence.

"After that, I enlisted in the army. I did one tour in Nam and then re-upped for another. I came home with two meaningless medals to pin on my resume. And here I am at Cornwall Angelica Hall. Does that answer your question, Spence?"

Logan stared at Tasker.

"Did you kill the bitch?" he asked, with an unemotional objectivity that caught the head of campus security off guard. He thought for a moment.

"Logan, I hate that girl far too much to even consider putting her out of the misery she calls a life."

The two friends broke into laughter. Although of different ages and backgrounds, they shared the cohesive bond of exile.

"Logan, the reason I stopped by was to invite you to a party, tonight."

"What kind of party?"

Tasker sipped his drink.

"It's an employee get together that has become a tradition on the Saturday night before the start of Spring Term."

"Where?" asked Spence.

"Where else?" he grinned. "Servants quarters."

"What time?"

Tasker polished off the rest of his vodka and stood up to leave.

"The party starts when you arrive and ends when you either get lucky or pass out," he replied, smiling.

"Sounds like my kind of affair," committed Logan Spence.

Jerry Tasker started towards the door. Suddenly, he stopped.

"Logan, I wasn't completely truthful with you earlier," he admitted.

Spence looked at the head of campus security and shook his head, not knowing what he was referring to.

"Talk to me, Jerry."

Tasker stared at Logan. He spoke, softly.

"If I thought I could off that bitch and walk cleanly, I would've done it years ago," he said and closed the door behind him.

Logan Spence sat in his recliner. He sipped the vodka and pondered Jerry Tasker's visit. His thoughts then drifted to his own current situation at Cornwall Angelica Hall. The words of Lewis Carroll popped into his head.

"Curiouser and curiouser!" he laughed and rose for another drink.

# CHAPTER SIXTY-FIVE

As Spence entered the employee dining room, the party was already in full swing. A DJ, backed by an impressive JBL sound system was spinning tunes for all tastes. A temporary bar had been installed on one side of the room. A buffet table lined the other side. Seeing the long chow line, Spence opted for the bar.

"What are you drinking tonight, Logan?" asked that evening's dispenser of the spirits.

"Absolut on the rocks."

The bartender scowled at Spence with feigned disdain.

"No rack rot for you, corn hole?"

"Not this evening, Charlie," smiled Logan.

The older man burst into laughter.

"Just so happens I managed to pilfer a bottle of Absolut from downstairs," he said and poured Logan's request.

Charlie was in charge of the kitchen staff. He appeared to be in his mid-sixties. He kind of looked like Popeye the Sailor, without the forearms. Charlie always had a Chesterfield tucked behind his right ear. Early on, he had taken Logan under his wing whenever Spence served time in the kitchen during that winter term's probation.

"If nothing else, you're going to learn a trade before you leave this place," he once told him. Charlie had been true to his word.

Logan Spence was now quite competent inside a commercial kitchen. He knew how to operate industrial stoves and ovens. He could accurately monitor commercial refrigerators and freezers. Logan was also adept at changing soda canisters for the dispensers. But, most importantly, Spence had mastered the mammoth dish washer.

"Washing dishes and silverware isn't a job, it's an art," tutored Charlie.

Spence sipped his drink and watched the buffet line dwindle.

"Charlie, I'm going to grab something to eat."

"I'll be here," said the man standing behind the bar.

Although not particularly hungry, Spence realized he had to eat something. Logan picked up a plate and started down the buffet table. Immediately, he noticed the quality of food being served that evening. Not surprisingly, it was far superior to the mess hall crap that the very same people dished out daily to the faculty and students of Cornwall Angelica Hall.

"Logan, sit with us," insisted Jerry Tasker.

Spence took a seat. As he began to eat, the music suddenly stopped. An eerie silence enveloped the room. The unexpected arrival of an uninvited guest had quelled the festive mood.

Patty White stood in the doorway.

No one was more surprised than Logan Spence. As he stared at her, Patricia had never looked more radiant. She was casually dressed in tight fitting jeans, heels, and a pull-over beige cashmere sweater. Patty wore no make-up. Cosmetics would have served no purpose other than to mask her natural beauty.

Instinctively, Logan Spence stood up.

"You're late," he improvised.

"I thought I'd keep you guessing," she grinned, impishly.

A person seated at Spence's table looked at the employee next to him.

"Who the hell is she?" he whispered.

"A faculty member," was the woman's discreet response.

"She don't look like any teacher I ever had!"

Logan Spence addressed the now hushed room.

"Patricia is a friend of mine."

That was all the employees of Cornwall Angelica Hall had to hear. Without further prompting, the crowd kicked back into party gear. Logan approached Patty.

"What are you drinking tonight?" was his only question, as he guided her towards the bar.

332

Patty White looked at Logan Spence. She was feeling a rare ease about just being, herself.

"What are you dinking tonight?" she asked.

"Vodka."

"Then that's what I'm drinking," she said, without hesitation.

Logan looked at her and laughed.

"What are you finding so amusing?" demanded Patty White, with a sudden brusqueness.

"I'm surprised, that's all. I pegged you for a wine sipping kind of girl."

Patty White looked at Logan Spence. Her annoyance had vanished.

"I'm full of surprises," she smiled.

"Charlie, two Absolut on the rocks."

"Coming right up."

"Logan, I want to talk to you," confided Patty.

With drinks in hand, the couple found a quiet corner of the room.

"I received your second set of test results," she said.

Spence shrugged, with disinterest, and stared at her.

"Do those results help your academic career?" he asked.

"To hell with my academic career!" she hissed.

Patty White knew Spence's current mind set. The permanent blot of probation on a school transcript was a very difficult thing to override when it came to college admittance and scholarship. She was there that evening to persuade Logan not to give up, on himself, or a collegiate future.

"Logan, I have contacts at several very good colleges. I'll use those contacts for you."

Spence looked at her.

"Are you hungry?" he asked, ignoring the words she had just spoken.

The young teacher realized her favorite student was not listening.

"No!"

Impressively, Patty White downed the rest of her drink in one gulp. She slammed the emptied glass on a table and stalked the exit.

Even more impressively, Logan Spence put down his drink, without finishing it, to follow her.

"Patricia, I'll see you back to your apartment."

The two walked in silence. Spence was the first to speak.

"So, where's your boyfriend tonight?"

"Which one?" she responded, with a cold sarcasm that hinted at loneliness.

"Wilkerson," continued Spence.

Patty made a dismissive gesture with the wave of her hand.

"That guy has been wanting to get down my pants since the first day I got here."

Her choice of words startled Spence. However, they also let him know Patricia trusted him. And where there is trust, there is usually friendship. Logan could not have asked for anything more than that!

"So has he?" persisted Spence.

"Has he what?"

"Gotten down your pants?"

Patty White stopped. She glared at Spence.

"That's none of your damn business!"

Again, they walked in silence for several minutes. Patty was the first to re-engage conversation.

"Do you think he has?" she asked.

"Do I think he has what?" replied Logan.

"Gotten down my pants?"

Spence answered her question, without hesitation.

"No."

"And what makes you so sure of that?" she questioned, smugly.

This time it was Logan Spence who stopped. He looked at her with the calm confidence of love.

"Because, Patricia, I don't think you've let a guy down your pants in a very long time."

Now, it was Patty White who was reeling. The funny thing was the young man's uncanny insight did not disquiet her. In some strange way, it actually gave Patty an unexpected reassurance about, herself.

They stood in front of her dorm.

"I guess I'll say goodnight," smiled Logan and turned to leave.

As she watched him start to walk away, the all too familiar feeling of emptiness began to engulf her. Patricia White made her decision.

"Where are you off to?" she asked, casually.

Spence stopped to look at her.

"Back to the party."

Her face frowned its disapproval.

"Logan Spence, a gentleman always escorts a lady to her door!" she admonished.

They entered the building and rode the elevator to her floor.

"We're at your door. May I now return to the party without you considering me less than a gentleman?" laughed Logan.

She paid no attention to his words and unlocked the apartment.

"Why don't you come in for a night-cap?"

It was more a directive than an invitation. However, it was a directive Logan Spence had no thoughts of disobeying.

# CHAPTER SIXTY-SIX

Patty had a one-bedroom apartment. The kitchen was small but the living room of comfortable size. What Spence found most appealing about the place was a tiny outside terrace that overlooked campus woods.

"Logan, I have red or white," she offered.

Spence looked at her and smiled.

"I knew you were a wine sipping kind of girl."

Patty White ignored his remark.

"Red or White?" she insisted.

"Patricia, I'm not much of a wine drinker."

She opened the door to the refrigerator.

"I have Diet Pepsi," she dead-panned.

"I'll pass, thank you."

Patricia then grinned at him, mischievously.

"Logan, forgive me. I nearly forgot."

She opened the freezer door and pulled out a bottle of Stoli.

"I know it's not your label, but you'll just have to suffer this evening!" she laughed.

Spence stood staring at her with bemused fascination. Patty White returned his gaze.

"I told you. I'm full of surprises." She was no longer laughing.

With drinks in hand, they walked into the living room.

"Please, make yourself comfortable," she smiled, warmly.

Spence looked towards the sliding door of the little terrace.

"Do you mind if we sit out there?"

"Logan, it's a little chilly, don't you think?"

"If you get too cold we'll come back in, okay?"

She looked at him, affectionately.

"Okay."

They sat down next to one another on a small outdoor sofa. Immediately, Patty White resumed their earlier evening's conversation.

"Logan, I will not allow you to let the probation interfere with your studies and college aspirations. You've come too far."

She sipped her wine and continued.

"As I've told you, when it comes gaining admittance to top tier colleges here in the Northeast, I have a number of connections."

Before Spence could respond, there was a sudden loud banging on the apartment's front door. Patty looked at Logan and shrugged.

"I have absolutely no idea who that could be."

"I'll find out," volunteered Spence.

"No! You wait here," she instructed. "Whoever it is, I'll get rid of."

Patty disappeared into the living room. Logan lit a cigarette and sipped the Stoli. After several minutes, he began to hear voices coming from the inside room. Those voices quickly escalated into shouts of argument. Spence flicked the cigarette over the railing and stood up.

Logan re-entered the living room just in time to see a drunken Tom Wilkerson slap Patty White across the face. Without a blink of thought, he was in motion. Logan paused in front of Patricia. There were no marks on her face. There were no tears in her eyes. Spence turned his attention towards revenge.

As he started towards Wilkerson, his advance was suddenly halted by the light touch of Patty White's hand on his forearm.

"Logan, let me handle this my way," she said, with a surprising calmness in her voice.

Logan looked at her but continued in the direction of Wilkerson. Patty's grip on Spence's arm tightened.

"Logan, go back out to the terrace. I'll join you there."

Spence was intent on punishing Wilkerson. Patty's nails started to dig into his forearm.

"Logan, please, do it for me!" she pleaded. Now, there were tears in her eyes.

Patty White knew what Spence was capable of doing to Tom Wilkerson. At that moment in time, her only concern was protecting Logan, from himself.

Spence stared long and hard at Wilkerson. With extreme reluctance, the young man turned towards the door of the terrace. Logan sat down on the outside couch. He drained the rest of his drink and lit a smoke. Within moments, Patricia was seated by his side.

"Thank you," was all she said.

Spence remained silent.

"Logan, do you understand that no matter how much you hurt Tom Wilkerson tonight you would've been hurting your future even more?"

Spence said nothing. Patty White sighed.

"Anyway, that jerk is gone."

Suddenly, Logan stood up. He looked at Patricia White.

"I think it's time I go, too."

Patty rose from the couch and smiled at him. She gently clasped both her arms around his neck and pulled his mouth towards hers.

"Not tonight," she whispered.

# CHAPTER SIXTY-SEVEN

Patty awoke the next morning. She was both surprised and disappointed Logan was no longer by her side. Quickly, she got out of bed and wrapped a bath robe around, herself. Patty entered the kitchen and surveyed the small apartment. He was not there. She was crushed.

A sudden movement from the terrace caught her eye. Logan was seated on the outside couch. Patty opened the terrace door to an unusually warm spring morning. He immediately rose to greet her. They kissed with a spontaneous ease that delighted the young woman. The emptiness that had plagued Patricia White her entire life was suddenly gone.

"Logan, what are you doing out here?" she asked.

"Thinking."

"About what?"

"You," he laughed and kissed her, again.

The two settled themselves on the couch.

"Logan, I'm going to make coffee. Would you like some?"

"No, thank you."

"Why not?"

"Because, I don't drink coffee."

Patty thought for a moment.

"I have orange juice," she offered, eagerly.

Logan Spence gazed upon the most beautiful face he had ever seen.

"Orange juice would be nice," he smiled.

As he watched her disappear inside, Spence found himself thinking about the vodka in the freezer.

"*A Screwdriver would taste real good,*" he mused and lit a cigarette.

A short time later, Patty returned to the terrace. She carried a small tray that had a carafe of orange juice and two ice-filled glasses in one hand and the bottle of Stoli in the other. Patty placed the items on the table and re-seated herself next to Logan.

Spence looked at the bottle of vodka and then at Patty.

"It's a little early for me," he claimed, with a straight face.

Why don't I believe that!" she said and stared at him until he grinned.

"You're something else!" laughed Logan.

Spence suddenly remembered something.

"Patricia, where's your coffee?"

She looked at him and smiled.

"I've decided this isn't a coffee kind of morning," she explained.

They poured drinks and sat back to enjoy the warm spring morning and one another's company. Theirs was an effortless relationship. Conversation flowed with a natural ease. Even more importantly, they were equally as comfortable during pockets of silence.

At one point, Logan thought of telling Patty about his business activities. However, seeing the newly found happiness in her face, he decided against it. Instead, he steered the conversation towards a more immediate concern.

"Do you think Wilkerson is going to cause any trouble for you?" he asked.

She looked at him with an expression of surprise.

"Why would he do that?"

"A woman scorned kind of thing" he replied.

Patty White broke into laughter.

"Logan, Tom's a lot of things, but a woman is obviously not one of those things!"

"He is as far as I'm concerned," he said, with disgust in his voice. "I still don't get why you didn't let me …."

She quickly stifled the rest of Logan's question by planting a kiss on his lips. Spence immediately understood her unspoken request. He complied. She looked at him with eyes he had never seen from her before.

"Logan, try to accept the fact that no matter how much you might have hurt Wilkerson last night you would have been hurting yourself even more; *us* more. As it stands now, what can he possibly say? That he barged into my apartment? That he abused me? That the student I'm held accountable for tried to physically come to my defense? No, he can't say squat!"

Logan listened to her words of reason. However, he still wanted to kick the crap out of Tom Wilkerson. Patty, instantly, picked-up on his frustration. She shifted gears.

"I'm famished! Logan, are you hungry?"

Although he looked at her, his mind was now other places.

"I can eat," he said, without enthusiasm.

"Good!"

Patty took him by the hand and led them into the kitchen. As she leaned over to peer into the refrigerator, Spence re-focused his attention on her lovely heart-shape. She came up empty.

"I'm afraid there's not a lot to eat in there," she said, apologetically.

Logan closed the door to the refrigerator. He gently put his hand on her back and started Patty towards the bedroom.

"We'll just have to improvise," he smiled.

She suddenly stopped and looked over her shoulder.

"Logan Spence!" she chided, with the pretense of outrage.

As he continued to guide her into the bedroom, Patty offered no resistance.

# CHAPTER SIXTY-EIGHT

Patricia White turned onto her side. She propped an elbow to cradle her head. Patty stared at Logan.

"I've broken every rule in the book," she said, wistfully. However, there was not a trace of remorse in her voice.

Spence sat up in bed. He looked at the woman he had adored from the moment he set eyes on her.

"That depends upon how you interpret the book you're reading," he smiled. "Or, at least, that's what you've taught me."

Patty White bolted upright. She glared at Logan Spence. She was angry.

"What I was conveying to you then was only fiction, not real life!"

"Explain the nuance between the two when I get back," he instructed, with a wink.

Logan swung his legs out of bed and on to the floor. He began to put on his jeans.

"Where are you going?" she asked in a suddenly, quivering voice.

"Just out for a cigarette and to get another drink," he explained.

Tears began to roll down Patty's face. Logan became ill at ease.

"Patricia, what's wrong?" he asked, with confused concern.

Without another word, she lied back down on the bed facing the wall. She began to quietly cry, to herself. Spence forgot about the cigarette and drink. He gently eased himself back into bed and curled up next to her. Logan was as close to tears, as he could remember. No words were spoken until Patty ended the silence. She rolled over to face him.

"I've betrayed a promise I made to myself," was all she said.

"And what promise was that, Patricia?" he asked.

She looked at him with bleary eyes.

"I promised myself that I would never need anyone more than me," she confessed. "That's no longer true. You've made me break my own promise," she said and started to cry, again.

Logan looked at Patty and smiled, serenely.

"What are you finding so humorous?" she sniffled.

"You," he said, softly.

"Why?"

Logan did not, immediately, answer her question. Instead, he paused to appreciate the woman he loved, so much.

"Patricia, you're shedding needless tears," were his only words.

"What's that supposed to mean?" she asked, with a welcomed defiance starting to creep back into her voice.

"It means that I need you as much as you need me. In fact, I probably need you more than you need me. What I'm saying is you haven't broken that promise you made to yourself," he said, quietly.

She stared at him, in silence. Patty was no longer crying. Logan studied her face.

"I'm hungry. Do you want to go out and get something to eat?" he invited and stood up to dress.

Patty White grabbed the arm of Logan Spence and yanked him back to a seated position on the bed. She stared at him with reproach.

"Logan, it's a Sunday evening on a three-day weekend. There's nothing open on campus," she reminded him.

Spence looked at her and smiled.

"Then, we'll just have to improvise, again," he laughed.

Patty quickly shook her head. She was now annoyed.

"Logan, your probation doesn't end until Tuesday. If you think I'm letting you off campus before then, you're sadly mistaken!"

"And what are you going to do to me if I try?" he teased.

She glowered with a vehemence that only love can provoke.

"*Anything* I have to!" she said, with commitment.

The irony of the situation was Logan Spence knew that the beautiful post-grad from New Haven would back up her threat. It made him adore her, even more.

"Okay, we'll eat on campus," he conceded.

"Where?" she asked, skeptically. "Some vending machine?"

Logan did not answer. Patricia White rose from the bed. She stood in front of him, unabashedly, displaying the full splendor of her nakedness. She took him by the hand.

"Come on, let's take a shower," she smiled.

Patty led him into the bathroom. After turning on the spigots, she picked up a toothbrush and tooth paste. Patty ushered Logan inside the now steam filled cubicle.

"So, where are you taking me tonight?" she asked, with a grin on her face and Aquafresh on her breath.

"The Key Club," he answered.

"The what?"

"It's a place on campus that I just found out about," he said.

"I've never heard of it."

"That's because you're not a member. But I'll get you in as my guest," he laughed.

Patty suddenly dunked her head under the stream of water.

"What are you doing?" he asked, with the impatience of already knowing the answer to his question.

"Washing my hair."

"And how long is that going to take?"

344

"Not too long," she promised.

Logan shook his head. He stepped out of the shower and grabbed a towel.

"Patricia, I'm going back to my room."

"Why?"

"To change. I've been in the same clothes for two days. I'll come back for you."

"Logan, you don't have to do that. I'll meet you at Squire House."

Spence thought for a moment.

"No, I'll come back and get you."

"Logan, I can take care of myself," she bristled.

"Like you did last night?" he asked, cynically.

"I got rid of him, didn't I?"

Spence chose not to challenge her. She gently kissed him on the lips.

"Besides, I know you'll be close by to protect me if I need it," she smiled.

Spence started the walk back to his dorm. He reached into his jacket pocket for a cigarette. He was out of smokes. Logan hastened his pace. The campus was deserted. He entered Squire House and climbed the stairs to his room. Spence sat down on his recliner and opened Pandora's Box. He pulled a pack of smokes and a bottle of Absolut. Logan then crossed the room to retrieve a glass and ice from the mini fridge. He poured a drink and lit a cigarette. He returned the bottle to its hiding place. He picked up a plastic packet.

*"No, I'm not doing that tonight,"* he decided and tossed it back into the secret cache and closed its panel.

Spence dressed, quickly. His intent was to get back to Angelica Hall in time to escort Patricia. As he exited Squire House, Logan was surprised to see Patty already waiting for him.

"I told you I wouldn't take too long," she grinned.

Logan looked at her and shook his head.

"You weren't kidding when you told me that you're full of surprises," he laughed and took her by the hand. They started to walk.

"So, where are we eating tonight?" asked Patty.

"I already told you. The Key Club," he answered.

"And what do they serve there?"

"Whatever you're in the mood for."

Patty White thought for a moment.

"I'm in the mood for steak."

"And how do you like your steak cooked?" inquired Spence.

"I like it medium rare. And while they're at it, I'll have onion rings and creamed spinach!" she ordered, with glee. "And a vintage bottle of red wine!"

"Coming right up," was all Logan Spence said.

In Patty White's mind, her dinner order was mere fantasy. She knew no Key Club even existed. However, she also knew that for the first time in her life she was with someone that she loved and felt safe with. For Patty, that was all the sustenance she needed.

"We're here," informed Spence, as he unlocked the back door to the Cornwall kitchen.

"Logan, what the hell are you doing?" she demanded.

"I'm opening the door, Professor."

"I'm not a Professor!" she objected, defiantly.

"Well, you will be one day," he said and spanked her ass inside the building.

Spence turned on the auxiliary lights to the kitchen. He then guided Patty to a door. He unlocked and opened it. Spence flicked the light switch.

"Go down there," he instructed.

"And what's down there?" she asked, with trepidation.

"Your vintage bottle of red. It's the faculty wine cellar."

"I didn't even know this place existed," she admitted.

346

"Well, you do now. Go pick out the bottles of your choosing," was all he said and turned to comply with her dinner request.

Logan ignited a gas grill and fryer. He then walked into a deep freezer to retrieve Patricia's food order. Spence emerged with a sirloin, onion rings, and a Stouffer's spinach soufflé. He punched the buttons on a microwave.

Patty White was mesmerized by the vast array of wine racks. She was fascinated by the labels and vintages. After finally selecting two bottles, she started up the staircase. As she reached the top of the stairwell, Patty was greeted by the head of campus security. She panicked.

"Ms. White, might I inquire what you're doing here tonight?" he asked, with a smile on his face and the resonance of law enforcement in his tone.

Patty was frozen with fear. She stood, silently, realizing that her academic career was now a thing of the past. Before she could respond, a voice of rescue intervened.

"Jerry, you're just in time to join us for dinner!"

Jerry Tasker turned to face the voice. Suddenly, he became awkward.

"Logan, I didn't realize it was you in here," he explained, apologetically.

"Well, it is. Now, are you going to be eating with us or not?" asked Spence, with a nonchalance that only intensified Patty White's consternation.

He eyed the couple.

"Ah, no. I've already eaten," responded the enforcer of the law.

Jerry Tasker looked at Spence.

"Logan, may I have a word with you?" he asked and nodded, discreetly, for space from the faculty member.

"Jerry, whatever you have to say to me you can say in front of her."

"Okay, just clean up and lock up before you leave."

"Done," was Spence's response.

The head of campus security turned towards Patty.

"It was nice seeing you again, Ms. White," he smiled and disappeared.

Patty remained a statue holding two bottles of wine.

"Shit! The steak is burning!" hissed Logan Spence and bolted towards the kitchen.

Patty followed him. She was still shell-shocked. Spence was busily finishing dinner. Patty placed the two bottles of wine on a counter.

"Logan, I just want to go home," she said, quietly.

Spence looked over his shoulder.

"You're not hungry?" he asked, with surprise.

"No."

Spence finished cooking and bagged the food to go. He cleaned the kitchen. Logan was mindful not to forget the two bottles of wine Patty had selected. He closed the auxiliary lights and locked the kitchen door.

The couple walked back to Angelica Hall in silence. Once inside the apartment, Patty made a beeline for the bedroom and slammed the door. Spence placed the bags of food on a counter. He went to the freezer and retrieved the Stoli. Spence poured a drink and retreated to the tiny terrace for a smoke.

*"Girls!"* he thought, with benign bemusement.

At length, the terrace light went on. Patty walked outside and sat down next to Logan. She was wearing only a bathrobe in the chilly spring night air.

"So, how screwed are we?" she asked, resignedly.

"We're not", he answered, with a surprising easiness in his voice that only vexed the young teacher even more.

"How can you be so sure?" she demanded.

Spence stared into her eyes.

"Because, Jerry is a friend of mine," he said.

Patty White returned his gaze and shook her head, dismissively.

"Logan, let me tell you something. Even the ones you consider friends can turn on a dime if the circumstance warrants it," she lectured.

Spence smiled.

"Not Jerry," he reassured her.

"And how do you know that?" she asked, with skepticism.

Spence polished his drink and stubbed the cigarette.

"Because, Jerry is the one who gave me the key to the Cornwall kitchen," he shrugged.

Patty White went slack-jawed. Logan looked at her and laughed.

"Patricia, you're not the only one full of surprises!"

The couple sat in silence for several minutes. Logan Spence made up his mind. He removed the necklace Sensei Tanaka had given him from around his neck and handed it to Patty.

"Patricia, I want you to have this," he said.

Patty was struck by both the beauty and obvious value of the piece.

"Logan, where did you get this?" she asked, with the uncertainty of fascination.

Spence ignored her question.

"It signifies quiet strength," he continued.

"Logan, I can't possibly accept this," she demurred and handed the necklace back to Spence.

"Stand up," he said, quietly.

The couple rose from the terrace sofa. With her back facing him, Logan gently clasped the necklace around Patty's neck. She turned to face him. The young woman was now trembling with a strange, intuitive feeling of foreboding.

"I love you, Logan," she said, softly.

Patty nestled her head against the chest of Logan Spence. She was crying.

# CHAPTER SIXTY-NINE

"So, who is he?" asked Chester White, with growing anger.

"Some student," replied Paul "Bounty" Hunter.

"When did you find out?" persisted an annoyed Chester White.

"I got the call from Junior about twenty minutes ago," replied Hunter.

White shook his head in disgust.

"These asshole kids never learn!" he fumed.

The two were in Hunter's car traveling to Carver's Bar and Grill. They had just found out that someone was selling coke on *their* turf. In the business of illegal drugs, that was the most heinous of crimes. White and Hunter were on their way to ensure that justice would be served.

"So, how long has this jerk been dealing at Carver's?" asked Chester White.

Paul Hunter kept his eyes on the road.

"Chet, I don't know. Ask Junior when we get there."

They pulled into the parking lot of Carver's Bar and Grill. The cars present indicated a brisk evening's business. They entered through the back entrance of the kitchen. The employees did not question their presence, as the two men walked towards the door leading to the barroom.

The place was jammed and cranking. Queen's hit single "Another One Bites The Dust" was pulsating from the jukebox. The two enforcers of street law stood at the server's end of the bar. Without prompting, one of the bartenders approached them.

"The usual, gentlemen?" she asked, knowingly, and began to prepare their drinks without waiting for a response.

The barmaid secured a metallic tumbler and filled it with ice. She placed it in front of Chester White. The young lady then turned around and bent over to intentionally showcase 20/20 hindsight, as she retrieved an unopened bottle of Jack Daniels from a lower cabinet.

"Here you go, Mr. White," she smiled. The young woman then poured a double Boodles for Paul "Bounty" Hunter.

"Will that be all, gentlemen?" she asked, teasingly.

"For now," dismissed Chester White.

Chester broke the seal to the bottle of Jack Daniels and melted ice. He took a long pull. He surveyed the packed barroom. White then stared at Hunter.

"So, which one is he?" he demanded.

Paul Hunter calmly sipped his gin before responding.

"Chet, I don't know. But he's here tonight."

Chester White yanked an ashtray and lit a Lucky Strike. Several moments later, a figure emerged from a door located behind the bar. He stopped to pour a drink and then made his way towards White and Hunter.

Johnny "Junior" Westfield was no longer the manager of Carver's Bar and Grill. He now owned it. His father, "Big John" Westfield had ceded that establishment and numerous other property holdings to his son and retired to Florida. Junior now walked with the swagger of finally being his own man.

"How are you, Chet?" he asked, already knowing the answer to his question.

"Not good," growled White and swallowed from the tumbler.

Although Johnny Westfield and Chester White had known one another since elementary school, Westfield had never considered White a true friend. That was because he had always been afraid of him. That evening was no exception. However, Johnny savored the revenue being generated by Chester's illegal drug trafficking business. He did not want to jeopardize that profitable relationship.

Chester White swilled the remainder of his Jack Daniels and stared at Westfield.

"So, Johnny, when did you figure out someone was dealing product on my turf?" he asked, with a quiet menace in his voice.

Junior Westfield drank from his glass before answering the question.

"Chet, I wasn't totally sure until this evening", he explained, defensively.

Chester White poured more Jack Daniels. He looked at Westfield.

"And what convinced you tonight?" he interrogated, with the intensity of a district attorney.

Junior Westfield was now nervous. He knew that Chester White would suspect him of double dealing. He downed the remainder of his cocktail and mustered the courage to look him in the eye.

"Chet, if I was working both sides of the street why would I have placed the call to Paul?"

Chester White ignored Westfield's words of self-preservation.

"You didn't answer my question. Why tonight?"

Johnny Westfield paused, before responding.

"Repeat offenders," he explained, with anxiety seeping into his voice.

"What's that supposed to mean?" demanded Chester White.

Johnny Westfield was scared. He began to stutter.

"It means that the same pa pa people are seeing the same per per person for the sa sa same reason, cocaine!" he stammered.

Chester White looked at the owner of Carver's Bar and Grill and smiled. He was now convinced Junior was not on the take from the newest dealer in town. His demeanor softened.

"So, where is he?" he asked.

Johnny Westfield poured himself another drink, for re-enforcement, before answering the question. He gulped half of it.

"He's over there," and pointed to a young man busily annihilating aliens on a video machine.

"Who is he?" questioned Chester White.

Johnny Westfield downed the rest of his drink.

"His name is Glenn Jenkins," he said.

Chester White eyed his latest competition in the world of selling blow. He was not impressed.

"Tell me about him."

Westfield looked at his inquisitor and shrugged.

"Chet, there's not much to tell. It's my understanding that up until till until recently, Jenkins was a low-level pot dealer peddling inferior weed. All of a sudden he's selling primo coke," shrugged Junior.

Chester White eyed Westfield.

"And how do you know it's primo product?" he demanded.

Westfield went to pour yet another cocktail. White suddenly grabbed Junior's forearm and slammed it on the bar. He stared at him with a face full of malevolence.

"You didn't answer my question!"

Westfield was now visibly rattled. He was shaking.

"Stre stre street noise," he confessed.

Chester White stared at Westfield. He was satisfied with the answer and released the forearm. Junior immediately poured more scotch into his glass. This time he did not bother with ice or mixer.

White thought for a moment. He looked at Westfield.

"Do you know who's supplying Jenkins with the coke?"

Junior sipped his scotch and made an attempt to compose himself.

"There was a kid in here once. I'd never seen him before. He and Jenkins sat together at that booth over there," motioned Westfield. "Anyway, after a while they went outside and then came back in. It looked to me like a drug deal going down. In fact, I called Paul that very night."

Paul "Bounty" Hunter shifted, nervously, on his feet. Chester White remained silent. He was contemplating his next move. Johnny Westfield downed his third cocktail. He looked at Chester White. He was now smiling and feeling looser.

"So, Chet, are you going to introduce yourself to Glenn Jenkins tonight?" he laughed.

Chester White stared at Westfield.

"Not tonight," he scowled. "But, the next time you see that other kid in here call me immediately. Junior, do you understand?"

Ye ye yes sir!"

# CHAPTER SEVENTY

"So, Paul, why didn't you tell me when Junior called the first time about Glenn Jenkins?" asked Chester White, in a surprisingly even tone of voice.

They had just left Carver's Bar and Grill and were driving back to White's warehouse. As always, Hunter was behind the wheel. He paused, before answering the question.

"Chet, at the time I didn't think it was worth mentioning to you. After Junior's phone call, I checked with the guys who handle the drops at Carver's. They reassured me that nothing was going down there that might threaten our business. So, I let it go. Besides, Junior said tonight that it wasn't until recently Jenkins started dealing coke," he explained.

Chester White stared at Paul Hunter, in silence.

"It's not *our* business! It's **my** business!" he seethed.

Not another word was spoken until they came to a stop in front of Chester's commercial building. White opened the passenger door and started to get out of the car. Paul Hunter looked at him.

"Chet, I'm sorry if you think I screwed up," he apologized. "It's just that I thought I had all bases covered."

Chester White stood outside the car and stared back at Paul Hunter with an inscrutable expression on his face.

"In this business, all bases are **never** covered!" he hissed and slammed the door shut. Hunter drove away wondering if he still had a job.

Chester White entered the building. He walked past a night guard who had just started to actively monitor the security screens on his desk.

"Good evening, Mr. White."

Chester did not acknowledge the man's presence, as he started up the stairs to his second-floor office. White unlocked the door and entered. He was quick to lock it behind him. Chester sat down at his desk and opened a drawer. He extracted a small ceramic box, mirror, and a sterling silver straw. Chester White had become a coke freak. The drug only inflamed an already combustible personality. After snorting his addiction, Chester sat back in the chair and plotted his next course of action.

Suddenly, he heard the lock to the office door being opened. Chester swiveled the desk chair and stood up. He had not been expecting anyone. Without hesitation, White pulled his knife to punish the uninvited intruder.

"Hello, Chet," smiled Kyle Overton.

Chester White did not relax.

"What the hell are you doing here tonight?" he asked, with knife still drawn.

Kyle Overton ignored the question. He casually made his way to the office bar and poured a drink. He turned to face Chester White, before sipping his glass.

"Will you be joining me this evening?" he asked.

"Of course," acknowledged White and pocketed the weapon.

Without needing instruction, Overton grabbed a glass, some ice, and poured a generous amount of Jack Daniels. He then carried both glasses to the office side table and sat down. Chester White joined him.

"To us," grinned Kyle and hoisted his drink.

Although Chester White raised his glass to toast, he was out of sorts with his friend's unannounced appearance.

"Why are you here tonight, Kyle?"

Overton sipped his cocktail and smiled at Chester White.

"Because, you need me tonight," he laughed.

"And why do you think that?" asked Chester, with growing annoyance.

Once again, Kyle Overton brushed off Chester White's question.

"Chet, may I bum a smoke?"

Chester White pulled a pack of Lucky Strikes from his pocket and tossed it on the table.

"And why do you think I need you tonight?" persisted White.

Overton blew a plume of blue and laughed.

"Because, you're smart enough to realize there's a new kid in town threatening everything you've built here," he said and looked around the office, in admiration.

Under normal circumstances, Chester White would have already dispatched with an uninvited guest. However, Kyle Overton had been Chester's best friend for as long as he could remember. He had no choice but to cut him some slack.

"I thought you'd have already relocated to, what did you call it? Silicon Valley," challenged Chester White, bitterly.

Kyle Overton laughed. He drained his drink and stood up for a refill. He walked to the office bar and looked over his shoulder.

"IBM corporate bullshit," he dismissed. "As soon as I've completed my latest project in Armonk, I'm bound for the West Coast!" boasted Overton.

Chester White remained seated in sullen silence. Kyle Overton returned to the table and sat down. He stared at his friend. Overton now felt a rare command of situation. It was that bravado that prompted his next question.

"So, Chet, why don't you simply off that bitch who calls herself your wife and move back into the house you bought instead of sleeping here every night?" he asked, with too much swagger in his voice.

Chester White's mood shifted. He stared at Overton with an unnerving expression.

"I've already told you. If I thought I could, I would," he said, and glared across the table at the uninvited guest.

Overton became nervous. Kyle was all too familiar with Chester's mood swings. He quickly changed the topic of conversation.

"Chet, I think I might know who's trying to take over your drug territory," he said, with a defensive smile.

357

Chester White sipped his drink and looked at Kyle.

"Tell me what you know!" he demanded in a low, guttural tone of voice.

Kyle knew he had crossed that dangerous threshold. He gamely tried to maintain the appearance of aplomb.

"Chet, it's the Delfino brothers who are muscling in on your cocaine operation," he said, measuredly.

This time, it was Chester White who stood up and headed to the bar. He did not return to the table.

"What makes you so sure of that?" asked White, spewing quiet toxin.

Kyle Overton shifted, nervously, in the chair.

"Because Angelo Defino is bragging on the street that he has turned you into a little paper boy delivering yesterday's news," winced Overton and rose to leave. Kyle closed the door behind him.

Chester White stood alone in his office. He had not been surprised by Overton's words. Chester had also heard the street talk. His coke ravished mind was now filled with nothing but anger and thoughts of revenge. He grabbed the bottle of Jack Daniels and sat down at his desk. He opened a drawer and drew new lines of attack.

"Guinea bastard!" he snorted, to himself. "It's about time I cut "The Angel's" wings off and send his ass to hell!"

Chester White was smiling for the first time, that night.

# CHAPTER SEVENTY-ONE

Mary Peterson R.N. had just finished a double shift at Rutland General Hospital. She stood alone in the foyer of her house parsing that day's mail.

Mary was exhausted. She was looking forward to a hot shower and cozy bed. As she headed for the bathroom, the phone rang.

"*Shit,*" she said, wearily, and picked up the receiver.

"Hello?"

"Mary, its Janet. We've got to talk!"

"Janet, we're talking now," responded Mary Peterson, impatiently.

"No, I mean in person!" demanded Janet Weiss, with growing tension in her voice.

Hearing the stress in her friend's tone, Mary Peterson immediately became alarmed. Janet rarely flustered. Of the three girls who had been known as "The Trio" since high school, Weiss had always been the strongest, emotionally. Mary, now had only one question.

"Jan, how long until you get here?"

"Twenty minutes," was all Weiss said and hung up.

Mary postponed her shower. She went to the kitchen and started a pot of coffee. The R.N. was now trembling. She sensed bad news was on its way. Peterson had never been good at coping with ill tidings.

True to her word, Janet Weiss arrived exactly twenty minutes later. Mary immediately saw anguish in the attorney's face. They sat down at the kitchen table.

"Jan, do you want some coffee?" she offered. "It's fresh."

"I'll pass."

"Can I get you anything else?" persisted Mary.

Janet Weiss stared at her best friend.

"A glass of wine would be nice," she said and smiled for the first time since her arrival.

Mary jumped to her feet. She was relieved just to be busying herself. Peterson returned to the table with two glasses of wine and sat down. Janet Weiss looked at her friend, quizzically.

"I thought you were having coffee."

"I'll pass," was Mary Peterson's response and half-hearted attempt at humor.

The two women sat in silence sipping wine. Oddly, it was Mary Peterson who spoke first.

"Janet, just tell me why the hell you're here!" she demanded, with quiet resignation.

Weiss stared into her now empty wine glass. She then stared into the eyes of her best friend. She was ready to talk.

"My office just completed the background check on Chester White's friend, Kyle Overton."

Mary Peterson was, instantly, riveted.

"What's the story with that guy?" she asked, with eager anticipation.

Janet Weiss looked at Mary and shook her head.

"Mary, that's the problem. Kyle Overton has no story."

"What's that supposed to mean?" asked Peterson, not understanding the words she had just heard.

Janet Weiss paused. She then continued with measured words.

"According to the IBM personnel department in Armonk, New York, one Kyle Overton is not now, nor has ever been in their employ," explained Weiss.

Mary Peterson was skeptical. She stared at Weiss.

"Janet, I find that hard to believe! From day one of their marriage, Chester White blamed Shirley for not being able to graduate high school and then attend college like his best friend did. He has thrown Overton's success at IBM in Shirley's face for as long as I can remember. She used to bitch about that bitterly to me," attested Peterson.

Janet ignored her friend's words. She rose from the table to pour another glass of wine. Weiss reseated herself and fixed her eyes on Peterson.

"Mary, have you ever met Kyle Overton?" she inquired, with the cold objectivity of an attorney.

Peterson did not need time for recollection.

"No."

Janet Weiss sipped her wine. However, her eyes did not stray from Mary's.

"To the best of your knowledge has Shirley ever met Kyle Overton?" she continued.

This time Mary Peterson took a moment to reflect. She began to shake her head.

"Now that you mention it, I don't think she has. In fact, I know she hasn't!" Mary then stated, with certainty.

"How can you be so sure, Mary?" pressed Janet Weiss.

"Because, Shirley once told me that if she ever met Kyle Overton the first thing she'd do is scratch his eyes out! And I know that hasn't happened," she smiled, weakly.

Mary Peterson stared at Janet Weiss.

"Jan, what are you getting at?" she asked, apprehensively.

Janet Weiss did not mince her words.

"Mary, the reason you and Shirley have never met Kyle Overton is because Kyle Overton doesn't exist. He isn't real!"

Peterson heard the words but was having trouble coming to grips with their meaning. However, once she understood the implications of what Weiss had just told her, she became, uncharacteristically, combative.

"Janet, just because Overton doesn't work for IBM doesn't mean the guy doesn't exist! Lots of people pad their resumes! They exaggerate about the positions they hold and the money they make! You should know that better than anyone!" she said, with conviction.

Janet sat, quietly, and listened to her best friend vent. Once Peterson fell silent, Weiss calmly continued.

"Mary, it's not just the fact Kyle Overton has never worked for IBM. Kyle Overton has never worked anywhere!"

"How can you be so sure?"

"Because, I've had my firm's background department on this case for nearly two weeks. They've turned up absolutely nothing on one Kyle Overton. There are no employment records, school records or tax filings. Hell, there's not even a driver's license. Mary, Kyle Overton lives solely in the twisted mind of Chester White!"

Mary Peterson began to tremble.

"So, you're saying Chester..."

Janet Weiss cut her off.

"I'm saying that son of a bitch is sicker than even I could have ever imagined!"

Mary looked at Weiss with moist eyes.

"Jan, what are you planning to do?" she asked, trying not to cry.

"The first thing is to get Shirley out of that house!"

Mary relaxed, momentarily.

"Jan, for all intense and purposes Chester doesn't really live there anymore," she said, with some relief.

Weiss scowled.

"But he knows *she* does. Now, try to reach Shirley on the phone. If she's home let her know we're coming over.

Mary Peterson jumped up to obey orders. As she watched Mary cross the kitchen to make the phone call, Weiss sat sipping her wine. Janet was also, quietly, fighting back tears.

Peterson returned to the kitchen table.

"Shirley's home and expecting us," informed Mary.

The two women rode in Janet's car to Shirley's house, in silence. Neither knew what to say to each other let alone what they were going to tell Shirley once they arrived. She greeted them at the front door.

"So, what's so urgent, ladies?" she asked, with a lopsided smile. Shirley White was already half in the bag.

As always, Janet Weiss took control of the situation.

"Shirley, why don't we sit down at the kitchen table," she suggested.

"Of course!" agreed Shirley and started, unsteadily, down the hallway. "Can I get you guys something to drink?" she asked over her shoulder.

"No!" they answered, in spontaneous unison.

Once in the kitchen, Shirley meandered towards a counter for another drink. Janet Weiss immediately took note of the fact her good friend's choice of cocktail was now scotch rather than wine. Janet looked at Mary and nodded towards the coffee maker. Wordlessly, Peterson started a pot of java. Janet sat down at the table.

"So, you didn't answer my question. What brings you guys here tonight?" asked a sloppy Shirley White, as she spilled herself into a chair and attempted to light a cigarette.

Janet Weiss stared at Shirley with a face full of reproach. However, friendship won out.

"Shirley, Chester White is one sick son of a bitch," she stated, calmly. "I've grown concerned about your safety."

Shirley White let out a high pitched shrill of drunken laughter.

"Jan, you've always been the smart one! Just think, it only took you all these years to figure that one out!" A lit match finally found its target.

Janet Weiss ignored the obvious dig.

"Shirley, for your own well-being I think you should move out of this house as soon as possible," she suggested.

Mary Peterson returned to the table.

"Shirley, I agree with Jan. Please, listen to her!"

Shirley White swilled her scotch and puffed on the cigarette. She then attempted to make direct eye contact with her two best friends.

"You guys don't have to be worried about me," she stated, with a hazy grin.

"And why's that?" coaxed Mary.

"Cause."

"Because why, Shirley?" pressed Mary Peterson.

"Cause I have a boyfriend who can take care of me," she said, as her head dipped towards the table.

Mary and Janet were stunned. They exchanged uneasy glances with one another.

"And who's the guy?" asked Mary.

Shirley tried to focus on her friends. White smiled, drunkenly.

"Johnny Westfield."

# CHAPTER SEVENTY-TWO

"So, Logan, where are you off to on your first weekend of freedom?" grinned Pete Ellison.

Spence's duffel bag was on his bed.

"Anywhere but this campus," was the terse response.

"Logan, my parents are due here any minute now. If you need a lift, I'm sure they'd be more than happy to oblige."

Spence looked at Ellison and smiled.

"Pete, I appreciate the offer. But, I've made other travel arrangements. Say, didn't you tell me your parents were having problems?" asked Logan.

"They still are, but they're now in counseling," said Ellison.

A car's horn sounded two crisp beeps.

"They're here. Are you sure you don't need a ride?"

"Positive."

Pete Ellison picked up his suitcase and bolted out the door and down the stairs into the warm and loving embrace of family.

Spence walked across the room to the mini fridge. He filled a glass with ice. Logan picked up his duffel bag off the bed and sat down in his recliner. Spence opened Pandora's Box. He pulled a bottle of Absolut and poured a drink. Logan tossed the bottle into the duffel bag. He then started to empty the secret cache of all its contraband. The last item was a small plastic packet.

*"What the hell,"* he decided, to himself.

Spence finished the drink and stood up. He looked around the room to make sure he had not forgotten anything. Suddenly, he spotted *Ulysses* on his desk. His thoughts, immediately, raced to Patricia. He picked up the book and stowed it in the duffel bag.

"I can't leave Leopold and Molly in the lurch!" he laughed, out loud.

As he descended the stairs, Spence was met by Susan Tompkins, a faculty resident at Squire House.

"Mr. Spence, I see you're leaving Squire House for the weekend."

"Yes."

"Well, enjoy yourself. Lord knows you've earned it," she said, with a surprising warmth in her voice.

"Thank you, Mrs. Tompkins"

As he walked off the Cornwall Angelica Hall campus for the first time in months, Spence felt a sense of comfort. The change of scenery, instantly, put Logan in a different frame of mind. It allowed him to block out the emotional turmoil and concentrate on the business at hand. It was a very needed departure.

Spence stood at the front door of the Kaminski house and knocked.

"It's open, Logan!" shouted Beth Kaminski, from the kitchen. Spence had called earlier that day to let her know he would be stopping by.

He entered the tiny foyer. There was no music blasting from the den. That told him Roger was not home. Spence walked down the hallway and into the kitchen. Beth was on the phone. To his relief, Valerie Larsen was not there. Beth quickly ended the phone conversation. She crossed the kitchen. The two good friends embraced, warmly.

"How are you?" beamed Beth, as she eyed him with an almost maternal-like concern.

"Just trying to stay one step ahead," smiled Spence.

"Would a drink impede those efforts?" she laughed.

"I should say not!" responded Spence, with mock indignation and sat down at the kitchen table.

Beth Kaminski returned with cocktails.

"To friendship," she toasted.

"A rare and precious commodity, indeed," added Logan.

The two clinked and hoisted. Spence stared at Beth.

"Where are the kids?"

Beth's mood grew somber.

"Roger took them to visit his mother. She's having an awful time getting over the loss of her husband," she sighed.

"Then she's one of the lucky ones," was his enigmatic response.

Spence pulled a pack of cigarettes from his jacket. He lit two and handed one to Beth. She took a couple of drags and then got down to business.

"The good news is we're nearly out of product. The bad news is we're nearly out of product," she said in a suddenly, business-like monotone that amused Logan Spence.

"All right, Charles Dickens, what's the profit margin?" he laughed.

She ignored his attempt at humor.

"Logan, we're approaching nearly sixty-five percent!" she reported, with excitement in her voice. "The quality of our weed is gaining rep on the street. People are more than willing to pay extra for primo. Pretty soon we'll be the only action in the area!"

Spence drained his drink and snuffed the smoke.

"Logan, do you want another drink?" asked Beth.

"Of course! But I have to use the bathroom."

"Meet me in the den," instructed Kaminski.

Spence emerged from the bathroom and headed down the hallway. Beth was already seated on the sofa in the den. Logan sat down next to her. On the cocktail table stood three impressive stacks of cash. They varied in height. Beth handed Logan his drink. She began her explanation.

"The tallest stack is cost of product. The next tallest is your profit. The last one is my profit."

"Why is your stack less than mine?" questioned Spence. "We're in this fifty-fifty."

Tears began to roll down Beth Kaminski's face.

"Because, I took some of my profit and opened an educational savings account for my babies," she explained. "I never thought I'd ever be in a financial position to do that. You're the only reason I can."

Logan Spence was moved. It was the first time, in a long time, he almost felt good, about himself.

"Beth, why don't you take all of your profit and put it in that account?" urged Spence.

The twenty-one-year old mother of two shook her head, vehemently.

"No way! I'm staying in this game for my children!"

Logan Spence had no rebuttal for a mother's love. He stood up to retrieve his duffel bag from the kitchen. He returned and started stowing the cash in separate compartments.

"Logan, your blazer and slacks are pressed and in the basement," she smiled.

"Thank you, Beth," was all he said.

Spence reappeared in the kitchen properly dressed, for travel. Without another word, he kissed Beth on the forehead, picked up the duffel bag, and headed out the door.

"Logan, I love you like a brother," were her final words.

Spence stood in the Kaminski's driveway, loading items of discretion into the hidden compartment of the Buick GS. Unexpectedly, a vehicle pulled into the driveway. It was Valerie Larsen. She got out of the car and approached Spence. Her face was etched with worry. They had yet to go out on that first date.

"Hello, Valerie."

She ignored his greeting. Larsen walked towards Spence. She stopped within inches of his face.

"Logan, I'm not feeling good about this run," was all she said.

Immediately, Spence realized it was Valerie that Beth had been on the phone with upon his arrival. He treaded, lightly.

"Valerie, this run is going to be like every other run. No more, no less," he reassured.

The young woman held her ground.

"Logan, I've got real bad vibes about this one. Please, just stay here for the weekend. I won't even fight with you over who gets the basement bed," she smiled, wanly.

Spence looked at Valerie Larsen. In spite of himself, Logan had begun to have vulnerable feelings for Beth Kaminski's younger sister. Valerie Larsen scared him.

"I have to roll. There are business commitments that must be taken care of," he explained.

Valerie paid no attention, to his words.

"Logan, it's my birthday on Sunday. My mom's going to be here. I'd like you to meet her."

"I'll do my best to be back here in time for your birthday party," he said, sincerely.

Valerie Larsen's mood shifted to anger.

"You're not going to make it back in time. In fact, you're not **ever** going to make it back!"

Valerie turned away from Spence and started walking up the driveway towards the house. She began to run. The young woman entered her sister's home and slammed the front door behind her. Valerie Larsen was in tears.

Logan fired up the Buick GS. As the engine warmed, he pulled the ever-present flask of vodka from a jacket pocket and took a swig. He then dipped into a plastic packet and took a few hits for the ride.

Spence was now breaking his own rules.

# CHAPTER SEVENTY-THREE

Logan opted for I-95 over the Boston Post Road for his trip to New York City. The thruway was a faster route. He was already running late for his pre-arranged meeting with Dwight Jefferson.

As he drove, Spence's thoughts raced between the future ramifications of school probation, Patricia White, Valerie Larsen, and an ever-increasingly profitable drug business. He was a conflicted young man. The blow only served to heighten his emotional disarray. However, he was careful to stay in the middle lane of I-95 and maintain the legal speed limit.

"Outlaws must always obey the rules!" he laughed, self-derisively.

As he crossed the Connecticut border into New York, Spence hit the radio button. Ace Frehley's "New York Groove" started blasting. The music lightened his mood.

Spence managed to secure a parking space directly across the street from the Harlem bar where he was going to meet Dwight Jefferson. He entered the establishment and scoped the room. Dewey was not there, yet. That surprised Spence. He walked to the bar.

"Long time no see, Logan," smiled the bartender and extended his hand.

"It's good to be back, Floyd," grinned Spence, as he shook the man's hand.

"The usual?"

"Yes," replied Logan and slapped a Grant on the oak.

The bartender returned with an Absolut on the rocks and placed it in front of Spence. He looked at Logan.

"Jefferson called a little while ago. Says he's running late, but he'll be here," relayed the bartender.

"I appreciate that information," nodded Spence.

Floyd lingered. Something was on his mind. Logan took immediate notice.

"What's bothering you, Floyd?"

The man hesitated, before speaking.

"I'd just like to know how you and Dwight became such good friends, that's all."

Spence sipped his drink and lit a cigarette.

"Common backgrounds," he smiled.

The bartender looked at Spence and shook his head.

"Logan, I'm being serious."

"So am I."

Floyd thought for a moment, before speaking.

"I'm just saying that your and Dwight's friendship is different. Hell, most white guys don't even have the stones to come this far up town!"

"Floyd, are you saying it's a *bad* different?" questioned Spence.

"Hell no, Logan! It's a good different! I'd just like to know how you guys did it. Because once I do, I'd like to spread it around. Lord knows this town could use a lot more of what you two have going as friends!"

Before Logan could respond, the front door of the establishment opened. Dwight Jefferson entered and walked towards the bar. Logan rose to greet him. The two comrades embraced, warmly. Logan, immediately, noticed two things. The first was the dour expression on Dwight's face. The second was the fact that Bria Cummings was not by his side.

"I'll have a Tanqueray and tonic," ordered Dwight Jefferson. "And back up my friend."

The bartender returned with the drinks. Spence tapped his cash on the bar indicating payment. Floyd did not touch the money.

"Logan, let's move to a booth," Dwight said, sullenly, and started to walk.

Spence sat down in a seat across from Dwight. Jefferson studied his friend, as if taking inventory. At length, he spoke.

"So, how does it feel to be out of jail?" he asked, with distracted politeness.

Spence sensed his friend's emotional distance. He came right to the point.

"Dewey, what's the problem?"

Jefferson did not answer the question. His eyes remained fixed on Logan. Suddenly, Spence felt a tap on his right leg from underneath the table.

"That's the problem," he said, softly. "It's the cash I owe you for the coke."

Spence, discreetly, pocketed the envelope. Before Logan had a chance to say anything, he felt a second tap on his left leg.

"That's your profit," nodded Jefferson. "The spread's nearly sixty-five percent."

Spence secured the second envelope and then stared at his best friend.

"Dewey, you really haven't answered my question."

Jefferson downed the rest of his drink and slammed the empty glass on the table. Without prompting, Floyd the bartender was at their booth with another round.

"Thanks, Floyd," smiled Logan. "My money is on the bar."

"I *know* where your money is," he said, cryptically, and walked away.

Dwight sat staring into his drink. Finally, he looked at Spence.

"Logan, Bria is an addict," he said, in a measured tone of voice.

Spence sipped his drink. He lit a cigarette and tossed the pack on the table. Logan stared at Dwight Jefferson.

"I assume you're blaming me for Bria's drug habit."

Jefferson's mood suddenly shifted. He smiled for the first time that evening and shook his head.

"Logan, I'm not blaming you for Bria's situation. Hell, the girl was already into Fets and Sopes long before I met her. That's just her personality. Thing is, the blow took her over the edge. Logan, Bria's into Crack."

"Crack? I've never heard of Crack," admitted Spence.

"You will," said Dwight Jefferson, with an ominous finality.

Dwight pulled a cigarette from the package on the table and lit it. He focused on his friend.

"Anyway, Logan, I don't know if I can continue to push a product I don't want my girlfriend doing. Don't get me wrong. I love the bread! But I'm having a real hard time handling the hypocrisy that goes along with it."

Jefferson sipped his drink and looked at Spence.

"That said, I harbor no such moral compunction when it comes to dealing your weed," he grinned.

Spence eyed Jefferson and shook his head.

"Well, Dewey, that's real big of you!"

Logan finished the rest of his drink and banged the emptied glass on the table. He stared at Jefferson.

"You know, I have half a mind to sic Sensei Tanaka on your overly moralistic ass!"

The two friends erupted in spontaneous laughter. Their merriment, momentarily, silenced the rest of the bar. Once again, Floyd the bartender arrived at their booth unannounced, with another fresh set of downs.

"These are on me," he smiled and hurried back to the now crowded bar.

Dwight Jefferson's mood, again, grew somber.

"So, Logan, where do we go from here?"

Spence lit another cigarette.

"Dewey, let me see how the rest of this weekend shakes out. I'll be in touch."

Dwight looked at his wrist watch. He was growing antsy.

"So, what's your next stop?" asked Jefferson.

"Rutland, New York."

"And what's in Rutland?"

"Carver's Bar and Grill" answered Spence.

Logan's answer got Dwight Jefferson's attention.

"Carver's? Logan, that place has a nasty reputation even here in town. Watch your ass in there, brother."

"I always do."

Jefferson looked at his watch, again.

"Logan, I've got to go. I'm meeting Bria at CBGB."

"Who's playing?"

"Talking Heads."

"I kind of wish I was going with you."

"Why don't you?" urged Dwight.

"Commitments," was all Spence said.

The two friends stood up and embraced. As Dwight Jefferson walked towards the door, Logan Spence headed for the bar to square the tab. He noticed that the fifty-dollar bill he had placed on the trough of enlightenment was still sitting there. A shot glass had been placed on top of it to ensure security.

"Floyd, what's the damage?" asked Spence.

"Logan, we're even," smiled the bartender. "You take your money and go."

Spence offered his hand. Floyd accepted it. Logan turned to leave. He, intentionally, left Grant buried underneath his tomb. Halfway to the door Spence turned, to face Floyd.

"Until next time," he nodded, with respect and disappeared into the night.

"*If there is one*," thought the bartender, as he picked up and pocketed the money.

Spence exited the bar and started the short walk to where he had parked. Two guys were loitering around his car. One was sitting on the Buick's hood. The other was slouched against the driver's side door. Logan approached and stopped in front of them. They appeared to be in their early twenties.

"Nice wheels, man," smiled the one leaning against the door. "Now, all you have to do is give me the keys and you can be on your way with no hassles," said the would-be carjacker.

Spence remained silent. He knew the two guys in front him had company. On the street, the unseen third person was known as the "Ghost". Sure enough, Logan heard someone closing in on him from behind, at too quick a pace.

Spence decided to take "Casper" out first. Keeping his eyes on the car, he smashed an elbow into the unseen face behind him. He then grabbed the head and pulled the guy to face him. A knee to the nose and another knee to the groin dropped him.

In one fluid motion, Spence was all over the punk leaning against the car before he had a chance to pull a possible weapon. With one violent thrust, Spence fractured the young man's windpipe. He then slammed his face into the roof of the car sending him and most of his teeth spilling onto the sidewalk.

The dude who had been perched on the Buick's hood was already off and running before Logan had a chance to formally introduce himself.

Spence got into the car and fired its engine. As he drove down 125th Street, Logan's thoughts drifted between Dwight Jefferson's plight with Bria Cummings' Crack addiction and that evening's next meeting with Glenn Jenkins at Carver's Bar and Grill. He took the exit leading to the FDR heading north.

*"Looks like a New Deal to me,"* he thought, to himself.

.

# CHAPTER SEVENTY-FOUR

"When was the last time you heard from Spence?" asked Angelo "The Angel" Delfino.

The younger brother did not hesitate with his response.

"Logan called me, yesterday. He assured me he'll be here sometime over the weekend with the money he owes us," said Carmine "The Cat" Delfino.

Angelo looked at Carmine and nodded, approvingly.

"I think you might have been right about this kid. He just may become a very valuable asset to our operation."

Angelo's office intercom suddenly, came to life.

"Mr. Delfino, there's a call for you," squawked the downstairs receptionist.

"Who is it?" demanded "The Angel".

"He says his name is Chester White."

Angelo looked at his younger brother and smiled the smile of a winner.

"The bastard knows he's beat!" he said and picked up the phone. "Hello, Chester."

Angelo listened into the receiver.

"When?" he asked.

As his brother spoke on the phone, Carmine shifted, nervously, in his chair. He had heard bad things about Chester White on the street.

"Where?" asked Angelo. "I prefer The Fontana," balked "The Angel". Okay then, one hour at The Fontana and hung up the phone.

"What's the story?" asked Carmine, with tension in his voice.

Angelo stood up from behind his desk and strutted to the side bar. He poured a drink.

"You going to join me?" he asked his younger brother.

Carmine looked at his brother and shook his head.

"No, I just want to know what's going down!"

Angelo returned to his chair behind the desk and lit a menthol.

"I'm meeting Chester White at The Fontana in one hour to discuss a possible merger."

Carmine shook his head, disapprovingly.

"Ange, I've heard nothing good about Chester White."

"The Angel" smiled, smugly.

"I've heard the same shit. That's why, when he suggested meeting at Carver's, I insisted upon The Fontana. Carver's is his personal hangout."

Carmine was leery.

"Ange, why consider a merger with him at all? We're doing just fine on our own."

Angelo sipped his cocktail and crushed the cigarette.

"Because, with White's better distribution operation and our superior product we'll all make a fortune!"

"I'm going with you," insisted Carmine.

Angelo downed the rest of his drink and smiled at his kid brother.

"The arrangement is I'm supposed to be meeting Chester White one on one. But, I'll let you drive. Besides, I won't really be walking in there alone," he smiled.

"The Angel" pulled a pistol from his desk drawer and slipped it into a jacket pocket.

"Let's roll."

The two brothers rode across town in comparative silence. They entered the parking lot of The Fontana. The place was jammed.

"I'll get out here and walk," said Angelo. "Find a place to park. This first meeting shouldn't take too long. I'll know real fast if a merger is even a possibility. If I'm not out of there in thirty minutes come in and get me," he instructed and got out of the car.

"Will do," agreed Carmine and drove off.

Angelo started to walk across the parking lot towards the entrance of The Fontana. Swiftly, a person appeared out of the darkness. It was Chester White. He approached with his hand extended.

"Hello, Angelo! What a coincidence, I just got here myself."

Suddenly, "The Angel's" eyes began to bulge. He began to grasp helplessly at his throat. Delfino was now choking for air. Paul "Bounty" Hunter had attacked from behind and secured a garrote around his neck.

In his extended hand, Chester White held a knife. He plunged it into the chest of Angelo Delfino.

"Die, you guinea bastard!" he laughed.

As quickly as that, the regional drug war was over. Hunter dragged the body to the rear of his car and wrapped it in a plastic tarp that had already been placed on the pavement. They stuffed the corpse into the trunk and were off. Hunter pulled to a stop in front of Chester White's office building.

"Make certain it's a *very* private burial service," instructed Chester White.

Hunter looked at his boss and smiled.

"They'll find "The Angel" the day after they find Jimmy Hoffa," he said, reassuringly.

Carmine Delfino looked at his watch. Thirty minutes had passed. He got out of his car and entered the lobby of The Fontana. He knew his brother was not there for dinner so he by-passed the dining room and walked into the crowded bar. It did not take him long to realize Angelo was not there. Carmine crisscrossed the lobby into a nearly deserted dining room. No big brother. Carmine's heart began to race. Out of desperation he barged through the door of the Men's Room.

"Angelo!" he shouted.

"Hey! Can't a guy take a dump in here in peace?" complained an unfamiliar voice from behind a closed stall door.

Carmine ran out of the building into the still crowded but now lonely parking lot of The Fontana.

"Angelo!" he wailed into the evening's darkness. "Angelo!" Angelo did not return his shouts. "The Angel" was gone.

Carmine walked numbly to his car and started the engine. As he drove aimlessly down the streets of Rutland, New York, he felt both scared and truly alone for the first time in his life. Carmine "The Cat" Delfino was crying.

# CHAPTER SEVENTY-FIVE

Spence was annoyed. After leaving the Harlem bar where he and Dwight Jefferson had met, Logan was stalled in traffic on I-95. It had been nearly an hour. He was running well late for his meeting with Glenn Jenkins at Carver's Bar and Grill.

*"Just sweep up the carnage and let us be on our way!"* he thought, angrily.

Spence lit a smoke. As he sat idling in the vehicular back-up, his train of thought shifted to Cornwall Angelica Hall for the first time since his departure earlier that day.

Interestingly, Valerie Larsen came to mind, first. Logan had been touched by her genuine concern for his well-being. Not many were. He decided to make an all-out effort to be back in time to help celebrate her eighteenth birthday.

"Older women are always trouble!" he laughed out loud.

Patricia then entered his head. Logan had no doubts that he loved her. However, he was confused and deeply conflicted by their relationship. Distance was a welcomed companion.

Finally, the traffic on I-95 began to flow. As he entered the parking lot of Carver's Bar and Grill, Spence parked at the far end. He climbed out of the car and popped the trunk. He stowed the money Dwight Jefferson had given him. He started towards the bar.

"Kid, you have ID?" asked an outside bouncer.

Spence handed the burly fellow a ten dollar bill and kept walking.

"Nice of you to join us this evening, Mr. Hamilton", smiled the bouncer and pocketed the money, without another word.

Logan entered the bar. It was, surprisingly, sparse of patrons. Spence scanned the video games looking for Glenn Jenkins. He was not playing. Suddenly, Logan felt a pat on his arm. It was Glenn.

"Man, I was beginning to think you weren't going to show up!" he said, in a shaky voice.

"Glenn, I got stuck in traffic. What are you drinking?" asked Spence, adhering to bar room protocol.

Jenkins looked at him with eyes of distraction.

"Whatever you're drinking," he said and plopped himself at a table.

Logan returned with two glasses of Absolut. Jenkins slurped, with an unsteady hand.

"Spence, I have your money."

Logan sipped his drink and stared at Jenkins.

"How'd you do?" he asked in a business-like tone of voice.

"Almost sixty percent on the bottom line! This shit is real good!"

Logan Spence lit a cigarette and nursed his cocktail, patiently, waiting for the punch line.

"Logan, do you have any more product?" questioned Jenkins, with desperation on his face.

Glenn felt a tap on his leg from underneath the table. He grabbed the small packet and stood up.

"I'll be right back!" he said, with relief in his voice.

While Jenkins was off in the men's room powdering his nose, Spence was trying to determine whether or not he could entrust an obvious Sno-Cone with another shipment. Logan decided to count the money Jenkins was going to give him before making that decision.

Glenn returned a new man. He sat down at the table and drained his drink.

"Logan, can I buy this round?" he grinned.

"Not before you give me the money owed."

Spence felt a tap underneath the table.

"It's all there, man," reassured a now buzzing Glenn Jenkins.

"I'll be right back," nodded Logan.

Spence stood up and headed for the door. A man standing behind the bar picked up a phone and placed the call.

"He's here," was all Johnny "Junior" Westfield said and hung up the phone.

Logan traversed the parking lot and unlocked the trunk of the Buick GS. Its light emitted enough illumination for him to count the money. It was all there. Spence stowed the cash and pocketed the remaining ounce of blow. Given Dewey's situation with Bria Cummings he had no choice but to deal with Glenn Jenkins, at least, on an interim basis.

Spence re-entered the bar and seated himself across the table from Jenkins.

"Glenn, nice work," he nodded.

Jenkins laughed.

"Now, can I buy the next round?" He was up and moving before Logan could respond.

Spence scanned the bar room. It was nearly empty. He had been in Carver's only once, before. On that weekday night, the place had been rocking. On this Friday evening, the place was dead. Something was wrong.

Jenkins returned to the table with cocktails and sat down.

"To a long and profitable partnership!" he toasted.

Spence lifted his glass and narrowed his eyes, on Jenkins.

"Glenn, why isn't there anybody in this place, tonight?

Jenkins sipped his drink and shrugged.

"Because it's early, I guess," he said, with uncertainty creeping into his voice.

Spence's eyes remained riveted on Jenkins.

"Glenn, never bullshit me!"

Jenkins looked around him to make certain no one was within earshot. He leaned over the table.

"Logan, to tell you the truth I haven't been in this place since the last time we met here. In fact, if you hadn't showed up when you did I was out of here!"

"Why?"

Jenkins pulled at his drink. He stared Spence in the eyes.

"Carver's has gotten a bad reputation on the street. Students are scared to come here. Hell, even most of the townies have found other watering holes," he said, candidly.

"Why?" persisted Spence.

Glenn drained his drink.

"Because, these days Carver's only attracts a nasty crowd looking for drugs and trouble."

Spence was satisfied with that explanation. Jenkins felt a tap from underneath the table.

"It's one ounce. Same terms," instructed Spence.

"Logan, you can count on me!" promised a grateful Glenn Jenkins.

Spence did not take his eyes off him.

"If I can't count on you, you can be certain that you can count on me, he threatened." "Now, get lost!"

Logan Spence sat alone, in a lonely bar. Sipping his drink, Spence reflected upon the previous six months of his life. The jury was still out on its decision. He reached for a cigarette. The pack was empty. Logan finished his drink and stood up. He walked to the bar. His intention was to buy some smokes and be gone.

"I'll take a pack of Marlboro," he said to the bartender.

Out of nowhere, a middle-aged man was suddenly next to him. He was standing just a little too close.

"Can I buy you a drink?" he asked.

"No." replied Spence.

The man ignored Logan's refusal.

"Bartender, buy this young man whatever he's drinking," he insisted. "And get me a Jack Daniels". The man behind the bar jumped to the demand.

Spence turned to directly face the unwelcomed presence for the first time. He was of average height and muscular build. His face was etched in venom. Their eyes locked for the first time. An immediate and mutual hatred was ignited. It was an animus that ran far deeper than the confrontation of the moment.

The bartender returned with the cocktails but no smokes. The older man downed half of his drink. He looked at Logan.

"You're not drinking with me?"

"No."

"Why not?"

"Because, I'm out of here," said Spence and turned to leave.

The older man finished his drink. He slapped the empty glass on the bar and pulled a knife.

"Oh, you're more out of here than you ever imagined!" he hissed.

The bartender interceded.

"Chet, please, take this thing outside!" he requested, in a quivering voice.

"No way. This ends right here and right now!"

Logan raised his arms in capitulation and started to back-peddle.

"I want nothing to do with you," he said, in a surprisingly calm voice.

"You have no say in this matter, little boy."

The older man started a slow advance towards Spence brandishing the blade.

"Kid, I never take no for an answer!" he glared, through blood shot eyes.

With stealth, Paul "Bounty" Hunter began to approach Spence from behind. He had garrote, in hand. Hunter started to move in for the kill.

Quietly, a figure emerged from the shadows and was now standing directly behind the would-be hangman.

"Don't even think about it, asshole!"

384

Paul Hunter slowly turned around to face the voice. He found himself staring up at the six-foot- five inch Dwight Jefferson who was grinning malice.

"Now, you hand me that rope and turn around."

Paul Hunter did as instructed. He was speechless, with fear. Jefferson hung the garrote around Hunter's neck.

"I see you so much as twitch, you're one dead mother-fucker!"

As Chester White advanced towards him, Logan Spence suddenly spun towards the bar. In one deft movement, he grabbed two long-neck bottles of beer and smashed them on the countertop. He now held two weapons of his own.

"Now, let's really start to play, old-timer!" and grinned with a confidence that infuriated Chester White.

Chester lunged forward with his knife. Spence easily side-stepped him and gouged White's right eye with one of the jagged bottles. The eyeball dislodged and splatted onto the floor. Spence circled to his left which was now, literally, the older man's blind side.

"You're disappointing me, old-timer!" chided Spence. "Come get what's yours!"

Chester White charged wildly flailing the knife. Again, Spence effortlessly avoided the advance and jammed the left eye with a shard of bottle. The eyeball was now dangling from its socket.

"Are you beginning to see things my way?" taunted Spence, with a sadistic smile.

In a final act of desperation, the blinded Chester White rushed towards his tormentor. Spence thrust one of the broken bottles into White's lower abdomen. The other one went down the back of White's neck. Spence lifted Chester White like a pig on a spit. He then let him drop to the bar room floor.

Immediately, Logan did a three-sixty expecting more company. No other guests arrived. It was then that he spotted Dwight Jefferson standing behind a guy he had never seen before. Spence walked towards his best friend.

"Who's your buddy?" he asked, staring at the older man.

Jefferson shook his head, with disdain.

"He's no friend of mine! Hell, he was looking to string you with this!" he said and removed the garrote from around Hunter's neck to show Logan.

Spence stared at the older man.

"What's your name?"

"Paul Hunter."

"Do you have an issue with me?" he asked.

Paul "Bounty" Hunter glanced at the body of Chester White, before answering the question.

"I did."

"Do you now?"

Hunter did not hesitate.

"No."

Logan Spence made his decision. He took the garrote from Dwight Jefferson and handed it to Paul Hunter.

"I suggest you get out of here."

Hunter started to walk. Suddenly, he stopped and turned to look at Spence.

"I owe you one," he said, with genuine appreciation in his voice and then disappeared.

Logan focused his attention on Dwight Jefferson.

"Dewey, what the hell are you doing here?"

Jefferson stared at his friend.

"Logan, after you told me you were going to Carver's I started to get real bad karma about the run. I just knew I had to be here! So, I hopped a train."

Spence acted as though he had not heard Jefferson's words. He reached into a jacket pocket and handed Dwight the keys to the Buick GS. He looked into his best friend's eyes.

"Drive the Buick home. Don't let it out of your sight. That car holds our future. Now go!"

Dwight Jefferson hesitated. He was on the verge of tears.

"Logan, I can't just leave you …."

Suddenly, Spence slapped Jefferson across the face.

"Dewey, leave now! For both our sakes!"

With reluctance, Dwight nodded his head.

"Word," he promised.

Logan watched his friend's safe departure. As he re-entered Carver's, the sound of approaching police sirens could be heard in the distance. Spence stood at the bar and glared at the man behind it.

"Now, I'll take those Marlboros! And while you're at it, a double Absolut on the rocks."

The bartender's eyes shifted nervously between the corpse of Chester White and the young man who had just killed him.

"Ye, Ye, Ye, yes sir!" stuttered Johnny "Junior" Westfield and quickly went to fill the order.

# CHAPTER SEVENTY-SIX

"So, why the pissy mood?" asked Kate Whitson.

"I've got to go to Rutland," replied Patty White.

"Well, that explains things" nodded Kate, with empathetic understanding.

The two young teachers were in Patty's Angelica Hall apartment. Patty stood in front of a mirror brushing her hair.

"Why the hell are you going back there?" persisted Kate.

"Because I have a doctor's appointment."

Whitson's eyes narrowed.

"Patty, is there something wrong?" she asked, in a concerned voice.

White put the hairbrush down and turned to face her life-long friend.

"I hate to disappoint you, but it's only an annual check-up."

The two friends burst into laughter.

"Patty, do you want me to go with you for the ride?"

"And tear you away from Seth? I wouldn't dream of it!"

Patty White was referring to Kate's boyfriend, Seth Abrams.

"Actually, Seth and I have already been torn apart."

This time it was Patty White who wore the concerned look.

"What happened?"

Kate shook her head and smiled.

"It's nothing like that," she reassured. "Seth is totally into his doctoral thesis."

"Oh, it must be yet another reprises on the Civil War," remarked Patty White, disdainfully.

Kate Whitson chose not to challenge her friend's foul frame of mind. Patty donned her coat and headed for the door.

"Are you sure you don't want me to come with you?"

"Quite."

Patty stopped and turned. Her face softened.

"Just make sure you're here to join me for a glass of wine when I get back," she said and smiled at Kate.

Patty White was on the Merritt Parkway heading south towards Rutland. Although her eyes were focused on the road, Patty's thoughts were not. Her relationship with Logan Spence was weighing heavily. Patty knew it was wrong. In the role model of teacher, she had failed, miserably. The problem was Patty loved and cared for the young man with emotions she could not control.

Patty White parked the car and wiped her tears. She entered the medical facility. An older woman sat behind the reception desk.

"You must be Patricia White," she said. "You're late."

Patty did not remember ever meeting the woman seated behind the desk. However, she looked eerily familiar.

"That's because I went to the old address. I forgot about Dr. Levine's new location," she explained, lamely.

The older woman stood up from behind the desk.

"Hang your coat over there and come with me," she instructed.

Patty followed the older woman into a small room.

"Roll up your sleeve," requested the physician's assistant and donned the latex gloves of indifference. After drawing three vials of blood, the woman handed Patty a plastic cup.

"A urine specimen is required. The bathroom is across the hall. I'll be waiting for you here."

Patty returned. The older woman then led her into an examination room.

"Dr. Levine will be with you shortly," she said and closed the door behind her.

'Shortly', was not so short. At length, the door to the examination room opened. A man walked in and closed it behind him. Dr. Elliot Levine was a short, balding man in his late forties. He was of kind disposition.

"Nice to see you again, Patty," he smiled. "How are you feeling?"

Patty looked at him and shook her head.

"A little embarrassed. I was late for this appointment because I went to your old location. I forgot you had moved."

He waved a friendly hand of dismissal.

"Don't give it a second thought. Actually, I preferred the other address."

"Then why did you move?" asked Patty.

Before he could answer her question, the door to the examination room opened. The older woman closed the door behind her and handed Dr. Levine a manila folder. She remained, unobtrusively, in the corner of the room. No doubt, to help preclude fraudulent malpractice accusations. Dr. Elliot Levine scanned the file. He placed it on a counter and looked at Patty.

"To answer your question, I had to move for larger office space. I assumed the practice of a retiring physician. Dr. Henry Spence is a dear friend of mine and I promised him I would," he explained.

"Spence?" asked Patty White. "I have a student that attends Cornwall Angelica Hall with the very same last name."

"No doubt that's Logan," confirmed Levine.

"Do you know him?" asked Patty, with keen interest.

"I've never met the young man. But his father tells me he's a handful. What kind of student is he?"

Patty White thought for a moment and then smiled.

"He can be a handful," she admitted.

Although seemingly busying herself at the examination room's counter, the older woman was hanging on every word of their conversation.

Dr. Elliot Levine stared at Patty White and, abruptly, popped the question.

"Patty, do you know you're pregnant?"

Patricia White did not immediately answer. She sat, numbly, trying understand why the doctor would ask such an implausible question. When she responded, it was with defiance.

"That's not possible!"

Dr. Elliot Levine looked at her with kind eyes.

"And why is that, Patty?" he asked, gently.

"Because, I'm on The Pill!" she screamed and started to cry.

The doctor gave his patient a little space, before speaking.

"Patty, no form of contraception is 100% infallible."

Patty left the examination room reeling. As she gathered her overcoat to leave the doctor's office, the older woman approached. She handed Patty a file folder and looked her in the eyes.

"I've decided you should have this. Only one other person in the world even knows it exists."

Without another word, Beatrice Strickland, long-time physician's assistant to Dr. Henry Spence turned and walked towards the reception desk. She was quietly crying.

# CHAPTER SEVENTY-SEVEN

Kate Whitson heard the news while having dinner with Seth Abrams at a local sports bar. The game they were watching was suddenly interrupted by Tri-State News Network:

**"In a grisly barroom confrontation in Rutland tonight, one man was killed and another taken into police custody. The incident took place at Carver's Bar and Grill. The decedent has been identified as Chester White. He was a prominent local businessman. His assailant has been identified as one, Logan Spence. We will keep you updated as this situation unfolds."**

As the game resumed, Kate Whitson looked at Seth Abrams. She was now trembling.

"Take me home."

"But Kate, the game isn't over," he objected.

Scott had half a jag on and, seemingly, oblivious to what had just aired.

"I said take me home. Now!" she demanded, with toxin spewing from her tongue.

The future Doctor of History felt, for the very first time, the life-long inner rage of Kate Whitson. It shook him. Seth pulled to a stop in front of her campus dormitory. Kate got out of the car.

"I guess I'll call you tomorrow?" he asked, sheepishly.

"No, I'll call you if I ever decide to!" she hissed and slammed the door.

Kate ran into the building and up the stairs. She knocked on Patty's door. There was no response. She turned the door knob. Surprisingly, it was not locked. Kate entered the apartment.

"Patty? Are you here?" she called out in a shaky voice. There was no answer.

Kate walked into the living room. Patty was sitting on the sofa. Papers were strewn all around her. She was drunk. Kate Whitson approached her best friend and sat down next to her.

"Patty, do you know?"

Patty White picked up a liquor bottle sitting on the cocktail table and took a long pull. It was the Absolut vodka she had bought for Logan.

"Know what?" she asked, with distraction.

Kate Whitson braced herself.

"Patty, I have bad news. Your father is dead. Chester was killed today," she revealed, softly.

Patty focused her eyes on Kate Whitson.

"That's the best news I've heard all day," she said, sardonically, and took another swallow of vodka.

Kate looked at her best friend. Whitson was uncertain whether or not to tell her the full story. The conscience of friendship prevailed.

"Patty, apparently it was Logan who killed your father," she revealed and broke down in tears.

The young woman seated next to her was unmoved.

"Like father, like son," said Patricia White, with an eerily foretold acceptance.

Through bleary eyes, Kate Whitson stared at her childhood friend.

"Patty, what the hell are you talking about?" she demanded, in a quivering voice filled with growing apprehension.

Kate was surprised to see Patty light a cigarette. She had quit years earlier. Patricia White smoked in silence. Abruptly, she stubbed the unfinished cigarette and gazed into the eyes of her life-long friend.

"You don't know what bad news really is! Do you want to know?"

Kate sat motionless on the sofa. Tears began to trickle down Patricia White's cheeks. She reached for the vodka. Patricia took a swig and then hurled the bottle, shattering it against a wall. She glared at her best friend.

"Bad news is finding out that you're pregnant with your own son's child!"

Kate Whitson could not respond. Although she had heard the words, her mind was having difficulty processing their meaning. As the reality of what Patty had just told her began to seep into understanding, Kate Whitson's face contorted in horror.

"Oh, my God!" she whispered.

The lines on Patricia White's face had aged a decade in a day. She stared at Kate Whitson through blood shot eyes and shook her head.

"What God?" she whispered, without really expecting any kind of answer.

# DAVID MOFFATT

David B. Moffatt is the author of ***Beltway Justice A Tale of Political Civility* ISBN-13:** 978-1596300859 BeachHouse Books (2013)